DIE AGAIN TO SAVE TOMORROW

DIE AGAIN TO SAVE TOMORROW

DIE AGAIN TO SAVE THE WORLD™ BOOK TWO

RAMY VANCE

MICHAEL ANDERLE

DISRUPTIVE IMAGINATION®

THE DIE AGAIN TO SAVE TOMORROW
TEAM

Thanks to our Beta Readers
Kelly O'Donnell, Rachel Beckford, John Ashmore, Larry Omans

Thanks to the JIT Readers

Veronica Stephan-Miller
Jackey Hankard-Brodie
Deb Mader
Zacc Pelter
Dorothy Lloyd
Debi Sateren
Diane L. Smith
Jeff Goode
Paul Westman

If I've missed anyone, please let me know!

Editor
The Skyhunter Editing Team

Copyright © 2021 by LMBPN Publishing
Cover Art by Jake @ J Caleb Design
http://jcalebdesign.com / jcalebdesign@gmail.com
Cover copyright © LMBPN Publishing
A Michael Anderle Production

LMBPN Publishing
PMB 196, 2540 South Maryland Pkwy
Las Vegas, NV 89109

Version 1.00, June 2021
ISBN (ebook) 978-1-64971-872-3
ISBN (paperback) 978-1-64971-873-0

DEDICATION

To Martha Carr and Subaru ... Martha knows why.

—Ramy Vance

To Family, Friends and
Those Who Love
to Read.
May We All Enjoy Grace
to Live the Life We Are
Called.

— Michael

CHAPTER ONE

Friday, May 19, 8:12 p.m.

Rueben Peet sat under the glittering chandelier in the ballroom of the Mount Olympus Grand Hotel and Resort Center. Tonight, the generic space had transformed into an elegant dining room with white linen-covered tables and waiters in full dress uniform bustling around, offering patrons choice filet mignon.

"This is quite the event." Rueben sipped a glass of wine. He puckered his lips. "Damn, this is good. They went all out."

His father narrowed his eyes in disapproval. "What would you expect? It's the police awards banquet. Don't you think the hardworking police officers of this city deserve one night in the lap of luxury?"

Rueben smirked and swirled his glass. There was no winning with Marshall Peet. It was best to stay quiet. A retired ex-cop, this was his version of the Academy Awards, and he had dressed tonight in his best jeans and expensive cowboy boots, which shone after a polish.

"I think it's a beautiful night." Aki Yamashiro smiled at

1

their resident cop, Martha Dragone. "And I'm proud of our little adventure."

Rueben gulped at her words. Aki was smoking hot, and he still wasn't quite over the fact that she was his date for the night. Really? She was here with him? Especially after she'd put him into the friend zone after their last adventure where she had told him that he was *too badass* for her. All after extensive training and, well, dying. It had been worth it even if he didn't get the girl because he'd saved the day...

He fought the urge to look around for her real date, frequently reminding himself not to stare. He had even considered putting it as a reminder on his smartwatch every twenty minutes.

Tonight, she wore a tight black sparkling dress and matching stilettos with black ankle straps.

Martha sighed and held her abdomen. "You only think it's a beautiful night because you're not the one giving a speech."

Everyone laughed, and Martha looked again through her dog-eared index cards. She was the reason they were all here tonight. She'd be accepting an award for exceptional service. Not only that, she'd be telling the story of what everyone here at Table Eight had helped her do.

Dressed for the part in a short A-line red formal, her long dark hair fell around her shoulder in soft, curled waves. Rueben realized it was probably the first time in years he'd seen her hair out of a ponytail and certainly in a dress. He would never expect she owned a curling iron. He thought of telling her as much but couldn't find that middle ground between flirty and insulting. He didn't want to do either, so he kept his mouth shut.

Martha sipped her wine and surveyed the crowd of cops and their families. "Seriously, guys. This isn't an honor. This is torture. Remind me not to give exceptional service at work again."

"You earned this." Marshall nodded gravely and wagged a finger at her. "It's an honor, and you should be proud of yourself."

The last patron at Table Eight, Buzz Lugger, chimed in with his two cents. "The trick is to take slow, deep breaths, which allows ample oxygen flow to the brain. This enables the neurons to fire slowly, effectively getting you drunk on air. Do it long enough, and you'll start to see things and—"

Rueben rolled his eyes. "Dude, if you don't shut up, I'm going to disable your neurons."

"Dude," Buzz said, "don't tell me to shut up when I didn't even want to come to this stupid dinner anyways."

Rueben raised both hands placatingly. "Whoa, whoa. We're cool. Just remember, we're going out to celebrate after this. That means more alcohol."

Buzz's eyes lit up, and he grinned.

"Well," Martha brought the table's attention back to her. "I've tried deep breaths, but they're not working."

Aki smiled at Martha. "Well, you could pass out. That's what I did when I didn't want to marry that guy in Vegas."

Everyone at the table stared at her, open-mouthed.

"You married a guy in Vegas?" Rueben didn't like the sound of that.

She picked at her fingernails. "No, I did not. That's the point."

Martha frowned. "Seriously, does that work?"

"Marrying a guy in Vegas?" Rueben clarified.

"No, passing out."

Aki winked at her. "Sure. You just 'plop,' hit the deck when you're ready."

"Huh."

Aki wagged a finger in instruction. "The secret to not getting hurt is to collapse at the knees—it will still look real. Then make up some bullshit story later about being anemic. Oldest trick in the book—worked for women since the invention of the corset."

"Ah, I could never do that. That's not how you stay off 'The Tampon Squad.'"

Aki grimaced. "The what?"

"Yeah. My sentiments exactly."

Rueben frowned at Aki. "You know, it concerns me the things I don't know about you."

"Occupational hazard. Secrets are kind of what we do."

Rueben laughed. He and Aki shared the dirty little secret that they both worked for the CIA. Buzz knew and they'd recently let Martha in on that, but Marshall still thought Rueben had some boring State Department job.

The lights dimmed, and the city police commissioner took the stage.

"Good evening." He warmed up the crowd, and the low roar faded into an attentive silence. "I'm glad you all could make it out on this beautiful May evening. You could be out enjoying this fine spring weather we've been having. Instead, you're stuck in here with a bunch of starched-shirt cops."

The audience laughed.

"Most people would call that jail."

Or, as Rueben mused, his childhood.

The commissioner stopped and let the audience respond again. Then he continued, "The truth is, this is probably the safest place to be in America tonight, and certainly in the city. Because if you want to cause any shenanigans here tonight, you're gonna get busted."

Little agreements rose around the room. "You said that right."

The commissioner paused for the laughter and winked at the crowd. "So criminals beware." He glanced down at his notes, and his demeanor turned professional. "In all seriousness, we appreciate you coming out as we honor the best of the best on the city police force. We have some of the finest men and women the United States has to offer, and we're here to recognize them for their acts of service throughout the year."

It was a long introduction with awards for the tenure of service, and Rueben's hands were sore from clapping by the time they got to the Twenty-Five Years of Service recognition. After that, they went through a couple of officers who had helped people through this or that.

Then the commissioner cleared his throat. "This next recipient is someone who has been instrumental in one of the highest-profile cases we've had in a long time."

Everyone immediately figured out who it was, and the room exploded with applause. For anyone that hadn't figured it out, Martha's police headshot appeared on the slideshow behind him. "It's truly been an exceptional case, and in some ways, it's still unfolding. Normally we do awards from the previous year, but because this case has been such a truly tremendous display of police work and investigation, we're going to recognize it this year. Please welcome Officer Martha Dragone."

Martha smiled meekly at Table Eight, and as she stood and made her way to the platform, the crowd gave her a standing ovation.

Aki turned to Rueben. "You should be up there, too."

Marshall overhead the comment. "Why? To make sure the projector works?"

Martha slowly took the stairs to the stage, and the crowd still roared with applause.

Aki narrowed her eyes at Marshall. "You don't get it, do you?"

"Get what?"

"Your son's a hero. He was instrumental in blowing this thing wide open."

Marshall snorted. "My kid? The only time he's ever been instrumental to anything was the time he played the oboe in the fifth grade."

Rueben blushed. "Dad, please. Not now."

Aki raised an eyebrow. "Well, he's a hero. I would know 'cause I only fuck heroes." Marshall's eyes widened, and he coughed while Aki stared him down.

"Not just for the whole Pout thing, either." She sidled up to Rueben and rubbed her breasts against him.

Rueben wasn't quite sure what to do, given he and Aki had barely so much as made it to first base.

How much did she want him to play along? He gulped. They were only friends, right? He couldn't bring himself to do much but sit there awkwardly. Not that he didn't want to. My God, he wanted to...but he also didn't want to get slapped, and Marshall sat there ready to spill all his childhood secrets.

She puckered her lips and gazed longingly into his eyes. "Given what he did to me last night, let's just say...he's a hero in more ways than one."

Marshall whistled low and shook his head in approval. He raised his palms in surrender.

Rueben blushed bright red and was grateful when the

ovation ended. Aki winked at him, and he fell back into his chair and finished off the glass of wine in one gulp.

Martha was at the platform now, and she smiled at the crowd.

"Thank you, thank you." She glanced down at her cards. "The week and weekend leading up to Valentine's Day for most of New York meant buying cards and booking five-star dinners that ended with diamond rings and midnight declarations of love between the sheets."

The crowd laughed, and Rueben winked at Aki. "You wrote that, didn't you?"

She nodded and smiled. "Her speech was dry. She needed a few jokes."

"Yeah, jokes aren't her thing."

"Not particularly."

The laughter died, and Martha continued. "Or if you're like me, you spend National Single's Awareness Day drowning yourself in chocolate and Chinese takeout and binge-watching Netflix."

More laughter.

"What am I saying? That's Tuesday night," she quipped.

Buzz turned to Aki. "These are good. You wrote this stuff?"

Aki shrugged modestly.

"What would you know about National Single's Awareness Day?" Rueben teased. Friendzone be damned. He was going to flirt. "Have you been single, like…ever?"

"Eh, I have friends."

"Ahhh, sure you have." Buzz nodded in unison with Rueben.

Martha's face brightened, and she visibly relaxed as the crowd decided they liked her. "For some of us, the week leading up to Valentine's Day was a little more." She paused for dramatic effect and glanced down at her notes before continuing. Reuben thought he saw her hand tremble.

"In America, it is one of our founding principles that we are *all*, whether rich or poor, equal under the law."

The crowd roared and gave her another standing ovation. They knew where she was going with this.

"Thank you, thank you." Her voice built momentum as her passion for the subject grew. Everyone sat back down, and she continued, "I received an anonymous tip that a certain high-profile member of the city was up to some activities he shouldn't have been into."

That wasn't quite the case, but her telling them about his ability to Time Warp back into himself probably wouldn't play well to this crowd.

Martha's eyes took on a dark and fiery look. "In the beginning, we didn't have proof, and as we all know, we are innocent until proven guilty. That's true, and we honor that. On the other hand, when you're proven guilty, you'd better hope there's a merciful God or Allah or Great Spirit Force or whatever floats your boat, 'cause the city of New York is coming to get your sorry ass!"

The crowd of police officers whooped and hollered, and Rueben whistled. He'd never seen her like this. Marshall gave her a lone standing ovation, and a few others joined him.

"So based on the tip, I took on a full-scale investigation of the high-profile investor and businessman, Alister Pout."

"Jail the Canadian!" someone yelled with a fist-pump into the air.

That set off a fresh round of cheering.

"Deport Pout!" another one yelled. That phrase had become a common local protest slogan and meme fodder.

Yes, Alister Pout was an almost-billionaire Canadian living

in New York for the last decade. Now, his sole place of residence was in the New York State Penitentiary. That was entirely the work of the band of misfits at Table Eight.

Martha regained the floor. "In my investigation, I found a man who is truly twisted and dark and belongs not exalted in city boardrooms, but rotting behind bars. I found a very sick man whose full roster of crimes we may never know. What we do know is that he left a trail of victims and their families heartbroken from sea to shining to sea and beyond.

"Who only knows what plans he had for his RedBook app and the software behind it. I mean, its software allows RedBook to activate its users' cell phone cameras and microphones. All in an effort to provide first responders quicker access and a first look at cities during a time of crisis. A major earthquake. A hurricane. An armed robbery at a bank. I don't know about you all, but this sounds like a front—spying on its users smells illicit in my book."

The sea of officers nodded in the audience like waves, and she continued, "For some reason, people continue to sign up for the app to get their social media fix. In fact, some estimates have it that RedBook has been gaining new users at an exponential pace since Pout was apprehended."

Someone in the audience shouted, "Shut RedBook down."

Martha silently nodded. Why did she get the feeling that they hadn't seen the last of RedBook or Pout's plans? "People gotta cash in on the newest fad, I guess. I, for one, will never fully understand some of those we've sworn to protect. It's people like them who probably think the upcoming world leader summit at the U.N. building here in NYC on Monday will come to something. Who knows, maybe it will. But one thing's for sure. We will not allow Pout and others like him to get away with illicit activities in our city.

"This man needed justice, and we brought it to him."

The crowd leapt up with another standing ovation, and Martha smiled and stepped away from the podium.

The police commissioner arrived back up on stage. "Officer Dragone, on behalf of the New York City Police Force, we'd like to present this award for Excellence in Service."

The commissioner handed Martha a plaque and an envelope. She smiled graciously and shook his hand as she took it.

She stepped off the stage and returned to Table Eight amidst the cheering throng.

The next speech involved the extensive police details of providing security for the upcoming U.N. meeting. The speaker joked that, of course, having the leaders of North Korea, China, and Russia in the same building was a splendid idea and nothing bad could come of that...

With the ceremony behind them, it was time to blow off some steam. Rueben and Aki piled out of a taxi onto the sidewalk in front of a small joint called the Exit Bar.

The Exit Bar was a square brick building with a highway theme. Outside, license plates and road signs decorated the front, and a restored truck from the 1920s sat on the deck with a century-old inspection sticker still on the window.

With the rest of the group lagging in traffic, they waited outside, and Aki ran her fingers across the truck's fire engine red paint job. "This is adorable."

The truck's door had been left unlocked for guest photos, so Rueben winked. "Yeah, why don't you get in it?"

She raised an eyebrow and jumped into the driver's seat.

She struck a suggestive pose, and he laughed and snapped photos.

He dug his hands in his pockets and looked over at her, dark folds of fabric on the brown leather seat and long manicured fingers around the wheel. God, she looked good in that truck.

She caught him staring. "What?"

He flashed her an odd half-smile. He couldn't take his eyes off her. That was what. Her arched eyebrows showed she knew it, too. She just wanted him to say it. Women. When would he ever get them? Oh well, had to try to play it cool. He smirked and affected a concerned face. "Sorry, is that a...bug in your hair?"

She batted at her hair. "What?"

"Yeah, no, it's on your dress now."

She wildly flicked at her dress, and he smiled and shrugged. "Yeah, it's gone now."

She glared at him. "Uh-huh. I bet it is."

"It was a big one. Like, uh…"

"Like, invisible? Nonexistent?"

He laughed, and she got out of the truck and smacked him playfully.

At that moment, Buzz, Martha, and Marshall arrived.

Marshall stepped out, mumbling about the taxi driver running a red light. "These guys think they can break the law, and it's okay if no one gets hurt. The law is the law, and you're supposed to obey it."

Rueben and Aki rolled their eyes, and she leaned in closer to him. He fought the instinct to wrap his arm around her waist. Not that he didn't want to. God, he wanted nothing more than to pull her close to him. But he didn't know what they were, and the fear that he might have it wrong made him err on the side of caution. The way she had fake-come onto him at the dinner table in front of Marshall... *Sexiest friend zone I've ever been in.*

Marshall rambled on. "It makes a mockery out of the law and the profession of good men and women who enforce it."

Aki pointedly ignored Marshall and wrapped her arm around Martha. "Well, this night is all about Martha. Let's get this celebration on!"

A cheer went up from the little band of partiers, and they all crammed in through the door.

Rueben was the last to file in, and as he did, a strange voice came from the street. "Nothing is what time allows, but the world is the same. Isn't that right, Mr. Hash Brown?"

Turning, Rueben saw a man in shabby clothes with crazy hair and greasy fingers. Tucked under one arm was a bucket of Hurley's chicken, a fried chicken fast food joint with a flashy logo and the slogan *Best dang chicken in the galaxy.*

Rueben studied the homeless man. "You again. The guy who's always eating a bucket of fried chicken."

"Infinite deaths become jumper's doom. You've lived what you knew to do. What's next is up to you."

He repeated himself twice, the third time in a sing-song voice. Then he went back to his chicken and ambled away down a darkened alley.

Rueben knew he shouldn't engage the man, but this was certainly odd. Did the man's words mean anything? What had Buzz said about those like the Chicken Man? He was part of the extreme minority of the population that experienced déjà vu-like symptoms, possibly due to remembering discrepancies from timeline variations due to Rueben's time warps. So, in other words, Rueben's time-warping had caused the poor bastard to go crazy.

But the thing about infinite deaths… "Hey man, you know, don't you? You know who I am? What I can do?"

The man stopped mid-step and turned his head toward Rueben. "I've seen you. Many different versions of you. I like this one the best." The homeless man took a bite out of a chicken leg and wandered off again, but not before adding, "He's coming. And he is the worst of you. Be ready, or don't. Either way, you're going to die…and die and die and die."

CHAPTER TWO

Friday, May 19, 10:05 p.m.

Rueben stood there before the door to the bar, angled away and facing the dark alley. The Chicken Man's words seemed too important to ignore, but Aki was inside.

How did the saying go? Hos before crazy homeless bros. Not that Aki was a—

"What was that about?"

Rueben turned toward the door where Buzz stood peeking back at him. "Eh, just a weird homeless guy. Creepy."

Buzz's eyes twinkled as if he knew something Rueben didn't, or maybe he was intrigued. "Infinite deaths? Jumpers?"

"Maybe he likes frogs. Come on. He's only one of those people who remembers fragments of my time warps. I'd rather not bother him."

"Because...you made him crazy? You feel guilty."

"I feel thirsty for a beer. You in?"

Buzz gave a nerdy laugh. "Dude. It's always beer-thirty in my mind. You know I do my best thinking with an elevated blood alcohol level."

"Yeah, and it worries me sometimes."

Buzz slapped a hand on Rueben's shoulder. "What is it that teenagers and reality stars are saying these days? YOLO?"

"Um. Something like that. Come on. Tonight's about celebrating. First beer's on me."

They both went inside. The lights were low, and the chatter was loud. The overpowering sound of a breezy Gin Blossoms hit—*Allison Road*, to be exact—seemed to fit with the highway theme.

The bar was full but not too crowded, and they made their way through booths made out of restored VW van seats against vintage motel signs on the walls. Rueben also noticed framed, oversized posters of road trip novels such as Jack Kerouac's *On the Road* and Robert Pirsig's *Zen and the Art of Motorcycle Maintenance.*

The ladies and Marshall were already ahead, chatting away, but Buzz seemed a little ill at ease.

Rueben slapped his buddy's shoulder. "You're quiet tonight, Buzz. I thought you said it was beer-thirty."

"I prefer fine wines in my company or in the company of choice others."

"In other words, you can't pick up a girl."

"Not to save my life," he replied quickly. "Terrifies me."

Rueben wrapped his arm around Buzz's shoulders. "Look, Buzz, I can tell you after living a hundred lifetimes that you've gotta just go out and do it. You embarrass the shit out of yourself, learn from it, and try again."

"First of all, you haven't lived a hundred lifetimes. You've only lived eighty-three, and they weren't lifetimes. They were the same week, played over and over again. Of course, you mastered it."

"Your point?"

"You are not a wizened sage qualified to dispense advice to lesser mortals."

"Fine. But the statistical probability that I will go home alone tonight is...eh..." Rueben glanced back at Aki, who chatted with Martha as they all made their way to a table. "Fifty-fifty."

"You delude yourself. Eighty-twenty."

"Eighty-twenty? In my favor?"

"You wish."

Buzz glanced back at Aki, who now posed with Martha beside life-sized figures of Bonnie and Clyde. It appeared they'd roped Marshall into reluctantly snapping the photo. Heaven forbid he have some fun.

She laughed, and even Marshall cracked a smile. Rueben watched her pose for multiple shots like a glamor model. Her short bobbed black hair shone under the low light of the bar, giving it an almost purple glow. "Actually, I'd say more eighty-three to seventeen."

"As opposed to your one-hundred percent?"

"Oh, now you're cruel."

Rueben slapped him on the back. "Come on, man, let me help you."

"I'm flattered, but I'm not your type."

Rueben laughed. "You know what I mean."

The photo op was over, and Rueben and Buzz followed the migration toward a table.

They found the Route 66 booth. According to a placard on the table, the bar's owner bought it from a liquidated mom-and-pop diner that had gone under when tourism lagged along Route 66 due to increased urbanization.

Aki sighed. "All the political shit I deal with daily, the last thing I want is to come to a bar to deal with it. I want to numb my brain and not think about how the entire world as we know it is a bunch of bullshit."

Buzz raised an eyebrow. "So I take it the CIA killed Route 66?"

Rueben and Aki groaned, and Rueben smirked at Buzz. "Don't try to divert the subject. You know what you're here for."

Aki glanced back and forth between the two of them. "What's going on?"

"Buzz needs to get laid."

Buzz looked miffed. "Excuse you!"

The ladies now appeared intrigued.

Marshall scoffed and snapped his fingers toward a waiter.

"Christ, Dad, this isn't France in the 1900s. You might as well yell, 'Garçon.'"

"There you go again, thinking you're hot shit cause you can remember some trivia fact from a history class."

Rueben mouthed his next line with him. "Damn Columbia education."

Buzz stiffened. "Pardon me, sir, but Columbia is a world-class institution."

"What would you know about the world? You can't even get a date without a username and password."

Everyone laughed, but Rueben knew the comment wasn't a jest. Marshall was being Marshall.

The waiter arrived in time, an energetic post-hipster with a scruffy beard, gauged earlobes, and no discernible work uniform.

Between them all, they ordered enough drinks and food to cover the table. The soundtrack switched to Tom Petty, and a group a couple of tables over cheered. A few of them started dancing. Aki raised an eyebrow at Rueben, and he made the famous John Travolta sideways-peace-sign-over-the-eyes dance move. She just laughed.

Martha started in on Buzz's problem. "So, what's your opening line?"

"I prefer not to disclose my strategy."

"You don't have one," Aki supplied.

Everyone laughed.

"Jesus." Marshall scoffed as he nursed his beer. "And I thought my love life was in the shitter. You kids are in the prime of your lives, and none of you know the basics of getting somebody to go to bed with you. I don't know how your generation is going to reproduce."

"Hey." Aki sat up straight and wagged her finger at Marshall. "We've heard about enough out of you. If you can't be nice, go home."

Rueben's mouth dropped. She had not just said that. Marshall made a face but said nothing.

The waiter arrived with drinks and appetizers. The hungry group dug in, reaching over each other for spinach artichoke dip, mozzarella sticks, and onion rings.

Marshall grabbed his beer and silently wandered off to another table.

"You're my straight-up hero," Rueben told her after Marshall had left.

"It needed to be said. Now, back to Buzz."

Buzz chugged his beer and winced. "I've not had enough cheap beer to have this conversation. What is this stuff?"

Rueben rolled his eyes. "Oh, please. Stop pretending you're a hardened bar snob. I've seen you get hammered on the cheapest shit every college bar had to offer."

"That was four years ago. I'm much more seasoned now."

"You're twenty-three. You've only been legally allowed to drink for two years."

Martha frowned. "You're only twenty-three?"

Rueben sighed. "He graduated high school at twelve and went to college at sixteen. He graduated at nineteen—double or triple major. I don't even know."

"I detest the sarcasm," Buzz said.

"Detest all you want. I'm okay with that."

Martha gasped and pointed at the overhead television. The news channel broadcasted the latest on the Alister Pout scandal.

A talking head spoke as the black-and-white captions followed. "The investment mogul is expected to get a sentence of two hundred years."

The camera cut to a press conference with Pout's legal team. "We are going to fight this sentence. Mr. Pout is not guilty, and we have the truth on our side."

Martha laughed. "The truth? The truth is you maimed and butchered people all over this city, masterminded a plan to hijack an experimental microwave bomb, and we caught your ass."

They all cheered and raised their glasses in a toast.

Aki sipped her drink and dipped a chip in the spinach artichoke dip. "This guy gets better and better every day."

Rueben saw Marshall sitting alone, hunched over his beer in a corner. He sighed, grabbed a plate, and heaped a handful of fries on it. He took it over to Marshall's table. "Here, Dad." He set the plate down.

Marshall glanced up at him as though he wasn't quite sure if he could trust the gesture.

"No one should have to drink alone."

Marshall started to growl something under his breath but stopped mid-sentence and said, "Thank you."

"You're welcome." Rueben sat and sipped his beer. There was a long, awkward silence, and Rueben sensed his dad wanted to say something.

After two false starts, Marshall said, "So you helped Martha, huh?"

Rueben nodded and perched precariously on his chair.

"Should have been a cop. You might have had what it takes."

Rueben couldn't believe his ears. An actual compliment. "Thanks, Dad," he started. "You know—"

"Then again, you have flat feet and the constitution of a gerbil, and who orders French fries at a bar? Peanuts, son. Peanuts," Marshall growled.

"There he is," Rueben muttered, and he took the offending plate of fries. "Now, if you'll excuse me, I want to celebrate. You want to sulk."

Marshall reached out and grabbed the plate. He gulped back his thanks, but Rueben saw it.

Rueben smiled and went back to his table. As he was about to sit, he felt a tiny sting on his neck. "Ouch."

When he reached up to feel it, a fly buzzed away from him. At least it looked like a fly or maybe a horsefly. It was hard to tell but what else could it have been? Those things could bite.

Oh well. He sat and turned to see what his friends were talking about now.

Aki was saying, "You would not believe how much work it is."

"What?" Rueben joined the conversation.

"The summit. I'm doing pre-security checks."

Rueben noticed that the TV was showing news coverage of the upcoming World Leaders Summit on Monday.

"You know," Aki continued, "only the event of the decade. Every world leader in one building. And it just has to be here in New York."

An exterior shot of the United Nations building downtown flashed across the TV. The World Summit had been in the national news media for months, and now it was all going down in three days. The main topic on the agenda: global peace and the looming threat of violence between certain neighboring countries, some of which had nuclear capabilities.

The entire CIA was overwhelmed with working all these angles on the conference. Nothing bad would be allowed to happen at such an important gathering on US soil. In addition to making sure the United States was clear of espionage and domestic and international terrorism at large, Rueben had been working on ensuring that air travel was secure for the event.

That meant securing private airports and staggering and scrambling dignitaries' travel plans, including staging decoy flights with full press at both public and private airports all week.

Aki was leading the entire operation, including working with the FBI and other intelligence and security agencies to ensure that the security at the event was clean, and there was no access to the buildings or hotels any time in the past week.

On the clandestine spy front, that included paying off hotel and business owners all over the city to shut down their businesses. She was far more senior than he was, and he didn't envy her one bit on this event.

"I'm up to my ass in security protocols for these guys," she said. "The prime minister of this, the president of that, the king of this, the queen of that...and everybody is convinced that *they* are the biggest security risk on the planet."

Martha frowned. "Well, they aren't wrong, are they?"

Aki sipped her cocktail. "Not exactly, but it's a pain in the ass. The prince of Saudi Arabia stipulates that 'no public affairs shall be conducted anywhere within five miles of where the prince will reside.'"

Martha cocked her eyebrow. "What the hell does that mean?"

"It means he's so paranoid about security, literally no one can live or even stay within a five-mile radius, or even have any kind of business within five miles. This is New York City —how do you have five miles of nothing?"

They all laughed.

"So the summit organizers finally found him a place upstate, but now the government has to bribe every mom-and-pop within a five-mile radius of the hotel, or the prince walks."

Rueben rubbed his head. "Jesus."

"So, the summit crew has been working on that, but of course, you've got the 'Murica mom-and-pops that aren't going to shut down for the week just because the government offers them a stipend. So, we have to send agents out there to 'persuade' them. That's just one example of the crap I've been dealing with."

Rueben raised his beer at her. "Props."

She returned his toast. "The whole thing starts on Monday. I suspect we'll all be doing overtime next week, so let's make this weekend last for as long as we can."

Martha gulped her beer and set it on the table hard. "Forever, if possible."

While she talked, Buzz stared off with an odd smile on his face. "Crikey."

Rueben laughed. "For the hundredth time, Buzz, you're American. Use American expressions, please. British or Australian ones don't work without the accent."

"The Raider Warlock pinball machine! Those are collector's editions. I can't believe they... How did they...."

Buzz jumped up and went to play the eighties collectible while Martha, half-drunk now, stumbled off to the bathroom.

Rueben was still concerned about Marshall sitting by himself. They had invited him back over, but he kept refusing as Aki had predicted. "Leave him be," she said, and even though Rueben agreed, he still felt for the old man.

Everyone needed someone, and Rueben was the only one Marshall had. It had been fifteen years since Carolyn had left and five since Marshall left the police force.

Marshall had been a hero then, and he'd had a hero's send-off. Now all those guys were gone, and young ones who only knew of him if they'd read the history files filled the force.

Rueben debated whether to talk to him again when he noticed his father staring at something at the opposite end of the bar. Suddenly Marshall rose and pushed his way through the crowd as if he'd seen someone or something, but Rueben saw nothing out of the ordinary. There were too many people standing and sitting and walking around in the bar. Maybe Marshall was tapping into his cop's intuition and following up on a "lead." Marshall did that occasionally, and it wasn't uncommon these days for that intuition to amount to nothing more than paranoia. It was kind of sad.

"Whatcha staring at?" Aki was a little tipsy now.

Rueben shook his head back to reality. "You think it's true that we end up like our parents?"

"Eh, I wouldn't know. Marge and Bob are hippies that moved to a cult in Sedona ten years ago. Changed their names to Sitar and Pegasus, and they don't believe in clothing. I could be wrong, but I don't see myself going that way."

"No clothing, huh?" Rueben smirked, steeling him for what he was about to say next. "I wouldn't mind seeing you do that."

He hoped that was the right thing to say, and he relaxed as she smacked his arm. They both laughed.

"Sitar and Pegasus. I wouldn't have guessed they would have a daughter who works in the CIA."

"Yeah, I keep up with them using company intelligence."

He plugged his ears with his fingers. "La-la-la, I didn't hear that."

"I told you my parents are nudists, and *that's* the part you didn't want to hear?"

"What?"

She laughed, then a shadow passed over her face.

"You worry about them, don't you?"

"Yeah. I could go to jail for checking on them with company intelligence, but it's the only way I can keep them safe. They don't talk to me because they disapprove of my involvement with the government. You know, according to them I'm very literally Big Brother."

She washed the words down with a long gulp of beer. "So, I keep them off the government radar when they pop up. And they do."

"They pop up, huh? What are they into, might I ask?"

"Nothing major. They're mild anarchists who wind up on watch lists every once in a while. You know, they follow all the wrong Facebook pages and will believe just about anything."

"Ah, yeah. Those types."

"Yeah. Those types."

"They weren't always like that?"

"No, they were once willing slaves to the 'real world.' Bob was a surgeon before he became Sitar and mom used to be a financial advisor."

"So money was never an issue for you growing up?"

"Would you believe I had a trust fund? Ha. I guess maybe that's one of the reasons why I was attracted to Mike. He and his family were pretty flush too."

"Right."

Mike Fury was her ex-boyfriend who was now in rehab for anger management. He had a complete meltdown at work and trashed the office in a fit of rage. Punched Sven, the head honcho in the face, too. It had been quite the spectacle.

A spectacle that Rueben was the unwitting catalyst for.

Wait, at least he had been in one version of the timeline. To prevent the microwave bombing of NYC, Rueben had warped backward to before Mike had his meltdown. Aki had still broken up with Mike, and he'd had taken it fairly well—all things considered. Instead of punching Sven, he'd chucked a coffee maker against the break room fridge. His punishment: mandatory anger management classes.

Aki drummed her long, manicured fingernails on the table. "I wasn't lying about what I said. Well, at least the first part. You are a hero, you know."

He raised an eyebrow, and his lips rose in a smirk. "Yeah? And the second?"

She laughed, and her eyes twinkled. "You might have what it takes."

"I might, huh?" He switched to an Australian accent only

slighter better than Buzz's. "Does he have what it takes to traverse the land down under?"

She snorted into her drink as she laughed.

He continued his *Discovery Channel* narration. "Or will he be engulfed by the raging fire of defeat, never to be seen or heard from again?"

"I guess we'll have to see, huh?" She sidled up close to him, and he could smell her perfume. Her voice lowered. "We'll have to tune in next week?"

"I don't know. I think next week might be too long."

"I don't know. After Mike Fury, I think I might be over dating other agents."

Rueben tensed. Man, he hated Mike and how he and Aki had dated.

Aki twirled a strand of her hair around her finger. "Oh, did I mention Mike is coming back to work soon?"

"He passed all his anger management classes?"

"Uh, most of them. I think. And just my luck, he got assigned to summit duty with me."

Rueben nearly spat out his drink. "Oh, uh, really? I've been meaning to challenge him at the shooting range."

Aki batted her eyelashes at him.

"It's a guy thing."

She nodded. "After working with you on the Pout case, you proved to me that you're a badass."

Rueben cupped a hand around his ear. "Can you repeat that, please?"

Aki snorted and smacked his arm.

Rueben cleared his throat as if putting on airs, glad to be talking about anything other than Mike. "The badass thing is a fraud, really. I'm an ordinary computer geek. I mean, I know what HTML stands for, and I can write in binary code about as quickly as I write in English."

"Oh yeah, that's geeky."

"Believe me, I know. So this is why I am most certainly not a badass."

"You're turning on the charm here, aren't you, Binary Code?"

"I'm just saying that the only reason you think I'm a badass is because I've lived a hundred lifetimes."

"What?" She doubled over laughing and snorted her drink. "You are a nerd! What kind of manga weird shit is that?"

He laughed along with her because she didn't know. She didn't know that he was a real-life superhero who had died and come back to life more times than he could count. She didn't know that he had only saved the world because he had so many chances to do it right. She didn't know how many times he had tried to win her heart before she'd finally given it to him.

She didn't know he was in love with her—the real her— not the fantasy of being with the hottest agent in the CIA.

"Don't worry about it." He smiled at her.

"You are a badass." She laughed. "How you singlehandedly took down Pout's three truckers at that warehouse... But, what can I say? Some girls never learn."

He tried to think up a witty reply, but Martha screamed from the other side of the bar. Rueben and Aki jumped up and rushed through the crowd.

"What's going on?" Reuben gasped.

A few feet away from him, a man in jeans and a white hoodie with stripes on the shoulders had Martha pinned against the wall, smashing her into the glass around the

Kerouac poster. He had his forearm pressed against Martha's throat, cutting off her air supply.

Fuck, Rueben thought, *is that the guy from the surveillance cams with Alister Pout?*

No time to think about that now. "Get off her!" Rueben yelled.

He grabbed the man and attempted to pull him off her. In the last few weeks, Rueben had been training hard. Jujitsu, target practice, and boxing. The aim: should his powers ever be needed again, he'd be able to save the world with far less dying.

That was the hope, at least.

Training or not, he could hardly grip the breadth of the man's massive forearms. They were rock-hard.

Rueben threw a punch at the man's lower back, aiming for the kidneys as Martha had instructed him during the Pout combat training. He figured the man's hoodie would be soft. It was, but some kind of metal armor concealed beneath it was hard. Rueben's knuckles popped, and he staggered back a step.

Damn, who was this guy? And what was he wearing—

Hoodie Man threw an elbow, and Rueben fell into the wall beside Martha.

The assailant continued to apply pressure to Martha's neck until her eyes rolled up in her sockets. Then he released her, letting her drop to the bar's floor. He turned to face Rueben, his face concealed by his hood and a pair of sunglasses. The man drew a silenced pistol from under his hoodie. "You want her? Come here and face me."

Everyone in the bar screamed and ran for cover, hiding under restored cars or booths.

Someone yelled, "He's got a gun."

The phrase resonated through the bar, and panic ensued.

The bartender tried to step in. "Sir, if you don't put down the gun—"

"What? You're calling the cops?" The gunman scoffed. "At this hour, it'll take them ten minutes to get here."

"What is it that you want?" Rueben asked the man.

The man in the hoodie laughed as he stood next to Martha's unconscious body. "A lot. I want a lot."

"Huh?" Shock started to grip Rueben as he tried to determine if Martha was still breathing or if she was dead.

Her assailant turned on Rueben with a huffing intake of breath. He jerked the silenced pistol at Rueben's chest and in a cocky voice, said, "You want to fight, kiddo? Let's see how much you've learned."

CHAPTER THREE

Friday, May 19, 10:41 p.m.

Buzz was the first to react. Without warning, he pulled out a homemade taser. "Take this, fucker."

Rueben was genuinely shocked.

The last fight they'd been in, Buzz had hidden in a closet and had been nearly traumatized by being held hostage. Things had changed in the last three months.

Go, Buzz.

With a confidence Rueben had never seen, Buzz shot the taser at the man, who grunted and recoiled.

Unfortunately, Hoodie Man quickly recovered. He tucked the gun back under his hoodie with one hand while reaching into his pocket with the other, and with one quick lunge, he punched Buzz in the chest. It didn't look like a particularly hard blow—as far as punches go—but Rueben saw the air knocked from his buddy's lungs as it propelled Buzz backward. He collapsed onto a booth table like a martyr.

"Buzz!"

Then Rueben noticed the futuristic gauntlet on Hoodie

Man's fist. In the fleeting glance he got of it, it resembled a metallic-colored thin nylon glove. For some reason, it reminded Rueben of the hard metal body armor or whatever was under the gunman's hoodie.

Who the hell was he and what beef did he have with Martha?

Rueben tried to focus and remember all his combat training as he prepared to rush the assailant. Before he could act, Aki planted her stiletto into the man's side with a swift kick. It *clicked* as it connected with the armor beneath his hoodie, and it threw her off. The man whipped around, and without hesitation Aki delivered a sharp left hook to his jaw, followed by a quick knee to the groin. The man fell back into a shiny stack of Goodyear tires, and they scattered and rolled. He quickly recovered and pushed Aki hard against the open door of a VW bus, and she rebounded to the floor in a heap as the door slammed closed.

Crap. Had Aki hit her head on the door? Was she okay?

How were they supposed to fight this man?

Rueben frantically scanned the bar for his dad but didn't see him. If anyone else was going to bullrush their attacker, it would be Marshall. His bite really was as bad as his bark—at least it had been during his father's days on the force.

All Rueben saw were people hiding and taking cover under tables and behind counters. These patrons were drunk, trapped, and scared. A couple of college-age party girls hiding in the Mercedes booth looked like they were about to have a nervous breakdown.

"Get these people out of here," Rueben yelled to the bartender.

"The cops are on their way, sir. I'm going to need you to calm down."

Rueben pointed at Hoodie Man and Aki, who had stood up and now tried to engage the gunman again in close combat. Whew. So she wasn't dead. But she was outmatched, and it would soon show.

Aki glanced Rueben's way. "Try to get these people out of here. I'll try to hold him off."

Rueben didn't want to leave her fighting this man by himself. But she was more experienced than he was. He shoved a finger at the bartender. "I know the police are on their way, but this guy's crazy. Is there a back door? Help me get these people out of here."

The bartender and bar manager looked at each other and shrugged.

The bar manager clapped his hands. "Okay, all of you, let's make our way back through this way."

Rueben and the waitstaff started gathering the patrons and ushering them through the employee areas and out the back door.

He was about to go to Aki's aid when he noticed one older woman crouched in a corner, visibly shaken. "Ma'am, you're going to have to leave," he told her. "It's not safe."

"I was in the first tower," she whimpered.

The first tower? His eyes widened. 9/11. PTSD. He had been too young to remember that, so he didn't know how to handle it. He followed his instincts and got down low with her.

She burst into tears. "I can't...I can't do it again."

His heart broke for this poor lady. He spoke in a soft, gentle tone. "This isn't a terrorist attack. This is a drunk man in a bar, and there are plenty of ways out. You don't have to be afraid." He offered his hand. "Come on. Take my hand. I'll get you out of here."

She grabbed it, and he helped her up. He ushered her through the crowd and out the back door with the others.

As they herded the stragglers out into the night, Rueben ran into Marshall. Rueben met his dad's eyes. "Are you okay?"

Marshall glanced down at the ground, then back up at Rueben. "Uh, yeah. I...I'll help get the rest of the people out the back."

Rueben nodded and flew back through the Exit Bar. After checking on both Martha and Buzz to make sure that they were still alive—they were—he rejoined Aki, never gladder for all the combat skills he had packed away back from the days when Martha and Buzz used to kill him repeatedly.

Aki was holding her own, considering her blood alcohol level at the moment, but she was slowly losing ground. Rueben saw her energy fading as she and Hoodie Man dodged blows. The man still wore the metallic gauntlet. Rueben figured that if it struck Aki, it would neutralize her just like Buzz. Sweat dripped down her forehead, and she panted harder.

Rueben rushed in at the man, but he easily sidestepped him and tossed Rueben sideways onto a table in the center of the room. It buckled under his weight, and he groaned as he connected with the floor and rolled off it.

The man in the hoodie, acting as if he'd just swatted a fly, directed his attention back to Aki. "You getting tired yet, Princess?"

"Never!" She spun-kicked him right in his abdomen.

Her kick deflected and *clanged* off his chest. A brief look of confusion appeared on her face, but she hid it quickly enough.

What the hell was this guy wearing beneath his hoodie? And who the hell was he? Some futuristic soldier or an armor-plated knight from the past? It made no sense.

Not at all slowed by her kick, the man chuckled and threw Aki against the brick wall.

She rose with scrapes on the side of her arm and a small tear in her dress hem. She punched him again in the jaw and drew blood.

Rueben clambered to his feet, suddenly realizing that he still hadn't gotten a good look at the gunman's face. All throughout the fight, his hood shrouded his sunglasses-covered face.

The gunman wiped the blood off his lips. "It just occurred to me that you think you can beat me, Lucy Liu!" He licked his lips with lust.

Rueben cringed. Sure, Aki was of Asian descent and the same age as the *Charlie's Angels* actress in her prime. But, wasn't Lucy of Chinese ancestry?

"I'm Korean, you racist bastard! And no, I don't think I can beat you—I know I can!"

Aki kicked him again, and he laughed.

He laughed so nastily that it turned Rueben's stomach. "All the better. You Korean girls—"

Before he could finish what was sure to be an explicit comment, she surprised him with a right kick under the knee. He folded a little but regained his composure and threw another punch at her. She blocked it and maneuvered away from him.

Suddenly, Aki darted close and leaned into her assailant while she tried to grab the man's pistol tucked back under his hoodie.

"Stop that," the gunman muttered, but it was too late. Aki got control of the gun. Her assailant twisted, and they both fell to the bar's floor. The spitting cough of the silenced weapon sounded, and Aki groaned. The man in the hoodie rolled her off him, and she lay on the floor with unseeing eyes and blood pooling out from a gunshot wound over her heart.

Rueben's mouth dropped. "You bastard!" With his heart about to burst, he charged toward Aki's murderer, full of adrenaline.

The gunman tucked the pistol back under his hoodie and met Rueben's attack, deflecting him and shoving Rueben to the side. "That wasn't supposed to happen," the man said.

But it had. Aki lay dead and bleeding a few yards away, and there was only one way to fix it.

Rueben had to die.

God, he hated dying. It wasn't like in a video game. It was a long process where overwhelming pain took over, and he had to fight back his instincts to stay alive—struggling to breathe and whatnot. They—the lack of oxygen, severe blood loss, bones piercing his lungs, etc.—eventually won, and he died. What fun it always was.

It had to happen. With enough calm and focused concentration, he could time warp back to before Hoodie Man ever stepped foot in the bar and call the cops to apprehend him before all this madness ever happened. Before his friends got hurt. Before Aki was...murdered.

Rueben drew a deep breath. In order to die, he needed a weapon—or at least someone else to kill him. The gunman was the perfect person. It was time to poke the bear. "Here goes."

In one quick, forceful motion, he grabbed a wooden chair, lifted it high, and smashed it over the guy's raised arms. Splintered wood rained down over the fight scene. Rueben expected—wanted—a fatal assault. Yet instead of fighting him, the man paused and turned to him with an odd smile.

His toothy grin and laugh sent shivers down Rueben's

spine. Although the hood and sunglasses covered most of Badass Hoodie Man's face, Rueben thought the guy was about forty years old. He cracked his knuckles as he stared down Rueben. "You looking to die, kid?"

"I could ask the same of you."

The man laughed. "I'm not going to make dying easy for you, you know."

"It never is."

The man sneered. Then police sirens rang in the background, coming ever closer. Blue-and-white lights shone through the windows. Rueben was running out of time.

He had to get this guy to kill him.

Rueben held up his fists. "You think you're big, tough guy? Going around hitting women. Come on, show me what you got."

Rueben was a lanky, computer-nerd type, and this dude, well, he was well-muscled, had a curious gauntlet and metal body armor, and a devil-may-care attitude.

This challenge was exactly what it seemed to any onlooker: a suicide mission.

Rueben gulped in anticipation of the intense amount of pain this guy was going to dole out. There was no way out of it. He danced around, waiting for a punch.

Instead of attacking him, the man used his remaining moments of freedom to pull out a syringe. He held it needlepoint up, pushed out a droplet, then tapped the cylinder of clear liquid with his finger.

Rueben raised an eyebrow. "A little heroin?"

The man laughed. "It's not for me. It's for you. With what I have in here, you'll wish it was heroin."

Rueben slowly backed away. Before he could wonder what was in the syringe, the man chased him. Rueben instinctively scrambled up on top of the Jaguar booth. He ripped off a gleaming metal wheel hub and held it before him like a shield. He didn't know what this guy was up to, but it didn't sound like this injection would kill him slowly.

At that moment, the door burst open and two cops rushed in, brandishing guns. "Freeze. Everybody freeze."

Rueben and the gunman held their hands up, and the cops quickly noticed Aki's body on the floor.

One of the cops stared wide-eyed at the unconscious body lying against the wall. "Shit, Martha?"

Hoodie Man ran toward the back entrance, and the two cops chased. When their line of sight was clear, they fired concentrated shots that found their mark but deflected harmlessly off the gunman's back.

Damn. What kind of hi-tech body armor deflected bullets?

It didn't matter. What *did* matter was warping back in time and preventing all this from happening. To do that, Rueben had to die.

Taking a deep breath, he sprinted into the firing range of the police officers' guns.

One of the cops waved his gun at him. "What the hell? You're obstructing justice, and that murderer is going down whether you stand in the way or not. Now, you got one warning. Move it."

Rueben backed off, mainly because it was pointless. The cop wouldn't murder him. Man, had that plan backfired, no pun intended. Maybe he could try again.

With Rueben out of the way, the two cops chased the gunman out the back door. Rueben followed them, hoping for another chance at a stray bullet. Luckily, the bar's staff had escorted all the patrons well away from the building so it was only the gunman, the two police officers, and Rueben. He saw a dumpster in an alley though, and huffing with a palm steadying himself against it was Marshall.

The cops chased the gunman down an alley, yelling and shooting. Rueben joined the chase, attempting to throw himself in the path of the bullets again.

"Damn idiot!" Marshall yelled from his spot against the dumpster. "You want to be civilian collateral damage? Get out of the way, son!"

The hooded gunman made it about half a block away from the bar when he came to a chain-link fence and stopped. Stowing the syringe under his hoodie, his hand went for his gun again.

"Drop the gun," the cop yelled.

The man drew a deep breath. Slowly he set the gun on the ground but hesitated with his palm still caressing the gun's grip.

The other cop squinted down the sights of his pistol, his finger poised over the trigger. "Let go of the gun and put your hands behind your—"

Then it all went down. The hooded gunman raised his weapon and nearly got his shot off, but the second cop had already pulled the trigger. Fire spat from the gun's muzzle, and Hoodie Man crashed backward to the pavement, striking the back of his head on a dumpster. Blood leaked from the man's shoulder under his hoodie, and he didn't move.

The first officer radioed in the situation while the second officer bent and checked for a pulse. Finding one, he kicked the gun a few feet away from the body, holstered his gun, turned Hoodie Man onto his chest, and cuffed his wrists behind his back.

Applying pressure to the wound, he tilted his head up from the unconscious man and toward the first officer who was speaking to someone on his radio with his back to him. Then he glanced back down at the shoulder wound. It wasn't bleeding too badly now, but he'd probably need medical supplies from the police car until the ambulance arrived.

When the officer rose from the apprehended man's body, Rueben had his chance. Neither cop was facing Hoodie Man, and Rueben snuck over and grabbed the gunman's weapon, noting a knife concealed inside the man's boot.

The cops turned, drawing their guns again. "Hey!"

One of them sighted down his gun, while the other warned, "Set it down, son. I don't know what's going on in your head, but you don't want to do it."

Instead, Rueben turned the gun on himself. This changed the whole scene. The two cops faced each other, and a sympathetic look crossed the first one's face.

He whispered to the other one. "Do you remember what to say from that counseling module?"

"Counseling module? Man, we got a dead cop killer in the street and another with a gun. Don't talk to me about no 'counseling module!'"

The first cop pursed his lips and appeared to be reciting from a script. "It's not worth it. You've got a lot to live for. We're gonna get you some help. Okay? Get you to see a counselor. Just drop the gun, okay?"

The other cop scoffed. "Ah Jesus, man. This is not the way we do this shit."

Before Rueben knew what was happening, the second cop had his hand pinned behind his back.

Rueben cried out as the officer's grip squeezed his wrist. "Owww."

Then the cop grabbed the other one and held it behind his back. It cut off his circulation, and Rueben felt that disconcerting dull ache that reminded him of the one time he got a really awful acupressure massage. "Look, you got the wrong idea, here. I'm not—"

The cop kicked his legs apart, and Rueben heard him reaching for his cuffs. "We're going to need you to drop the gun, son."

Rueben tried to talk fast. "It's not what it looks like."

They didn't listen. With both hands pinned behind his back, Rueben knew he had no choice but to release the gun. The cop already had his hand on it. He just had to let go. He wriggled his fingers free of the weapon, which the officer promptly confiscated. The grip on his wrists only lessened and didn't release. The cop sounded like he was having a hard time with the cuffs.

The cop replied soothingly, "There you go."

These guys were an obvious and literal interpretation of the good-cop-bad-cop routine, and if Rueben wasn't so worried about going to jail, he would have found it funny. Now he was just scared out of his mind.

Once, when he was a teenager, he had been behind the school with a couple of kids who were getting drunk and high. He wasn't doing either but trying to interview them for the school newspaper about their rock band.

The interview wasn't going so well. His voice recorder kept screwing up, and he was trying to take notes but having a difficult time transcribing the frontman's speech about, "Don't be into labels and just let the music happen, man. Music comes from our primal souls, the part of us that we share with nature. We can't label that instinct to make sound and art through our cultural biases of what we understand sound to be."

"I'm sorry, can you repeat that whole 'primal souls' part? I didn't get the rest of that."

It had been at that moment the cop sirens had sounded. Before Rueben had even known what was happening, the band had all dropped their spoils and ran like hell.

This had left Rueben with all their evidence of vices. The truth eventually won out in the eyes of the school and the law, but Marshall never believed it. He made Rueben spend an hour in jail to scare him straight. The highlights of that hour included a drunk named Paco who defended his honor against a meth head named Speedy, who had allegedly just bitten off a guy's ear.

Marshall's plan had worked.

Rueben never did a bad thing again after that. Or at least he was paranoid as hell about it. Now, the prospect of going to jail made him break out in hives, and he was suddenly fourteen again, trying to explain the instinct to create sound or something. He never did understand what that frontman meant.

But then the cops started talking about a fate worse than jail.

The first cop continued, "Come with us. We're going to take you to the hospital, where you can talk about what's going on, all right?"

Shit. There would be no place to die in the psych ward.

"I'm sorry, I'm not suicidal. I just—"

The cop led him away from the scene toward the waiting car. "It's okay. We all have things going on in our lives. Situations we feel like we can't control. Right?"

"Sure, but—"

The cop searched for his script before cutting Rueben off. "But hurting yourself is never the answer. You've got so much to live for. So much potential. It might seem hopeless right now, but it's always darkest before the dawn. Things can turn around in an instant. We just have to remember to make the right choices."

"I'm really not suicidal, I—"

The cop spoke over him in a patronizing tone. "Of course not. Sometimes we all need to take a step back and reevaluate our choices and our responses."

God, he was going to have to play to this guy. If he told him the real reason he'd just tried to off himself—that he had a superpower and when he died, he went back in time—yeah, he'd be going to the nuthouse for real.

And they made sure there was no way for those guys to die. He could be in there for years and stay alive.

Rueben sighed and studied the ground. "You're right. I don't know what came over me. That man attacked my friends. Shot one of them...oh Jesus, and I...lost it all a little. I freaked out. I made a bad choice."

The soft cop patted him on the shoulder, and his face beamed that his pep talk had worked. "Yeah, yeah, that's right, let it out."

The other cop muttered almost unintelligible swears as he led Rueben to the squad car.

Rueben had visions of Speedy licking his lips. "Look, really, I'm not suicidal. I'll see a counselor on my terms. Really. Look, you've uh, got a lot of paperwork here. Come on, do you need any more on this case?"

The two cops stopped and glanced at each other. Paperwork. The universal kryptonite of cops, Rueben knew from Marshall. Marshall even hated signing his permission slips when he was a kid.

The hard one turned to the soft one. "He does have a point."

"All right, we're going to let you go. But please, see someone."

"I will."

The cop let him go, and Rueben twisted away and darted toward Hoodie Man's body.

"Agh, that sonofabitch was lying!"

With the police's footsteps falling heavily behind him, Rueben felt at the gunman's boot. Bingo. The knife.

He grabbed the knife and grimacing with sweaty palms, squeezed his eyes shut and plunged it hard into his chest.

Rueben writhed in the excruciating pain, and the cops rushed toward him. As the light faded, the last thing he saw was Marshall. And the anguish on his face as he stared at him.

Then he died.

CHAPTER FOUR

Friday, May 19, 10:46 p.m.

Rueben reinhabited his body and found himself in the Exit Bar. It always took a moment for him to reorient himself after he'd died. He arrived as the assailant pinned Martha against the wall.

Okay, so this was where they were. Not necessarily where he'd wanted: before Hoodie Man even showed up, but this would do. When training for the Pout mission, Rueben had learned to focus and control how far back in time he traveled whenever he died. He hadn't exactly done that when he'd killed himself this last time.

He glanced at his smartwatch, knowing that it would have recorded his death and time warp for later analysis at Buzz's mansion. Before the Pout mission, Buzz had automated a process that sent himself and Martha an email alerting them that Rueben had just warped as well as notes from before the warp.

However, they'd all agreed to turn that feature off for the foreseeable future to give Rueben some privacy if he wanted to warp back for personal reasons—not that he ever had. Which meant that Buzz and Martha had no clue he'd just died and warped. He could catch them up later, but right now, he had to act and try to save his friends before someone got killed.

Aki.

Rueben's eyes shot to Aki standing amid the crowded bar. Oh, thank God. She was alive. He could kill himself again and go back farther to before this happened, but for now, he wanted to kick Hoodie Man's ass. To do that, he needed a weapon. His eyes locked onto the bar. Perfect. He jumped behind the counter.

The bartender yelled at him, "What the hell? You can't be back here. We have insurance, man."

When Rueben didn't listen and kept throwing stuff around, the bartender kept yelling. "Hey, hey, stop."

Rueben nodded toward the fight, still unseen by the staff. "Yeah? Your insurance cover that?"

The bartender peered in that direction. "What the hell? I'm not dying for this job!" He yelled at the other employees. "We've got a fight. Call the cops! Get Joe!"

Joe, Rueben surmised, must be the manager and wouldn't be much help. While the waitstaff scurried around trying to handle the situation, Rueben rummaged under the counter.

It was a food service establishment. There had to be something. He noticed the lemons chopped in a container and threw them on the ground. Bingo. Right behind the container glistened a serrated steak knife. Had the bartender been eating steak back here while on duty? Eh, better than nothing. He grabbed it, ran back out from behind the counter, and rushed toward the fight scene.

By now, several bar employees were trying to break up the

fight, but no one was getting anywhere. There was mainly a lot of yelling and tussling. The whole bar had noticed, and a couple of vigilante customers had joined the fray. Someone was trying unsuccessfully to pound the assailant with the rim of a Goodyear tire. It wasn't working.

Joe was on-site now, a skinny man with glasses, an untucked dress shirt, and jeans. The only thing that seemed to qualify him to manage a bar in the city was a nose ring. Otherwise, the guy looked like he belonged in an accounting office. "Sir, the cops have been called. Drop the gun."

Oh, Rueben scoffed in his mind. *You didn't add the 'Drop the gun' part before. Way to change things up. He'll drop it now.*

Things were going a bit differently this time, as he'd learned could happen during the Pout mission. Two bouncers from the next bar over had stepped inside at the sound of the noise. They wore security windbreakers, and each had pistols raised, their eyes trained on the guy.

Holy shit. If they had carry permits, at least one of them might have served in the military or on the police force at one time. That was good. The customers slowly backed away, and a tense hush fell over the scene.

The gunman shoved his hip against Martha to keep her from fighting him while he cut off her air supply, and Rueben saw her bite her lip to avoid giving him the satisfaction of letting him know he'd hurt her. "Pretty little young thang, ain't she? Would be a shame for her to die a death of 'friendly fire,' now wouldn't it?" Martha's assailant made eye contact with one of the security guards. "You would know about that, wouldn't you…Lieutenant Roberts?"

The security guard's face turned white. "Fuck you. You don't know what you're talking about." His shaking voice betrayed him.

The gunman laughed maniacally. "Don't I? Tell me now, what really happened out in Kabul?"

The security guard gulped and deflated. Everyone turned to look at the guard, who simply holstered his weapon beneath his jacket and left the restaurant.

Whoa.

Rueben took advantage of the distraction. He held the steak knife up high, and with a good running start, slammed it into the man's back. It tore through the man's white hoodie and penetrated the thin, form-fitting metallic body armor beneath. The blade stabbed into muscle, and the gunman grunted with pain. That was all the satisfaction Rueben got.

Even with his running start, the knife didn't go nearly as far as Rueben hoped. At least Rueben now knew that the man's hi-tech body armor deflected bullets but not blades.

Hoodie Man let Martha go, and she gasped for air, but then he reached behind him and ripped the knife out of his back. The blade dripped red drops onto his boots and the black concrete.

Rueben expected to see a manic fury in his assailant's eyes. Instead, he saw an eerie calmness that fury slowly swallowed. Was he hyped up on drugs?

He laughed at Rueben. "Is that all you could think of? A steak knife? What am I? Chopped liver? Or maybe a nice sirloin?" He scoffed. "Clearly, you haven't repeated this enough times. What is this, your first trip back? Maybe second?"

Oh shit, he's a time warper.

He approached Rueben with the red-tipped knife, and Rueben knew this guy was capable of anything. From behind them, a bar patron screamed, and Rueben scrambled with the rest of the crowd, but the man was faster. He grabbed Rueben by the shirt and slung him face-first against the wall.

"How about I do you a solid and give you a chance for some more practice? You know what they say. Try, try again..." he sang. "If at first you don't succeed."

Then with a harsh laugh, the man slit Rueben's throat.

Serrated blades aren't for slicing—they're for sawing—but Hoodie Man needed only one powerful jerk. Internally screaming at the excruciating pain, Rueben's head lolled to the side, his eyes landing on his smartwatch as his consciousness faded.

Then he died.

Friday, May 19, 10:32 p.m.

Martha was sitting at the table in the bar with Buzz, Aki, and Rueben. Suddenly, she was struck by an uneasy feeling of déjà vu, as if she'd already relived this moment. But she hadn't. She'd never been to this bar in her life until tonight.

Oh shit. Unless Rueben had died and warped back to this spot, and now she remembered bits and pieces.

It usually didn't hit her so strongly. Hell, during the Pout mission, the déjà vu had mainly involved her remembering a van she'd seen in a previous timeline.

She turned to her friends. Aki was saying something, and Martha turned from her to Rueben, who suddenly looked very confused, then frustrated.

Maybe it was nothing.

Buzz's eyes shot wide. "A Raider Warlock pinball machine!" He jumped up and started toward it. "Those are collector's edition. I can't believe they... How did they..." For all Buzz's intelligence, sometimes he seemed like he was ten.

Now it was only the three of them, and Rueben was muttering something to himself. Now it was Aki's turn to look confused.

Shit, shit, shit. If this was a time warp thing, she'd find out soon enough. She pulled up her email on her phone, but she didn't see an automated email from Buzz's computer alerting her to a time warp. Then she remembered they'd agreed to discontinue the email method to give Rueben some privacy.

She sighed.

Life had changed a lot for her since February when they'd busted Pout. For the first time in a long time, she was happy.

Work was good.

She had finally made it off "The Tampon Squad." Now the douchebag post-jocks at work listened when she talked. As a matter of fact, she thought she'd caught a look of intimidation on some of their faces, at least from time to time. She tried not to make much of it.

Her boss kissed her ass these days, which was a far cry from a few months ago when he told her to get a massage and let the veteran cops handle the big cases. Things with her work partner Jake had gotten a lot better, too. He worked with her instead of trying to work around her whenever he thought she was chasing aimless leads.

All in all, she had become a hero in her own right. And everyone had noticed.

Her social life had improved. Only a few months ago, her best friends were old college chums who had turned into what Bridget Jones would call "smug married couples" who wanted to talk about their pregnancies and their Lamaze classes. Her nights were spent with Jimmy Fallon in LCD and harmless flirting with the takeout guy.

Now she had a ragtag group of friends that, while a little

odd and quirky, were turning out to be a good bunch. That, of course, was what happened when you made a score as they had. They had bonded while preventing a national crisis and countless deaths, and they had also put Alister behind bars.

Trying to smuggle in and detonate an experimental microwave weapon...

Martha shuddered. If Rueben had time-warped, surely the situation this time wasn't as grave as that.

They wouldn't have prevented it without Rueben and his time warp ability. She still didn't understand it, but now she believed it. Aki didn't know about it. Buzz loved it and damn near pissed his pants every time anyone brought it up.

Now, in the bar, Buzz stood in the corner hunched over a pinball machine, getting ready to insert a coin to play.

"I'm, uh, gonna go catch up with Buzz," Rueben hurriedly told Aki as he stood. "Find out about the Raider pinballs."

Aki laughed. "There's a dirty joke there." She didn't notice that he cocked his head at Martha, motioning her to the pinball machine with him. He exaggeratedly blinked as if sending her a coded message.

Then Martha knew. Yep, this was a Rueben time warp thing.

She glanced around the room and didn't see much to worry about. Everything seemed normal. Of course, she was more than a little drunk at the moment.

Rueben turned to Aki, placing a tender hand on top of her hand. Even though she was inebriated, Martha's cop instincts saw through Rueben's hollow smile to the somber expression beneath. "You cool to chill here?"

Aki didn't notice. "Sure. Don't be too long."

He winked, and both he and Martha left the table. Martha pretended to head toward the bathroom. As soon as she was out of Aki's line of vision, she hurried toward the pinball machine. She wore heels about twice a year and had never learned the art of running in them. How did Carrie Bradshaw ever do that?

Buzz and Rueben were already in conversation at the pinball machine—which now resembled the miniature whiteboard of a college physics class marked up by the frantic scrawl of dry erase marker in Buzz's hand.

Martha tapped an equation full of Greek letters and angle markings. "What is it this time?"

Buzz gave Martha an irritated look before turning back to Rueben. "It's not like we haven't already discussed the possibility of multiple time warpers."

"Yeah, but right now?" Rueben threw up his hands. "And I think he's connected to Pout."

Pout. Martha raised her eyebrows. Not only had Rueben warped, but it might be connected to Pout.

Turning away from Rueben and Buzz, she let her eyes wander over the bar's interior until they landed on a guy standing near the back entrance, wearing a white hoodie. A white hoodie with stripes on the shoulders.

"Man in the white hoodie." The words slipped from her mouth, and Rueben nodded uneasily.

"That's right. Um, déjà vu?"

Martha nodded, then felt at her neck. "What does he do?"

Rueben studied her for a few moments. "I think I know what set him off. You recognized him, probably went after him. Then he…"

Now Martha grabbed Rueben's wrist. "What happens? What does he do to me? Shit. Does he kill me?"

Rueben swallowed. "He chokes you until you black out."

"Egads," Buzz blurted.

Rueben continued. "We've got about seven minutes before Hoodie Man starts shit and people start getting hurt."

She had learned to trust Rueben, but it was never easy to think or hear about these things without thinking she was in some sort of Bizzaro World. For God's sake, she was a cop. A practical thinker. There was nothing practical about how time travel worked.

Buzz stroked his chin. "All right, what's the plan, then? We take him down?" He pulled out some sort of homemade weapon, and Martha stared at it.

"What is that?"

Rueben was quick to answer. "It's a homemade taser, and it's not going to work."

Buzz frowned as Rueben tossed the device behind him. "Shit. There went three days of product design at the lab."

"No, no, no, it works. It just won't save you. This dude is the badass to end all badasses."

Martha scowled. "There must be something we can do."

Rueben ran his tongue over his teeth in thought. "That's what we have to figure out. And we have less than seven minutes to do it."

CHAPTER FIVE

Friday, May 19, 10:46 p.m.

At the behest of Rueben's hasty instructions, Buzz, Aki, and Martha headed for the bar's entrance. On the way toward the door, Rueben "borrowed" a steak knife from a patron's plate and slid it into his pocket.

Outside the Exit Bar, Friday night in New York City was in full swing. The live music bar next door played loud unintelligible rock, and pierced and tattooed patrons wandered in and out, joining and leaving the throngs as they pleased.

Rueben and his friends had other plans than to enter another bar. Or at least they had *a* plan. It wasn't the brightest of ideas, but with less than seven minutes to both decide and execute it—and with alcohol in all their bloodstreams—it was the only one they could come up with.

A few moments later, they were standing at the mouth of an alley with a line of sight on the Exit Bar. "Rueben," Aki said, slightly tipsy. "If you're pulling a prank..." She batted her eyes at him, and Rueben swallowed.

"I wish it were, but this is no joke."

In the darkness, Buzz postulated. "So let me get this straight. We plan to lie in wait for this unidentified gunman in a white hoodie, and then we four ambush him?"

Rueben watched the crowds filter in and out of the bar. "That's the short and long of it."

Buzz frowned. "What about the metallic body armor he's wearing and that hi-tech gauntlet you said he has? And you mentioned he carries a silenced pistol."

Throwing up his hands, Rueben turned to Martha and Aki. "Anyone have any better ideas?"

Aki giggled, and Rueben thought it was about the sexiest thing he'd ever heard. He shook his head to clear it. Then Aki made things worse by planting a palm on his shoulder and meeting his eyes. "Good plan, boss man. Now let's kick some ass."

Buzz tugged his shirt collar at the public display of affection, then pulled up a phone app. "I'm calculating our respective body weights, and if this man is the height and breadth that you describe, I would say that together we equal only slightly more than him. Of course, that's not accounting for muscle mass, which can be quite tricky to determine without the proper—"

Rueben ran his hands through his hair. Buzz was a great guy, but sometimes Rueben needed him to shut up. This was one of those times. "Look, consider that your X factor, okay? Muscle mass."

Buzz typed away. "Well then, I would say that we would have to approach him from a velocity of... Hmmm..." Buzz scratched his chin as he made calculations and grabbed sticks and rocks to lay out angle variations. Based on Rueben's experience with their opponent, they had much bigger problems than velocity.

Martha adjusted her dress in a futile attempt to be less formal and more utilitarian. She took off her earrings and laid them neatly on a ledge. "Don't want them to get in the way. Costume jewelry, anyway. You're sure you saw him leave?"

"Yes, I did," Rueben said definitively. "I specifically saw him come into the bar. He looked around the room and walked out. I don't know where he went or why. But he wasn't with anyone and didn't seem to talk to anyone."

Aki nodded as she took in the information. "Then he's probably working alone."

Rueben answered, "As far as we know, but he'll be back. He has something he has to do in here. Trust me."

Buzz toyed with his homemade taser and propped it up in the holes of a chain-link fence. "This thing is controlled by an app I wrote. So, if I have it here… Everyone step back."

The whole group nearly jumped out of the way of his invention. He pushed a button, and the taser emitted a terrific electric blast. "See, it works."

"That ought to do it," Martha observed.

"Right. Now, if I rig it against this wall this way, it will stun at a forty-seven-degree angle. All he has to do is come past that crack, right there"—he shone his phone flashlight at a small sidewalk crack—"and I can activate it from here, and boom. He's toast."

Aki nodded approvingly. "That's great work, Buzz. What are you? Some kind of mad scientist?"

Buzz chuckled nervously, and Rueben cleared his throat. "I told you, it's not going to work as a sole weapon. You'll buy some time, but you'll need a backup plan."

Buzz whined. "I'm not comfortable with hand-to-hand combat."

Rueben scoffed and was quick to answer. "Yes, you are."

"I am?"

Rueben produced the steak knife from his pocket that he'd pilfered on the way out of the bar. "Trust me. Use it."

Buzz frowned, grabbed the knife, and inspected the serrated edge. "There are seventeen points on this knife, each one capable of making an individual incision."

There's Buzz the sadist, Rueben thought.

Buzz fingered the knife. "But serrated blades aren't meant for stabbing—they're for sawing and cutting. However, with the proper angle of incision..." He held the weapon awkwardly and made a clumsy lunge. "I can't do it."

Rueben smirked. "Deep inside you, Buzz, is a much more violent man. Reach inside. You'll find him."

"I resent that remark."

"Me too."

Aki corrected his stance. She was starting to take things seriously, which was good. "If you want to disable an enemy, you need to do it like this. Weight evenly distributed on both feet."

"Okay." Buzz stared down at his feet, and Aki directed him on how to stand.

"You have to use your body weight to your advantage. You would know all about that. Velocity."

"Velocity I get, but how to harness that power? I'm afraid I'm at a loss."

Buzz and Aki worked on knife lessons while Rueben continued to watch the sidewalk for the gunman. There was no sign of him. He had to come back, didn't he? Rueben didn't know why he'd left the bar, but he was sure he had seen him walk in and out. Obviously, he had done that before without them noticing, so he clearly was on his way back. Did he come to check that they were there and leave to get his gun?

Aki had finished the knife lessons, and now she looked irritated and cold. Winter ran late this year, and in May the evening breeze still had a sting to it. "I wish you would tell me this anonymous tip that you keep getting intel from. It would help us both."

He repeated what he had told her a dozen times. "I can't. I told you, you'd be uh, implicated, and I can't put you in that position."

"I have a higher security clearance than you."

He blushed. "Don't make this about that."

"Then tell me. You don't think I can handle it?"

He couldn't explain to her the truth about himself. Not yet, anyway. When Rueben had first found out about his ability, Buzz had accepted it pretty quickly. Martha...well, Martha still gave him looks every time he mentioned time warping, but at least she went with it.

Aki wasn't ready, and he knew it.

One day, maybe, but not today.

He shoved his hands deep in his pockets. "Look, I care about you..."

She drew a deep breath, and her expression rang with little patience. He talked over her, not wanting to hear any objection she might counter with.

"I mean, like, you know, as a friend and all—or more than that, if well, I don't know. Look, that's not the point. The point is, I don't want anything to happen to you. Not that you can't take care of yourself or anything, but I feel like it's better this way."

She didn't respond to that but rubbed her arms in her sleeveless formal. "It's freezing out here."

It was. He slipped off his sport jacket and handed it to her. "Here." The cool spring air cut through his dress shirt.

She scanned the sidewalk and pushed the jacket away. "You don't have to do that. It's fine."

Aki's words came in hard. She didn't trust him. Why would she? She barely knew him, but he knew her.

They'd had many conversations about so many different things, not that she remembered.

They'd kissed, not that she remembered.

He'd had almost a dozen interactions that she didn't remember.

He did, and her brushoff hit him hard.

She folded her arms across her chest for warmth. The wind blew her dark hair as she studied the sidewalk outside of the alley intently. A car of drunk partiers flew by them, and a young man hung out the passenger window. "Hey there baby, looking good!"

Aki shot him a look so withering, even Rueben felt like slinking away. She pulled out her phone.

"What are you doing?"

"We should call for backup. If the intel is as good as you say, we're not going to be able to take him alone. We'll need to follow protocol and get Sven—"

Sven Larson was the division director and their boss. If he got involved, it would become a formal operation, with accountability reaching the Pentagon and even to the president.

The last thing Rueben wanted was the president of the United States weighing in on his actions.

"Would you please trust me on this? I got us Pout."

She turned back to face him. Her eyes burned with frustration before they softened. If only slightly. "Okay, but I need to know what's going on. You can't keep me in the dark."

"I'm not. There's just shit going on that—"

"You want me in the dark on. I get it. But without more to go on, we're stuck."

"We had less on Pout."

"Are you kidding? We had a ton on Pout."

"By the time I got you involved, yes. Before you got on board, it was only the three of us."

She raised her eyebrows and studied the little band of three amigos. "Rueben, I'm a field agent."

"So am I."

"Yeah. Now. After Pout, you got promoted. But I've been doing this for a long time, and I've watched dozens of agents come and go. Look…" Her words trailed off, and she searched for more. "I know they leave this off the trainee pamphlet, but we're expendable."

"I know that."

"No, you don't. Not really. If we fuck this up—"

"I don't think Sven would have us assassinated over—"

Aki shook her head. "I'm not saying that. Although…well, never mind. What I mean is that if we fuck up, there's no 'innocent until proven guilty' for us. It's more like 'justice is blind.' It would be a threat to national security to give us a fair trial." She leaned against the fence and glanced over at Martha and Buzz. Neither were listening to her.

"What are you saying?"

She studied her fingernails and continued in a lowered tone. "I've seen things, Rueben. I know things. I've watched as the agency had to deny involvement with agents caught behind enemy lines. They've had to sit by and do nothing while agents have rotted in Chinese prisons. Right and wrong, good and bad in this industry, it isn't always so clear. There was stuff they had Mike do…"

A motorcycle roared by, and the music in the bar next door quieted.

Aki spat out her words as if they tasted bad. "I'm saying you got lucky with Pout. But this isn't a game. I get secrecy, and I get the virtue of not giving up your sources. But I need to know that you understand what you're doing and that you take it seriously."

Rueben nodded soberly. He thought about trying to tell her his secret, but there was anger in her expression that showed she still wasn't ready. He simply said, "I get it. I'm asking you to trust me. Can you do that?"

She studied his face and finally answered, "Okay."

He leaned against the fence with her, and she didn't say anything else.

"Aki?"

"What?"

"The phone?"

She looked down and was still holding her phone. Division director Sven Larson's number was ready to be dialed. She put the phone away. "Sorry, it's been a long night for all of us."

Even longer for me.

The discussion over, the four of them stared down the sidewalk, waiting for the guy who still hadn't arrived.

The street was empty except for a drunken old man stumbling through the street wearing a sign reading, "The end is near," and babbling about John 3:16. Rueben thought about Pout and mused that the guy had no idea how near the end had been for the people of NYC.

Buzz cleared his throat. "Dude, it's been twelve minutes. I think you might be off about this one."

Rueben kept his eyes on the Exit Bar. "No. He has to be here."

Martha asked, "What if us being out here changed every-thing and he left?"

"Couldn't be. He has to be here."

They stood in the alleyway, and a couple from the bar stumbled past them in the heat of the moment. They found a dumpster about ten feet away and started to make out.

Just great, Rueben thought as he listened to their pre-coital bliss.

Martha stood against the wall, slipped off her heels, and massaged her feet one by one.

He couldn't have missed it, right? Maybe Martha was right. Maybe he'd altered the entire event by having them wait outside. Maybe the gunman had returned and seen they weren't there and left.

"All right, guys." Rueben clapped his hands, ready to abort the mission.

A souped-up low rider blaring rap music pulled up to the bar, revved its engine, and blared its horn. Rueben grimaced from the blast.

"Damn you," the drunk by the dumpster yelled at the car. He reached into the dumpster and threw an empty beer bottle at the vehicle, and in a clatter of footsteps, the couple took off for another not-private place to make out.

A couple of young women came out and joined the loud driver out looking for fun. The car left, and Rueben shook his head of the noise. He turned to face the rest of his group—only to see the man in the white hoodie standing behind them.

He had on his metallic nylon gauntlet and struck Aki in the back between the shoulders. The air around her distorted as she flew forward and collapsed on the alley pavement. Martha turned, saying, "Freeze—" but White Hoodie had already backhanded her across the shoulder, sending her crashing against the alley wall.

Buzz watched as Martha's unconscious body rolled to a stop beside a dumpster. "Oh fuck."

White Hoodie flicked one finger outward, connecting with Buzz's temple. The genius slumped to the ground.

All this had happened within five seconds. Then White Hoodie turned to Rueben. "Too bad about your friends." He harshly laughed as he surveyed his handiwork.

For some reason, his attacker had incapacitated his friends instead of killing them. Well, Aki and Martha had died in two of the previous encounters, but it seemed like White Hoodie was actively trying to avoid killing them. Why?

Rueben's eyes narrowed on White Hoodie's gauntlet. "What is that?"

"An amazing piece of tech."

Yeah, like that was helpful. "Who the hell are you? Are you from the future or something?"

The hoodied man considered this. "Interesting concept. Not entirely correct." He took a step closer to Rueben and Rueben recoiled the same amount.

Rueben stared hard at the man, his features illuminated only by a yellow streetlight out on the sidewalk. Then he understood something. "You're here for me, aren't you?" When the man smiled grimly, Rueben clenched his fist. Behind Hoodie Man, his friends were starting to move. "What do you want with me?"

The gunman chuckled. "You're getting smarter." He pursed his lips. "That's what you'd like to know, isn't it? Why I'm here. Why I'm targeting you?"

"Yeah, asshole. So why don't you tell me?" Rueben hoped

his voice didn't betray his worry as he recalled his combat training.

White Hoodie didn't seem to be in the mood for combat. At least not yet. He opened his mouth, his voice taking on a chilling tone. "There will be time...time for you and me...in the room the women come and go, talking of Michelangelo..."

Rueben narrowed his eyes. The refrain sounded oddly familiar. "T.S. Eliot."

"Right-o," the gunman said. "'The *Love Song of J. Alfred Prufrock*. I guess that Columbia education did you good after all."

"What the hell?" Rueben's eyes burned hot. "Who are you?"

"It doesn't matter who I am," he said. "What matters most is that I know who you are, Rueben Peet."

Rueben's stomach went ice-cold at the mention of his name from this man. How the hell...

Clambering to her feet, Aki sidestepped White Hoodie and stood by Rueben's side. She wiped some bits of asphalt from her cheek with her palm. "You clearly want him to know that you know who he is. Why is that important to you? Tell me, what is it you're after?"

He chuckled again. "Don't try that terrorist negotiation bullshit on me, honey. It doesn't work."

"I'm not negotiating. I'm trying to work this out. We can help each other, you and me. Mutual goals. Let's talk about them."

"Your little girlfriend's good," he told Rueben. "The answer to your question, sweetheart, is far, far more complicated than you can understand."

"Try me," she said.

"No." His tone was decisive. "I'd rather not. Thank you for the offer, though. It's ever so sweet of you, but—"

"Then why?" she interrupted him. "Why all of this?"

"Silence!" he demanded. "I've had enough questions for one night. Don't make me hurt you more than I have to. It's not part of the plan."

With that, their attacker flexed his fingers beneath his flexible metallic gauntlet.

Rueben rushed forward, but White Hoodie whirled him around and pinned his arm behind his back.

"Like a patient etherized on a table," he continued to quote from *Prufrock*. Suddenly, Rueben recalled the syringe Hoodie Man had held up the first time around.

"Go ahead, kill me," Rueben muttered as he fought to escape the hold on him. "See if I care."

The gunman laughed, and Rueben's heart froze in his throat. There was something familiar about that laugh. "You think I'd give you the satisfaction? Playtime is over. I have other plans for you."

Why was the man's laugh familiar? *Think, Rueben, think.*

Suddenly the gunman cried out. Aki had zapped him from behind with Buzz's taser. She'd also inadvertently zapped Rueben in the process. He blinked back stars. *Shit...*

"Not so fast, asshole." She pouted her lips and swished her hips. In that black dress with a taser in hand, Rueben couldn't keep his heart from racing.

"Oh, sweetheart," the gunman jeered. "You think you entice me with that charm? Not even close."

She zapped him again. "I don't give a shit." The blast of electricity jolted Rueben again as well. *Fuuuck...*

The gunman dropped Rueben, and he fell hard onto the asphalt and scraped his forehead. He got back on his feet—his knees felt like rubber—and found Aki had already engaged in hand-to-hand combat with the man. She dodged his supersonic glove or whatever that gauntlet was but then, with an elbow swing, he knocked her to the ground and the taser from her hand.

He sneered. "Nice precision, huh? I've had a lot more practice than you will ever know."

In the dark, Rueben couldn't see White Hoodie's face, but he swore he recognized that voice. He didn't have much time to contemplate it as a speeding punch hurtled toward his face. He dodged it barely in time.

The gunman snorted. "Oh, you're getting good. Daddy helping you, now?"

"I don't know who the hell you are or who you think you are, but you have no idea who you're messing with. You're going down."

"Oh, I think I know every bit of who I'm messing with. That's the whole point."

Rueben blocked a vicious kick, his combat training taking hold. He evaded a punch and crouched, landing two quick jabs to White Hoodie's calf. White Hoodie barely grunted and kicked Rueben back onto his butt.

"What is it you want from me?"

The next thing he knew, a wooden broom handle snapped across White Hoodie's shoulder, and Martha came forward, wielding the bottom half of the broom like a sword. Behind her, Buzz was back on his feet and digging through the trash for a weapon.

Martha put up a good fight while dodging the man's metallic glove, but the man hardly seemed to tire. In all their combined efforts, they weren't even slowing him down any. And they were wearing themselves out.

Rueben was aware that he had blood running down the side of his face, and he panted as he blocked a kick.

Without warning, White Hoodie's gauntlet slugged him in the cheek. Rueben blinked and found himself on the ground in the alleyway. He was vaguely aware of the *thumps* and *thuds* of his friends continuing the fight behind him. With his body drained of energy, his eyelids closed as smells of the dirty pavement, and the nearby trash dumpster entered his nostrils.

A full minute seemed to have passed before the effects of the supersonic punch started to wear off. Rueben opened his eyes and stiffened at the sight of White Hoodie kneeling beside him now, a syringe in his upraised hand.

"Now..." The man flicked the syringe's body before stabbing its needle into Rueben's neck. "Three days, my friend. Three days. Sleep for three days."

Before Rueben could think of something to say, the world went black.

CHAPTER SIX

Monday, May 22, 6:47 p.m.

What the hell happened?

Rueben blinked, trying to figure out where he was. An unfamiliar room. Concrete floor. Exposed wires dangled from the unfinished walls and ceiling.

He was lying on a cot, his wrists tied to metal railings at each side. Across from him sat crates and buckets of nails and screws. Lying on one of the crates was a metallic nylon glove.

Where the hell am I?

Rueben's mouth was parched. He was about to open his mouth and run his tongue over his lips, but then he saw him.

His attacker.

The muscular man in the white hoodie had his back to Rueben. He was sitting on a swivel chair facing a computer monitor, keyboard, and mouse setup sitting on a desk in front of him. At intervals, he typed out rapid commands, and Rueben noticed the scars on some of the man's fingers.

Who the hell was this guy?

A TV screen next to the computer monitor showed a news

program offering coverage of the upcoming World Leaders Summit at the U.N. building downtown. Rueben squinted. Why were there so many people gathered out front of it? It was like they'd gathered there for a celebration or something. Reporters. Spectators. Bodyguards wearing tuxes and earwigs.

White Hoodie glanced at the news coverage, then back at his computer monitor. It looked like a spreadsheet program with oversized cells labeled one through two hundred. When he clicked on one of them, the screen changed and complex lines of code scrolled upward. White Hoodie navigated the cursor to sections of the code and changed inputs.

Rueben could read and write code, but he couldn't read the fine print. He stiffened as White Hoodie glanced back at the TV screen and back to his computer monitor. He cursed and started muttering. "Dammit. I should have capped his abilities here instead of back at that wretched bar."

White Hoodie fell silent as he caught Rueben's reflection on the computer screen. He grinned, and after completing his current coding sequence, he sighed and locked his computer. "Ah, you're awake."

"Where am I?"

White Hoodie spun his swivel chair around so that he was only a few feet from Rueben. He still wore his hood and sunglasses, but they did little to conceal the large scar running across the man's cheek. Something about the contours of his face reminded Rueben of someone he knew. Who? He couldn't say at the moment. His head hurt, and he was being held captive by a madman.

The man cleared his throat. "You're in the basement of an empty skyscraper owned by one of Pout's conglomerates. Only you and me in here."

Rueben winced. "Why are you telling me this?"

White Hoodie shrugged. "Because it's too late for you to stop me. What do I have to lose?"

Too late for what? Rueben wondered.

As if reading his mind, White Hoodie motioned to the TV screen where a foreign dignitary was standing on a stage full of lights and waving to the reporters and spectators out front of the U.N. building. That's when Rueben read the date and time at the corner of the news feed.

Monday, May 22, 6:45 p.m.

Rueben's eyes contorted. "Is this some kind of joke?"

"Whatever do you mean?"

"Monday? It's Friday night."

White Hoodie raised a finger. "It was Friday night. That was nearly three full days ago. Today is Monday—summit day."

"But that—"

"I knocked you out with a sleep serum. The injection I gave you put you in an artificial coma while I fed you via IV." White Hoodie nodded to the floor beside Rueben's cot, and Rueben strained against his restraints to peer over the edge. Sure enough, a metal stand with several IV bags lay upon the floor. That explained his parched throat.

That meant that whatever his kidnapper was planning, it probably had something to do with the summit. Restrained as he was, Rueben was helpless to help stop it. What he needed to do was to die so that he could warp back in time before any of this happened. Unless White Hoodie was lying. Could this all be an elaborate setup? That made no sense.

Rueben's brain tried to find a flaw in the man's words. "Let's say I believe you that today is Monday. If this is an abandoned building, where are you getting the electricity?

Wouldn't someone come to investigate an abandoned building?"

White Hoodie chuckled softly. "I spliced into the city's electric grid. I only needed it for a few days. No one has noticed. I'm smarter than you think."

Rueben considered this. His kidnapper did seem quite intelligent. Plus, he had that metal body armor and hi-tech glove sitting on the crate.

"You think I mean to hurt you," the man said, "but the truth is, I've been taking care of you."

On the TV screen, the camera footage played over the stage out front of the U.N. building as well as the people gathered. There was a big police presence and Rueben's breath caught in his throat as his eyes locked in on Aki talking to a police officer. There was no way White Hoodie was faking that. Today really was Monday night. Rueben suddenly did a double-take as he realized Mike Fury was standing by Aki's side as he surveyed the crowd for threats.

White Hoodie placed a hand on Rueben's shoulder. "Trust me. She's better off with that guy than she is with you."

Rueben tried to shake the man's hand off his shoulder. "Shut up. Quit trying to mess with my head. You murderer."

"Murderer?"

"Yeah. You killed Aki back at the bar."

White Hoodie thumbed his chin. "Did I? I wouldn't have meant to. I mean, why would I want to hurt her? She has the curves of an angel."

Rueben didn't know what to think about this guy. Something about him gave Rueben the creeps and yet also seemed familiar. "What's your name?"

"Why should I tell you?"

"Um. I don't know. Maybe so I don't have to keep referring to you as 'White Hoodie' in my inner monologue."

The man scoffed. "Very well. You can call me Pete."

"Is that your real name?"

Pete's lips curled. "Now, what do you think?"

"I think you're not from around here."

Pete's eyebrows furrowed over the rim of his sunglasses.

"That metal body armor of yours."

"Oh. Pretty neat, huh?" Pete lifted the front of his white hoodie, revealing a form-fitting body armor that hugged his lean, defined abs and chest with a metallic gleam. It seemed almost organic, but a few tiny red and green lights spotting it hinted at some kind of battery power or something. Pete lowered his hoodie.

"And that 'supersonic glove' of yours…" Rueben let his words trail off as he tried to read Pete's expression from behind his sunglasses.

Pete rubbed his chin again. "Supersonic glove. Now that's an accurate description. I call her Doris. Sure packs a wallop, doesn't it? It's got some surprises too. I'd show you, but it's charging."

Rueben followed Pete's gaze off to the side at the metallic glove resting on the crate. Now that Rueben squinted at it, he saw a tiny red light on it too. Charging…

"So, what? Are you from the future? Or a parallel universe or something?" Rueben couldn't help it. The words slipped from his mouth.

But Pete wasn't listening. He'd already turned back to face the TV. "Hush. It's about to start."

Rueben was about to ask what was about to start when Pete picked up a black backpack that had been sitting on the other side of the desk. The man retrieved a bulky satellite phone and a notebook filled with names. Rueben could read a few of them, but he had an idea: if the camera in his smartwatch could take a picture of the notebook, Buzz could enlarge them back at his mansion—assuming Rueben was able to escape, die, and warp back to before this happened, whatever this was. He still didn't know Pete's plan. But with all the world's leaders gathered in one place at the U.N. building, it couldn't be good.

Rueben fidgeted and adjusted his wrist to try to get a clear shot of Pete's desk and notebook.

Pete glanced at Rueben again from the reflection in the monitor. "If you're trying to take a picture of me with your fancy smartwatch, I already disabled it."

"You're bluffing...shit." A glance at his watch showed only a blank screen.

"Don't underestimate me, Rueben."

Something was happening on the TV now. The volume was turned low, but an attractive reporter with blond hair was gesturing at the sky off-camera. The camera then shifted upward and in the opposite direction of the U.N. building to reveal a swarm of bright lights floating toward the building.

Highly Anticipated World Summit Drone Light Show... the words at the bottom of the screen ticked by. Now the camera view tracked the lights as they stopped in front of the U.N. building just off to the side from the stage now containing over fifty world leaders and other dignitaries. Everyone stared in awe as the drones formed a giant "peace sign" forty feet in the air. Mouths opened. Hands clapped.

That's when the bombs started to drop from the drones' underbellies.

CHAPTER SEVEN

Monday, May 22, 7:30 p.m.

The camera shook as bright flashes of light exploded on the ground outside the building. People shouted and raised their hands as they tried to flee, but some of the drones were spitting dark blobs at the ground. When the blobs hit the ground around the stage, they detonated. Debris and shrapnel filled the air as flames rose.

Rueben suddenly realized that his body was shriveled up on the cot. He felt sick to his stomach. He felt like dying. "You bastard. This is your plan? You won't kill me, but you'll kill all those people at the summit?"

Pete sighed and slowly shook his head. "You couldn't possibly understand. Not yet."

"Not yet?" Rueben struggled against his arm restraints, but it was no use. "I used to think you were just crazy. Now I know you're a homicidal psychopath!"

Pete didn't say anything and Rueben realized that his kidnapper was searching the TV screen for something or someone. When the shaky camera zoomed in on some of the police officers at the scene, Aki came into view. Pete maintained a grim face.

"Aki," Rueben shouted. "You're going to kill her again, aren't you?"

"Not as long as she stays out of this, but I'll do what I have to."

"Oh, so you'll kill all these people, but you don't want to hurt her? What's she to you?"

Pete didn't answer, only shook his head as the camera tracked Aki sprinting toward a child searching for her parents. A bomb exploded, and its force flung Aki to the side where she lay in a lifeless heap.

"Aki!"

Grim-faced, Pete rose from his chair. He slid his notebook into the black backpack and then raised the pack to his shoulders.

"What are you doing? Leaving?" Rueben asked.

Pete picked up his satellite phone from the desk. Then he turned to leave.

On the TV screen, bodyguards were ushering the world leaders into the U.N. building. Rueben didn't think any of them had been hurt in the blasts. But the drones were starting to bomb the doors and windows as if to get inside, presumably to hunt down the leaders.

"Come on, tell me why you're doing this. I'll try to understand."

Pete made to leave the basement room.

Rueben tried to think of a way to get Pete to stay. He had to prevent this all from happening but in order to do that, he had to get more information. He suddenly recalled something Aki had said in the alleyway outside the Exit Bar. Something about the man in the hoodie probably working alone. Rueben could use that to his advantage. Maybe.

"You're all alone. Aren't you?"

Pete hesitated.

"You're lonely. You have a plan. I get that. But you have no one to talk to about it…" Rueben eyed Pete's knuckles turning white as they gripped the satellite phone by his side. Shit, maybe he does have someone to talk to…

"You're right," Pete said. "I am alone."

Rueben relaxed. The sat phone wasn't to call up some evil buddies of Pete's.

"Then tell me what's up. I want to try to understand you." The next words out of Rueben's mouth almost physically pained him to say. "I don't think you're evil. You've got a side, and I want to hear it."

Pete turned to face him. "I don't have to—"

"You said it yourself. I'm not getting out of these restraints." Rueben made a show of struggling against the bindings.

Pete studied him for a few moments and then sighed. On the TV screen, the carnage continued but it was all in Rueben's periphery. Pete was his objective. And more information.

"I do have a few minutes to kill before I start checking on things across the globe." Pete slid the sat phone into his hoodie's front pouch.

"Huh? Checking on things across the globe?"

Even Pete's sunglasses couldn't hide Pete's irritation. He jabbed a finger toward the TV. "What is it you think I'm trying to do?"

"Uh, kill a lot of people?"

"Wrong. I'm trying to start a war."

"A war?" Rueben glanced over at the TV as the last of the world leaders entered the building, and a bodyguard sealed the door behind them. "The world leaders. All together in one place…"

Pete nodded. Rueben didn't know why Pete wanted to initiate a war between nations, but his mind started to string some things together. "This has to do with Alister Pout and his RedBook app, doesn't it."

Rueben took Pete's silence as confirmation and continued. "Buzz said that Pout had sold some of RedBook's spying software to North Korea, China, and some other countries." He recalled security camera footage outside a dry cleaners that Buzz had been able to find where Pete in his white hoodie was conversing with Pout. "Wait, are you working for Pout?"

Pete scoffed. "Hell no. Pout worked for me—he just didn't know it at the time. He was a puppet."

"Wait, so you're probably pissed at us then for ruining your microwave bomb scheme."

"That was all Pout. When I found out about his little plan, I…well, I didn't have to do anything. Because I knew you were in the bomb's blast radius and now was as good a time as any for you to begin your, how should I put it? Training."

"You knew I could and would go back in time to fix it? Wait, since you can warp too, could you sense me or something? Is that why you know so much about me?"

Pete scoffed. Then he stepped over to Rueben and checked his restraints. "Look. I've told you enough. I need to get to the roof."

"Why?"

Pete tapped the sat phone inside his hoodie's front pouch. "I already said. To check on things. Technology is limited here."

Here?

He made to leave again, then paused and turned back to face Rueben. "Actually, there is one more thing you should know."

Rueben waited.

"There's something familiar about me. Isn't there?"

Rueben didn't say anything. Pete reached up and pinched the hood of his hoodie. Then with the finesse of a magician, he pulled it back. He removed his sunglasses too. Then he laughed.

Rueben's skin paled like frosted ash. "You. You..."

"What?" Pete laughed again, and the voice chilled Rueben's veins. "I look like you do when you look in the mirror? Well, an older version of you." Pete lifted a hand and traced the scar on his face. "And my voice. My laugh. It's yours too. Annoying, am I right?"

Rueben's mouth dropped open, but he couldn't seem to form any words. Pete was right. He was looking at an older, mirror-image version of himself. Minus the face scar and the scars on his fingers.

But how? This wasn't how time worked. How could he be looking at his future self?

His mind began melting into madness as Pete exited the room.

CHAPTER EIGHT

Monday, May 22, 7:42 p.m.

"No. No, no, no."

It was a few minutes later, and Rueben still couldn't believe it. How could he be talking to his future self? Didn't that wreck the physics of reality? Didn't one version warp into the other? He wished Buzz was here to explain things to him. He needed some damn rules written down so he knew what was and wasn't possible for time travel.

Even worse was the question of how his future self could commit such wanton murder and destruction on a global scale. He would never do this. Yet, at times during their conversation, it was almost as if Pete had read his mind. Made sense if he truly was him.

Ugh. Rueben felt like grabbing his head in his hands, but he couldn't. His restraints still held him. He also had no energy to try to figure out a way to escape, let alone kill himself so he could warp back to before Pete kidnapped him. Glancing at the time on the TV screen, he saw that his three-day warp limit wasn't up yet. Even if it had been, all he had to do was keep dying and warping back until he'd made it to before this all went down so that he and his friends could stop it.

His friends.

That explained why Pete—future him—was so reluctant to kill them at the Exit Bar. Because they were his friends at one point. And Aki. Pete had loved her at one point, maybe still did.

Rueben blinked and shook his head. Unless there was some other explanation for everything. Again, he needed Buzz here. For a moment, Rueben wondered if Buzz had been able to triangulate Rueben's smartwatch for his location before Pete had disabled it. Then Rueben dismissed the idea. Pete had already proven he was smart. He'd have disabled the GPS before taking him here.

So that meant Rueben was on his own. It was up to him to figure out how to escape and die so that he could warp back and fix this mess.

Even if he could, should he?

After all, Pete was him. Urggh. Time.

Wait, why was he even having this debate? If Pete weren't evil, he'd have approached Rueben and his friends and calmly tried to explain his situation. Instead of trying to kidnap him.

Yes. Pete was obviously crazy or demented or something.

He was evil. And Rueben had to go back and stop him.

He recalled a few months ago when he'd first realized his time warp power and thought of himself as being a super-hero. Well, superhero or not. Aki had died. So had countless others.

Rueben glanced back at the TV. The blond reporter was now covered in soot and helping survivors away from the fires as Mike Fury stood in the background with a machine gun tucked against each shoulder, going full-Rambo on the remaining drones hovering around the scene.

God damned Mike Fury.

With renewed energy surging through his veins, Rueben started to work on an escape plan. Testing his restraints, he found that they were still tight against his arms.

Well, he had a trick that might work, and it involved dislocating his elbow.

He'd discovered he could do this back in the days when he and his then-fiancée Rachel had been taking ballroom dance lessons. Rueben had discovered he enjoyed it and was stressing his body to its limits one day in rehearsal when he'd slipped and fallen wrong on his elbow. It had popped out of its socket, and Rachel had gasped and said she was going to throw up.

She didn't, and Rueben managed to pop it back into the socket all on his own. As far as he knew, he was the only one who could do that. Hell, the elbow wasn't even a ball and socket joint like the shoulder or wrist. So maybe technically, it hadn't popped out of the socket. But that's what he was calling it.

He now tilted his head downward for a better look at his right elbow. Then, grunting, he popped it out of joint and wiggled his arm against his bindings. A couple of minutes later, he had his arm free, and he quickly re-popped his elbow and extricated his other arm. Then, wasting no time, he bolted forward off the cot.

In retrospect, he kicked himself for not anticipating his legs wouldn't be able to support him after being confined to a cot for nearly three days.

His legs wobbled, his knees buckled, and he sprawled forward toward some crates. He smacked the concrete floor with a hard slap, and one of his outstretched hands knocked over a bucket of nails that scattered on the floor like metal ants.

He was trying to scramble to his feet when he heard a spitting cough from the doorway and an excruciating pain bit into his thigh. Rueben glanced down to see the outside of his leg bleeding. Then Pete stepped into his peripheral vision while holstering his silenced pistol.

"Should have known you'd try the elbow trick." Pete felt his elbow. "It's been so long since I danced. I'd forgotten about that. No matter. That's only a flesh wound…"

Rueben caught the look of fear darting across Pete's face. It was only there for an instant. "Hold your hand on the wound," he barked.

Rueben's hand went instinctively to his wound. He didn't want to die after all…

Actually he did.

He removed his hand.

"You little bastard. You're not dying on me. I knew I shouldn't have capped you at the Exit Bar. I should have capped you here."

Capped? Pete had mentioned that when Rueben was waking up. What did it mean?

Pete removed his backpack and unzipped it. While he rifled through it, Rueben played his hands over the red slippery floor beside him and closed his fingers around a nail. He slipped it into his jeans pocket as Pete withdrew some gauze wrap and some medical tape. "Now hold still, or I'll really get mean."

That's what Rueben wanted—for Pete to get mean and kill him so he could warp back. He suddenly felt very lightheaded. He'd bled a lot.

Rueben's head tipped back and the next thing he knew, he was lying back on the bed with Pete leaning over him and checking his straps. Now, he realized, Pete had bound his arms *and* legs to the rails of the cot. He wasn't going anywhere this time. He was trapped.

Pete stared down at him, scrutinizing him.

Well, he wouldn't stay trapped for long. He had a nail in his pocket. All he had to do was wait for Pete to leave and angle his wrist up against his jeans pocket.

Pete smirked and bent over the cot. He then performed a thorough search of Rueben's clothes and pockets, eventually finding the nail and raising it in front of Rueben's nose. He tossed the metal behind him where it clattered upon the floor.

"Nice try."

"How'd you know?"

"Because I'd have done the same thing." He pointed at his forehead. "We're both smart."

Rueben's chest collapsed in defeat.

"Seriously. Nice try." Pete left, removing the satellite phone from his hoodie's pouch before disappearing through the doorway.

Nice try...

Rueben cursed under his breath.

CHAPTER NINE

Monday, May 22, 7:58 p.m.

The reporter on the TV said something Rueben couldn't hear because Pete had never turned the volume up. And Rueben was still restrained. To a cot. In the basement of an empty skyscraper.

At least, that's what Pete had said. Why would he lie about that? About anything? He had Rueben well and truly screwed.

The shaky camera played over some of the wreckage and firefighters putting out some of the fires, but all Rueben could see was the image of Aki's still body, imprinted in his mind.

God damn this man. It didn't matter if Pete was somehow an older, alternate version of himself. He'd killed Aki. Again. Rueben had to go back and fix that. He needed to find a way to kill himself.

Maybe if he jumped out of a window on the fifth floor? But he'd have to free himself. And Pete took his nail.

Also, how would he walk with an injured leg?

He glanced down at his patched-up thigh, the taped-up gauze a bright red but no longer leaking. A sudden thought entered Rueben's mind. Had Pete sterilized the wound? What if he caught tetanus or gangrene? It didn't matter. He needed to die now.

The easiest way would be to step out the front door of this building and throw himself in front of traffic. A pain shot through his thigh, and he grimaced. Again, he had to get free first, and how was he to make it up the stairs to the first floor with—

He could die, and he could do it right here in this bed. The key was his leg wound. He'd bled a lot—Pete's bullet had probably nicked an artery. But how to start the bleeding again?

Tensing against the restraints holding his limbs against the cot's rails, he realized he wouldn't be able to tear open the patches that way. Besides, his previous blood loss down on the floor had depleted his energy.

He'd lost so much blood already. Surely it wouldn't take much more to kill him. Right?

He recalled the scared look that had flashed across Pete's face when he'd told him to apply pressure. *This wound is worse than Pete let on. Yep. Probably nicked an artery.*

Rueben was surprised the gauze was doing as good a job as it was. He wondered if this unexpected development would prompt Pete to take him to the ER. No. Probably not. Too many people there to see him.

Panic gripped Rueben. No, Pete wouldn't take him to the hospital. He'd simply kill himself and go back in time to before he'd shot Rueben. Why hadn't he already? Rueben guessed it was because Pete wanted to ensure that his plan had worked as intended by calling across the globe to other countries or whatever he needed the sat phone for. In fact, Pete would probably be rushing back down here any moment to figure out his next move, AKA time warp if he needed to prevent himself from shooting Rueben.

That meant Rueben had to work fast. Except he had no nail.

Marshall's face popped into his mind. *What would Marshall do?*

He'd probably rant about how back in his day, he walked uphill both ways in the snow just to get to school, and he was a tough bastard so he'd figure out a way to get out of some lousy cot.

How? Rueben wondered what his best buddy Buzz would say if he were here.

Science, my friend. Science is the answer. It's always the answer. Have I ever told you that when I was in first grade, I built a 64-bit, custom OS for a—

"Thanks, Imaginary Buzz, you're a genius," Rueben said to the space before him. Science was the answer. At least, he hoped so.

His eyes darted to the crates in front of his cot and to the metallic glove still resting there. Charging.

Pete had mentioned that the supersonic glove had some surprises. No. What had he called it? Doris?

This might not work, but he had to try.

The glove was hi-tech so there was a good chance that it was voice-activated. Since his voice was Pete's voice…

"Hey, Doris."

A sexy robot voice answered from a tiny speaker embedded into the glove's fabric. "Yes, Master Rueben?"

Master Rueben? Ha! It worked.

"Oh, um, yes, Doris."

"I'm still here, Master Rueben. What is it you'd like me to do?"

"Um, do you...see my bleeding leg?" Rueben reckoned it wouldn't take much pressure to reopen the wound so that he could bleed to death.

There was a pause, and Rueben realized how stupid he'd been to assume that a glove could "see" him.

"Yes, Master Rueben. I see it. You are much younger, and it threw me off for a moment."

"Oh, right. You know about my abilities."

"Of course."

"You've helped me, um, kill myself before?" He was making his words up as he went along. It was almost too unbelievable that Pete had left him alone with such a powerful device.

"Of course. Did you get knocked in the head, Master Rueben?"

"N-no. No, I did not. Well, maybe I did. Yes, I did. Ha, you caught me, Doris. And um, I need to go back in time to before I hit it. Are you fully charged to, um, shoot a blast at me or whatever surprises you're capable of?"

"Pulse? Or obliterate?"

"Excuse me?"

Doris sighed. "Do you want me to use the pulse feature? Or do you want me to use the obliterate feature?"

Shit, Rueben thought. But he didn't appreciate the over-enunciating tone Doris had responded to him with. Like he was some kid.

"Obliterate."

"Okay. Let me check my battery reserve. I am quite low."

Footsteps sounded from the other side of the basement's door.

Shit. Shit. Shit.

"Can you hurry with your calculations, Doris?"

"Can you please mind your manners, Master Rueben? How many times have I had to tell you?"

Geez. He was talking to a robot. No wonder Pete was so messed up. Of course, Doris was a rather intelligent AI or whatever she was. It felt as if he was talking to another person. It was almost as if Buzz had designed her.

The footsteps were louder now, more rapid.

"Hey, what's going on—"

"Doris, obliterate my leg. *Please*," Rueben blurted as Pete rushed into the room.

"As you wish."

Rueben was expecting the supersonic glove to emit some invisible, focused sound blast that would tear loose the gauze and tape so that he'd bleed out and die. What he didn't expect was for his entire goddamned leg to explode apart from his hip.

"Holyshit!" he let loose in a rush of breath.

Pete swept into the room. "What did you do!"

Rueben's consciousness felt like a professional boxer's glove punched it repeatedly as his hip bled profusely onto the basement floor. It was difficult to think, but what was it Pete had told him earlier? That they were both smart? "Doris, deactivate yourself."

"As you wish, Master Rueben."

Pete roared, "No!" as he threw himself to the floor and began scrabbling for one of the spilled nails.

Rueben smirked through his intense pain as Pete attempted to kill himself with nails. He didn't exactly know how this time thing worked for sure, but he figured it would be a race against time to see who could die and warp back in time first. If Rueben succeeded, Pete wouldn't even remember being here, thus giving Rueben a huge advantage in stopping him.

Rueben's body was numb now, and he suddenly remembered that he had to stay calm and focus on what time he wanted to go back to. As his consciousness faded, he thought of Aki sitting in the old car out front of the Exit Bar and her smile as he snapped pics of her with his cell phone. That was a relaxing thought. It would be plenty of time to call the cops and have Pete apprehended before any of this went down.

Yes. He visualized her face.

Then there was blackness.

CHAPTER TEN

<u>**Friday, May 19, 10:35 p.m.**</u>

Rueben came back to his body at the Exit Bar. Not outside, but inside, seated at the table with Aki, Martha, and Buzz. Odd. Had he not been calm enough to warp back to him snapping photos of Aki outside?

He immediately felt his leg to make sure it was still there and that this wasn't a fever dream and he was still trapped with Pete, only now, legless. His fingers felt solid flesh and bone beneath his pants. He relaxed a bit. A fly buzzed near his head, and he swatted at it but missed.

His friends laughed at something Aki had said, and it startled him. At the other side of the bar sat Marshall, drinking alone with his wild silver hair, age-lined face, and permanent scowl.

Buzz jumped up and yelled, "The Raider Warlock pinball machine! Those are collector's editions. I can't believe they... How did they...."

Rueben sat still, deep in thought. He glanced up at the TV, which showed preparations for the World Summit on

Monday. Good. It hadn't happened yet. They now had the full weekend and part of Monday to stop it.

Aki watched the TV with a shake of her head as Buzz excused himself to play the pinball game. Martha stood to go to the restroom.

He thought about stopping Martha, but they'd need time to formulate a workable plan to stop Pete before he attacked them and tried to kidnap him. Rueben needed to inform his friends about what Pete had in store for the U.N. building summit in three days, but there wasn't enough time now. What they needed was for him to warp back even farther in time to before he'd even stepped into the bar.

To do that, he'd have to die again and go back to when he was snapping pics of Aki outside. His eyes scanned the bar. What would be the easiest way to die here?

He spotted two guys he'd never seen before at the bar, talking to a pretty blond. He could go over there and get in the middle of that and let his ass get kicked. But then he might not die, and it would be a long and slow death, and what if they put him into a coma—a real coma this time? He wouldn't be able to stop Pete then.

How else could he die?

Back in the basement with Pete, he'd considered running out into traffic if he'd been able to walk up the stairs to the first floor. He was now at ground level and had a fully functioning leg. "I'm going to go for a run!"

Aki frowned. "Whoa. Slow down. A what?"

"A jog. I think I'll go for a jog."

"You're drunker than I thought you were."

"You stay here. I'm going to go for a run." Rueben rose from the table and dashed outside.

Aki yelled after him. "Rueben, what are you doing?"

He heard Marshall answer her from across the bar, "Being a dumbass."

Of course, Marshall had to get one last dig in.

Rueben raced outside, closed his eyes, and darted into the street, ignoring yells, horn blasts, and screeching tires. Eventually, he got what he wanted: the hard impact of a speeding van knocking him down. He grimaced under the crushing weight.

Then he died.

Friday, May 19, 10:35 p.m.

Rueben came back, and he was oddly sitting in the booth at the Exit Bar. He checked his hands and felt his chest. He was all in one piece, but he hadn't gone back any further than the last time. Damn. What was going on? He'd been as calm as he possibly could've been as the van had mowed him over.

A fly buzzed near his head. Rueben didn't bother swatting at it.

Buzz jumped and yelled, "The Raider Warlock pinball machine! Those are collector's editions. I can't believe they... How did they...."

Rueben jumped up from the table. "I'll go with you."

"You hate arcade games."

"I love...this one."

Buzz shrugged, and they wandered off to the pinball machine.

"I've got a problem," Rueben said. "There's a psychopathic madman about to attack us here in the bar. In three days, he's going to bomb the World Leaders Summit and kill a lot of people in the hopes of starting World War III, and I'm not going back far enough when I die."

"Really? How curious. What do you mean you're not going back far enough?"

Leave it to Buzz to only be concerned with the science of the problem and not the looming threat of global war. Rueben searched his friend earnestly. "I killed myself twice and went back to this moment each time. What does it mean?"

Buzz dropped a quarter into the machine. "It means you need to take your mind off your work and live a little." Buzz suddenly reflected seriously. "Rueben, buddy. You gotta stay calm and warp on. You learned that before we took down Pout. Heh. Stay calm and warp on. I oughta put that on a t-shirt."

Calm? Stay calm? A psycho version of myself is trying to turn the world into a nuclear wasteland!

Rueben shook his head of the thought. "No, Buzz. See that man in the white hoodie over there?"

Buzz glanced around. "What man in the hoodie?"

Pete was nowhere in sight.

"Never mind. There's a friggin' terrorist here that wants to blow up the U.N. building in the city three days from now. And he, um, wants us out of the way because we're the only ones who can stop him."

Buzz looked irritated. "Rueben, can we not do this now? Can we have one night of enjoying our sweet victory?"

"I'm telling you, I've been here at least three times. This guy is going to attack us within minutes. He's going to inject me with some kind of knockout drug and kidnap me and keep me in the basement of an empty skyscraper belonging to Pout for the next three days."

The pinball machine came to life as Buzz pulled the knob to shoot his first ball into play. Then Buzz dropped his hands from the machine's sides and turned to face Rueben. "You couldn't have made that up if you tried. Okay, I believe you, buddy. So what do we do about it?"

"We've tried everything. It doesn't work. And, when I kill myself, I don't go back far enough."

Buzz turned back to the machine. "Then kill yourself again."

"I was really hoping for some better advice."

Buzz turned back to the pinball machine and sent his second ball into play.

"Right." Rueben jumped behind the bar, and the staff started to yell.

"You can't be back here! Insurance, man."

He quickly found the serrated steak knife and thrust it into his chest.

Then he died.

Friday, May 19, 10:35 p.m.

When Rueben came back, he was sitting at the booth again. The fly buzzed away. Buzz jumped up and yelled, "The Raider Warlock pinball machine! Those are collector's editions. I can't believe they… How did they…."

"You've got to be kidding me."

Buzz furrowed his brow. "What? It's only a game."

"Damn it. Let me see your taser."

"My what?"

"You know, your homemade taser."

"I never told you about that."

Rueben waved dismissively. "Hand it over."

Buzz reached into his pocket and handed Rueben the taser.

Rueben turned it on himself and pushed the button.

Aki screamed. "What are you doing? Are you crazy?"

Everyone in the bar rushed to Rueben, and he even heard shouts to call 911. But Rueben endured the pain and kept the taser on himself.

Then he died.

Friday, May 19, 10:35 p.m.

Rueben returned to his body and found himself sitting in the booth at the Exit Bar. The fly buzzed away. *Damnit!*

Was he truly stuck in the same spot? Maybe if he kept dying more rapidly than usual, he could jar himself loose.

Without waiting for Buzz to exclaim about the pinball game, Rueben jumped up and darted back to the bathroom. There had to be something to kill himself in there, right? He entered the empty men's room and surveyed the sinks, urinals, and stalls. He could drown himself, but that would take too long. There had to be something. He opened the cabinets under the sink and found a stash of cleaners. That would work, but it would likely be too slow and painful.

At that moment, one of the guys hitting on the blond girl entered the bathroom. Rueben noticed the form of a handgun bulging from beneath the man's glossy, untucked dress shirt. He'd tucked the weapon into his belt. Perfect.

He taunted the man. "Hey, I saw you hitting on her."

"Yeah, so what of it? It's a bar."

Rueben affected an exaggerated swagger and leaned against the wall. "Yeah, well, that's my woman, man."

The guy frowned and looked Rueben up and down. "You gotta be kidding me."

Rueben swaggered a little more and tried his "cool guy" tone. "Nah, man, we been together for a while. That's my girl."

The man held up his palms peaceably. "That's cool, dude. Look, man. It's all good, you know. I know how it is."

Rueben frowned. This wasn't going how he'd expected. "And I'm going to kick your ass for talking to my girl."

The man held up his arms in complete surrender. "Look, I don't want no trouble, man. I'll leave her alone."

"Oh, so just like that, huh? My girl's not worth it? Is that what you're saying?"

"Nah, that's not... I'm just trying to live right, stay out of trouble. Straight and narrow, all the way. Look, if you're with her, that's cool, man. I won't talk to her."

With that, he left the bathroom.

Rueben stood in the bathroom, hands on his hips. That didn't work. He thought about how else he could die. Another guy came into the bathroom, a burly tattooed man with piercings on his lips and eyebrows. This one would be perfect. As the guy sidled up to a urinal, Rueben ran up behind him and kicked him as hard as he could.

The man smashed into the urinal with a grunt. Then he whipped around, and Rueben ran like hell. He got back into the bar, and within seconds the man had chased him onto the floor, tossing punches. Rueben grabbed at the man's piercings and ripped them out of his face. "I've always wanted to do that."

The man grumbled in his face, "You want to die, kid?"

"Wouldn't mind."

"What the hell is wrong with you?" The man shook his head, clutching at his bleeding face. "This just isn't worth it. I've...got to piss."

With that, the tattooed man walked away. By then, Martha was coming out of the ladies' room, and she saw Pete. Rueben was out of time. This time, though, Pete noticed Rueben standing there first.

He sneered at him. "You look like you've repeated this scene a few times."

"You don't remember?"

"Remember what?"

"You drugging me and taking me to your little basement hideout."

Pete scowled. "I must have been sloppy to allow you to come back here."

"Oh, I'm sorry, my bad. Have I hurt your feelings? I mean *my* feelings."

"Oh. So you know the truth? How interesting that I revealed that. Also, you're really starting to piss me off."

"I'm pissing you off? You can't kidnap me."

"I don't have to kidnap you. I thought we could both coexist together." Pete narrowed his eyes at Rueben like a gunslinger. "Maybe I was wrong."

Well, that was unexpected. Rueben was trying to think of something witty to say when Pete beat him to the punch.

"I might not be able to kill you, but I can kill your friends."

"Then I'd just kill myself and undo it."

Pete laughed. "At an impasse, are we?" He drew a syringe from under his hoodie, and Rueben backed away.

"You're not going to do what you want to do."

"And what is that?"

Without taking his eyes off Pete's syringe, Rueben pointed at the TV on the wall. Surely it was still showing coverage of the upcoming summit.

"Hah. You think you know what's going on here, don't you? Well, you know shit."

"Enlighten me, then."

"I'm not going to enlighten you, child. I'm going to get you out of the way."

Suddenly, Martha dove toward Pete from out of nowhere. Pete grabbed her, and they grappled. Then Pete drew his gun, discharging it into Martha's chest. She collapsed backward to the floor, her hands clutched over her heart, a mass of red darkening the fabric of her dress.

The entire bar erupted in screams, and people ducked under the tables. Rueben and Pete stood staring each other down.

Shit. I've got to die and go back to save her... Without wasting a breath, Rueben dashed out into the street, and Pete followed him.

"Don't think I'm going to let you do this."

"You're not my dad," Rueben said.

"God, you're an annoying little bastard."

Rueben winked and jumped out into traffic. It was mere seconds before a speeding Porsche crushed him. *It wasn't the least stylish way to go down.* The weight of superior German engineering bore down on his gut.

Then he died.

Friday, May 19, 10:35 p.m.

Rueben came back to his body and was sitting in the booth again. The fly buzzed away. He slammed the table so hard it shook. "Damn it!"

Aki looked concerned. "What's wrong?"

"It's not working. None of it's working."

Aki pulled her eyes off the TV screen showing the World Summit preparations. "What are you talking about?"

"I have an evil psycho doppelganger!"

Aki massaged her forehead. "Huh?"

Rueben looked around the table. Buzz was already standing but had stopped at his friend's desperate expression.

Rueben scratched his head. "Look, there isn't time." Why the hell wasn't he going back any farther in time? Then it hit him. During his basement imprisonment, Pete had mentioned something about "capping" Rueben at the Exit Bar. What if "capping" meant... "Hey Buzz, you think it's possible to 'cap' my uh, special power?"

"Theoretically speaking, with the right application of science and technology..."

Rueben looked at him.

"...yeah. I'd say it's possible. Are you saying that you can't go back any farther than right now?"

Rueben nodded.

"Hmm. Then my best guess is that someone implanted you with a nanobot that counteracts your ability to warp back at the genetic level, thus rendering you unable to warp back before the time of implant."

"Implanted? Buzz, I'm sitting at a bar." Then it hit Rueben. "Shit. The fly."

"The fly?" Buzz said.

Rueben dropped his head in his hands. "Yes. It bit me and flew off." He considered dying and warping back again to kill the 'fly,' but it would already be too late. There'd be no warping back to before it had bitten him or implanted him with the "capper" or whatever.

That meant there'd be no stopping Pete before he got here. His adversary was smart. *And* had some crazy-advanced tech —was that even a fly or some kind of tiny robot?

Aki raised her eyebrows. "Special power? Rueben, are you on drugs?"

Rueben let his hands fall to the tabletop. "No. It's just that we gotta... Just...*run!*"

They all stared at him.

"What are you looking at? *Just run!*"

At Rueben's command, Martha and Buzz looked at each other knowingly. With a glance at Rueben for confirmation, they took off for the front door.

Rueben grabbed Aki's wrist and followed them.

"Stop." She slipped off her shoes. She started running in bare feet toward the entrance as Rueben now struggled to keep up with her. "Now, what the hell is going on?" She couldn't quite run in a straight line—what with all the alcohol coursing through her system—but she still ran faster than he did. Running and endurance had never been big priorities for him, and he thought that had been a mistake.

He caught up with her as they reached the door. He took in her inquisitive and intelligent dark eyes and felt a pang of guilt. She was too smart to allow him to keep stringing her along in the dark about his powers. "Just trust me. Can you do that?"

"Well, you got us this far."

Rueben shrugged and remembered all the doubts she'd had several time warps before. "I know the stakes are high, and I know that you have a lot of doubts and questions. I can't tell you everything. But, I also know that justice is blind for people like us. Whatever I'm putting us through, I'm not taking that lightly."

She nodded. "Thank you, Rueben. I needed to hear that."

He held out his hand. "I know you did."

She took it, and they ran to the street curb. Rueben bent to catch his breath. At the moment, the only person in sight was the wild-eyed homeless man from before that he seemed to keep running into on the streets. The man sat on the ground, munching on a fried chicken thigh from a bucket of Hurley's Chicken: Best dang chicken in the galaxy.™ "He's trying to kill you to keep you distracted," he mumbled.

Rueben raised an eyebrow. "What?"

The homeless man picked himself up and wandered off.

Buzz and Martha rejoined Rueben—they'd originally gone the other way—and Buzz pointed at Chicken Man's departing back. "Haven't we seen that guy before?"

As Rueben was about to respond, he saw Pete five yards away from him, peering inside the Exit Bar's front window.

Martha pointed at Pete with one hand while she dug in her clutch for her badge with the other. To Rueben, she said, "Isn't that the guy who was talking to Pout…"

Pete turned then, and he saw them.

Martha drew out her badge like a gun. "Sir, I'm going to have to ask you to raise your hands slowly."

Pete shook his head, disappointed. Then he glared at Rueben. "I see this isn't our first interaction. And politely conversing as adults didn't go so well…"

"Politely conversing?" Rueben clenched his hands into fists. "Eat shit."

"I see. So sad we've come to this path. But I will carry out my plan. One way or the other."

Rueben started backing away until he came to the sidewalk's curb. Behind them there was a gap in the traffic. "Go to hell."

"Your friends first."

Aki turned to Rueben. "What's going on?"

"Run!"

As Pete silently reached under his hoodie, Rueben leapt out into the street. His friends followed. "Come on!"

They'd made it to the other side when traffic started flowing again. After a garbage truck roared past, Pete stood on the other side of the street with his silenced pistol extended.

"Down!" Rueben ordered. They hit the ground as Pete pulled the trigger. A car passed between him and his target, and there was a screeching of burned rubber.

Buzz yelled from the concrete as they all picked themselves up. "Holy shit, Rueben. What have you gotten us into now?"

"Trust me. Now move. Run!"

"Wait." Martha stooped over on the sidewalk. "I dropped my badge."

Rueben grabbed her arm and yanked her away from the badge, glittering under a street lamp. "No time."

For a moment, Martha resisted, then she turned away from her badge, and the foursome took off at a sprint around a street corner to put some distance between them and Pete, who had started across the street.

Aki sucked in a breath and blinked as she tried to shake off her alcohol. Too bad it wasn't that easy. "Who is that guy? How did you know he was going to be out here?"

"Aki. Right now, I can't tell you how I know. I just know, and I need you to trust me."

"Trust isn't in my nature."

They kept moving at a fast jog. Rueben huffed in a breath, wishing he was in better shape. "Yeah, but staying alive is. Let's get out of here—it's not safe."

Rueben knew that Pete was smart, and he'd find them eventually. He had advanced technology and stuff on his side. What they needed was an advantage.

What they needed was a set of wheels.

Rueben led them out of a back alley and up to a street and stopped.

Martha's eyes were wide. "Why are we stopping?"

Rueben ignored her and snapped his fingers at Buzz. "Where's your taser?"

"My what?"

Rueben sighed. "I know you have a homemade taser. Let me see it."

Buzz produced it, and Rueben grabbed it.

"Shit," Aki said. "He found us."

Over his shoulder, Rueben glimpsed Pete forty yards behind them, entering the alley they had recently exited. "You can't run forever," he roared.

Rueben turned his back on Pete and stepped into the street. Approaching him was a red Camry. It slowed, and a man leaned out the driver's side window. "Do you want to die?"

"No, not this time. But you're about to." Rueben showed him the taser through the front windshield and hoped it looked like a gun in the night.

The man's eyes widened. "Shit. What do you want?"

"Unlock the doors." The car's doors *clicked*. Rueben motioned to Aki, Martha, and Buzz, and they all hopped into the back seat. Rueben climbed into the front passenger's seat and held the taser to the man's head. "Just drive."

"Absolutely."

The man floored it as Pete reached the sidewalk. He fired a barrage of bullets that embedded themselves into the car's rear end and was left standing in the rearview.

"Anyone hit?" Rueben called to the back seat.

When his three friends said they were all good, Rueben turned back to the driver and noticed he was trembling. He was young, not a whole lot older than him. "What's your name, man?"

"Ben."

"Hi Ben, I'm Jim."

Jim Lewandowski was his fake name when cyberstalking and going on tech jobs for the CIA. He figured it was the kind of name most people wouldn't bat an eye at.

Ben nodded, still scared shitless. He glanced at Pete shaking his fist and standing on the sidewalk in the rearview. "Friend of yours?"

Rueben answered, "No."

"Where, um, to, then? Uh...please don't kill me. Please—"

"I'm not going to kill you. He might. Just get us out of here."

They drove in silence for a few minutes until Aki called attention to a small blue Nissan that seemed to be following them. Rueben turned to see Pete's muscled body crammed into the tiny vehicle. The Nissan accelerated as if to ram them from behind.

Ben gasped and began in a terrified ramble. "Look, man, I don't want to die. I just... You know, I don't even drink or go to clubs. I'm a geeky guy who plays World of Warcraft on a Saturday night. I thought I'd mix it up and try to meet some girls. I clearly picked the wrong night, or the wrong bar, or the—"

Ben screamed again and swerved to miss Pete's latest attempt to disable their vehicle. If Pete succeeded, what was he going to do? Kill Rueben's friends in cold blood and drug and kidnap Rueben? Lock him up in the basement again, but this time with enough serum to keep him sleeping past the beginning of World War III?

Rueben felt guilty. They had to get Ben out of this. They'd figure this out on their own. He ordered, "Turn here."

It was a quick turn, one that Pete wasn't able to take on such short notice. After Ben made the turn, Rueben instructed, "Floor it like hell."

It was good that the streets in this section of town were mostly deserted at this hour, and luckily, they didn't run into any police cars. A few minutes later, they arrived at a mini-mart. Rueben told Ben to stop the car. "Let us out."

"Uh-huh." Ben accelerated past a Ferrari filling up on gas at one of the pumps outside and promptly stopped the car. The four of them piled out, and Ben sped off into the night. Rueben doubted he'd ever try to get laid again.

Buzz shook his head. "Poor guy."

Aki snorted. "Poor guy? Poor us. What the hell is up with that hoodie dude following us?"

Rueben answered quickly, "Terrorist. Wants to blow up the World Summit on Monday night."

Aki's eyes widened. "The U.N. conference?"

Rueben nodded and searched for a way out of the mini-mart. Aki wasn't going to let that go.

"How do you know this?" she said.

"I can't tell you. I need you to trust me."

She was quiet, and Rueben suspected that a long lecture about the dark side of the CIA was on the tip of her tongue. He beat her to it. "I won't let you rot in a Chinese prison."

She gulped, and her dark eyes fired with intensity. "You can't guarantee that."

"I know who we work for and how dangerous our job can get when they have to maintain plausible deniability. And I know you're worried, but trust me—I know what I'm doing."

"I hope you do."

Buzz cleared his throat as he paced in front of a stack of propane tanks for sale. "I hate to interrupt this Hallmark moment, but we're stuck outside a mini-mart without any wheels and a trigger-happy asshole on our sixes. Can we please think of a way out of here?"

At that moment, the blue Nissan squealed into the mini-mart parking lot, window down. Pete had his gun pointed out the window, and the foursome dropped to the concrete. He pulled the trigger, and one of the mini-mart's windows exploded. "I'm getting tired of playing," Pete hollered.

Rueben spotted the mini propane tanks beside him. *Worth a try.*

He might not have had running endurance, but he had moves. Using his dance prowess and muscle memory honed during his competitive ballroom dance days, Rueben grabbed a propane tank and launched it at Pete's car.

He wished he had a gun to fire at the tank—would it have exploded like they always did in the movies?—but Pete sped off around the block, rubber squealing. They all panted as they rose from the concrete.

Aki dusted the dirt off her dress. "That's not all we'll see of him."

Rueben answered, "No, it's not. Not by any stretch. Now we need another vehicle."

"You're too good a man, Rueben," Aki said. "Which I admire. But we should have kept Ben's ride."

Buzz eyed the four-seater Ferrari sitting at the gas pump. In his haste to seek cover when Pete had shot at them, its driver had abandoned his vehicle.

"Oh, I've got something better." Buzz winked at Rueben, Martha, and Aki, and with a grin, jumped in the driver's seat.

The keys were still in the ignition, and Buzz gunned the engine. "You guys coming?"

The mini-mart door burst open, and the Ferrari's owner, a middle-eastern man in his fifties, came running out. "Get out of my car! I'm calling the police!"

Aki, Martha, and Rueben all shrugged at each other. Then, without a word, they all jumped in, Rueben and Aki squeezing into the back, Martha in the front, as Buzz took off in a squeal of tires.

It wasn't a moment too soon because Pete circled back in his Nissan, prepared to finish the job. He cruised up to the store and stopped, searching and not noticing his targets were in the Ferrari.

It didn't take him long to figure out what had happened, though, and he pivoted in his seat and fired at the Ferrari's side. Buzz jolted out of the parking lot and out onto the street. The blue Nissan was soon hot on their bumper.

Buzz scoffed. "Really? A Nissan against a Ferrari? Come on, let's see what this baby can do."

Buzz punched it, weaving in and out of the sparse late-night traffic. The little blue Nissan tried to keep up as they wound through New York City's streets, dodging traffic and cabs. Unfortunately, traffic eventually grew thick, and the other cars leveled the playing field. Ferrari or not, Pete soon gained on them.

Martha shook her head. "We gotta get out of the city."

Aki nodded and checked her phone's GPS. "She's right. If we go up that way, we can get to an open road out of the city."

They made a quick turn to confuse the Nissan and lost Pete for a moment. That was when Aki's phone rang. "What is this number?"

Rueben watched her decline it, but the phone rang again

and again. They all looked at each other. They knew what this was, but they couldn't begin to fathom the how.

Rueben grabbed the phone. He answered it and put it on speaker. "What is this?"

Pete's laughter always sent a chill down his spine. So sinister and dark, and his own, and Rueben knew Pete was using it to his advantage.

"Hello, Rueben."

"Leave us alone."

"But if I do, you won't leave me alone."

"You don't know that," Buzz said. And then, "Hey, his voice kinda sounds like yours, Rueben."

Pete's laugh came over the phone's speaker. "You going to tell them? Or shall I?"

Rueben terminated the call.

Aki pierced him with her dark eyes in the dimness of the back seat. "What the fuck is going on?"

Rueben didn't know how to answer. Up ahead was an exit leading toward the countryside of upstate New York. Buzz only needed to maneuver around one car hogging the wide exit lane in front of them, and they'd be off to the races with them in a Ferrari and Pete vastly outmatched.

"Well?" Aki said.

The Nissan's engine revved, and there was an impact from behind.

Buzz cringed as he gripped the steering wheel. Tires squealed. The Ferrari's front end nearly ran under the rear fender of the car in front of them, but Buzz managed to control the sports car.

The car in front of them did a three-sixty and came to a stop against the concrete retaining wall. Buzz accelerated past, following the exit's curve and entering a long, wide-open road. There was only one problem: part of the car's quarter panel thumped against one of the rear tires as they accelerated, torn loose from Pete's impact.

Rueben checked on the foursome. "Everyone okay?"

Aki winked. "Not the first car chase I've been in."

Martha laughed. "Me neither."

"No shit?"

"I'm a cop. We kind of invented them."

Buzz passed the back of his hand across his sweating forehead. "Uh, guys. I'm not. Hear that sound back there like a rabbit tossed into a cycling clothes dryer? By my calculations, the driver's side rear tire will deteriorate to the point of failure within…two hundred and ninety seconds."

"So we've got less than five minutes to outwit Pete?" Rueben said.

Aki punched Rueben's arm. "Pete? Why didn't you tell us that you know this dick's name?"

"It's…"

"A long story? Rueben, you and I…you're really straining our relationship right now."

"Relationship? I didn't think we were in a relationship."

Aki rolled her eyes. "Well, you know what I mean. Our, uh, work thing. You know."

Rueben didn't know. Women were so hard to understand. "Wait, so are you saying there's a chance—"

"Uh, guys," Buzz interrupted. "T-minus four minutes and counting."

Rueben sat up straight and drew a deep breath, trying to focus. It was hard with that awful flapping sound coming from the tire. "Guys, I need to tell you something, and I need you not to think I'm crazy." He didn't wait for his friends to respond. "The guy chasing us. The one who calls himself

Pete. I don't know how exactly, but he's an older version of me."

"What?" Aki said.

Buzz slapped the top of the steering wheel. "Bingo."

Rueben screwed his eyebrows together. "Bingo?"

"Yeah. Totally makes sense. His voice. It kinda reminded me of yours."

Martha shuddered in her seat and raised her hands. "I'm not even going to argue it."

"But," Rueben said. "It makes no sense. I mean, time travel doesn't work that way—"

Buzz looked like he was about to scream in irritation. "Look, people. If you think about it too much, you'll break it. Three minutes, twenty-seven seconds!"

Aki's face lit up in the glow of her cell phone as she studied her GPS app. "Take the next right turn, then the next left."

Buzz did.

"Careful. There's a curve coming up."

Rueben watched out the window as the city's bright lights began to fade behind them, and fields and vineyards started to open ahead of them under the moonlight.

They took the curve, and Buzz followed a few more directions from Aki. All the while, the flapping sound increased in intensity and sound.

Rueben turned and glanced at the headlights far behind them. It was Pete. He was still on their tail.

Buzz called over his shoulder. "Hey, buddy. You think of a plan yet?"

"You're our resident genius," Martha countered.

"Woman, I'm driving!" Buzz blurted, and that reminded Rueben of how scared Buzz had been on the Pout mission at the Canadian border when things had gotten hairy.

Rueben groaned. "I'm thinking."

Buzz slammed on the horn for good effect. "That's your problem, son. Sometimes you gotta learn not to think. That man in the Nissan is you. Which means he thinks like you. This means you gotta do something he wouldn't expect. Forty-two seconds left!"

"Good idea, Buzz. Good idea." But what could Rueben do that was completely out of character and thus unpredictable to Pete? There had to be something—

"Buddy," Buzz said. "You're thinking too hard again. Blurt out the first thing that enters your mind...now!"

"I sometimes pleasure myself to Aki's photographs!"

"Ew, gross," Martha said.

Ah shit... There was dumb, and there was dumber. Why had he said something so stupid? He turned to Aki as he scratched behind his ears. "I er, uh..."

"Ten seconds!"

She wasn't mad at him. In fact, by the sexy pout on her lips, she looked turned on. "It's cool. It's cool. You do know that half the guys in our division probably do that. You're just the only one with the balls to admit it."

Whoa. So it looked like he'd scored major points with Aki.

Suddenly, a loud *thudding* smacked up and down beneath the car's low undercarriage.

"Ahh!" It was Buzz.

Rueben swallowed. "What? Did time run out?"

"No. Squirrel."

Then time ran out, and the back tire exploded, sending them swerving and careening off the country road.

CHAPTER ELEVEN

<u>**Friday, May 19, 11:13 p.m.**</u>

The Ferrari eventually came to a stop in the ditch off to the side of the road. Since it was now facing the way they had come, they had a good view of Pete's Nissan speeding ever closer to them. Its twin headlights cast an eerie glare through the dark countryside.

From the back seat, Rueben rubbed his forehead and unbuckled his seatbelt, hoping the rest of his friends had buckled in as well. "Guys?"

"Still here," Martha said.

Aki unbuckled her seatbelt. "Yep. Ditto."

"I'm alive too," Buzz said. Followed by, "Wait. You masturbate to Aki's photo?" as if his brain had only now processed Rueben's words. He beat the meat of his fist against his forehead. "TMI, Rueben. TMI."

Rueben sighed. He had a feeling this little tidbit would become a recurring jab. *If we all survive and I don't have to die to warp backward and do this all over again...* "I'm glad everyone's all right. Now we've got to scram. And fast."

Two car doors *clicked* open almost in unison, and they all got out. Luckily neither of the doors had jammed in the wreck. After a glance at their dark surroundings, Rueben stumbled away from the road and toward what appeared to be a vineyard. He ducked under a vine as he sidled between two rows of trellises. "Follow me."

They did, and they stumbled through the rows of grape plants. Behind them on the road, they heard Pete's car screech to a halt, followed by the opening and closing of a car door.

Rueben and company meanwhile continued through the vineyard, their hands held out before them and guiding the way in the dark. The moon was bright, but the trellises cast some awful-looking shadows into their path. Once, Rueben glanced over his shoulder and thought he saw a spider crawling on his arm. He swatted at it in case it wasn't a shadow and it wasn't. It was a spider, and it happened to land on Aki's chest. She yelped, then punched Rueben in the arm, a little harder than Rueben would've liked.

"Sorry," he whispered.

"I hear you." It was Pete's voice, coming loud and clear from somewhere in the rows behind them.

"I'm too young to die," Buzz whined and took off with a burst of speed in front of them.

Rueben huffed and panted. His legs were about to give out. "Wait up. Buzz, we can't get...separated."

"We're separated." Martha pulled up beside Rueben at an easy trot. *Damn her and her police training.* "I'll go ahead and catch him before he does something stupid." She took off.

Aki slapped Rueben on the elbow. "Then there were two. Hope you're a fan of horror movies."

"Uh, I don't particularly like them."

"I didn't know that."

Rueben nodded as he continued to move forward. "There's a lot we don't know about each other."

"I have a feeling you've got a lot more to hide than me." There wasn't exactly condemnation in Aki's voice, but there was impatience.

"That's why I'm glad you're such a great friend who understands that I'll tell her shortly. We have to survive this psycho chasing us first."

Aki reached toward her back pocket for her phone. "We need backup. I'll call Sven."

"Sven? No—"

"Damn. There's no signal out here."

That's odd, Rueben thought. They weren't too far out from the city. Was something else in play out here? Was Pete somehow blocking the nearby cell towers with some hi-tech device under his hoodie?

Rueben and Aki passed an open area in the grape trellises and came to a tall wooden stake with a scarecrow stuck to it.

He braked and did a double-take. "Who puts a scarecrow out in the middle of May?"

Aki stopped beside him, and her hand brushed his. "Creepy."

The scarecrow suddenly moved. Buzz popped out from behind it, followed by Martha.

Rueben shook his head and whispered, "Not funny. Especially without any cell service out here."

"I know." Buzz nodded, the moonlight reflecting off his dark eyes. "And I think I know why."

"Cell jammers," Rueben said.

"Right," Buzz said.

"Pete."

"Wrong."

"Wrong?" Rueben studied his friend. They had to keep moving.

Buzz scratched behind his head. "They're one of my top-secret government clearance-only proprietary cell jammers."

"Um, okay...We need to go." Rueben turned away from Buzz to continue running in the direction they'd headed before they came across the scarecrow in the open area.

Buzz's voice came as a harsh whisper. "No. Rueben. Follow me. I know the way."

Frustrated—and more than a bit worried his friends were about to get slaughtered by Pete—Rueben turned back to Buzz, surprised when he saw the screen of Buzz's smartphone held in his hand. Its screen resembled a submarine's sonar display—probably one of Buzz's proprietary phone apps. A blip on the screen flashed every time the clockwise-spinning "sonar line" passed over it.

Buzz started off at a jog in the direction of the blip. Instead of running parallel with the trellises, Buzz's path shot through a wide-open aisle running perpendicular to the trellises. That meant they wouldn't have to worry about ducking under vines and swatting spiders.

Rueben grunted and caught up to Buzz while Martha and Aki followed on his heels. He glanced over at Buzz. "What are you smiling about?"

"These are my favorite type of grapes we're running through. Merlot. I'm a fine wine connoisseur."

"Dude, you're a drunk."

"Heh. Whatever. You dork."

"Uh, you're also a dork."

"Geez, Rueben, can you let me have a win now and then?"

Rueben winced. He tried to think calmly. "What if we're running blind into a trap? Some government facility where they experiment on aliens or something, and they subdue us and keep us in cages...?"

A lot of good Rueben's warping ability would do for him there.

"It's not a government facility. It's...well, that's my jamming signal. As in..."

"As in what?" Rueben said.

"Well. I...don't know. I don't remember ever coming out here."

"Great. Just great."

From behind them, Aki and Martha pulled even with Buzz and Rueben, and a few moments later, the four of them passed the last row of grapes. They entered a giant clearing, with a medium-sized metal pole barn painted black like the night standing before them.

"I don't know what's inside, but that's where we need to go," Buzz said excitedly.

Rueben leaned forward with his hands resting on his knees as Martha peered distrustfully at the black barn. "We're not going inside there, are we?"

"I'm coming for you!" Pete shouted from the grape rows behind them.

Aki met Martha's eyes. "I think we are."

They sprinted up to the barn.

CHAPTER TWELVE

Friday, May 19, 11:42 p.m.

Buzz was standing at the barn's front door. His friends gathered around him as he flipped open a keypad concealed on the wall. After a moment, he tapped out a four-digit code. A red light beeped beside the keypad, and a small speaker squawked. A robotic voice said, "Incorrect."

Red laser lights blinked on from somewhere high on the wall and trained down on each of their four torsos like sniper lasers.

"You have ten seconds to vacate the premises before the self-destruct protocol activates. One. Two. Three."

"Buzz," Rueben said.

"Hold on, hold on." He quickly tapped out another code.

"Incorrect. Targets acquired."

Gun barrels slid out from the wall above them, and Rueben gripped his buddy's shirt. "Buzz…"

Buzz tapped a third code, and a green light flashed on the keypad. The gun barrels slid back into their housings, and the laser lights blinked out so that all that remained was a harmless-looking barn wall. The door slid open with a *hiss* of air. This was no normal pole barn.

The interior was pitch black, and Buzz stepped inside. "Umm, after me."

After exchanging looks, his three friends followed.

Soft ceiling light panels came to life as they entered, revealing a futuristic airplane-hanger interior. There were no planes, but there were plenty of metal workbenches lined with hi-tech-looking gadgets and instruments. At the back of the room were several bookcases lined with hardcover books.

Rueben rubbed his eyes to make sure he saw correctly. "Uh, Buzz?"

Buzz was already inspecting a small box-like device with a tiny needle projecting from one reflective metal surface. It was about the size of a small Rubik's cube with several tiny ports for hooking it up to some kind of electronics. "Yeah, buddy?"

"I think it's time for you to explain."

From behind them, the door slid shut, and Aki and Martha went to inspect it.

Buzz slipped the shiny cube into his pocket and whistled. "I wish I could."

Rueben scowled. "What do you mean you wish you could?"

"As far as I know, I've never been here before. I don't recall ever creating any of this." He gestured at an item lying upon one of the benches. It looked like a cross between a futuristic weed-eater and a portable vacuum cleaner. "But this is all my handiwork."

Martha rejoined Buzz and Rueben. "What do you mean?"

Buzz picked up a sleek-looking spinning top and held it upside down. There was a tiny BL insignia at the bottom. "That's my secret logo. It's trademarked. And clearly my design. But I never built it."

Now Aki stepped up to them. "A top? You're building children's toys for the government or something?"

Buzz smirked and pressed a tiny button on the top of its spinner before balancing the top upon the workbench. "Ready for this?" He gave his thumb and forefingers a hard twist, and the top began to spin. Suddenly, razor blades clicked out from the top's sides as it spun, and they all stepped back a step in surprise except for Buzz, who only stood and watched like a proud father.

"You knew that was going to happen, but you didn't build it?" Rueben asked.

His friend nodded. "It's how I would've designed it." He tapped the side of his head. "It's how my brain thinks."

Martha made a face. "You have a dangerous brain."

"Why, thank you."

"That wasn't really a compliment."

The sound of a gun blast interrupted her words. It had come from right outside the barn. A moment of silence followed and then, "Come out, come out, wherever you are!"

Aki eyed Rueben closely. "Your buddy Pete. Or is he some kind of future you?" She stood with her hands on her hips. "It's hard to keep all your secrets straight."

"Look, I—"

Martha stepped between Rueben and Aki. "That madman has us cornered. We've got to do something."

Aki nodded and noticed a computer monitor on the opposite side of the floor. It looked like security footage split-screen. "I'm going to check that out. See if I can get a fix on that asshole's location out there."

She took off for the monitor. Rueben turned to Buzz and jabbed a finger at his shirt. "I don't like the coincidence of being chased by that man and you stumbling upon some secret barn in the middle of a field containing a bunch of secret tech you built but didn't build. What the hell am I missing?"

Rueben released his grip, and Buzz straightened his shirt. "If Pete is you and you're both warpers, it's possible that this has already happened and you just don't remember."

"Huh?"

"This is speculation, but maybe Pete has already chased us way out here. And now he's trying to do it again, to see what happens or to get a different outcome."

Rueben shook his head. "Then why don't I remember?"

"Because. If he died and warped back, you wouldn't have remembered." Suddenly a futuristic-looking tablet caught his eye on the next bench over. He swept it up into his hands and unlocked the screen with a password on the second attempt.

"Buzz, what is it?" Rueben asked hurriedly.

"Ho-ly shitstorm!"

Martha huffed. "Well, don't leave us in suspense. We're running out of time."

Buzz tilted the screen down so that Rueben could see. It contained a few lines of text, but they made no sense. They were in code.

"Buzz," Rueben said.

"Yes, yes. I know what this place is and how it got here. Sort of. This is a coded message from myself. It says: 'I, Buzz Lugger, sent these tech barns out into the multiverse to aid my fellow Buzzes and Ruebens.'"

"What the hell does that mean?" Martha said.

Buzz slapped his forehead. "It means we're not only dealing with time warps. This is a multiple-universe issue. Rueben, I think you might be an interdimensional being."

"I was born in New Jersey."

Buzz continued. "I don't think Pete is Rueben from the future at all. I think he's from another universe like ours, but it's somehow older. Maybe there's another Buzz out there who is trying to help the universes fight Pete."

Martha shook her head. "I am so lost."

"He's out there," Aki called. "We better get ready to defend ourselves."

As Rueben tried to wrap his head around this new development, he thought of one last question. "Assume that for the moment, I don't think you're crazy about the multiple universe thing. What was that shiny cube you placed in your pocket earlier?"

Excitement shone in Buzz's eyes. "I'm not one hundred percent sure. But did you see the needle on it? I think it's a prototype nanobot injector—the design is like twenty years into the future… Once I get it back to the lab, I'll be able to hook it up to my computers and know more. Who knows, maybe I could use it to 'cap' Pete like he did to you, but only permanently. No promises, though."

Buzz angled his head at the top, still spinning on the bench with extended blades. A moment later, he carefully pressed a button on top, and the blades retracted. He picked it up and tossed it to Rueben, who carefully slid it into his pocket. "Don't say I never gave you anything." The scientist chuckled.

Aki called, "He's approaching the front door."

The barn's walls muffled Pete's cold laughter outside. "I know you're in there!"

They all hurriedly searched for makeshift weapons on the benchtops, but they were interrupted by the squawk of an intercom and the robotic voice saying, "Incorrect." Then a moment later, "Incorrect." Finally, "Incorrect. This barn will self-destruct in thirty seconds. Thirty, twenty-nine, twenty-eight..."

"Oh shit," Rueben muttered. "We've got to get out of here."

Aki was already at the front door. "It's no use. It's sealed. And Pete is probably a safe distance away, watching and waiting for us."

Rueben wanted to pull out his hair. Instead, he turned to Buzz. "There has to be a back way out of here."

"Perhaps."

"I know you didn't design this barn, but if you did, where would you put it?"

"Um..."

Martha got in Buzz's face. "Damnit, man. Use your dangerous mind!"

"Oh, um, right—"

"Sixteen, fifteen, fourteen—"

Buzz scanned the barn's back wall, and his eyes lit up. "Follow me."

He sprinted toward a bookcase resting in front of the wall. Rueben and the gang followed on his heels. They were cutting this dangerously close.

Buzz stopped at the bookcase and glanced over the book titles.

"Eleven, ten, nine—"

Buzz pulled on the spine of a book titled *Theoretical Physics in a Theoretically Non-Existent World,* and it tilted toward him like a lever. The bookcase slid to the side on oiled rails, exposing a gap in the wall and the freedom of the night outside.

"Go, go, go!" Buzz screamed, and they all ran.

"Three, two, one."

Rueben threw out his arms and knocked all his friends down and forward onto the ground.

Behind them, silence filled the night air. Then the robotic voice said, "Goodbye," and clicked off.

They all turned to face the barn from their position on the ground.

Rueben expected the barn's roof to blow sky-high. Instead, an intense white light shone out from all of the barn's corners and edges. With a barely audible *poof*, it reduced the barn to a flat rectangular pile of steaming ash.

Rueben blinked. "Damn…"

He suddenly stiffened as a harsh voice echoed through the night air toward them from behind some old tractors. "You better watch your back. I won't let you ruin my plan."

Pete. Why wasn't he rushing in to get them now while they were vulnerable and sprawled out on the ground?

That's when they turned to face the dirt lane off to the side and the flashing lights of police cars bearing down on them.

CHAPTER THIRTEEN

Saturday, May 20, 1:17 a.m.

Rueben grimaced as the police officer pushed him over the hood of the car and frisked him.

"You got any weapons on you, son?"

The officer found the harmless-looking razor blade top in Rueben's pocket and chuckled, placing it into an evidence bag along with Rueben's phone and wallet.

"No," Rueben answered, scanning the darkness. Pete was still out there, and he said he'd come for them.

The officer finished with him, and Martha, still in her torn red formal, got searched next by another officer. Rueben caught her eye over the hood of the car and mouthed the words *Sorry*. She rolled her eyes. "Thanks for this."

He felt the hard pinch of metal as the cuffs clicked over his wrists.

"Mr. Peet, we received a call from the farmer who owns this land. Were you aware that you were trespassing on private property?"

Rueben frowned. Rueben and his friends had commandeered a car at taser-point and stole and wrecked a Ferrari. If trespassing was all the cops had, he certainly wasn't going to open his mouth and give them any more.

"Uh, no, Officer. I sure mean it when I say we're all quite sorry. We'd like to get on our way if we could."

A third officer walked over to them after examining the perfectly rectangular smoking ashes where the barn had previously stood.

"Think they did it?" a fourth policeman asked.

"Nah. The geometry's too perfect. If anything, it was aliens."

"Shit, man. Don't joke about that stuff. UFOs give me the willies."

Beside Rueben, Martha tried to explain how this was all a big misunderstanding and that she was with the NYPD.

But, having dropped her badge on the sidewalk back in NYC, the cop handcuffing her snickered. "Yeah, and I'm with the Secret Service. You're under arrest, lady. And you're lucky we don't take you seriously enough to bust you for impersonating an officer."

"But, I really am. We were trying to apprehend an attempted murder suspect."

"Lady, get in the car."

Martha got shoved into a waiting squad car while Buzz and Aki were searched and questioned. Aki tried the ol' cleavage trick, but it didn't work. The cops had confiscated all of their cell phones so they couldn't call Martha's precinct or the CIA for help. Too bad he and Aki didn't carry badges outside of work.

The cops radioed back and forth, and Rueben was shocked that the news of the stolen Ferrari or the blue Nissan hadn't reached them yet. Both vehicles were only about a mile down the road. It seemed the cops were mainly concerned about the trespassing charge.

Regardless, they were all on the hook now.

It would seem he had to die to fix this mess. That would likely mean he'd go back to the bar at 10:35 last night, and he'd have to confront Pete all over again. It had been difficult enough to get him this far.

Rueben suddenly felt very tired. They were all still alive, and Pete hadn't kidnapped him. It was probably for the best that Rueben let things play out. They still had the weekend and part of Monday to stop Pete's plans. It didn't matter if Pete was Future Rueben or Rueben from another universe. They'd find a way to stop him—they had to. The thought of global nuclear war was too much to fathom.

A few minutes passed before the cops herded them into two squad cars, with Rueben sharing the back seat of a car with Aki and Buzz and Martha occupying the other.

Aki met his eyes seriously. "That creep is still out there."

"I know. I know."

Aki sighed. "Remember when life used to be simple?"

"No. Not really." *If she only knew.*

At least they were moving. Also, Marshall was safe and wasn't involved in any of this. That was kind of a silver lining. Asshole that he was, Rueben felt bad enough for endangering his friends—he didn't want to have to worry about Marshall's safety too.

Rueben lay against the inside of the car door, his cheek smushed against the window as he watched the countryside go by.

What a night. You just couldn't make this stuff up.

Rueben lay in a cell bunk, staring up at the ceiling. The county jail was like an army barracks, rows and rows of metal bunk beds under glaring fluorescent lights.

The officers had taken Martha and Aki to a separate section of the building. Buzz was on the next bed over from Rueben. The genius was sitting on his bed with his arms wrapped around his raised knees as though he was afraid to touch anything.

Rueben sighed. "Too bad the barn got destroyed. It could have had more answers for us. I just can't wrap my head around the fact that there are alternate universes out there with alternate Buzzes and Petes and Ruebens and—"

"Are you guys high?" a man asked from the next cot over. He wore a dirty turtleneck and his breath smelled like alcohol.

"No, Barry," Rueben said. "For the last time, go back to sleep."

Barry scratched his beard stubble. "How can I when you two have been babbling nonsense for what seems like hours?"

Barry was the only other person in the cell with them. He was intoxicated so Rueben hadn't worried about him over-hearing him and Buzz discussing their time warper situation.

Rueben turned to the man. "It's not nonsense—"

"I get it. I get it." Barry made a rolling gesture with his hand. "You two are writers, aren't you? Writing a book on time travel and such?"

Rueben exchanged glances with Buzz. "Um—"

"It's too complex!" Barry shouted. "You can't just make stuff up. You got to stay grounded. Got to have some rules."

"Rules…" Rueben glanced over at where his friend still sat

on his bunk. "Buzz, you're the genius of the group. What are the rules?"

Buzz cleared his throat and began to lecture. "Rule number one, on average, when you die you can warp roughly between ten minutes and three days. Rule number two, only you remember what happens when you warp back. Rule number three, it looks like you're not the only warper. Rule number four, when there are two warpers, only the one who warps back first remembers. Rule number five, there appear to be multiple or parallel universes out there. Some of them may have warpers as well whose powers only affect the world they are currently on. Rule number six, there are probably going to be more rules."

Rueben thought them over. "You know, when you lay everything out like that, it's quite simple—"

"Exceptions to the rules," Buzz went on. "Exception one, ordinarily, you can warp back multiple times in a row. However, Rueben, you can't warp back farther than the Exit Bar because Pete implanted a nanobot 'capper' in you that interferes with your warp ability at the genetic level. Exception two, while the warper is the only one who remembers when warping backward, some individuals experience déjà vu-like sensations and can recall bits and pieces of some of the timelines that no longer exist. Over time, it can be enough to drive them mad. For example, Martha and possibly that one homeless man you keep running into." Buzz sighed. "There. That's all we know. I'll write up a full report when I get back to the lab. You both happy now?"

Rueben and Barry both nodded in satisfaction. Barry said, "There. Now things make a bit more sense to the common man."

Buzz turned to Barry, who'd been grumbling ever since

they'd entered the cell and started disturbing the peace. "Good. Now, where's my fucking prize?"

Barry grinned and stood from his bed. "Here, let me give you what you really want."

Buzz recoiled as Barry stepped up to him and lifted his hand above Buzz's head. Then he slowly patted Buzz on the shoulder. Buzz relaxed.

"Better?" Barry said.

"Yeah, actually."

Barry returned to his bunk. "Good. Now, I'm going to try to get some sleep. Keep it down, please?"

Rueben had finished talking about their problems. He felt like there was still so much to learn and he was dead tired. It had to be after three in the morning, or maybe it was four. There was no way to tell since there were no windows or clocks anywhere. The concept of time in jail had a sort of creepy mystery to it.

He laid down, but there was no way he could sleep in here. If he did manage to fall asleep, he feared he'd wake up with Pete looming over him with a syringe of knockout serum.

A short while later, a police officer yelled, "Rueben Peet and Buzz Lugger."

Rueben jumped off his bed, but Buzz had already beaten him and was standing at the bars.

The officer found them and handed them papers through the bars while he unlocked the door. "You're being released."

Rueben's bleary eyes suddenly shot to life. "Huh? How?"

The officer didn't respond, only opened the door. Then he handed Rueben and Buzz clear bags containing their phones, wallets, and other personal items, including the experimental spinning top. They accepted them and wasted no time stepping out of the temporary holding cell. Following the officer,

Rueben wiped the sleep from his tired eyes. "What about Aki and Martha? Where are they? Are they free too?"

Still, the officer said nothing. About a dozen signed papers later, Rueben and Buzz walked outside as free men, stopping on the front steps of the jail.

Aki and Martha also waited on the steps, and they talked in low tones. It was still dark, and it had been a long night for all of them.

Rueben's voice was thick with lack of sleep. "How did we manage to get sprung from the pokey? Tell me someone didn't call Marshall."

Aki winked at him. "No—Sven."

Martha rubbed her arms in the cool of the dawn. "Sven?"

Aki and Rueben both sighed. Sven was their boss and the division director. He could get witnesses out of a Chinese prison and on a plane with a provisional passport within twenty-four hours. Of course, he could get a couple of field agents out of a county jail.

Rueben, however, didn't like the implications. "How? They didn't give us our 'one call' like they were supposed to."

Aki only winked and rolled her shoulders, shifting her bosom beneath her dress.

"Right." Rueben admired her winning smile. "What do we owe him?"

"I told him we were chasing a mark and it went bad. I tied it to another case I'm working on, and he's fine with it. Also, the CIA is providing a security detail for all of us for the next couple of days."

A black limousine pulled up beside them, and the driver's window rolled down. A skinny man in dark shades sat behind the wheel. "Get in the car."

Rueben stared at the man and didn't move.

Aki stepped confidently toward him. "Good morning, Jack. You can drop the cover."

Jack looked disappointed. "Really? I was just getting going."

Aki opened the back door. "Good work, though. Feeling the vibe. But sunglasses at four a.m.?"

He took off the glasses. "Yeah, it's kind of hard to drive with these things."

Aki turned toward the rest of the group. "You guys coming?"

Martha was the first to respond. "Uh, yeah."

They all piled in the limo, and Rueben tried to piece it together. "Sven sent you?"

"I'm not at liberty to say."

Aki sighed. "Recruit."

A collective, "Ah," rose from the back seat.

Jack started rolling up the divider between them. "The less information I know, the better."

When the divider was up, Rueben leaned back in the seat and was glad he didn't have to talk. Buzz found the mini bottle of wine and chugged it. Aki and Martha pulled out their cell phones and started scrolling through them while Rueben sat and worried about Pete's plans for them and how they were going to stop him.

Jack broke the silence through the intercom. "Where to?"

Aki sat up. "Should we debrief at one of our places?"

Buzz grumbled, "I'm tired, and I think I might have contracted a parasite or two in that hellhole. I can feel it burrowing into my intestines."

Rueben rubbed his face. "Buzz, you can't feel parasites. That's the whole point."

"These I can feel. I can feel these things multiplying and

shutting down my organs. I think I'm losing air." He started gagging and thrust his head between his knees.

Rueben smacked the back of his buddy's head. "Pull yourself together, man."

Buzz spoke from between his legs. "That's it. I'm going to do a natural cleanse once I get home. Then I'm going to take a lingering bath and get wildly drunk and forget this all happened."

Rueben snickered, but Martha groaned in agreement. "Every one of those things sounds good. Do those cleanses work?"

Aki sighed. "With Pete at large, we all need to be careful. Even with the security details assigned to our homes, we don't know what he's planning. We know he has a target on all of us. As long as we're alert and armed, we should be fine. Anyone need guns or ammo? I have enough at my place to knock down a city block."

Rueben knew Marshall did too, and so did Martha. Buzz had, well, more gadgets than the Department of Defense. So, he should be fine.

The scientist whined as much. "I'm more worried about being killed by a variant Ebola strain than a terrorist."

Buzz moaned, and Rueben smirked. "Hey Buzz, it looks like there's a little dirt in your hair."

"What?"

"Oh, yeah. Little black speck. Let me get it for you. Oh wait, I think it moved."

"What?"

"Oh, look, there's more of them. They're all moving. They're alive!"

Buzz scratched erratically at his head and fell screaming

on the floor of the limo. The rest of them doubled over laughing.

Aki high-fived Rueben. "Best thing all night."

Buzz sat back up, face flushed. "You guys are assholes."

Rueben laughed. "Yeah, well, we're not the ones with parasites."

Martha teased, "I don't know, maybe we need masks and gloves to be around you."

Buzz frowned and folded his arms. "Haha, very funny. You know, intestinal health is not a joke. Our intestines show us a lot about what's going on in our bodies. When they are compromised, it can wreak havoc on our systems. Do you know that gastrointestinal—"

Aki smacked him this time. "Buzz, do you ever intend to have sex in this lifetime?"

"Huh, what?"

"You've seriously got to lay off of words like 'gastrointestinal.'"

"I do just fine with the ladies, thank you."

Jack buzzed in on the intercom. "Where to?"

Aki answered, "Let's all go home, get some sleep. We'll rendezvous back at Buzz's this afternoon for a debrief."

Jack answered, "Copy that. Also, I have a lemon-based cleanse I do twice a year. It's very healing. You can prevent a lot of illnesses by paying attention to your gastrointestinal health."

Buzz threw his arms in the air. "Thank you!"

Jack came back through. "You can't ignore your gut."

Aki rapped on the divider window. "Jack, roll down the window."

Rueben was the first one to arrive home. As much as he had been confident about Marshall's ammo supply, now he wasn't so sure as he spotted the two capable-looking men in black stationed outside his apartment building. *Real subtle...real subtle...*would they deter Pete? He had a futuristic glove with an "obliteration mode."

Rueben took the stairs up to his apartment and noticed his downstairs neighbors Midge and Sheera sitting outside on their front patio, drinking their morning coffee.

They shot him a withering glance. He offered them a fake-pleasant smile and continued up the stairs.

He arrived in the small two-bedroom apartment he shared with Marshall. Plush orange couches and a fifty-two-inch plasma TV took up an entire wall. Marshall lay asleep and drunk in front of the TV. The news reports profiled the agenda at the upcoming U.N. World Summit.

"The delegates have been arriving in New York for the last two days for the U.N. World Summit that will start Monday. Topics under consideration include climate change as well as global poverty. Delegates have indicated they'll address plans to stimulate the economies of underdeveloped countries."

Stock footage flashed across the screen of children with swollen bellies with flies buzzing around.

An American politician came on the screen. Yolanda Martinez, the American ambassador to the U.N. "We have a responsibility to work together with these countries to make sure every man, woman, and child has equal access to clean water, food, adequate shelter, and basic healthcare."

Applause.

"Every person on this planet, rich or poor, young or old, should have access to basic human rights."

The talking news head returned. "Martinez's One World campaign has faced challenges."

A wiry politician with dark circles under his eyes and tiny spectacles spoke from an armchair. Oliver Westin, Senate Committee on Foreign Aid. "No one wants to see people—especially children—suffer, and I've seen the video on the One World campaign, and the footage is devastating. Heartbreaking. My wife couldn't even sit through it because it was so disturbing. The reality is, we have problems here in the United States that we need to fix before we can look elsewhere. We have a national debt that's so far out of control that it will take generations to fix. We have poverty, homelessness, unemployment… What Martinez's plan advocates is diverting American tax dollars away from our national programs to help the economies of other countries."

Rueben listened to the debate about the One World campaign rage on and shook his head. From the news footage he had seen during his basement captivity, Pete's drones were going to attack the summit on Monday at 7:30 p.m.

He didn't think Pete's plan was because of the One World campaign. Pete seemed unhinged, but not in a politically extremist way. At least, that's what Rueben's gut was telling him.

Unless maybe Pete was part of some kind of conspiracy-theorist group that thought the One World campaign sounded too suspiciously globalist and believed there was a nefarious intent behind it?

He'd been in the CIA long enough to know there was some truth to some of the more popular conspiracy theories. Although to his knowledge, it didn't go as deep as people thought. Still, he'd be lying if he said that he believed countries were run only by their respective governments.

Pete had specifically mentioned that he wanted to start a global war—which most likely meant nuclear war since nuclear disarmament between high-tension nations was a big topic at the Summit. He planned to go up to the roof with his satellite phone after the summit bombing to confirm it had worked.

Why a nuclear war? Rueben eventually gave up trying to figure out the reason why. He knew Pete was behind it, and he had to figure out a way to stop it. Of course, what unnerved Rueben even more than the threat of impending global war was the fact that Pete was some kind of alternate future Rueben. Even if Pete was from another universe, it was hard to believe a version of himself would turn to the Dark Side.

Rueben massaged his head. On the limo ride, he and his friends had decided to meet at Buzz's to formulate a plan Saturday afternoon after they each got a few hours of sleep. There they would discuss everything they knew—including Buzz's new rules for warpers—and Rueben feared he'd probably have to come clean to Aki about his time-warping ability. The prospect of this sickened Rueben's stomach. What would she think?

Seeing Marshall asleep, Rueben clicked off the TV. Marshall grumbled and stirred.

"Where the hell have you been?"

Rueben hadn't anticipated how to answer that. "I...I was out."

"Out?" Marshall pushed his recliner in. "Don't bullshit me, son. I know exactly where you've been."

Rueben sighed, and a small ache formed in his skull. "Coffee?"

"Don't try to change the subject. I didn't appreciate the guys at the precinct calling to tell me you got mixed up in some shenanigans and popped up on the radar in some county lock-up. What the hell? I raised you better than that."

That meant Marshall had very little knowledge of what had happened and pretended to know, to milk him for information. Rueben wouldn't give it to him. It was too complicated.

"I didn't see you rush to bail me out."

Rueben grabbed the coffee bag out of the cabinet. Marshall still hadn't come around to the single-serve coffee movement. Red can of Folgers, just like the old days. Of course, single-use coffee was so bad for the environment…ugh, that One Global campaign must be getting to him.

Marshall followed him into the kitchen and stood on the other side of the counter. "Bail you out? Why should I? You were at the bar acting like a goddamned idiot, going around getting yourself into all kinds of scrapes. And what's worse, dragging Martha into the middle of it."

Rueben spooned the grounds into the paper filter. "Ah, yes. Martha, the daughter you never had."

"Don't change the subject."

"I'm not. Don't you think she can make her own decisions?" Rueben placed the full coffee filter into the machine, filled the reservoir with water, and flipped it on.

Marshall growled. "She's a decorated officer and deserves your respect."

"I do respect her. You're conveniently avoiding the question."

"Don't sass me. It's bad enough whatever you're involved in. You can ruin her career by bringing her into whatever kind of mess you're in. What were you thinking? Were you on drugs? Huh? And way out there, trespassing on some farmer's property? You care to explain that?"

Rueben pursed his lips and leaned against the sink, his father on the other side. "Dad, I promise you, I'm not on drugs, and you have no idea what's going on."

"I would hope so, with the way you're acting. There had better be more to this story."

Rueben poured the steaming coffee into a mug and set it down so hard it splashed droplets on the counter.

Marshall pursed his lips and twisted his neck. "Do you know how terrifying it is to get a call from a cop in the middle of the night? I do… I was usually the guy making the call."

Rueben blinked twice. Was that Marshall telling him he was worried? Lately, Marshall wasn't his usual old self. He showed moments of kindness these days, and Rueben wondered if this was just more of New Marshall coming out. "I'm fine, Dad. You can trust me." Rueben gave his father a soft smile.

"That's rich," Marshall spat, his old self tumbling out with his words.

Rueben shook his head and pulled his lips into a tight line. "Never in my life have I ever done anything to cause you to distrust me. I never even skipped school. So why can't you trust that I know what I'm doing?"

Marshall was quiet, then rubbed his nose. His words were barely audible. "Because you're too much like her."

"Her? Mom?"

His mother, Carolyn, had suddenly and mysteriously left when Rueben was ten.

"You're more like her than you know. Mr. Hash Brown."

"Hey," Rueben said. "You don't get to call me that. Only Mom could."

At that, Marshal swallowed, then turned and padded down the hall to his room. "Turn off the kitchen light when you finish. The electric bill was through the roof this past month."

"I know, Dad. I pay the bill."

"Don't act like I'm a charity case. I pay my half."

Marshall shut the door to his room, and Rueben sipped his coffee. He added more cream to mask the bitter taste. Folgers had been the smell of his childhood, his parents happy and in love over the scent of coffee and bacon.

Carolyn had left after the "incident." It had started as a normal day of fifth grade. Well, sort of anyway. Rueben had replayed that day over and over in his head and found more odd inconsistencies with each passing year. But at the time, it had felt normal.

Rueben had stayed up late the night before writing some paper he'd waited until the last minute to finish. Carolyn had lectured him about the quality of his work and sent him off to the school bus. But her goodbye hug had lingered too long, and she had seemed desperate and sad when she told him, "You know I love you, right?"

He wiggled out of her embrace. He was too old for this kind of stuff. "Sure, Mom." Then he left for the bus.

When he got on the bus, Martha was already there. She lived the next street over. Most of the ride was uneventful, but toward the end of it, a crazed gunman hijacked the bus.

In later years, Marshall's cop buddies would tell Rueben that Marshall had overheard the dispatch and recognized the bus as Rueben's. He'd jumped up and run out the door without even being assigned the case.

Some reports had him jumping over a desk, yelling, "I'm saving my kid."

Marshall denied that part and said he was assigned the

case and did his duty for the kids of New York. "I have a responsibility to all the citizens of this city."

In any event, Marshall apprehended the gunman and saved the children on the bus. But as they evacuated, Rueben swore he saw Carolyn at the scene. She wore the same light floral print dress she'd had on that morning, with the same sandals, and her wavy red hair blew in the wind. That was odd because all the parents had instructions to wait at the school and that the police had the situation under control.

All he saw was her walking away, and he instinctively ran after her, yelling, "Mom."

An EMS worker herded him back to the safety zone of the officers standing around the bus, understandably trying to maintain order between thirty traumatized schoolchildren. From the bus window, Rueben watched her departing back. As the bus pulled away, she turned toward it one last time. The wind blew her hair and obscured her face, so Rueben was never completely sure what he saw or if it had truly been her or an overactive imagination. If it had been her, it was the last time he saw her.

When they reached the school, Marshall was still at the station filing paperwork, and Carolyn was nowhere around. Martha's mom took Rueben home to an empty house.

Carolyn had packed her clothes and left a weird note that Rueben didn't understand.

And that was it.

The first Christmas without her, Marshall threw the note in the fire. "Fuck that."

It killed Rueben inside to watch the note burn, but Marshall had turned into such an ogre, he didn't dare argue with him over something like that. From time to time, Rueben tried to remember what was in that note, thinking that maybe adulthood would give him better insight into what had happened. The whole thing was cryptic and weird. But, he still never had real answers.

He sipped his coffee. "Whatever."

After setting his empty mug in the sink, Rueben headed to the shower to wash off his jail funk. *Maybe Buzz was onto something about the whole parasite cleanse.* The warm water eased the tension of what he had been through. It couldn't hurt.

CHAPTER FOURTEEN

Saturday, May 20, 3:30 p.m.

Later that afternoon, Rueben pulled up at Buzz's mansion in his Mazda, unsurprised when he saw the CIA men in black standing outside. It was a stately home, originally built by an investment banker with roots in the Vanderbilt fortune. He had subsequently lost the house in a messy divorce, and his ex-wife sold it to unload the emotional baggage.

Having become an overnight millionaire after selling some proprietary video game software he'd developed, Buzz had swooped in on the sale. Now the picturesque columns, rising arches, and dignified brick had become a bachelor's pad.

Rueben parked in the cul-de-sac and rang the bell. For a moment, he wondered if Aki knew how to get here. So far, they'd never invited her over here to join him and Buzz and Martha. Aki had been completely in the black during the Pout operation at the Canadian border.

A large Hispanic maid answered the door, wearing a black and white skirt and apron combination. "Mr. Rueben."

"Hello, Rosa. Is Buzz here?"

Rosa paused a little too long for Rueben's liking as if her processor was stuck. Not that he knew for sure if she was a robot. *Jesus, being friends with Buzz fucks with your head.*

After a long moment, Rosa finally said, "They are all here, even the new girl. Come in."

Rosa held the door wide, and Rueben walked into the expansive marble lobby. A winding staircase led to the upper floors, and Rueben smiled as he remembered Buzz and Martha chasing him around these stairs with swords, guns, knives, and there was once a guillotine attached to the door. Of course, he'd time-warped backward each time he'd died, so there wasn't any evidence of any of his messy deaths. So Buzz and Martha remembered none of it. Luckily the two of them were able to watch the nanobot footage of his deaths in Buzz's secret computer room—the room that housed a recording of all Rueben's adventures in the timeline before his numerous deaths.

Rosa yelled across the lobby in heavily accented English, "Mr. Buzz, Mr. Rueben is here."

That seemed to be about the extent of Rosa's job—that and buying Twinkies.

Buzz yelled from the living room, "Thank you, Rosa."

Rosa nodded to Rueben, and he turned to her. "How's Pedro?"

She clasped a hand over her heart. "Ohhh, Mr. Rueben... remember how he died on the hospital bed?" Rosa twisted her body both ways as if to check if anyone was eavesdropping. "He faked his death! He's alive, and guess what? Now he has found himself in the arms of another woman. These twists and turns. Dios mio, the writers have no mercy on my soul."

Rueben found it almost comical, the parallel between Pedro's cheating death and Rueben's time warp ability or genetic mutation or whatever it was. "Remind me. How did he wind up in the hospital bed?"

Her eyes grew wide. "Because he impregnated his sister."

Yeah…luckily his life didn't share that in common with Pedro's.

She continued. "But he didn't know it at the time. She was his partner's daughter, and his partner was Pedro's father, but neither of them knew it." She drew a breath. "Then, Pedro faked his death and left her for Catalina, a…how you say… hussy…from Mexico City."

"Damn, that's cold."

Buzz yelled from the living room, "Rueben? Get in here."

"Right."

She winked at him. "I'll get you some Twinkies."

Rosa left, and Rueben went into the living room, passing under the massive rising dome. The dome was a wildlife fresco with zebras prancing through the Sahara.

Rueben stared up at the dome and whistled. "What a shame."

He entered the living area, a huge cozy room decorated in exquisite detail with cream couches and plush rugs under a glittering chandelier and strategically placed lighting.

Martha and Aki were already sitting on the couches, and Buzz flitted around in his usual bathrobe and silk pajamas.

"You may not be getting laid anytime soon," Aki said, "but this is a damn nice mansion."

"Why, thank you." Buzz handed out tumblers filled with a fluorescent yellow liquid. "All right ladies, drink up. This is a specially formulated potion to clean out your intestines and balance the pH."

They tentatively sipped their drinks.

Martha spat hers out. "Buzz, what's in this?"

Aki squealed and jumped up and searched for a napkin. "This is awful. Where did you get this recipe?"

Buzz sank into a leather chair and crossed his ankles as he swirled his glass. "It's a formula I concocted myself."

Martha stared at the glass suspiciously. "Formula? Concocted? Did you create this in a test tube?"

"Of course. What, you don't think those health food corporations make theirs in a test tube first? They add artificial flavoring and water it down to make it sell. Both techniques compromise the strength of the formula. So I created a concentrated cleanse with the same basic ingredients that doesn't cater to nanny government FDA regulations and will restore your health instantly."

Buzz snapped his fingers for emphasis, and Rueben entered the room and wryly eyed the drink.

"Ah, Rueben. I have one for you as well."

"I think I'll pass. I believe in the FDA."

Buzz held out the frighteningly unnatural-colored drink. "No, no, after the ordeal we went through, it's a must."

Rueben took the drink away from him and set it down. "Buzz, we spent an hour in the county jail. We'll be fine."

"Really, I insist."

Rueben raised an eyebrow, and Buzz took a long gulp of his glass. He violently spat the liquid out, gagged, and screamed, *"Con permiso, mujeres.* My apologies, ladies."

They all laughed, and Buzz set the glass down. "Rosa."

Rosa appeared in the doorway. "Yes, Mr. Buzz."

"Drinks all around."

"Ah yes, Mr. Buzz. I had a feeling you'd say that." She lifted a tray containing fully prepared martinis. She winked as they took them all.

Rueben laughed. "Thank you, Rosa."

"My pleasure, Mr. Rueben."

Rosa grabbed the colon cleanses and whisked them away.

The foursome settled nicely into their martinis and began talking.

Buzz started the discussion. "Okay people, let the debrief begin. What have we learned?"

Martha sipped her drink, set it down, and rubbed her hands together. She looked a lot more refreshed in a blue-and-white striped shirt and jeans. "A man named Pete, who may be Rueben's older self—*or* from another universe—is trying to kill or kidnap us."

They all laughed nervously except for Aki. Buzz raised his drink. "Hear, hear." The rest of them brought their drinks to their lips.

Aki narrowed her eyes while she sipped. When she set it down, she rubbed her chin in the way she did when presented with a clue. "Is anyone going to fill me in?"

Buzz and Martha looked at Rueben in a coded way, and Rueben struggled with how to answer. He didn't think Aki was ready to hear the truth, and he didn't believe she'd get it anyway if he told her. He knew Martha was still rattled and confused by the whole time warp ability even after seeing the proof in Buzz's special computer room. What if Aki thought he was crazy, even after seeing the proof?

Buzz reached into an end table drawer and pulled out a cigar. He crossed his legs and lit it, and the smell filled the room. He held the box out to the rest of the group. "Anyone?"

The rest of them declined, and Rueben crossed the room and stared out the window. "Pete is going to bomb the World Summit."

Martha was quick to respond. "That U.N. thing? Monday night?"

Aki groaned, momentarily dropping the "out of the loop" routine. "Ugh. I've been doing security for all of that. So far we've stopped a Real IRA bomber from rigging a hotel room and a Russian mobster with a bomb. We're not sure what the Russian had planned. But, he's in custody." She stared at Rueben suspiciously. "I know you have your 'sources,' but do you know how he's planning to attack it?"

Rueben shoved his hands in his pockets. "He has an army of drones that drop bombs—"

Buzz jumped on his computer. "Drones. What type?"

Rueben fished in his memory for the news footage he had seen in the basement during his captivity by Pete. "They're ordinary-looking drones. A boxy center with four propellered arms. They were part of a light show."

"Ah." Buzz clicked away at his keyboard. "Shouldn't be too difficult to track down the make and model. Unless they're custom-made...hmm, leave it to me. Anyway, I'll work on a program to hack into the drones' navigation system. In case it comes to that."

Rueben tapped his finger against the side of his drink. "Good idea."

Martha pulled a small notepad from her purse and a pen to take notes. When she was repositioning her purse beside her, her keys fell on the floor. She picked them up and dropped them back into her purse, but not before Rueben saw the red toucan figurine dangling from her keychain. Petunia, Martha's good luck toucan. Martha cleared her throat. "These drones have bombs in them?"

"Yes."

Aki jumped up. "Rueben, drones with bombs? This is bad. I'm calling Sven."

"No, Aki, you need to trust me."

"You just told me that you have these 'anonymous sources' that say the World Summit will be blown up by drones Monday night. I can't sit on that kind of information."

"I'm not asking you to. That's why we're here."

Martha held out a palm toward Aki. "Calm down, Aki. You have to trust that—"

Aki pushed her hand away. "Quite honestly, Rueben, I hate to put it this way, but you leave me no choice. I outrank you. This is a matter of global security. I need to know your sources."

Rueben and Aki stood in the living room, enveloped in tense silence. Rueben ruffled his hair, and Aki's dark eyes searched him. "If you can't give me your sources, it implicates you in the attack, and I have to treat it that way."

"No, Aki. I'm not involved."

"Then give me your sources."

Buzz interjected, "He can't."

Both Aki and Rueben turned to look at him. He stared at his laptop screen, his chin cupped by his palm. The cigar burned in an ashtray beside him.

Aki turned to him and flipped her bobbed dark hair. She strode up to Buzz. "Are you involved, then?"

"Sit, Aki. There's a lot you don't know."

She swiveled around Buzz's laptop screen. "What are you —" She paused. "This is my agency profile. What the hell? How did you get this?"

Buzz stood and paced the room. "You're not the only one with security clearance around here. I'm on the president's payroll as an advisor on artificial intelligence. I likely outrank you."

"I highly doubt that."

"Well, fortunately, I don't care enough to find out. It

appears you have enough security clearance to know what's going on."

"I agree."

"Good, then we're on the same page."

Rueben was surprised to see this side of Buzz, this sort of in-charge Buzz.

"Take a seat, darling."

Aki reluctantly obeyed. Rising, Buzz took the floor, pacing, and theorizing in professor mode. "I looked at your history with the agency. It looks like you were part of the security detail of Dr. Eduardo Nunez. Does the name ring a bell?"

She sipped her drink. "Sure. A physicist specializing in temporal displacement."

"Ah, yes. About four years ago?"

"Yes. I've heard rumors about it, but you know it?"

Buzz nodded soberly. "I worked on it. I was a consultant to his scientific research team."

Martha raised her palm. "So for the uninitiated among us, Dr. Nunez was…"

Buzz answered quickly. "Involved with highly classified government operations having to do with manipulating the dimensions of time and space. Two people died in the beta phases, and Dr. Nunez himself disappeared and was never heard from again. While they scrapped the project shortly after, it did prove the possibility of time travel: they managed to send a banana back three days."

Rueben narrowed his eyes. "You knew all this?"

"Of course. Why do you think I was so quick to believe you when you first came to me a few months ago?"

Aki regarded Buzz seriously. "I'd heard rumors of the banana experiment."

Rueben gulped back shock. Buzz was one thing, but Aki knew of experiments involving time travel too?

Buzz continued his lecture. "Rueben is something like that banana."

"Capable of simultaneously experiencing multi-dimensional realities?" Aki swiveled her body toward Rueben.

Rueben's eyes widened. "Huh?"

Buzz closed his eyes for a moment, then opened them. "To put it quite simply, he can't die. We can kill him over and over again, but he always returns to life within seventy-two hours of when he died."

Aki took Rueben in, looking him up and down, and he shrugged. The cat was out of the bag now. Rueben cleared his throat ceremoniously. "I know it's hard to believe. When I told Martha, it took a long time for her to accept it. Sometimes I think she still doesn't. So, if you need time for it sink in or—"

Aki shrugged. "No. I get it. Makes sense."

Rueben pursed his lips. "It just... Like that?"

"Yeah. It's the only explanation I can think of for how you turned into a badass overnight."

Rueben scratched his head, not quite sure what to make of that. Buzz straightened his shirt collar and rubbed his hands together. "Well then, that was easier than I thought. Now that we've got that out of the way, can we get to more important matters, like stopping the bombing of the World Summit?"

Aki went into full professional mode. "I agree, now that we're clear on what Rueben's 'source' is. You've lived through this attack, then, Rueben?"

"Uh, yes."

She snapped around, looking for pen and paper, and

Martha tossed some spares to her. "Approximate time of attack?"

"Seven-thirty p.m."

"And you said drones?"

"Correct."

"How many?"

Rueben didn't know. He thought back to Pete's computer screen in the basement. Pete had been viewing a spreadsheet with two hundred cells.

"Two hundred. I think."

"Wow. That's a lot. And the million-dollar question: why is Pete doing this? Do you know?"

"He wants to start a global nuclear war."

"Egads," Buzz said.

Martha shook her head sadly. "But why? Rueben, do you remember anything else?"

Rueben thought about it. Pete had pulled a notebook out of his black backpack. A notebook with names. He could only remember a couple of them. "Pete had a notebook with names and numbers in it. Do Jackson Ford and Patricia Mendel mean anything to anyone?"

Buzz did a quick Google search on his laptop. "One of the country's leading civil engineers. And...hmm. One of the nation's leading doctors."

Martha tapped her pen against her knee. "What might Pete want with them?"

An idea came to Rueben. He didn't like it. "What if he's trying to start a nuclear war. And he's got a list of some of the people he wants to save. Maybe the rest of the notebook contains the locations of fallout shelters." He might be just grasping for straws now, but maybe not. Damn, Pete was a real bastard. But why did he want to start World War III in the first place?

Aki pursed her lips. "Doesn't sound good. We don't know where Pete is right now. Rueben, can't you die and go back in time to right before the bar? So we can stop him?"

Rueben was quick to answer. "Can't. He implanted me with a nanobot that has 'capped' my warping abilities at the genetic level. I can't go back farther than 10:35 p.m. on Friday night." He proceeded to give his friends an abbreviated version of his captivity at Pete's hands in the basement of the empty skyscraper.

Afterward, Martha threw her hand over her mouth. "You had to blow your leg off to die? That's a horrible way to…"

"And you think I have a dangerous mind?" Buzz smirked. "Pretty ingenious, I say. High five, buddy."

Aki made some notations on her notepad and looked at Rueben as if examining a clinical test subject. "Futuristic tech. You mentioned that he is you, but older, right?"

"Actually," Buzz said, "I believe Pete is Rueben from another universe. So an alternate Rueben, not a future Rueben." He then proceeded to give them his "rules for warpers" that he had conceived at the jail.

Afterward, Aki studied her notes. "Here are the facts as we know them so far. The U.N. bombing involving two hundred drones is a little over two days away. Rueben can't go back in time far enough to apprehend Pete. And Pete appears to be Rueben from another universe."

Buzz shrugged as if this was an ordinary Saturday afternoon for him. "Yeah, I think that's everything."

Suddenly, Rueben didn't feel so good. He stood. "I need some air."

He left the living room and heard Aki say, "Where's he going? We need the subject. I mean, Rueben."

Rueben cringed as he continued walking away. Last night he had been her date. Platonic-friend date, but one with the potential for more. Now he was "the subject?"

What the hell?

He made it outside and headed toward Buzz's manicured garden. As he walked into the hedged mazes, hands in his pockets, he thought about Aki. The truth was, he was madly in love with her.

He'd been in love with her for a long time, and that love had only grown as he had died eighty-three times when trying to stop Pout, and he'd tried to woo her anew several of those times.

She had found him exciting and mysterious, and he had thrived on that. Now that his secret was out, it was everything he had feared. She was over him. He would lose her, and that would be that. He'd go back to being the dorky guy in cubicle thirty-three who repaired people's computers.

Or worse, he'd be the freak who had some kind of weird genetic mutation possibly due to some drug he never remembered being exposed to. Who would want to date that guy? And how would he fight his way out of the "friend zone" now?

He sat against the hedge maze for a few minutes and thought over what to do next. Then his phone chirped with a text. Aki.

Where are you? Marshall is in trouble.

CHAPTER FIFTEEN

Saturday, May 20, 5:36 p.m.

Aki and Rueben sat at a table in Buzz's garden. Rosa brought them tea and pastries.

"Anything else, Mr. Rueben, Ms. Aki?"

Rueben smiled and bit into a scone. It was horrible. She should definitely stick to store-bought twinkies. "That's it, Rosa. Thanks."

Aki smirked and tossed her scone back onto the plate. "Buzz trying to be pretentious, I guess?"

"What would possibly give you that idea?"

They both laughed.

"Okay, so tell me," Rueben said. "What's the deal?"

Aki leaned forward. "The CIA has noticed some unusual activity. Someone's tapping Marshall's phone line."

"His phone line?"

"Yeah. His cell phone. You have the same phone account, right?"

"Yeah. He has a pension, but he also has memory problems, so I took over all the bills to make sure they get paid each month. I consolidated our phone lines, which was one of my harder victories in the ongoing saga of Handling Marshall Peet."

"I can see how that would be."

Rueben sipped his tea. "Yeah."

"Well, I had Tech check your phone number to see if Pete was tracking yours too. He's not. But, he is tracking Marshall and has been for a while."

"You thinking what I'm thinking?"

"Bait. He's going to kidnap Marshall and use him as bait somehow to get us off the board. And with 'endgame' being Monday and Pete probably needing to make a lot of last-minute preparations…"

"…he's probably going to make a move soon," Rueben finished.

"Right."

"So, what do we do?"

"The agents stationed outside your apartment building aren't adequate. We've got to keep Marshall busy with us. Not let Pete get a chance at him."

Rueben burst into laughter. "You do realize what you're suggesting, right? You've interacted with Marshall before. At the police dinner."

"Yep."

"All right, let's go."

Aki and Rueben went back into the mansion to say their goodbyes. Buzz and Martha were staring at a screen that appeared to be blueprints.

Aki recognized it immediately. "That's the U.N. building."

Martha now had half a legal pad full of notes. "Uh-huh."

Aki gestured toward the screen. "Where did you guys get this?"

Buzz shrugged. "Oh, I called the White House. I told them I wanted to make sure the security system was working properly for the summit. They sent them right over."

Martha flipped through her legal pad. "We're getting the lay of the land, and Buzz is trying to locate the drones by searching the city for possible signals. Nothing so far, but Buzz thinks maybe he could plant a virus that confuses their signal and repels the drones. Or at the least, slow them down once they're in the air."

That plot sounded familiar to Rueben. "Did you steal that from *Independence Day?*"

"Yeah. It worked for Will Smith, and it can work for us."

Rueben shrugged. "More power to you. We think Pete may be trying to kidnap Marshall."

"Good luck, you two. Don't have too much fun without us."

Outside, Rueben shrugged at his Mazda. "I guess we'll take your car."

She laughed and clicked the remote for her Porsche. "I think that might be a good idea."

He slipped into the leather seat, and she put on her Versace shades and gunned the engine. God, she looked good behind that wheel.

She pulled out of the driveway and out onto the road and picked up speed. "So, what's the plan?"

"You want to know something? I genuinely have no idea."

"Come on. He's your dad. You've got to have some idea how to coax him into listening to us."

He laughed. "You obviously don't know him."

"At the police dinner, he didn't strike me as particularly friendly."

"That's a delicate way of putting it. In short, he's an asshole."

"Well, I think we should be straight with him. Just tell him we know he's in danger."

Rueben laughed. "Do you have any idea how he would respond to that?"

"How?"

"He would go out, buy an entire box of ammo, and sit in the apartment with the shotgun pointed at the door all night."

She laughed. "Based on what I've seen of him, I think you're probably right." She wound through the city streets and put her playlist on the stereo.

Rueben smiled. "Je Ne Sais Pas."

She smiled at him, surprised under her dark shades. "You know them?"

"Yeah, I know them."

They were an art-rock band out of Montreal that he had discovered after his breakup with Rachel. Their entire second album was the ultimate breakup anthem, and he had fallen so much in love with their music he had almost gone to Montreal for the quintessential fan experience, May Fest. When he first started talking to Aki, he found out she had gone almost every year since college. In fact, she and her college friends had been just short of Je Ne Sais Pas groupies. But he had died multiple times since their first conversation about it, and it hadn't come up since.

She navigated the road with one hand and leaned the other against the door, clicking her acrylic fingernails. "I can't believe you know them. I used to—"

"Go to May Fest."

"Yes! Oh my gosh, you went?"

"No, I never made it. But I know you used to go all the time."

She sat quietly for a few minutes, then turned the music down. "What else do you know about me?"

He gulped. "What kind of a question is that?"

"I figure you've probably spent time with me that I don't remember, right? Because you've time-warped back to the past?"

He answered simply and honestly. "Yes."

"Okay, so tell me what you know."

"I know you weren't really in love with Mike Fury. I know that you knew it hadn't been working out long before he started having anger management issues."

She didn't respond. She only watched the road.

Rueben wasn't quite sure how much more to say or when was too much. He opted for more trivial information. "I know that your parents were wealthy, and you have a trust fund. Then they decided to sell their house and move to Sedona, Arizona and be in a hippie cult. They changed their names to Sitar and Pegasus. I know you check on them using company resources, and you keep them safe."

She shifted in her seat, and he knew he had hit her heart. He stopped talking, and they drove in silence for a while.

Finally, she asked, "Have we ever…"

He blushed and scratched the back of his head. "Uh, no… we've never… But we did make out a couple of times."

She laughed. "Is that right?"

He blushed and smiled sheepishly. "Yeah…in a car on a stakeout and during the Pout thing. It was in a warehouse."

"In a warehouse, huh? I wish I could remember that."

He scratched his forehead. "I wish you could, too. It's a good memory."

She was quiet for a while. "It's weird, you know. You wonder where that part of you went."

"Yeah. I know. I think about that all the time with Buzz and Martha, especially. Buzz seems to get over it pretty quickly. I think Martha has a harder time with it. It seems almost like an invasion of privacy that they did things only I remember."

"Yeah, I can see that. It's cool, though." She nodded as she contemplated the thought. "It's pretty sexy."

"Really?"

"Yeah. It makes you mysterious and somehow more badass than anyone I've ever met."

He smiled, and all the frustration of being a science experiment faded away. She still thought he was badass.

She slowed as they hit a traffic jam. "Damn. It's the summit."

"Summit traffic already? That's not for two more days."

"Trust me, they're already all in town with all their security details, and all their staffers, and all their staffers' staffers. There are only two hundred delegates, but there will be close to a thousand people in that building on Monday."

"Pete knows what he's doing."

"Terrorists usually do."

They got stuck in stop-and-go traffic, and Rueben noticed a limo in the next lane over with *Just Married* scrawled on the back of it. He thought about Rachel and if they ever would have made it down the aisle even if she hadn't found that other guy. That stupid, stupid dancer who was better than him.

Oh well, she wasn't worth it. He recalled how his secretive

work with the CIA kept cutting into their "alone time" when he was on big cases and how irritated Rachel was that he couldn't tell her anything about it.

Aki had expressed that she thought two agents couldn't be in a relationship, but the way Rueben saw it, two agents made the best partners. They would understand each other's work better.

The traffic inched forward at an agonizing pace. Suddenly the door to the limo flew open, and the bride, in full dress, jumped out of the car.

Aki whipped her head around. "What the hell?"

The bride leaned her head back into the limo and yelled, then stormed off down the side of the road, holding her skirts and train the whole way.

Rueben laughed. "Trouble in paradise, I see."

"No kidding. What do you think he did?"

"Ohh, that's a tough one. It could be anything."

She flicked her tongue over her teeth. "Come on, take a guess."

"Ah, off the top of my head, I would say he texted another girl."

"So uncreative. Come on. You gotta come up with something better."

"Okay, let's see...ooh...she complained that the dress was bothering her from sitting the whole time in that limo."

"I can see that."

"So, then he said that she over-ate at the wedding reception."

She laughed and smacked the steering wheel. "That's great. That would do it."

"All right, you do one."

"Okay, let's see...her dad drank too much at the reception

and got in an argument with the groom. Not only that, he trashed the groom's dad, and it went from there."

"I can see that one. Oooh…what about this? It just came out that once upon a time, the groom slept with her sister."

"Oh yeah, that would do it, too."

The bride stood on the side of the road, head buried in her hands and crying with traffic at a virtual standstill.

Finally, the groom got out of the limo and dodged through traffic to get to her. The groom helplessly placed his hand on the small of her back.

Rueben pointed. "She didn't push him away."

"Oh, then it couldn't have been too bad. She wanted to make a point."

After a few minutes of talking, the bride reluctantly followed him back to the limo. She passed right by their windows this time, and tears streaked her face. The groom apologetically waved to the honking vehicles along the way.

Aki laughed. "Yeah, that won't last. That's a bad omen right there."

"Yeah, you're probably right."

The bride and groom got back in their vehicle, and the traffic picked up in pace.

Aki's lips twisted to one side. "But it does give me an idea."

"Oh yeah? What's that?"

She smiled mischievously and turned to Rueben. "You want to get married?"

Rueben's eyes widened. "What?"

"I mean, not for real. But as a sting."

"How would that work?"

"Well, we stage a fake wedding, and of course, what would a wedding be without my new father-in-law?"

"You want to lure Marshall in with a fake wedding?"

She winked.

"You know I have to live with him after this, right?"

"Yeah, but he'll make it out of this alive."

Rueben scratched his head when he thought of what Marshall would do once he found out he was lying. Of course, maybe Marshall would finally stop acting like less of an asshole all the time if he thought Rueben was going to marry somebody as hot as Aki. This plan might work.

She winked. "Have a little fun. Perk up. We're getting married."

CHAPTER SIXTEEN

Sunday, May 21, 6:30 a.m.

It was early Sunday morning, and Martha arrived at the precinct with a mental to-do list and a cup of steaming hot coffee. She would need it for this.

She was going to have to get on her A-game for the rest of the weekend. Alister Pout was the past. There was no phoning this in or coasting on past accolades. This new terrorist Pete meant business, and she needed to find out everything she could to stop what he had planned. She now had less than twenty-four hours until the day of the summit officially began.

She summoned the elevator and muttered, "You can do this, Martha. You're a hero, right?"

Knowing what she knew about Pete, she didn't feel convinced.

She arrived on the precinct floor to find the office nearly empty, as she had hoped. There was an open receptionist desk, and fluorescent lights ran on low power over rows of abandoned cubicles in the bullpen.

The overnight staff still mingled over coffee and chatted in low tones, and the morning crew wouldn't be in for another hour at least.

Good. She didn't need any distractions this morning.

By the time the day shift started, she wanted to have enough of a lead on the terrorist attack to get the captain on board with the case. If all NYPD was on alert tomorrow, they stood a better chance of catching the bastards. She made her way down the long hallway to her office.

Her office.

Just the thought gave her step a little spring. Yes, she had an office now. It wasn't much, merely a glorified closet with a table, a swivel chair, and a laptop. Compared to what she had before—a cubicle about the size of a bathroom stall—this was a penthouse suite.

The best part was, she had her name on the door.

She smiled and ran her fingers across the letters. *This was what happened when you took down an international criminal.*

She dropped her bag on the desk, sank into the vinyl orange-and-brown chair, and powered up the laptop. Today's goal: stop the attack.

It was a tall order, and she didn't have the slightest idea how to break it down into smaller pieces. That was the problem with "Rueben cases." Criminal investigations based on nothing but Rueben's time warp ability were difficult to start. There were always clues, but they weren't easy to spot. You had to keep looking every time you hit a dead end. In Alister's case, dead ends were about all they had the whole way through. But they had managed to bring that one in on an explosive, fiery home run. Figuratively speaking, of course. No bombs had detonated, thank God.

They could do this one, too.

Rueben had said the bombing would be during the keynote address. So, when was the address, and what were the weaknesses during that time?

She ran an online search for background information on the World Summit. By about the twentieth news article, her head started to hurt. "I need more caffeine for this."

Martha headed down to the break room. It was getting later, and the day shift early birds were already in. Everywhere she walked, colleagues nodded and smiled at her.

Two officers, Tom and Mark, stood talking in the hallway. As soon as they saw her, they quieted and stepped aside, raising their coffee mugs in her direction.

God, that felt good coming from them. She smiled and breezed past them. "Hello, gentlemen."

Tom nodded vigorously to her. "Martha. Hey, hey, good to see you. You doing all right?"

She kept walking as she answered, "Well, there's air in my lungs and sunshine outside. What more can I ask for?"

Mark laughed too loud at that. The twenty-three-year-old baby-faced officer was the human embodiment of a "follower."

Tom winked at her inane comment. "I hear ya."

Martha swished on, making Tom basically jog to keep up. She barely contained a smile. Three months ago, Tom and Mark had been stalwart members of the precinct "boys' club" and had relegated her to "The Tampon Squad."

They told her to stay focused on her beat—petty theft and little old ladies getting flashed. Leave the real cases to the big boys. Watching them eat their words made her day, all day, every day.

Tom cleared his throat from behind her. "Hey, Martha. Uh,

you know, if you were working on another big case at all, let me know. I'd love to chip in."

She turned to face him. "I think you've got your hands full with your beat, Tom. Aren't there some little old ladies getting flashed or apartment tenants with noisy upstairs neighbors? We couldn't have anyone disturbing the peace, now could we?"

He sipped his coffee, and a smile played about his face. "Look, Martha, I know we all like to bust balls around here. It's part of the job, you know."

"No, I don't. I don't have balls, and I don't appreciate the sexist reference."

Tom grimaced. "Point is, everybody messes with everybody. At the end of the day, we're all on the same team out there. We're all the good guys."

She arrived at the break room, a roomy, glassed-in kitchenette. "What do you want, Tom?"

He leaned against the glass wall. "I feel bad about the way things went before. I was a dick, all right?"

She raised an eyebrow, and he caught himself. "Apologies for the sexist reference. I was an asshole."

She cocked her head in agreement.

"And you know, I'd like to help you out a little."

She pursed her lips. He'd had her until that last sentence. "What makes you think I need your help?"

"I mean, come on. Well, first of all, props, man, props. Alister Pout, that was...that was something. Damn. Respect." He made a bowing motion with his hands, but she still didn't buy it. He continued, "It's just...beyond that, you haven't been on the force that long and—"

"Oh my God, Tom."

Granted, she had been on the force for just over a year

compared to his decades wearing the badge. But then, why was she on that stage Friday night and he wasn't? Why did she have an office and he still had a cubicle? After ten years?

She jerked the door to the break room open and stormed inside.

He followed her, grabbing the door just before it hit him. "Hear me out. I think we can mutually benefit from working together."

Martha grabbed the coffee carafe and ran it under the faucet. "Mutually benefit? Now I get it. This is what this is all about. You need something to impress Kenneth."

Captain Ken Kenneth was their boss. It now occurred to her that ever since Martha's promotion, Kenneth had distanced himself more and more from "the boys' club." In fact, Tom was already there when she came in early. That meant only one thing. "How's the graveyard shift working out for you these days?

Tom didn't say anything but leaned against the counter.

"Nice to get your workday all over with and done before eight a.m., right? Then you can have your days to yourself to get a massage or catch up on your Netflix. Who needs a career when you've got *Cobra Kai?*"

Tom buried his tongue in his cheek and smiled. She owned him. "You're good."

She found a filter and searched for the coffee, pretending she wasn't enjoying the moment as much as she was.

The precinct hadn't yet upgraded to the K-Pod movement, and it was the one thing around here that she would love to change now that she had achieved semi-celebrity status. She made a mental note to bug Kenneth about it.

Tom slid a red can of Folgers across the counter toward

her. He caught her eye, and she took the can but didn't say anything.

He finally spoke. "It's not about that. Well, not entirely about that. I can help you—we can help each other. I mean, honestly, how long do you think you can dine on Alister Pout?"

"Oh Christ, Tom. Do you even hear yourself?"

At that moment, the door opened and Zach the intern burst in, all smiles. Zach was a tall, lanky twenty-year-old and the type that should skip the morning coffee run in favor of a daily tranquilizer.

He also fancied himself a young James Patterson, which rendered him utterly useless as a street cop. But his penchant for conspiracy and scandal made him adept at cases like Alister—a fact that made him a particularly attractive candidate for the tedium she faced today.

Zach sauntered up to the coffee bar. "Good morning, gang."

Tom pushed the Folgers canister out of sight, and Martha purposely hogged the carafe.

Zach grabbed bottled water instead. "How is everyone this fine day?"

Tom shoved away from the counter. "Shut it, kiss ass." Then he walked out of the room.

Zach glanced back at him, then at Martha. "What was that about?"

Martha shook her head and poured her cup. "Nothing. I think the better question is what are you doing in here on a Sunday? Your internship is unpaid."

Zach inhaled deeply and threw back his shoulders in a proud pose. "Oh, you know. Saving people. Hunting leads. The police business."

"So…book research."

Zach's shoulders slumped. "Yeah. Book research."

"Good. Then you have time on your plate to help me today."

Martha and Zach sat at the table in her office. She had a dry erase board propped up on a chair against the wall and made another notation.

Zach whistled as he read from a printout. "Okay, this is going to be a massive event, you know. There are over a thousand attendees alone, and that's not including the staff. There's no way we can map out all the associations."

"I know. I want to make sure we know as much as we can in case something fishy goes down."

Zach laughed. "Fishy? I mean, you've got, like, two hundred world leaders and all their security details. I'm sure the security and background checks are airtight. They've got to have the entire global intelligence community involved, including our CIA and everything."

Martha answered with certainty. "They do."

"Then what does that have to do with us? They know what they're doing. All their super-cool Jason Bourne-hanging-from-ceiling spy antics and shit."

Zach mimicked ninja moves with jerky arm motions. Martha couldn't tell him she knew CIA agents, and that was hardly what they were like.

She explained it the only way she knew how. "This is our city and our jurisdiction, and we need to prepare and be on alert in case something does happen."

"Cool."

She could tell he didn't buy her whole spiel, but he didn't press further. He kept reading the promotional printouts. He tossed them back on the desk. "My buddy's company is working on the pre-show events."

She collapsed into her chair. "Which pre-show events?"

With virtually all the world's political powers—and their wallets—congregating in one physical space for half a week, there was money to be made, and a whole lot of it. Everyone that was anyone was trying to cash in. Unofficial pre-pre-pre-pre-show events had been happening all month.

Zach leaned forward. "Dude, it's gonna be sick. You know, this whole thing is a big deal and all. Like, never has this happened quite like this."

Martha made a so-so gesture with her palm. "This is New York City. These kinds of things happen."

Zach blushed. "Oh, I'm from Alabama. So these kinds of things don't happen."

"Right. Except at a Lynyrd Skynyrd concert, I assume."

He shot her a go-to-hell look, and she laughed. He cleared his throat and continued. "So there's this official kick-off event happening in Times Square tomorrow night, after the first session."

She smiled wryly. "I think I've heard of it a time or two... or twelve."

"Are you going?"

"Are you kidding? With all of this? No. I don't really even know anything about it. Just that the city has blocked off Times Square for about a week."

"Are you kidding? Dude, it's, like, a *thing*."

She studied attendee lists and ran background checks on all of Yolanda Martinez's staff.

Zach kept going. "They've got Bruno Mars headlining, and

they're going to do a fireworks show, there's going to be cannons, tons of stuff. They keep talking about 'surprise' events. Tickets are, like, wicked expensive, but my buddy's hooking me up. I'm thinking of taking that girl, Claire."

"Claire? Alister Pout's assistant? Or former assistant now."

Claire and her misplaced iPad had been unwitting accomplices in bringing down the mogul earlier in the year.

Zach smiled. "Yeah. We hit it off pretty well."

"After you stole her iPad to indict her boss?"

"Well...I've glossed that over with a little finesse, so she doesn't see it that way."

"Uh-huh. You haven't told her, you mean."

He looked away guiltily. "Look, she's way hot, and you know, I'm lucky a girl like that even looks at me. The only reason she's with me is because she thinks I'm a crime novelist, so I have to keep that going, too."

"A relationship built on lies and deception. Sounds like a recipe for happiness."

"Fingers crossed."

She laughed. "So tell me about this pre-show."

"That's about all I know. And that it's going to be tomorrow night, two or three hours before the keynote speech. My buddy's going to send me an e-mail with more details."

Martha perked up. The keynote? "Do you know what time the keynote speech is?"

"7:30 p.m."

Shit. That was the time of the attack. "I want to know everything there is to know about this show. We need to be on top of what's going on."

"Sure. I can call my buddy. He can hook you up with his

boss or whatever. I'm sure they'd love to get NYPD on their side."

"Well, I'm sure we already have a squad assigned to the event for crowd control. What we need to be careful of"—she tossed the marker in the air and caught it, and made hard eye contact with the intern—"is that we don't step on their toes."

She winked for emphasis, and he nodded slowly. "Right."

"The police force can be a very political place."

"I've seen it already."

"You piss off the wrong people, all of a sudden evidence goes missing, or you don't get reports when you need them. This is a good lesson for you." She tapped the marker on the desk. "You should write this down as part of your internship."

Zach erratically rifled through his papers and produced a small green leather journal.

She held back a smile. She needed to keep him quiet because if word got out that she was investigating a possible terrorist attack with no evidence, it could have disastrous effects on her career. Not the least of which would be accusations of involving him.

He found a page, and she paced the small space and toyed with the marker. "There is a thin line between playing politics and pandering. Successful officers know how to do both and get the job done."

She watched him draw an asterisk on her statement and knew she had gotten through. She sat on the edge of the desk. "Now tell me, who do you know?"

CHAPTER SEVENTEEN

Sunday, May 21, 11:30 a.m.

Martha drove the squad car around a corner while Zach sat in the passenger seat, simultaneously munching on a hot dog and scribbling notes in his green leather journal.

She sighed. "Tell me about where we're going."

He put the book away and talked around a mouthful of food. "So, the name of the company is One Republic Entertainment. They do major event planning, but this is a big deal for them."

Martha made a left turn toward the One Republic office as instructed by the GPS. "Planning the entertainment for the World Summit? That would be a big deal for anyone."

Zach sipped his drink and wagged his finger. "No, no. This is, like, different. So, you know the event company that usually does the New Year's Eve thing?"

Martha groaned with disgust. "Please."

"Right? So, everyone originally assumed they would do this event. But, One Republic outbid them for the account. It was cutthroat, dude. One Republic eventually won, but this is a make-or-break moment for them. From what my buddy says, they're going broke on this account, thinking they'll make it all back."

The GPS directed her into downtown, and she navigated through the city traffic. "So, who are we going to see?"

"So, my buddy got me in contact with his boss, Lucas Cameron. I talked to Lucas, and he'll be in the office all afternoon. He's totally into talking with cops. I played it all like, 'Well, you never can be too safe.' He was totally on it. So, we can drop in anytime."

"Good work."

"Thanks."

Zach finished the last bite of his hot dog and wiped his hand on the side of the paper bag. "Can you be honest with me about something?"

"Shoot."

"You think I'd make a good cop?"

She looked him over, a clean-cut and freshly scrubbed intern. Zach was a good kid. Too good for all of this. He belonged in a cubicle somewhere, not out here in the trenches of daily police work. She gave him the most honest answer she had observed about him. "You don't want to be a cop, Zach."

"I don't?"

"No. You think you want to be a cop because there's some once-or-twice-in-a-career payoff that makes it all worth it. But bottom line, this is gritty work. Long hours with often-times no recognition. And sometimes people shoot at you. You're...too smart for that."

He sipped his straw until it gurgled. "You sound like my parents."

She smiled. "Go work for some lawyer's office as an investigator or something. You'd be good at that and make a hell of a lot more money. Would make great fodder for your crime novels too."

He contemplated that, and she snapped for his attention. "Tell me everything about Lucas Cameron."

"Oh, right, right." He pulled up a page on his phone. "Okay, so he was a record producer for a while and lost a lot of money in the digital music revolution, I think."

"Record producer? All right. So he's a music business type."

"Yeah. From what my buddy says, he's kind of a dick."

"Good to know."

Zach skimmed the page on his phone and summarized as he read. "Once he went belly-up in music, he used his old music contacts to create an event planning company, and now it looks like they do pretty good. Some Hollywood music premiers, a lot of big music festivals. Ooh...they were somewhat involved in the Met Gala…"

"Not a bad resume."

"Not bad at all." He looked puzzled and tapped around on more pages. "It looks like he's invested in some kind of science company? I don't understand."

"Science company? What would an event planner want with a science company?"

"I don't know. But it looks like there's a lot of little ties to this place. Global Research Initiatives, out of Palo Alto."

She pulled out her phone and texted Buzz while she drove. *What do you know about Global Research Initiatives in Palo Alto?*

They arrived at the office, a tower downtown. She pulled into the parking garage. "Here we go."

He frowned. "So, what exactly are we going to ask this guy?"

She hadn't gotten to that part yet. They exited the vehicle and started through the garage toward the tower. "Mainly, we want to find out what his security plans are and see if anything sounds out of the ordinary."

Zach didn't look convinced. "What do you mean 'out of the ordinary?' What could be wrong?"

She stopped and looked him over. She couldn't tell him the truth about Pete and Rueben, but he had gotten her Lucas Cameron, so he deserved a tiny slice of the pie. "All right. I have an unconfirmed—repeat, *unconfirmed*—and anonymous tip that there might be a terrorist attack on the summit."

Zach's eyes widened, and he ruffled his hair. "Whoa."

"Yeah. We get these reports all the time, and that's one thing you'll have to learn as an officer—how to give these threats the 'attention they deserve.'"

He pursed his lips in thought. "Right."

"Because we can't divert all our resources into investigating every teenage prankster on the phone."

"That makes sense."

"We can't ignore them, either. So right now, with how flimsy this report is, it could be a bunch of hacks looking for attention, and they chicken out or get high and sleep right through it."

Zach laughed. "I could see that happening."

She amazed herself at how logical she sounded. "Right now, I want to find out if this event has any security weaknesses that terrorists could possibly take advantage of."

She resumed their pace through the garage, her boots resonating against the concrete.

He wrote in his leather journal as he walked. "Is this how you found Pout?"

"How?"

"Following an anonymous tip?"

They arrived at the elevator leading up to the building. "Something like that. Now, enough questions for me. What about Cameron?"

"Right, right."

Martha and Zach stepped off the elevator and into a world they had only seen on television. One Republic Entertainment occupied the entire sixtieth floor, designated by a glossy silvery plaque that took up the main wall.

It was an expansive open-plan office, all done in contemporary minimalist design. The furniture was all sleek white, bathed in natural light with shimmering chrome and glass walls. Young, sexy, upwardly mobile New York business types flitted around, occasionally typing on MacBooks.

Zach scrawled in his leather journal, then turned to Martha. "So this is all that gritty police work you were talking about, right?"

She didn't reply but grabbed the attention of a tall Swedish-model type in Jimmy Choos. "Excuse me?"

The blonde stopped dead in her tracks as soon as she saw the cop uniform. "I just work here. I don't know anything."

Martha smiled. "No one's in trouble. We only want to talk to your boss. Lucas Cameron?"

The blonde nodded slowly. "Yeah. Yeah." She scurried off to another blonde, a strikingly beautiful woman in a red dress.

The woman met up with them, looking them up and down with disdain. "What can I do for you, officers?"

Martha raised an eyebrow and refused to let this woman intimidate her. "We want to talk to Lucas Cameron."

Her tone was condescending and cold. "Do you have a warrant?"

"No. He's expecting us."

Zach jumped in. "I called ahead. We want to make sure everything's good with summit security."

The woman looked at Zach like he was an insect, and Zach smoothed his sweater and stuffed his journal into his blazer.

She pursed her lips. "Charming. I'll get him."

The woman left, and Zach turned to Martha. "What was that?"

"That is what some people think of cops."

"Geez."

He adjusted his hair in the glass reflection on the wall. It bothered Martha. "Stop."

"My hair gets—"

She ordered him more forcefully. "Zach, don't do that."

He froze with his fingers still in his hair. "Why not?"

"That's part of her game, to throw us off."

"Throw us off what? We don't have anything on her."

"No. It's a power play. She's trying to show us that she's rich and invincible, and we don't have any real jurisdiction over her. We'll be intimidated and stay out of her way."

"Well, the whole intimidation thing is kind of working."

"Don't give in to it. You'll have to know how to handle these New York society types if you want to be a good cop. They all think police only have authority under certain tax brackets."

Zach clasped his hands in front of him and tried to look

serious. He was an intern, so he didn't get a uniform. Right now, he wore his characteristic style: an argyle blazer, khakis, and Converses. He was right. He didn't fit in.

The woman in the red dress floated back up to them with a plastic smile. "Mr. Cameron will see you now. Right this way."

Martha and Zach followed her down a long hallway full of glass offices, Apple-designed workspaces, beanbag conference rooms in bright pastels, and a kitchenette with brick walls, low track lighting, egg barstools, and artisan coffees offered from a touchscreen.

Martha pointed at a worker making notes on an electronic wallboard that looked like a high-tech Etch A Sketch. "See, this is where you belong."

Zach smirked with disdain. "You don't think I know that?"

Martha raised an eyebrow. There was more to Zach than met the eye.

Finally, they reached the corner office. "Mr. Cameron?"

"Ah yes, Allison. Show them in."

Allison gestured into the room, and Martha and Zach stepped inside. The floors were polished concrete with a brick wall rising to a high, vaulted ceiling. Paper lantern-style lamps hung from the ceiling on long silver poles dotted at intervals like abstract art installations. A large white table served as a desk, and the whole sidewall was a window overlooking the city. An industrial staircase in metal and glass rose behind the desk and led to a loft area, where Martha saw the rim of a pool table.

Lucas was an attractive man in his early thirties. He had carefully disheveled dark hair, intense blue eyes, and a dimpled smile showing off a row of perfectly pearl-white teeth. He wore black slacks and a white dress shirt with the sleeves rolled to his mid-forearm, and Martha glimpsed a tattoo peeking out.

He shoved his hands into his pockets and smiled as he approached them. "Hi, come in, come in." He gestured them toward a black leather sitting area, and they shook hands and introduced themselves. "Sit. Can I get you something to drink? Coffee, water?"

Martha sat, and Zach followed. She pulled out a notepad. "No, we're all right."

He sat opposite them. "Are you sure? We make a mean boba tea."

Zach perked up. "Boba?"

"Yeah, we've got a great kitchen. In fact—" Lucas pushed a button on the phone next to him. "Molly, could you send Zach here one of those new boba teas?"

Martha sighed as the voice came through the intercom. "Absolutely."

She was a little annoyed at Zach. They weren't here for snack time. She took a moment to make notes of anything she saw around the office.

"What flavor?" Lucas asked.

"Uh, I don't care."

He winked and made the "perfect" gesture with his fingers. "Watermelon's our new flavor. We got it in from the vendor this week. Terrific. You'll love it."

"Uh, yeah."

Lucas popped back on the intercom. "Make it a watermelon. And—" He pointed toward Martha. "Are you sure I can't get you anything? I mean this new flavor, it's great."

"I'm fine, thank you."

He narrowed his eyes and pointed toward her. "I'm going to take you for a strawberry, right?"

"I—uh… I'm not thirsty."

"Molly, get Officer Dragone a strawberry tea. Blended. Whipped cream."

"Got it."

Lucas got off the intercom. "You're going to love this new drink. We're getting a great deal on the machine, demoing it for inclusion in events. Our staff is going crazy about it. It's boba-mania around here. We've already set up stations at the One Response."

Martha was a little agitated that he'd ordered her a drink anyway but let it go. "One Response?"

"That's the name of the show we're producing for the World Summit in Times Square. But you knew that. You wouldn't be here if you didn't."

"Yeah, I didn't know the name."

He made a banner title motion in the air. "We're calling it 'One Response' because it's the global celebration of the people whose leaders have come together as one world. We're celebrating taking the first step toward the end of wars, global famine, poverty, and economic inequality. It's a cultural celebration of unity and hope."

Martha thought she'd gag on the buzzwords, and Molly, another tall, leggy blond Swedish-model type, came in carrying two frothy drinks on a tray.

Lucas graciously pointed toward the two on the couch. "Ah, thank you, Molly."

Molly bent down over the coffee table and set down Zach's drink, and Martha's mouth dropped when she realized Molly made a conscious effort to let Zach see some cleavage. She rolled her eyes as the move practically incapacitated her intern.

Molly set Martha's unordered drink down. "And here you

go, Officer Dragone. Great mention in the *Times* this week, by the way. You're a real patriot, bringing down scumbags like Alister Pout."

Martha smiled wryly. Okay, this woman knew what she was doing. "Thank you."

Molly winked at them both and left the office.

Martha sipped her tea and found it was quite good.

Lucas watched them drink. "Great stuff, huh?" They simultaneously agreed, and Lucas clapped his hands together loudly. "So, what can I do for the NYPD?"

Martha set down the drink and got down to business. "We're here about One Response. Obviously, with such a large-scale event, we want to make sure that you have security as your utmost concern."

Lucas nodded vigorously, although Martha noticed the tiniest glint of irritation in his face. "Security is a top concern for us, clearly. We've complied with all city and state regulations in regard to providing necessary security measures. We've hired a private security firm. They are truly the best in the business.

"You can't tell me who that is, though?"

"I'm afraid not. Not without a warrant, anyway."

"Right."

"They're doing the usual: installing metal detectors at all entrance points, facial recognition video surveillance at every angle, and they're making sure we stay in compliance with the ratio of attendants to security personnel. We're also working with..." He searched his memory. "His name is Officer Bramley at NYPD. You know him?"

Martha smiled at the name of the showboat cop who had been on reality TV. "Yes, I know him."

Lucas scratched his head. "Yeah, we've been working with

him on and off, filing security permits. He's sending us some guys, I think. You might want to check with him."

Martha took all this information down. Everything seemed to check out, and Bramley's paperwork would likely have the security firm's name. That would be useful information, and she didn't like Lucas being evasive about it. Other than that, everything here seemed clean and aboveboard. So, how did the summit get attacked during the keynote address?

"Okay, that all sounds on the up and up. May I ask what One Response entails?"

Lucas smiled and scratched his head again. "Well, we've got everything in the ads. I'll—"

Molly knocked on the glass door. Lucas turned toward her. She stood in the doorway. "Sorry to interrupt, but the guys from the light show are here."

Light show, Martha thought. Rueben had said the attack drones were part of a light show. Was it possible that Lucas and his company were part of this?

Lucas stood. "Thanks, Molly."

Molly left, and Lucas gestured Martha and Zach toward the door. Martha didn't move. "Light show, huh?"

"Oh yeah, that's one of the surprises. We're going to pull this out at the finale. One of the most high-tech light shows ever. You have tickets?"

"No. He does, I don't."

Lucas raised an eyebrow at her. "Oh, you should. You can't buy tickets now, but I'll tell you what…" He popped over to a desk drawer and rifled through it. He came back and handed Martha four laminated lanyard cards. "VIP. On me. Both of you and your dates. We appreciate NYPD checking in on us, and it never hurts to have more officers on the ground. We hope you enjoy it."

Martha glanced at the cards with the One Response logo and a barcode, and he slipped his business card in the middle. "Thanks."

He winked at her and opened the door. "No problem. Let me know if you have any more questions. You have my number."

"I do. Thank you."

Martha and Zach left the office, passing a handful of tech guys congregating in the lobby. She told Zach, "I take it those are the light show guys."

"I would assume so."

She noticed as she passed that one of them had the Global Research Initiative logo on his shirt. What was that company?

Martha sat alone in her office with Buzz on speaker. "Global Research Initiative? Where did you hear about them?"

"One Republic Entertainment invested in them, and they're putting on a light show. I don't see anything wrong with any of it. It's the only thread I have, and I'm pulling on it."

Buzz was quiet for a minute.

"Buzz?"

"Yeah, yeah. I'm still here. Just processing this."

"Processing what? Is it something?"

"Yeah, it's definitely something. GRI has gone before the scientific research association for several ethics violations over the last decade."

"Really? Like what?"

"Fuuuuucked-up shit."

Martha's eyes widened, and she leaned over the phone. "Oh yeah?"

"Yeah. A lot of what they're doing is classified, but it's all shady, under-the-table human rights violations."

"Human rights violations? In what way?"

"Like....umm...experimenting with what they call 'disposable peoples.'"

"Disposable peoples? I would assume that would mean the very ones the One World Campaign is supposed to help."

"Exactly. They offer orphans and the poor of underdeveloped countries small amounts of money and decent housing, or jobs, or cars for them or their family members to undergo very experimental clinical trials."

Martha felt sick to her stomach. "Like Nazi doctors."

"Sort of. Only it's voluntary. There's nothing wrong with clinical trials. People do it all the time. It's just they can do much more aggressive trials, and much, much cheaper, with people that are desperate or don't know any better."

"Oh my God."

Buzz was quiet for a few minutes. "It's some dark stuff. They're into other weird stuff. Like using high-level frequencies to interact with the brain waves of an entire city and reroute them to make independent people think how you want them to."

"Wha—you can do that?"

"Sort of. It's out there. It's based on the idea of matching the electrical frequency of brain waves. Human brain activity is only ever a series of chemical and electrical impulses, anyway."

Martha never was comfortable with that assessment, but how else would Buzz see things? "Right."

"So, if you can tap into that electrical impulse in a subject's brain and match it...theoretically, you could manipulate it."

"Manipulating brain waves?"

"Yeah. I don't know if it works or not. But they're into that, and they have whole research centers in Thailand and places in Africa where they try it. They're doing that and some other stuff that Aki probably knows about and can't discuss."

"So it makes sense why they might be involved with the summit attack?"

"I choose not to speculate."

"We've got to get back into that office. Do some detective work and find out how deep this thing goes."

"I can't go. I'm double-booked tonight."

She made a face into the speaker. "What are you doing tonight?"

"I have other plans."

"Buzz, a terrorist is going to destroy New York and kill much of the world's leaders in about twenty-four hours. If we don't—" Water gushed in the background. "Are you in the bath?"

"I'm taking a dip in the jacuzzi. If these terrorists succeed and anarchy and looting come to destroy all that I've worked a lifetime to build, I'd rather spend the last night pampering myself in luxury."

"You're twenty-three."

"Lifetimes are relative. You can ask Rueben about that. Besides, I don't do break-ins. Or jail. I'm much too delicate for all of that."

She groaned and ended the call.

She would have to do this alone. She used a trick Buzz had showed her to download the One Republic Entertainment building's blueprints. However, when she stared at them, she couldn't figure out how to break in. Too bad Aki wasn't here. She'd know. Martha's job was to keep people from breaking in, not do it herself. That gave her an idea.

She paged Zach. "Come in here."

Zach arrived in her office, looking bright-eyed and excited. "We got any new developments?"

"We're going to break into One Republic."

Zach grinned. "I'm so down." Then his eyes darted back and forth. "How?"

"I haven't decided yet."

"My friend has a key card."

She shook her head. "Too traceable. Get your stuff—we're going to the jail."

"The jail?"

"Yeah. First, we have to stop at the comic book store."

Zach clutched his head between his hands. "You're right. I'd make a bad cop. I have no idea what's going on."

***

Martha pulled the squad car in front of Comic Geek, a tiny comic book store next to a CBD distributor. As soon as she did, everyone on the street and in both stores magically disappeared.

Zach laughed. "What the hell?"

"Yeah, that happens when you're a cop. You get used to it. Come on."

Martha and Zach entered the comic book store, and the smell of marijuana greeted them.

Zach took in the frightened look on the faces of the customers. "Ah. I see."

"Yeah. I could go to town in here if I wanted."

She approached the counter, and the twenty-year-old kid with the Dungeons and Dragons t-shirt stiffened. "What can I do for you, ma'am?"

"Where's Don?"

"Don, the manager? He's in the back."

"Can you get him for me?"

"Yes, ma'am."

The kid ran to the back, and a few minutes later, Don showed up. He was a tall, lanky man with glasses, a shaved head, and a live boa constrictor around his neck.

"Hello, Officer Dragone. What can I do for you?"

"You know what I want."

Don cocked his head toward the manager's office. "We keep it in the back for you."

Zach shot Martha a confused look, but she didn't respond. She followed Don to the manager's office. It was a tiny, cluttered room with comic book posters, an old beat-up desk, and a chair that looked like it had come out of a dumpster.

He sat and gestured at Zach. "Shut the door. We don't want anyone knowing about this." The manager reached under the desk and pulled out a cardboard box, and tossed it onto the surface.

Martha peered in and gravely thumbed through it.

Zach peeked in. "Archie comics?"

Don placed his finger over his mouth. "Shhh. People around here believe we're a serious comic book shop. If they knew we were selling this kind of stuff..." He shook his head and sighed deeply. "It would be the end of us. They'd never take us seriously again. We could be labeled a 'hobby shop.'"

Zach flipped through a box and shrugged. "What's wrong with being a hobby shop?"

"It's the end. Once you're a hobby shop, people don't sell

you the collectors' stuff anymore. When you can't get the collectors' stuff anymore, then to survive, you have to 'go corporate.'" He shuddered at the thought. He grabbed a lid and shoved it over the open box. "Use the back door."

Martha winked and grabbed the container. "Thanks, Don."

He gestured toward the snake. "We're still good, right?"

"As always, Don, no one will bother you."

Don nodded and smiled, and Martha and Zach left the store by way of the back entrance.

As soon as they got outside, Zach laughed. "What was that all about?"

"It's an old deal. Sometimes you have to make deals to get deals." She shoved the box into the car and made a call. "Hey, Robyn. Get me Slasher. I'm on my way."

She got into the car, and Zach sat with his green leather journal. "Who's Slasher?"

"You'll see."

They arrived at the prison and entered through the back entrance, box in tow. As soon as they walked in, a young black woman at the receptionist's desk who appeared bored out of her mind greeted them. "Morning, Robyn."

"Hey, Martha. How's life up on top?"

"The same as life on the bottom. Just more paperwork."

Robyn laughed, and Martha set the box on the desk. "Check this for me."

Robyn went through the box, fanning through the pages of each magazine. "Good."

"Great. Is he ready?"

"Yep. Down in interrogation three."

"Great." Martha grabbed the box and motioned for Zach to follow.

"So, where are we going?" he asked.

"To see Slasher. He's a Ukrainian butcher connected to some of Pout's shady operations. He's useful to law enforcement from time to time."

They arrived in interrogation room three. It was a small space with double-sided windows, a table, and a couple of folding chairs. Slasher sat on one side, his hands clasped, his beefy handcuffed wrists chained to a metal ring on the table. He was an older man, maybe sixties, tall—too tall—and hunched over in his orange jumpsuit. He had dark eyes and a face that looked like it had seen too much, with tufts of black hair framing the mostly bald spot on his head.

Martha shut the door behind her. "Hello, Slasher."

"Officer Dragone. What do you have for me today?" His accent was thick and to the point. She set the box on the table, he opened it, and his face lit up like Christmas morning. "Oh, that Archie."

He fanned through the different issues, and Zach and Martha sat.

"You have to love that Jughead. I can't wait to see what hijinks they get into next."

He scanned one strip and laughed hard. He showed them the comic. "That Moose. He's so dumb. He will never get Veronica. You Americans have the best sense of humor."

Zach and Martha looked at each other.

Finally, Slasher set the magazines down. "What can I do for you now?"

Martha pulled out some rolled-up copies of the blueprints to the One Republic Entertainment skyscraper. She leaned in and slid them over to him. "If someone wanted to break into that tower, how would they do it?"

Slasher leaned back into his chair and grinned. "I know exactly how to do it. I used to work in that tower."

Martha raised an eyebrow. "Pout was connected to One Republic Entertainment? I should have guessed."

CHAPTER EIGHTEEN

Sunday, May 21, 7:11 p.m.

Rueben and Aki had decided not to tell Marshall the news of their upcoming "wedding" right away. There was too much work to be done. They'd instead gone to CIA headquarters to crack down on researching and to use all the resources at their disposal to try to stop Pete. That meant Marshall got about twenty plainclothes agents outside the apartment, as well as an increased police presence in the neighborhood. If Pete made a move, they'd notify Rueben and Aki immediately, and the pair would rush to Marshall's aid.

As it happened, Pete made no move on Marshall Saturday night, and Rueben and Aki ended up sleeping at their desks. They resumed work the next morning and throughout Sunday. Now they were preparing to give Marshall the news.

An hour ago, CIA Tech had reported that the signal tracking Marshall's phone was on the move and could be heading toward Marshall's apartment. They didn't know yet.

As soon as Aki finished up what she was working on, she and Rueben would head out to Marshall's and "break the news." With the possibility that Pete might make a move on Marshall at a moment's notice, they'd be able to keep Marshall in their sights. They would have plenty of CIA agents on standby too, and if they needed to whisk Marshall away for safety, they could claim they needed him for some last-minute wedding activity.

Rueben sat with Aki at her cubicle and listened to the buzz around them.

The real IRA bomber had just cracked and given his sources. As promised during his interrogation, authorities were extraditing him back to Dublin. Sven was on the phone negotiating the deal with the Irish prime minister. The Russian mobster had escaped from custody in Langley, and heads were rolling on how that could have happened.

Sven was about to burst a vein over that. His voice on speakerphone carried through his closed door and halfway through the bullpen. "I hand-delivered you an international terrorist with a confession, rap sheet, and idiot-proof evidence. How could you have possibly screwed this up?"

Then there was an unrelated threat where someone had apparently shot up a Dunkin Donuts in Florida, and the guy had a swastika tattoo.

The local authorities neutralized the threat, but it still had to be thoroughly investigated. Rueben was reading the memos on his laptop when Sven whisked by.

He stopped at Aki's cubicle where the two sat working on their wedding plans. "You guys made it out of jail."

Aki nodded. "Yes, sir. Now we're working on a possible security breach at the summit. We have a lead, and we're on it."

Sven nodded vigorously. "Keep up the good work." Then he noticed her screen. "Wedding chapels?"

She smiled. "Possible sting operation."

"Check out The Waterfall upstate. We've done a sting there before."

She looked intrigued. "The Waterfall?"

"Yeah. It's a tributary of Niagara Falls. We have a good relationship with the owner. What are you guys up to?"

She answered quickly. "Too early to tell. I'll let you know when we have something concrete."

"Good. I don't need any more complications today."

With that, he left.

Rueben shook his head at her. "You handle him well."

"I've worked closely enough with him for a while. The trick is to make him think you have everything handled and play to his ego from time to time."

"Good tips. He scares the hell out of me."

She laughed. "He's not so bad once you get to know him. He tries to play the old-school spy games, but he's too much of a softie to pull them off."

Rueben raised an eyebrow. Sven pulled off the spy games successfully when he was around.

She pulled up the website for The Waterfall and whistled when she saw it. "This place is nice."

Indeed it was. Amidst a backdrop of a tranquil waterfall, there were picturesque bridges and floral arrangements. A pavilion with wood floors offered dance space and seating, and photos of past weddings showed the place decked out in silk, beads, and lace.

Rueben winced. "They'll let us do an impromptu wedding there?"

She picked up the phone. "Of course they will." Aki dialed the number with one manicured finger and coyly smiled when someone answered. "I need to book a wedding."

Rueben overheard the man through the phone line. "I'm sorry, ma'am, our reservation desk is closed for the evening. I'm only at the office because we're so booked up and behind schedule. Yep. Booked clear with appointments for the next few weeks, I'm afraid."

Aki laughed. "Uh, I mean I need to book a wedding now."

"I'm sorry, I can't—"

"What's your name?"

"Uh, I'm Glen, but the reservation manager is—"

"Glen, Glen, I don't think we quite understand each other."

"Uh, okay."

She changed her voice to a sultry tone. "What can you do for me…say…first thing in the morning?"

"Well, I…uh…"

"Come on, Glen, you can do it for me."

Rueben listened as the conversation turned. By the end of it, they had a wedding appointment for 10:30 the next morning.

As soon as she got off the phone in victory, he applauded her. "So, what do we do now?"

"Well, that's the best part. Now we go home and announce our engagement."

Rueben gulped. "Right."

It was dark by the time Rueben and Aki left. They got back in her Porsche, and she programmed his address into her GPS.

He felt a little nervous taking her to his humble home, but she had already met Marshall, so what else could he be afraid of? He called Marshall to make sure he would be home.

Marshall was as gruff as usual when he answered the phone. "Yeah?"

"Hey, Dad. I'm on my way home from work. I wanted to make sure you were going to be there."

"Yeah. What of it? You're not coming home from jail again, are you?"

"No, Dad. I wanted to talk to you. Make sure you were there."

"Talk? We're talking right now. What do you want?"

"It's not that kind of talk. I'll see you when I get home."

"Tell me now. Did you get fired or something?"

"No, nothing like that. Look, I'll see you in a few."

Rueben ended the call and shook his head. "I hope you're ready for this. It isn't going to be easy."

Aki threw her head back. "I love it. This kind of stuff is the reason I became an agent."

"What? Dealing with half-senile old coots?"

"No, playing roles. You know, I wanted to be an actress when I was younger."

"I did not know that about you."

"I can't believe I didn't tell you that in one of our 'forgotten' timelines you warped back from."

"You did not."

"Yeah, I was a theater student in school. Pretty good at it. But there's no future in acting unless you make it big in Hollywood. So, I ended up here. This is the part I love. Being undercover." She winked and took his hand. "With my new husband."

He gulped at that last part, and she laughed. "We have to get our story straight. How did you propose?"

"Uh...don't make me be cheesy, with the pathway full of rose petals and the wine and all of that."

She laughed. "Come on, you're not a romantic, huh?"

Oh, geez. That was the wrong thing to say. "No, it's not that, I just…"

He wanted to say that his feelings for her were too real and that he didn't dare entertain all of these ideas.

"Okay, so how did you propose to Rachel?"

"Rachel?" Rueben didn't remember ever telling Aki about his ex-fiancée.

"Yeah. I've done my research on you."

"You pulled my record at the CIA?"

Aki rolled her eyes at him. "No. Facebook."

"Oh. Right. So you want to know how I proposed to her"

Aki nodded interestedly.

"Let's see. It was so cliché. We did a picnic in the park, and I got down on one knee, and I asked her there. Not very creative. Marshall would remember that story."

"Okay, let's make it fun. You proposed on the way to jail."

He laughed really hard. "That's great."

"So we were in the squad car, and we couldn't keep our hands off each other."

"Except that they cuffed us."

"Oh, right. Okay, but while the sirens were blaring, you told me that I was your partner in crime, and as soon as we got arrested together, you knew you wanted to be with me forever. Then you asked me to marry you."

He choked back the lump in his throat and laughed weakly. That was pretty much how he felt about her. He knew they weren't ready to get married, but yeah, the whole part-ner-in-crime thing read pretty real.

She laughed it off, though. "We need a ring."

He pursed his lips. "Pull over at that bank."

City Wide Bank sat on the corner near his and Marshall's apartment. "This one?"

"Yeah."

"It's almost eight o'clock on a Saturday night."

"Right," Rueben said. "Working for the CIA has its perks. Back at the office, I made some calls while you were checking on things. The bank is open for us only, but we have to be quick."

Aki studied him curiously and decided he wasn't joking. She parked, and they jumped out. A CIA agent stood inside the locked glass doors. After verifying that it was indeed Rueben Peet, the man unlocked the entrance. Rueben ran inside, and Aki followed him. He gestured toward a couch. "Wait right there."

She sat, and he ran up to the teller, an irritated middle-aged woman who looked like she'd rather be anyplace other than back at work after the vault had been sealed for the rest of the weekend and then reopened by order of the CIA. Oh, the perks of being a bank manager...

"I'd like to get something out of my safe deposit box."

"Absolutely." Sarcasm. "Fill out this form."

He filled out the form, and she brought out a small metal box. Inside, there it was.

Rueben lifted the black velvet jewelry box carefully. When he opened it, it sparkled. "That's all I need."

"Thank you for your business, Mr. Peet." More sarcasm.

The bank manager took the safe deposit box away, and Rueben approached Aki at the couch.

She looked up. "You get what you need?"

"Almost."

Then, there in the bank, he got down on one knee, and she

gasped. "Aki Yamashiro, will you fake-marry me?" He opened the jewelry box, and the ring glittered in the artificial light.

"Oh my gosh. Yes, I'll fake-marry you!"

She grabbed the ring, and they both laughed as he rose to his feet and dusted off his knee. "That's the second time I've done that, the whole one-knee thing. I think I'm getting too old for it."

She laughed and slipped the ring onto her finger. It fit perfectly. "It was hers, right?"

A shadow passed across his face. "Rachel's? Yeah. You're supposed to spend a month and a half of your salary on a ring."

"Really? I didn't know that."

"Yeah. I read up on it. So I saved up and bought it and did the picnic proposal. Six months after that, she threw it back at me. Luckily I caught it." He shoved his hands in his pockets and shrugged. "I've held on to it all this time. I couldn't bear to sell it. I guess I kind of thought she'd come back one day, and we could pick up where we left off. Stupid, I know."

"Well, she missed out."

His heart leapt into his throat. Did she mean on the ring or him?

She let the diamond catch the light, and he smiled at his ring on her manicured finger. "Now we're legit."

She crooked her arm in his. "Let's do this."

Rueben and Aki arrived at the apartment building shortly after eight. They got out of the car, and he clarified, "We're going with the jail story, right?"

She shut the door, and they headed up the stairs. "Right.

But you didn't give me the ring until just now. We can go with that story. But not that it was Rachel's ring. It was…"

"I bought it on Valentine's Day after we busted Pout."

"Sure, we'll go with that."

Rueben had butterflies in his stomach as he approached the door. He had never lied to his dad, mainly because he always knew he'd get caught. Now, here he was, about to execute the biggest lie he'd ever concocted. He was sure Marshall would see right through him. But with Aki standing right beside him, wearing Rachel's ring, he couldn't exactly back out.

He opened the door. "Hey, Dad? You here?"

The TV blared Fox News. The lead story was a running commentary on the summit, the One World campaign, and Yolanda Martinez.

"Dad?"

"Yeah, I'm here, I'm here." Marshall came into the living room, popping open another bottle of beer. It was clear he was already one or two beers in. He stopped when he saw Aki. "Son, what's going on here?"

Rueben motioned at the easy chair. "Yeah, Dad, maybe you should sit."

Marshall didn't say anything—he just sat. Rueben figured he was putting a lid on his assholery in front of Aki.

Rueben took Aki's hand, and they sat across from him. The feel of Aki's soft hand in his sent his heart racing. He toyed with her fingers, and she smiled at him. He had to remind himself it was all fake. "So, Dad, umm…I know it's a little sudden."

He couldn't look at Marshall while he said it. He was certain his dad would see right through him. Then he remembered from his CIA training that was the first indicator of a liar—they couldn't make eye contact. So Rueben forced himself to look his dad in the eye.

Marshall inquisitively stared back and forth between them.

Aki squeezed his hand, and he could feel her staring adoringly up at him. He knew it was all fake, but it felt so real. That's when he blurted his announcement. "We're getting married."

CHAPTER NINETEEN

<u>**Sunday, May 21, 8:30 p.m.**</u>

Marshall spat out his beer. "I'm sorry, I thought you said you're getting married."

Aki squealed and squeezed Rueben's arm. "We are." She held out the ring long enough for Marshall to see what it was but not long enough for him to recognize it as Rachel's. She squealed again and looked adoringly at Rueben. "We're so happy."

Marshall sipped his beer and glanced back and forth at them. "What is she, pregnant?"

"No, Dad. It was just...the right time for us, and we didn't want to wait."

He studied Rueben for a clue, and Rueben knew his face would give him away, so he turned to Aki. His first thought was to kiss her, but given that they weren't really together, it was likely to come off as awkward and give them away. So instead, he went for the regal gentleman route. He held his hand against her palm, slowly brought it to his lips, and pressed them against it while staring adoringly at her.

She blushed and turned to Marshall. "He's such a romantic."

Oh, shit. She was going to blow it with that.

Marshall appeared confused. "How long has this been going on?"

Both Aki and Rueben glanced at each other and laughed awkwardly. They hadn't rehearsed this question. Rueben tried. "Well, it all started when, well... You tell it, baby."

The word 'baby' fell out of his mouth like lead, and he was sure Marshall would pick up on it. But Aki covered it with her blushing bride act. Then the undercover actress blossomed. "So, it started when we were working on the Pout case. We stopped for lunch at the cutest little cafe on the border... You remember that, right?"

She pointed at him and laughed, and he nodded. "Yep. The cafe. That's where it all started."

There had been no cafe on the border. There *had* been a McDonald's drive-thru with Buzz sulking. But no picturesque cafe.

Aki kept going. "And there was this gorgeous lake, with ducks and benches. And we kept throwing crackers at the ducks, and they would fly up and catch them. It was so cute."

Marshall contorted his face and repositioned himself in his easy chair. "You're not supposed to throw food to the animals. It can poison them. It's a wonder you didn't get caught."

"Well, we didn't, Dad."

"No, it only took another three months for you two idiots to get to jail. Is this what I get to look forward to in my old age? Bailing my idiot son and his bride out of jail every few months?"

It seemed his father's assholeness was back.

Aki pursed her lips, and Rueben smirked at her. *See?*

She continued her story. "Anyway, after that day with the ducks, Rueben and I have been spending a lot more time together, and things have been progressing."

"Really? What are you, religious or something? Why's he sleep here every night?"

Aki and Rueben both stammered for words. "Dad, that's none of your business."

Marshall kicked his recliner upright. "Well, whatever. Best wishes and congratulations." He stood and shuffled out of the room.

Rueben turned to Aki. "What do we do now?"

She glanced at her phone and then grimaced. "Shit. The agency has intercepted communications that show Pete might be about to make a move on the apartment now. We need to leave ASAP."

Rueben's eyes widened. "I thought we had more time."

"Me too." She nodded and showed him the agency alert on her phone. It was strange seeing his home address on a CIA alert.

Aki nodded. "Yes. This could work. All we have to do is lure Pete somewhere we have the advantage. We can apprehend him—alive—before he attacks the U.N. building on Monday."

"Where would we go on such short notice?"

Aki flashed him a wink. "We move our plans up a little."

"What do you mean?"

"Well, we were set up to keep Marshall under surveillance by having him look at a wedding venue in the morning."

"Right."

"Instead, we have him go wedding shopping tonight."

"Wedding shopping? You want Marshall Peet to help you pick out a dress?"

She scrunched up her face and shuddered. "God, no. I meant a cake."

"A cake? You want Marshall to go into a bakery and try a dainty little cake?"

"He eats, doesn't he?"

"Well yeah, but…"

She pointed toward Marshall's room. "You go back in there and tell him we need him to go cake shopping with us right now. I'll arrange everything else."

Rueben stared at Marshall's closed door and gulped back fear. She'd given him one job, and he didn't think he could do it. "All right."

She nodded and got on the phone.

He hesitantly approached Marshall's door. He paused before he rapped lightly on it.

The reply was annoyed. "Yeah?"

"Hey Dad, can I come in for a sec?"

The silence on the other end reminded Rueben that he didn't think he had ever asked to do that.

"What do you want?"

Rueben cracked open the door, and the low lamplight fell into the hall. He stepped into the room. Once in a while, Rueben came in here to put something away, but other than that he didn't enter. It was dusty and full of books, old newspapers, and beer bottles on the floor. It kind of smelled like skunked beer. It was also kind of sad.

Marshall sat in a stuffed chair on one side of the room and shrank back a little with each step Rueben took. His son was invading his territory, and he wasn't sure what to say about it.

Aki laughed on the phone in the other room.

Rueben decided he needed to get on with his one assignment. "Listen, Aki and I wanted you to help us with the wedding."

"Damnit. Is that what this is about—money? You need money?"

"No, no, not at all. She comes from a wealthy family, and between the two of us, we've got it covered."

"Then what do you want?"

"We want you to… We'd like you to be… Well, it's important, especially to Aki, that you be part of the wedding."

"Sure, if that's what you want. Just let me know where to go for a tux fitting, and I'll show up."

"No, no. That's not what I'm talking about."

"Damn it, son. Would you say what you mean, then?"

"You're not making it any easier."

"Oh, Christ. Did you come in here to pick a fight?"

"No, no, not at all." Rueben gestured toward the bed. "You mind if I sit?"

Marshall made a face that he very much did mind, but the brazen suggestion was such a shock that he didn't know how to say no.

Rueben took advantage of his confusion and perched on the corner of the bed. He rubbed his palms together. "Look, we're getting married fast. Real fast."

"I knew she was pregnant."

"No, she's not. I'm telling you, it's not about that. Like, we're getting married at the end of the month." He made that part up without Aki. They had the venue booked for the next day, but if all went well tonight, they wouldn't need it.

Marshall's eyes grew wide. "The end of the month? In two weeks?"

"Yeah. She's getting transferred to Sri Lanka." It shocked

Rueben how easily the lies rolled off his tongue. "And we couldn't wait any longer."

"You're going with her, then?"

"Maybe. We're not sure if we can get me a transfer."

Rueben let the news sink in. Marshall shifted in his chair, and Rueben picked up a sentiment he never thought he'd get from Marshall.

Would Marshall miss him?

"Well, it would be good to get some peace and quiet around here."

"Yeah. I know you want that."

Marshall searched Rueben's eyes, and Rueben caught a hint of something in them. Fear? Was Marshall afraid of being alone? "Maybe I'll turn your room into a TV room. I've always wanted one."

Rueben's heart sank a little. This was as close as he would ever get to an emotional moment with Marshall, and it was all based on a lie. He gulped back his guilt.

Marshall's eyes narrowed. "What was that?"

"What?"

"You always do that with your throat like that when you feel bad about something. What's going on?"

"Nothing, Dad. It's an emotional thing, is all."

"What's to be emotional about? So you're getting married. You're not still hung up on that old Rebecca or…"

"Rachel."

"Yeah, her."

"That's not why I came in here."

"Damn it, son. I'm tired, and it's late. Why don't you get to your point already?"

"I want you to come cake shopping with us."

"Cake shopping? That's for the girl and her mom and her little bridesmaids."

"Look, Aki really wants you to like her. She wants to spend time with you. She's heard what a great influence you've been on Martha and wants to get to know you better."

Martha was the keyword, and Marshall's face softened. "Okay. Just let me know when."

"Now."

"Right now?" Marshall glanced around the room. "Son, I'm getting ready for bed."

"I know. But we're going to the venue tomorrow, and they want us to have a cake at least. It's important."

"No, Rueben. I'm tired. This kind of thing isn't for me in the first place. If you want to get married, go ahead. It's your life."

"You also get to sample the wine."

Marshall stopped.

"You don't want me to have to pick the wedding bar by myself, do you?"

"What do you know about bars? All you drink is cheap shit beer."

"I know. And if you want your opinion on the bar menu, then you'd better come."

Marshall sighed. "Fine. If it means that much to you that you'd use that lame line, then I'll come. But really, you've got to get better at your persuasiveness."

Rueben clasped his hands together and bowed them in a motion of gratitude, then left the room while his father rooted around in his dresser.

Aki was in the living room and finally off the phone. "Is he coming?"

"He's coming."

"Great. The sting is in place. The agency is hacking into the security cameras for surveillance, and we're switching out the staff for agents as we speak."

"That was fast."

She winked. "Welcome to being an agent. All we need is the subject."

"Right. Um…" Rueben shuffled on his feet as he considered Aki's choice of word, 'subject.' So sterile sounding, and she'd called him a subject at Buzz's mansion earlier. Was that all he was to Aki? A subject? No chance of a romantic connection?

Rueben suddenly realized Aki was standing before him with her hands on her waist. "Well, where is he then?"

Rueben shook his head to clear it as an idea flashed into his head. "He's uh, getting dressed. FYI…we're getting married this fast because you're transferring to Sri Lanka. I want to join you, but we're still working on the transfer."

"Got it."

A few minutes later, Marshall shuffled out of the bedroom.

Aki smiled at him. "Thank you so much for doing this. We wanted to get this done fast before I leave, and we need all the extra help we can get."

"Yeah, Rueben tells me you're going to Sri Lanka?"

"Yep. It wasn't my decision. When you work for the government like this, you learn to move fast."

Marshall frowned and didn't say much more about that. They all left the apartment, and Aki clicked the remote on her Porsche. Marshall raised an eyebrow at his son, and Rueben shrugged and got into the passenger seat.

Aki smiled at him, and Marshall clicked the remote on his blue Toyota. As soon as she and Rueben were safely in the Porsche, Rueben remarked, "I think he likes you already."

"Well, the objective is to keep him safe."

As the two vehicles pulled away from the curb, so did a third one behind them. Rueben eyed the headlights. "Who is that?"

"That's Jake, remember? The guy who drove the limo."

"Right. Jake the agent."

"He's following us to the pastry shop to make sure nothing happens on the way." She pulled out her phone and switched to a walkie-talkie app. "You there, Jake?"

"Yeah, I got you."

"Is that his real name, 'Jake?'"

"No. I don't know his real name."

"You're sure Pete is moving in on Marshall?"

"Yes. Tech pinged Pete's general location. They can't pinpoint it exactly, but it's closing in on the apartment right now."

Rueben set his jaw. So much for not putting Marshall at risk. "Okay. So what is this bakery?"

"It's open a little later; that's why we chose it. It's called Laura's Pastries. They do wedding cakes, and they're setting some samples up for us now. But..."

"We have our agents in there now."

"Exactly. Everyone's ready to make a move."

"Let's make sure there's plenty of booze for him to sample, too. That's what sold him."

Aki laughed. "Why am I not surprised."

Rueben pulled up the number on his phone. The receptionist answered with a trembling voice. "Laura's Pastries?"

"Hi, this Rueben Peet. I'm the groom in the wedding we're coming in for tonight."

The receptionist halted. "Hold on, just one moment."

"Thank you." He was on hold for several minutes.

"This is Laura. How can I help you?"

"Laura, this is Rueben Peet. I'm—"

"I know who you are. What can I do for you?"

Her tone confused Rueben. He wasn't sure if she was annoyed or ready to help with the sting. "My father is coming in to sample cakes."

"I'm aware of that. We have the samples ready, Mr. Peet. When can we expect you?"

"We're minutes away. But if we could have some different samples of bar items, that would be helpful, too."

Laura hesitated. "All I knew about was cake. My staff is gone, and all I've got are—"

There was a muffled sound in the background, and Rueben knew an agent had overheard and was telling her someone might've tapped his line.

"I'm sorry," she continued. "I meant most of my staff is gone for the night. We don't get this much business this late, so we're not equipped to handle full wedding packages."

"I understand."

They would not be getting much more help from Laura. They arrived at the pastry shop, and Aki parked in full view of the cameras. Before they got out of the car, she pointed them out. "There's one here, here, and…here. Great, that should give us a good view of Pete once he shows up."

Aki and Rueben exited the car, and Marshall was right behind them. Jake stayed in his car for the moment. Rueben had never been on a sting like this before, so he could hardly sit still with the rush of adrenaline.

Laura's Pastries was a beautiful little silver-and-white shop with bridal cakes on display in the large bay windows, draped with tulle and satin. It was the perfect ruse for what they needed to do.

Laura greeted them with a large, tense smile. She was a tall, well-dressed blond woman in an elegant cream pantsuit, and her makeup was way too put-together for this hour. It was obvious the agents had called her into work for this operation. "You must be the happy couple."

Rueben draped his arm around Aki's shoulder and pulled her close. "Yes, we are." It felt so awkward that he let it drop and moved to wrap his arm around her waist. Even that was a quick jerky movement, and Aki nearly tripped as he pulled her closer.

Laura pretended not to notice any of that. "Oh, so young and in love. We're excited that you chose us."

Rueben could see right through the shop owner's plastic smile.

Marshall shuffled around the shop as Laura launched into her rehearsed sales speech. "As you might have read in our marketing material, we donate one percent of all of our profits to charity. This month, all of our donations go to the One World campaign. You've heard of that, right?"

Rueben nodded, and Marshall groaned. "You're into that socialist, one-world government crap?"

"Excuse me?"

"It's all about equalizing the world's economies so we can live in a one-world communist Russia, while the rich elite sit fat and happy on their asses with all the wealth in the world."

"Dad, please. Can we talk about my wedding right now?"

Marshall looked at Rueben and Aki as Laura's jaw practically sat on the floor. "Fine. I'll behave."

Laura fake-laughed and looked like steam was about to come out of her ears. Rueben could tell she couldn't concentrate.

There were also too many staff members for the number

of customers in the store. There must have been six or seven waitstaff in the shop, and they all did things like wipe down clean tables and dust blinds. A few were behind the counter.

"So, as I was saying, when is the date?"

Rueben answered quickly. "We're looking at the end of the month."

"The end of the month? Well, that doesn't give you much time." Laura didn't seem fazed by this, mainly because she wouldn't be doing anything.

The store was way too quiet. Usually, if a store were this slow, the staff would be busy chatting amongst themselves, not mindlessly performing repetitive chores on an already spotless interior.

Marshall looked around at the shop. "Good place here. Never seen this store before."

"Yes, we've been open a few years."

"You ever have any trouble? This neighborhood has a lot of crime in it."

"We've had a few scrapes here and there, but..."

Laura tried to keep her composure. Rueben could tell she was already scared—now Marshall was just making it worse.

"Forgive my dad. He's a retired cop. This is the way he thinks."

Laura laughed weakly. "Oh. So you're going to be the proud papa-in-law, right?"

Marshall shoved his hands into his jean pockets. "That's what they tell me, anyway."

Laura glanced out the window and seemed to be stalling for time. "Okay, well, let's talk about the big day, shall we?"

Aki squealed, and Rueben finally got the bravery to fake-kiss her. Only she wasn't expecting it, and he accidentally smashed her nose with his chin.

He rubbed his chin and mumbled, "Sorry."

She winced and tried to keep her smile in place. Fortunately, Marshall—the only one not in on the ruse—didn't see it.

Laura grabbed some pamphlets off a counter, her hand trembling a little. "So, shall we sit and go over the packages?"

Aki squealed. "I can't wait."

Rueben scratched the back of his head, wondering if Aki might be overdoing it with the squeals. "Yeah, let's go over the packages."

Laura led them to a small pink table in the back of the room. "So, we have the gold package. This is our most exclusive." Her voice faltered, but she continued and pointed at a photo of an elaborate cake.

Rueben whistled. If he ever did get married, he was sure he couldn't afford that one.

Marshall didn't pay much attention to any of it.

Laura rambled on and on about the cake packages, quickly losing Rueben's attention. "Let me go get you guys some samples."

She disappeared into the back, and that's when Marshall started in. "This place is a pussy-ass bunch of social justice warrior crap. There's probably not a gun in this place. You know how many times this street has had robberies?"

Rueben sighed and glanced at Aki, who shook her head.

Marshall pointed outside toward a building across the street. "You see the black mark on that building?"

Rueben peered through the window but didn't exactly see what his father was talking about. However, it was dark out, and the street lights did seem awfully dim.

Marshall didn't wait for an answer. "That's a bullet mark. I arrested scumbags for armed robberies three times on this street and got called out here for multiple more. Yet they're all about this liberal pussyfoot bullshit, with Yolanda Martinez's One World campaign. It's all socialism."

Aki groaned and pulled out a makeup compact.

Rueben turned to Marshall. "Would you please try, and I mean try really hard, to be happy for me?"

"Try? Son, I'm in a goddamned bakery with fluffy wedding cakes sitting in a pink chair. This is as low as it gets. I might as well cut off my balls right here and hand them to the feminazis that run this country now, turning the whole nation into a bunch of special snowflake liberals and their 'safe spaces.'"

Rueben rubbed his face and half-wondered if he should have let Pete blow him up.

Marshall sighed. "Yeah, I'm happy for you. I'm here, aren't I?"

"Are you, though?"

"Don't get smart with me. I swear, if my old buddies on the force were here right now, what they'd say to me…I don't even want to know."

"Okay, Dad."

Aki squealed as a large fly flew into her compact. She swatted at it. "Gross."

Marshall took a moment to pontificate. "See, this is what happens. When you start on this scale toward socialism, there's no money to maintain the buildings that there used to be, and our quality of living goes down. And we've got flies."

"Dad, Yolanda Martinez is not to blame for flies."

Laura returned with a tray of cake samples. "Okay, are we ready to try some cake?"

Aki put the compact away, and her smile had a little more edge than it did earlier. "Let's try some cake."

Laura expectantly put the samples in front of the trio. "This is our plain vanilla. Many people like this for the bridal cake because it's not so noisy and can accommodate a wide variety of preferences of wedding guests. One of the concerns we always have to be aware of is dietary needs, like peanut allergies and chocolate allergies."

Marshall scoffed around his cake. "Made-up bullshit. Meant to turn an entire generation into pussyfoot whiners. In my day, there weren't these bullshit allergies every which way. People ate their food, and they lived with it."

Laura chortled. "Oh, I'm sorry you feel that way. Let me... step back into the back, and I'll get some more flavors out for you. You...take your time with that vanilla and really taste those flavors."

Rueben swore he saw Laura close her eyes and take slow, deep breaths as she walked toward the back. If this hadn't been a prearranged operation, she would've thrown Marshall out of the store.

"Dad, you're going to get us thrown out. You have to watch what you say."

He slammed his plastic fork down. "No, I don't. This is America. Land of free speech. I should be able to say what I want to say."

Rueben sighed long and deep. "Yeah, but free speech doesn't mean you don't have to be polite."

"I'm polite enough, and don't you dare try to teach me manners. I'm your father, for Christ's sake."

The three sat in tense silence as a fly buzzed about the room.

Laura came back with another tray. "Okay, well, I've got you guys some punch to wash that down with. This is our classic wedding punch. We have multiple flavors, and we'll get you to sample those, too. And I have some coconut creme cake samples and some chocolate."

Each plate had a piece of cake with white coconut flakes peeking out, covered with white icing, and then a piece of chocolate cake with half a strawberry with glaze dripping off it.

Aki grabbed a plate. "Now, this looks good."

Laura smiled. "Doesn't it?"

The bell above the door clanged, and a young teenage boy entered.

Laura jumped up. "No, no, go, go."

"But I want to buy a cupcake."

"No, no, go. We're closed. Get out."

His friend came in after him, and the two boys stood in the doorway.

Laura shouted. "Go. I said go."

The two boys shrugged and left the store on their bikes.

Laura clasped her hand over her heart. "Excuse me. I—yeah, excuse me." She left the main floor and went into the back.

Rueben caught Aki's eye and made a questioning gesture toward her. Where was Pete? She shook her head and checked her phone.

Marshall continued to rant. "See, that's liberal hypocrisy right there. They want to say all are equal, but those two boys come in, and because they look like they don't have any money, what does she do? She runs them off. They're not worth her time. But oh, she wants to donate to the poor economy when it's the American tax dollars."

Aki dropped her fork and gave Rueben a look. "Tell you what, Marshall. You do us a favor. You taste this stuff and tell us what you think when you're finished. In the meantime, Rueben and I are going to fuck in the bathroom."

Marshall nearly choked on his cake, and Rueben's eyes widened. He had to remind himself it was all fake. It was all fake. *She doesn't mean it. She doesn't mean it.*

Aki stood and tapped her fingernails on the table, showing off her ring. "While we're gone, try not to piss anyone off. Oh, and pick chocolate. None of the snowflake vanilla shit, either." She crooked her finger toward Rueben, and he followed her.

Marshall laughed behind them. "Well, she sure as shit ain't Rachel."

Aki took Rueben into the hallway, and Rueben dug his hands in his pockets. "So where are we really going?"

"We're going to wait in the kitchen and watch for Pete on the security cameras."

"I gotta admit, fucking sounded more fun."

She laughed. "We may get to that later."

He cocked a sheepish smile. "Really?"

"Don't get too excited now. We have a lot of work ahead of us."

"Like not getting blown up or kidnapped by a psychopath."

"Yeah, that."

He followed her into the kitchen, where nearly a dozen agents in waitstaff uniforms stood around security cameras. They were bulky, and they carried tranq guns. They might stand a good chance at taking Pete down.

Aki was the first to speak. "Where are we?"

An agent wearing the nametag *Ernie* was the leader under Aki. "We haven't seen anything. Not on the street, not on the sidewalk. I don't know where this guy could be."

"Keep looking. Our intel is reliable."

"I'm looking, but we're not getting anything."

"Are we tracking Marshall's signal?"

Another agent who wore the nametag *Gus* sat on a counter with a laptop. "I'm tracking it. It's broadcasting, and someone's intercepting it, but right now the intercepting signal is scrambled. We've lost the triangulation and have no way of knowing where it's coming from."

Laura emerged from the back office. "Tell me we have something. Can we all go home soon?"

Fake Gus answered, "Not yet. We're still tracking the subject."

Laura sighed. "Can you please not sit on my food preparation space? If the health department came in right now, I could lose my license."

Fake Gus jumped off the counter. "Sorry."

"That goes for all of you. Hats or hairnets. Gloves, please."

The agents scrambled around trying to make their cover look more credible.

Laura stood against the counter and watched the security feed. "Please tell me there's a real reason you guys had to disrupt my business."

Aki tried to reassure her. "Ma'am, we can't tell you everything, but we're disrupting your business for the sake of the summit."

She sighed. "I sure hope that's the truth. Your dad is eating all my cake. Are you two even a couple?"

Rueben started to answer no, but curiously noticed that Aki avoided the question. Wait, was some of this real?

They watched the security camera more, and nothing happened. Marshall started to look bored.

Laura mumbled, "Archie Bunker needs more cake." She grabbed a tray and trudged out to the table where Marshall sat. Once she was in his eyesight, though, she perked up and switched to sales mode.

Fake Ernie nodded and watched the security footage. "Atta girl. Sell that cake."

Laura sat at the table with Marshall and talked to him for a while. He started to warm up on the camera, but there was still no attack. They waited. Rueben glanced up from the camera footage. It was after ten. They had been here for over an hour.

Fake Gus pulled out a deck of cards. "Anyone up for a game of poker?"

A couple of the agents joined in as they all waited.

Laura came back into the kitchen. "Any news?"

They all shook their heads.

"So when do we call it enough?"

"Not yet."

Marshall stood and straightened his belt and pants to leave. Aki and Rueben looked at each other. Aki messed up her hair, disheveled her clothes, and stumbled out onto the main floor, her face looking like she had slept with a coat hanger.

Marshall greeted her with a curt, "I'm ready to go."

"Just…just give us a few more minutes."

He took her in and raised an eyebrow.

She bit the side of her finger and stumbled backward. "Just a couple more minutes."

He smirked.

Aki disappeared back into the kitchen, and the agents applauded and whistled.

Fake Gus nodded approvingly. "Hey, next time can I fake-marry you?"

Everyone laughed except Rueben. This was all getting a little too messy and real for him.

The poker game continued, and they all watched the monitors. The fly buzzed around again, and Laura sighed. "What is the deal with this fly? We don't have a pest control problem here."

Suddenly a figure appeared on the camera outside the door. Rueben recognized him immediately. "It's Pete."

The agents dropped the card game and grabbed their tranq guns, tucking them inside their uniforms. They all inconspicuously found jobs to do on the main floor. Dusting, straightening, arranging the tables and chairs.

Pete stepped inside the cake shop and surveyed the room from under his hood and behind his dark sunglasses. Satisfied that no one was watching him, he walked up to Marshall. "Hello, Marshall Peet."

"What the hell do you want?"

Pete's mouth curled into a smile. "I'm looking for your son."

He drew his silenced pistol and guns cocked all over the room in Pete's direction. "Freeze."

CHAPTER TWENTY

Sunday, May 21, 8:30 p.m.

It was getting late, and Buzz had his mansion to himself. He'd worked most of the day on research about Pete as well as on some of his projects. He'd checked in on Rueben and Aki, and he wondered how the Marshall babysitting thing was going. That, he knew, was probably going to end badly.

Buzz leaned back in his cream leather armchair and sipped a drink. He closed his eyes and savored the vodka as it warmed his body and calmed his nerves.

Buzz suffered from severe anxiety. He often described living in his head as being trapped in an amusement park. Every waking minute, hundreds of ideas and thoughts and facts and theories and numbers and scientific laws bounced around, bumping into each other. He had learned that this was anything but normal.

In fact, if there was anything Buzz knew in life, anything at all, he knew that he was not...normal. Whatever that was. He'd known that when he was four and in preschool.

While the other kids played with blocks in Ms. Jessica's

classroom, he was bored out of his mind. He eventually wandered off, and when they finally found him, he wasn't outside on the playground.

No, Buzz Lugger ran away from preschool to hide in the book closet. He had stolen Ms. Jessica's college math book and laid on the floor and read math theory.

He found it scintillating to try to grasp the principles of college algebra. Numbers weren't just numbers. It wasn't just one, two, and three like Ms. Jessica tried to make the class believe.

Numbers were so much bigger and more exciting than that. They were dynamic entities moving about on a number line on a balanced scale of equality. They were quantities, objects, even ideas. It was like math was a language, almost an art.

Although much more controlled and predictable than the Crayon washable paints in Ms. Jessica's classroom, math was like a painting, but with known quantities.

The first thing he asked when they discovered him was, "So, how can changing the quantities of X and Y move the bell curve?"

Ms. Jessica, the slender, blonde twenty-three-year-old teacher, grabbed the text from his hand and scanned the page. "You want to know the truth? I don't know."

Buzz was the only kid in the history of St. Bartholomew's Day School to get kicked out for being too smart.

No, Buzz was far from normal. So neither was the noise inside his head. Most people did not have Ali Baba's circus tramping about upstairs every waking minute.

He had learned to relate to normal people by understanding that if total brain usage were a scale, most people spent their daily lives operating on a level five. When they were at the point of extreme concentration, all neurons firing, and their brain pathways lit up like an airport runway, they were at level ten. These were the kids who were fine with painting in Ms. Jessica's class.

Then there was him.

Buzz estimated that daily, he operated at about a level thirteen or fourteen. When he was at a point of extreme concentration, he ran at a level seventeen or eighteen. As such, the sensory input was more than he could take and gave him grave anxiety.

It was exhausting being Buzz.

When he was a kid, he had been medicated and seen dozens of therapists who put him on all sorts of experimental drugs. None of which did anything except give him a taste for reality-enhancing chemical reactions.

As an adult, he had since found that no prescription could calm the noise in his brain quite like the buzzing warmth of alcohol.

So Buzz sat surrounded by the plush leather, silk, and velvet, and all the fineries that money could buy and enjoyed the chemical reaction in his brain. He flipped on a David Attenborough nature documentary and let the British narrator massage his aching neural pathways.

Now he could think.

He thought about this Pete character. Maybe he wasn't related to Rueben somehow. He had to cover his bases, so he ran a comprehensive series of AI profile searches across all the country's criminal databases. Nothing. He had expected as much. With the futuristic tech Rueben described Pete as having, this man was either actually from the future or some parallel world.

While he thought on it, Buzz deleted his and his three

friends' arrest records from the corrections system. Now their arrests had never happened.

Maybe he could get lucky and catch Pete on video feeds from NYC city cams. He could have hacked into the system, but there was no need. He picked up the phone and called Erica in D.C. She was always good for help.

"White House Technology Advisory Department, this is Erica speaking."

"Hi Erica, it's Buzz Lugger over in New York."

"Oh, hi, Buzz. Did you get the blueprints I sent over for the U.N. building?"

"Yeah, I got them. I need you to do one more thing for me."

"Sure, what do you got?"

"I need you to patch me into the security feed for the NYC CCTV. We need to catch this bastard."

"Absolutely." There was a brief pause, and she returned. "There you go. You should be clear. Let me know if you need anything else."

"Thanks, Erica."

"You bet."

He ended the call, and sure enough, logged right into the NYC CCTV cams. The feeds filled up his laptop so he would need bigger screens.

He grabbed his computer and headed down to his basement.

The basement lair in Buzz's mansion was a massive room with vaulted ceilings and over two hundred monitors covering the walls. Long marble counters with computers of every kind filled the room's floor. Boxes and boxes of old computer parts lined the walls. This was where he tinkered with new AI devices. So various experiments lay around in different stages of completion. One day, when Rueben stopped needing him to kill him and all, he'd go back to tinkering with robots. But this part was fun, too. Saving the world and all had its charms.

Yeah, he could have worked for the CIA like Rueben and Aki. They'd offered. In fact, he'd been offered it before Reuben. Only after he turned it down did he recommend Rueben.

Buzz loved what the CIA had been at its creation. It was a clandestine organization designed around the development of new technology for political purposes. Now it had become all about counter-terrorism and global initiatives. They were no longer at the cutting edge of the science and tech field. In Buzz's mind, the CIA was irrelevant and growing more obsolete each year.

He was glad he never took the job and instead started as a science researcher at NYU. From there, the possibilities skyrocketed and the next thing he knew, he was flying on Air Force One advising the president's advisors. Well, that was partly because one of the president's advisors had stolen his research to get the job and now needed his input to keep her job.

But, he was happy with where life had taken him. And ever so grateful for the Road Not Taken at the CIA.

Rueben, for example, spent forty-plus hours a week over there and didn't know how to work even half of Buzz's equipment. The future of global security scared him.

He pulled up the CCTV footage on the screens and filled his lab with live images of the streets of New York. He had to find this guy. Based on his memory, he would have been at the Exit Bar at around 10:30 last night. He pulled up the archived footage and watched the evening. In grainy black-and-white video, he saw himself enter with Martha, Rueben, and Marshall.

Rueben stopped to talk to a homeless man. Buzz recalled seeing him before but couldn't quite place him. That guy was weird. But, weird piqued Buzz's interest, and he enhanced the image. He took down a description of the homeless man. He sure seemed to like his bucket of fried chicken...

Finally, Pete showed up in his white hoodie.

"There you are, you bastard."

He wore his hood up and seemed to be fully aware of where the cameras were. He moved his face this way and that, and Buzz couldn't get a full look at it. Even if he'd been able to, he knew what he'd find if he ran it through facial recognition: nothing.

He forwarded through the footage and saw the foursome run out the door, then Pete chased them. They all disappeared from the footage at that point. "Damn."

Buzz gathered still frames of Pete on the streets and tried to analyze them for clues. Nothing so far.

There was a knock at the door. "What is it, Rosa?"

Rosa came in carrying drinks. "I thought you might want your cleanse now that the others are gone."

He smiled at the maid and grabbed the drink off the tray. "Thank you, Rosa." He downed the drink all in one gulp. Yeah, it tasted awful.

"Is this the mysterious Pete?"

He turned to the screen and washed the bitter-tasting drink down with flavored water. "Yeah. I don't know what to make of him. He's a Repeater."

"Like Mr. Rueben."

"I'm trying to analyze footage of him for clues, but he always seems to know where the cameras are."

"Hm," Rosa said. "Play the footage for me."

When Rosa talked, Buzz had learned to listen. "Okay."

He did, and after a few moments, she gestured toward the computer. "May I?"

"Sure, have at it. I can't get anywhere with it."

Rosa leaned over and selected a photo of Pete and enhanced an image of him standing sideways. "He is wearing some kind of hi-tech body armor, yes?"

Buzz squinted at the screen. In the still shot, he could just make out the outline of the body-conforming armor beneath the hoodie as Pete turned. Damn, Rosa was good. "Yes. Among other pieces of advanced tech."

She narrowed her eyes in thought. Then with a quick key sequence, she enhanced the photo even further. Rosa peered at the photo. "See that little dot, Mr. Buzz?"

He scrutinized the pixels on the screen, and that's when he noticed a black speck on his white hoodie. "Looks like a fly. That's some impressive resolution blow-up."

"And not just in this one," Rosa continued. She flicked through the rest of the footage, pausing and zooming in to expose a tiny black fly resting on Pete's hoodie or buzzing about him. "It's in every one."

Buzz stared at Rosa. "He has a tiny drone."

CHAPTER TWENTY-ONE

Sunday, May 21, 8:30 p.m.

Martha and Zach pulled up near the tower in the unmarked police car. She felt a little uneasy driving it to commit a crime. Still, she couldn't think about any of that right now. The world depended on her and Zach to help stop a nuclear war.

She vented her guilt to Zach. "Sometimes, you have to bend the rules a little."

He gave her a puzzled look. "Yeah, John Grisham does it all the time."

"Uh...something like that."

They put on their hoodies and sunglasses and exited the car about a block from the tower. They walked the last stretch toward the back of the building. The tower at night was largely empty but still lit up with the cleaning crew and the workaholics burning the midnight oil.

Her heart raced. Slasher told her it would be like this. He also said the cameras at the back of the building didn't work, so she should try to stay on that side. She hoped the cameras still didn't work.

They arrived at a single-pane glass door, and Martha tried it in case it was open. It wasn't.

Zach pointed out the keypad. "That's what he was talking about."

She nodded. Slasher had said all the building workers carried a key fob that allowed workers in after hours.

But in the occasional instance that a key fob didn't work or was missing, or an after-hours delivery arrived, there was an emergency backup code. The code was #8800.

She glanced around and entered the code.

Pop. It opened.

She pulled open the door and glanced back at Zach in disbelief. He grinned with a full face. She whispered to him, "You're getting off on this, aren't you, Grisham?"

"Oh, this is seriously the coolest thing I've ever done...like, ever."

She made a face at him, and they approached the elevator. She pushed the button, and it wouldn't move. She noticed the keypad and fob sensor.

She wondered, "How did we get up here earlier?"

"Maybe it works on its own during the day."

She tried the #8800, but it didn't work on that elevator.

Zach looked confused. "What do we do now?"

It would have been nice to do this with Rueben and Aki. When they'd all gone to Canada together to capture Pout, the two CIA agents had called the shots and knew how to get around stuff like this. Right now, they were pretending to get married to keep Marshall busy. She thought about texting them, but a rush of pride kept her from it. She could figure this out on her own.

It was then she noticed the receptionist's desk down the hall and had an idea. "Take off your shades, but keep your face hidden. Come with me."

"Where are we going?"

She sauntered up to the desk and noticed the night guard. He was a young, dark-haired guy in a full-dress uniform that didn't suit him, and he pored over a college textbook. Perfect. She affected a really bad British accent, albeit the best she could do.

She knocked on the marble counter to get his attention. "Hullo?"

His head snapped up, and he shut the book. His dark eyes were fuzzy with concentration. "Hi."

"Hi, don't let me stop you. What are you in uni?"

She had once read that British college students referred to their time at university with the shorthand "uni." She hoped she was right, or at least that this guy didn't know the difference.

He cleared his throat and glanced down at the shut book. *Principles of Accounting.* "Uh, yeah, I…uh, I'm a business major. I've got finals tomorrow."

"Business? Brilliant. My husband, God rest his soul, was a businessman. He worked for Rupert Murdoch before he was Rupert Murdoch."

The kid's eyes lit up. "Really?"

"He's got successful media companies all over the world now—different BBC affiliates. I don't know about the organizational structure of it all. I just know every time I walk into the BBC, I get my arse kissed."

She laughed too loud, and his mouth dropped.

"Your husband owned BBC affiliates?"

"He did. I'm Rosie, by the way. Rosie McClintock."

She held out her hand, and he shook it. "Josh. Josh Montgomery. I'm a senior business major, and I've been looking for an opportunity or a foot in the door. You know, with the economy the way it is…"

"Never blame the economy, dear. It's laziness."

He blushed and shook his head. "Right."

"Of course, you've explored the internship here in New York, right?"

"Uh…I've not heard of that one."

"Oh, well, that's the place to start if you want to get into the BBC. Word to the wise, the BBC hires from within, so don't expect a recruiter or an advert."

"Got it." He scrambled for a piece of paper. "How would I apply?"

She smiled. "Well, dearie, I'll tell you what. You send your CV directly to me, and I'll see that it gets to the right hands."

He nodded vigorously and poised his pen. "Yeah, yeah. Where should I send it to?"

She made up a professional-sounding e-mail address, and he jotted it down.

"Now, dearie, can you do me a favor?"

"Yeah, yeah, anything."

"I've just been to the optometrist, these lights, ohh…" She pointed toward the fluorescent light fixtures above. "They give me a migraine."

"An eye doctor appointment on a Sunday, ma'am?"

Martha batted an eye at him. "For me, yes."

"Oh, right," the man said quickly and then glanced up at the ceiling lights. "Should I turn them off for you?"

Martha inwardly smirked. She had this guy. "You're such a doll, dearie. No, I just left something up at One Republic, and I can't seem to remember the key code."

He frowned and picked up the phone. "Well, I don't think there's anyone up there right now. Let me..."

She placed her palm over his hand. "I'd really rather not bother any of them up there. I just forgot my address book, and it would be a shame if that fell into the wrong hands, let me tell you. I know they're all busy. I just need to dash up there and get it."

He laughed uncomfortably and then glanced back up and down the e-mail address on his notepad. "What the hell." He caught her eye and then scrawled four digits onto a sticky note. 5399. He handed it to her.

"Well, thank you, Josh. I'll forward your CV to the internship director."

"Thank you, thank you."

She winked at him, then turned to Zach. "Come along, Robert."

They moved quickly down the hall toward the elevator, and she typed in the code. The elevator popped open, and she and Zach entered the car.

Zach replaced his shades and leaned against the back of the elevator as it rose to sixty. "Pretty good story."

"I thought so. I doubt he'll believe it for very long, but it bought us time up there, anyway. We'll have to be quick."

The elevator stopped at the sixtieth floor, and Martha and Zach stepped out into the One Republic lobby for the second time that day. This time it was dark and empty.

Martha breathed a sigh of relief. It would have ruined everything if one kiss-ass worker had pulled an all-nighter. They took for granted that there were likely security cameras all through here. This meant they had to keep their eyes covered. Walking through unfamiliar hallways in dark shades was much more difficult than she expected.

Zach followed her, glancing around for security cameras, and whispered, "Where exactly are we going?"

"Lucas' office. If there's something shady, it should be in there."

They found the room easily enough, and she tried the door. It was locked. "Damn." Martha inspected the construction. It was heavy double glass, and there was no visible lock. "It must lock electronically."

Zach peered into the office and pointed at a sensor in the ceiling. "Yep. That locks it on a timer."

"But how does he get in?"

On the side of the wall was a key fob, and Zach smiled. "This worked one time for me by accident. I'm going to see if it works this time." He pulled his keys out of his pocket and passed it over the fob pad. With a *beep*, the door popped unlocked.

Martha gasped and opened the door to Lucas's office. "How did you figure that out?"

They walked into the office, and he glanced around the expansive room. "Promise me you won't arrest me?"

Martha nodded.

"I won't explain how it works, but it's a universal fob key. Umm...not exactly legal, and it works on most smart locks like this one."

Martha bit her lip. "Shit. I didn't know such things existed. Where'd you get it?"

Zach swallowed. "A prize for winning an underground hacking competition. It was research into the criminal underworld. For the crime novel I'm writing. I swear I'm not..."

When she saw the nervous puppy dog look on Zach's face, Martha chuckled. "Your secret is safe with me. You and Buzz would get along nicely. Okay, what we need to find is everything on the One Response event."

Zach let out a breath and wiped his forehead with the back of his hand. "Right."

Zach and Martha crept around, not sure what they were looking for. There was a small filing cabinet and a desk with space for a laptop. A cube-style bookshelf held volumes on PR, and on the floor in a stack was a binder with the GRI logo.

She grabbed it. It was full, about five inches thick, and she flipped through it. It talked about "research for a global world" and "sustainability models for the human race." Was this a part of Pete's plan?

Martha didn't know, but the book in Lucas's office was proof that he was working with GRI on something. But what? Zach pulled a laptop out of a drawer and was trying to break into it.

She asked him, "Find anything?"

"Not yet. You?"

"They're definitely working with GRI on something."

"What's wrong with that?"

"GRI has a reputation for shady science, using the people of poor countries as cheap guinea pigs for scientific research."

He turned to face her, and his grin couldn't get any bigger. "Wow. This is a scandal."

"Keep looking. We don't have any proof that he's up to anything just yet."

Zach tried to restart the computer in safe mode, and Martha rifled through the filing cabinet. Client forms, invoices, everything looked good. She slammed the cabinet in frustration and placed her hands on her hips. She had to find something.

She paced the floor and tripped over something in the dark. "What the hell?"

Zach turned as she got off the floor. "What is that?" He picked the device up and risked turning on a desk lamp. It was gray, about a foot wide, with a boxy central housing containing a small storage compartment beneath it and four strut-like arms with propellers. "A drone." Zach played around with it, and it lit up with a bright blue LED light, a light so brilliant it would be worthy of being in a...

Martha's mouth dropped. "The light show. That's it. The light show. The drones are part of the light show."

"What do you mean?"

"The drones. That's how the attack goes down. The compartments underneath, they're for holding bombs—"

The hallway lights flipped on, and they heard yelling. "Rosie? Rosie McClintock?"

Zach and Martha stared at each other. "Oh shit."

They tried to slip out the office door, but that's when they saw them. Josh and a big burly security guard with tattoos and a nightstick. Josh pointed at them. "That's them."

The security guard charged in their direction. "Halt."

Josh sneered at Martha. "Nice try using the word 'uni,' and your British accent was mostly convincing. Once that e-mail bounced back, I knew you were lying. Oh, and that phony optometrist appointment on a Sunday...please. Who are you, and what are you doing here?"

Zach and Martha glanced at each other, and then they both ran for it, darting to either side of the guard. Josh and the security guard chased, and the guard radioed, "We've got a runner up on sixty. Get me some backup."

They ran down the maze of hallways with the two security guys in tow. There had to be a back entrance to the suite that would lead out into the main hallway. It would be a fire hazard to have this many workers and only one entrance. She searched for stairwell exit signs as the guards panting behind her yelled. She finally found one and yelled at Zach, who was running in the other direction, "This way."

She pushed open the door, and an updraft of chill air met her as she glanced down the stairwell's center past sixty landings. Would it kill building contractors to put insulation in stairwells? Not everyone took the elevator.

The blaring fire alarm jarred her from her thoughts, and she shrugged at Zach and the sixty stairwell landings below. "More workout than the treadmill."

She bounded down the stairs with Zach following behind her. "We're sitting ducks here, you know."

"They're not going to fire blindly down a staircase for breaking and entering. If we were injured, it would be too messy with the cops later on."

"Are you sure about that?" Zach looked up at the hefty security guard, who *thudded* down a few flights above them.

"No. Keep moving. Pick up the pace."

Zach channeled his inner schoolboy and started sliding down banisters—careful not to topple over the railing where he'd plummet to his death—and gained two or three staircases on Martha.

"Good. Just do that, like thirty more times or something."

Zach gave her a dirty look and motioned at the door of the thirty-fourth floor. She nodded, and he tried the door. It was locked, but Zach's magical key fob saved the day again.

They opened it and dashed inside, and quickly found the elevator.

Zach pressed the down button as she leaned over and heaved for breath. Yep, this was why people took the elevator. As they waited for the car, a door opened down the hall, and Josh and the security guard charged through the building. Zach and Martha stared at each other, and Martha cringed at the loud *ding* of the elevator bell. The metallic doors slid open, and they stepped on.

The yelling wasn't far off. The burly guard depressed a button on his radio. "Shit. They're on the elevator. Go, go, go."

She cringed and jammed the Door Close button, and it finally shut. Zach had it set to go to the ground floor, but she shook her head. "No, they'll be waiting for us there. Let's go somewhere they're not expecting. Like, six."

Zach panted. "Six?"

Martha nodded. "Then we take six flights down the stairwell and come out where they're not expecting."

"You're the boss."

The elevator stopped at six, and as they disembarked, she pressed all the other buttons to stall the elevator. "That way, it will take longer to come down."

The sixth floor was a publishing house, and Zach stopped and stared longingly at the empty bullpen.

"Hey Grisham, if you want to live to see your book published, I suggest you get running."

"Right, right."

He ran, but he stopped when they found the editor's office. He looked at Martha longingly, then pulled out his phone and snapped a photo of the nameplate. "I'll look him up later."

"Great. We don't have time."

"Right."

They found another interior stairwell and ran the last six stories to the first floor. By the time they reached it, Martha was out of breath and dizzy. "Look, a doorway to the outside. Let's go."

They stepped outside, this time on the ground floor. Martha quickly ascertained her surroundings. They weren't too far from the car. "This way."

They ran at full speed and made it to the car as police sirens pulled up to the building. Zach looked scared. "We're all over those cameras."

"We were pretty disguised, I think."

"I hope."

"Calm down. I know some people on the force. We'll be good." She hoped.

Zach didn't appear convinced. Martha calmly pulled out onto the street as two police cars whizzed past. Without drawing any unwanted attention, she eased away in the other direction, and they merged into traffic.

Once they were out of danger, Zach laughed. "That was cool."

"You think so?"

Her heart was beating out of her chest. But now she knew.

One Republic and GRI were going to bomb the World Summit using a drone light show.

They weren't going to get away with this.

Or were they?

CHAPTER TWENTY-TWO

Sunday, May 21, 9:49 p.m.

The scene at Laura's Pastries had now turned pretty tense. Nearly half a dozen waiters had blown their cover and trained their tranq guns on Pete, still hooded, still wearing sunglasses. Marshall sat at the table, palms raised, unmoving, and the gunman stood with his weapon jammed into Marshall's neck.

Pete sneered beneath his hood and sunglasses. "Well played, well played. I wouldn't have guessed that one." He held up his silenced pistol in pseudo-surrender.

Aki sauntered onto the main floor, her weapon—loaded with bullets, not darts—held high. "Drop the gun."

He winked. "You know I like it when you talk dirty to me."

"You wish. You're going to jail, asshole. For a very long time."

"No, I won't. But, I guess it's all part of the script, isn't it now?" Stepping away from Marshall, Pete delivered a lightning-fast spin kick, sending the weapon flying out of her hand. Everyone in the room hit the floor as the loaded gun crashed against a wall and clattered against the floor.

Marshall yelled at him. "Are you fucking nuts?"

The man laughed. "Of course I am. Then again, so are you. And I guess so are we all, really. Sanity is the crutch of an infertile mind, I say."

Fortunately, the weapon didn't fire as it fell onto the floor with a loud spinning clatter. Rueben rushed over to check on Aki.

With that, all hell broke loose. Fake Ernie jumped over the counter and tried to pin the gunman down, but Pete was quicker. He delivered a hard right to the jaw and a simultaneous kick to the gut that sent the agent reeling.

"Ah, I thought you would be more interesting as an opponent. That quick?"

Two agents shot at the moving target. They'd swapped their tranq guns for pistols. Several bullets deflected harmlessly off Pete's hi-tech body armor, tearing holes in his hoodie, and several more missed him and hit the windows instead.

In one fantastic moment, the storefront glass shattered, and the shards fell like raindrops to the white linoleum, along with splintered pieces of wood.

Laura screamed and ran for cover, yelling something about insurance. "Are you people all crazy?"

The distraction of the exploding glass bought Fake Ernie enough time to recover his footing and grab Pete from behind. He wrestled him to the floor, and with a little help from some of the other agents, they all pinned Pete's wrists behind him.

Ernie jerked Pete's restrained body up off the floor to look at his face. "Who are you?" Pete sneered and, now in a standing position, tried to wrest away.

"Let me go," Pete said calmly. "Or I'll blow your scrambled brains all over this goddamned room."

Laura screamed. "Please, no scrambled brains."

Multiple guns stayed trained on Pete and Ernie while they wrestled, but none of the agents fired for fear of hitting Ernie.

"Just shoot!" Ernie said.

"Doris, pulse," Pete said, and invisible shockwaves blasted outward from the metallic gauntlet in his hoodie's pouch. The agents went flying, as did cake stands and fancy glass vases filled with mints positioned throughout the room. Pete took the opportunity to slip the gauntlet onto his hand.

Rising like a bull elephant, Marshall went completely ballistic and tore into Pete from behind in a dirty street fight move. They crashed to the bakery floor. Marshall threw a solid fist into Pete's chest and grunted when his knuckles connected with metal. Laura yelled about blood on the floor, and a couple of the agents rushed forward. They restrained Pete and pulled Marshall away.

Marshall wiped the blood off his lip. "Fucking pussy. You wouldn't last one day on the force."

Pete laughed. "I'm not trying to. Being a cop doesn't seem like a worthwhile occupation."

Marshall glanced down at a tranq gun on the floor in front of him, dropped by one of the agents. He stared at it longingly, and an agent stopped him. "Let's get you out of here."

Marshall reluctantly let the agent escort him out of the bakery.

Pete laughed and struggled against the agents restraining him. "You don't know who you're dealing with."

"Is that right?" An agent held a tranq gun extended.

"Doris, obliterate!"

A rush of invisible energy brought part of the ceiling down

on Pete and the agents. The latter fired tranq darts, but they all missed.

Rueben knew he had to act fast. "Doris. Disable."

A tiny green light on Pete's glove tuned red. Pete scowled. "I see you've met Doris already. Oh well."

Aside from Rueben and Pete, Aki was the only other person still on her feet. Pete turned to her, and in a flashy move, threw back his hood and tore off his sunglasses.

Aki flinched. "Rueben. It *is* you."

Pete grimaced. "You told them already? You ruined my fun." He turned back to Aki, his serious face lightening. "Well, at least now you get to see what you're getting if you choose to be with Rueben. He'll eventually turn into the bad boy you're always looking for."

"Will not!" Rueben shouted.

Pete cocked his head toward Rueben. "I think you will. I did, after a few hundred jumps."

Rueben gulped. "Jumps?"

"Yeah, jumps. You call them time warps. Somewhere about two hundred jumps ago, I just decided to start living exactly how I wanted and turned to the dark side." He laughed. "Luke, I am...well...*you*."

Rueben scoffed. "That was the worst Darth Vader parody I think I've ever heard."

"I think you are the worst parody of you."

"Huh? What? I'm never going to turn into you."

Pete rolled his eyes. "You know what they say about 'never say never.' You'll turn dark."

Rueben realized his hands were shaking. "I would never. I repeat, *never*, try to start a nuclear war that would kill millions of people."

Pete shook his head glumly. "You don't get it. You can't. Not yet. But you will. You will."

Rueben shoved a finger at Pete in defiance. "I'm not you!"

Pete sneered.

"What happened to you? Why are you like this?"

"You don't know what you're missing. I tried to follow the rules once. I was uptight and scared all the time. I was always worrying about shit like, 'What will she think,' or 'Did I say the right thing?' or 'What should I tell my boss'? Ugh. It was exhausting as hell. And quite frankly, boring as fuck. I sure as hell wasn't getting any action alone in my twin bed. So finally, I shoved one massive middle finger into the face of all that is right and good, and look, now I own all of you. I've got every one of you turned upside down wondering what the hell you should do with me."

"You're full of shit," Aki said as she edged toward a tranq gun lying on the floor.

He turned to Aki and licked his lips. "Go ahead. Go for it. You know, we have our little fun, you and me. But, eh. You're not half as interesting as you think you are. You're a cheap, knockoff Bond girl."

Real Rueben stammered for a reply, but nothing came out but empty grunts. From behind them, one of the agents groaned.

Hot tears of anger welled up in Aki's eyes. "I am not a Bond girl." She kicked Pete square in the crotch, and he cried out. "That interesting enough for you?"

He laughed. "You're so boring and predictable. You really only have a few moves, you know. After that, you're like a bad Kesha song. Blah, blah, blah. Me? I have a wide variety of different tools."

With that, the annoying fly from before buzzed past

Rueben's and Aki's faces before coming to a perch on Pete's shoulder. "Meet this world's smallest drone. Good for remote surveillance, and it alerts me to the presence of security cameras. It also has a handy nanobot injector."

Rueben cursed under his breath, recalling the "fly" that had bit him at the Exit Bar, implanting the nanobot "cap" in him. He and Aki made to rush toward Pete, but their opponent had already picked up a display table and launched it at them. They both went down in a tangled heap as Pete jumped out the broken storefront window.

Laura dashed out from the kitchen and threw a piece of shattered glass in Pete's direction. "Asshole!"

The agents picked themselves up, grabbed their weapons, and ran out the door.

Laura plopped down amidst the broken glass and whimpered. "I poured my whole life savings into my shop. Everything I had..."

*Damn...*Rueben picked himself up and watched the shop owner lamenting on the demolished floor. He turned to Aki and told her he'd catch up. Aki followed the agents outside as Rueben helped Laura up. He had to do something to help her —he was the reason Pete had come here in the first place. Why couldn't the CIA agents have been more prepared?

Oh, right. Because Pete is me and thinks like me and outsmarted us again.

Rueben kicked a shard of glass. It skittered along the floor until it cracked against a table leg. Then Rueben retrieved his business card from his pocket and handed it to Laura. The card didn't have his real name or phone number or anything associated with the CIA on it, but it would help her. "Call this number sometime this week. The government will reimburse you for everything."

She took it and didn't say anything.

Rueben shuffled out through the door to join Aki and the rest of the team.

He moved slowly as if in a daze. As he searched for Aki and the other agents, he couldn't help but review Pete's words and explanation of how he would eventually go bad. He wouldn't do that. He wouldn't. He wouldn't let himself become addicted to warping or jumping or whatever the hell it was that messed Pete up. He wasn't going to warp back in time to fix every little wrong thing he said or did.

But what if he had to keep saving the world from the likes of Pout and Pete and who only knew who else?

Rueben sighed and started jogging down the sidewalk.

When he first realized his powers, he'd never thought this might go on for decades. He'd always thought that one day he'd quit warping and live a normal life. Maybe with Aki.

He was in love with her, and he was tired of hiding how deep his feelings for her were. He'd spent so much more time with her that she would never know about—when he died and warped back. The whole engagement façade had made him even more confused, which made matters worse. Sure, it was a game. His feelings for her weren't. How did Aki really feel about him? He'd gotten to see the flirty, actress side of her as of late, but was it all a show? A performance?

Suddenly he thought about the implications of having a family. Could he raise kids and live with the ability to time warp? How would that work? Every time his kids got themselves into trouble, would he kill himself to go back and fix the problem? That couldn't be right.

One day he'd want to settle down and live a normal life, spend the weekends mowing and the summers at Cape Cod. Or wherever normal people spent summers. He wouldn't know. It wasn't like Marshall had been big on summer vacations.

Of course, for all that to happen, he'd have to quit dying. For him to stop dying, crazed killers would have to stop hijacking and blowing things up. That sure would help.

Spotting Aki and the agents across the street, Rueben rushed after them.

CHAPTER TWENTY-THREE

Sunday, May 21, 10:26 p.m.

Rueben leaned over and panted. "Where is he?"

Aki pointed at a street to their left, with a small schoolyard out front. "He went that way. The other agents cut him off and cornered him, but he managed to dodge capture." Aki looked around. "We need a car."

Rueben shook his head. "We know what happened last time we stole a car."

She cocked her head. "I'm not losing this one. *We* can't lose this one. This guy's going down."

He wasn't quite sure what to make of her resolve. This was his futuristic self they were pursuing so the whole chase bothered him a little.

Marshall pulled up on a stolen golf cart. "Let's get this bastard. Hop on."

Rueben made a face. "I thought I saw some agents escort you away—"

"Hah." Marshall raised a meaty palm as if taking a solemn oath. "I don't run from a fight, son."

"Um…okay. But a…golf cart?"

"Yeah. I know some people on this block from when I patrolled it back in the day. Guy half a block down from here owed me a favor—I asked to borrow his golf cart." He snorted. "Rich people. Buy whatever they want. Not like you can play golf in the streets of NYC. But I digress. You want to keep trying to get there putting one foot in front of the other, or you want to jump in?"

"Sure, but…"

"What? It's a damn golf cart. Oh hell, is this about the time when you were ten?"

Rueben glanced embarrassedly at Aki. "Dad, we don't need to share the details—"

Aki hopped onto the golf cart. "I'd like to hear—" She stopped talking when she saw Rueben's pale face.

"It'll be fine, son. Just get on."

Aki leaned out and touched Rueben's shoulder. "We have to catch Pete."

Marshall growled. "Son, the midnight train don't wait forever. Get on."

Rueben bit his lip and hopped on. Marshall floored it, and the thing lurched forward faster than Rueben would've guessed. Suddenly, Rueben and Aki crashed awkwardly into each other's arms as Marshall jerked the wheel to the side and pulled up onto the sidewalk. "Which way?"

Aki weakly smiled as she pulled herself away from Rueben and pointed. "Left turn."

Marshall veered in a sharp left and sailed through the schoolyard on the golf cart. His two passengers tried not to fall on top of each other, but the speed made it practically impossible.

Rueben asked, "Couldn't we have taken one of our cars? Aki has a Porsche."

"Don't spit on the cart, son. Traffic. Ever hear of it? God, you and your Columbia education. It's called common sense. Walk if you want. I don't give a shit."

Marshall accelerated the cart down an abandoned alley, squeezing between two buildings, circumventing half a block of street driving in the process.

"I'm not spitting on the cart. I'm just wondering why we couldn't—"

Marshall's impatience was thick. "Because we'd have to find it first, and when you're on a foot pursuit, having a car slows you down cause you've got to find a place to park, and you get stuck in traffic and at stoplights. You get stuck at one stoplight in a foot chase and your suspect's history. Gone, scattered to the wind. And no Porsche can do this."

A shabby warehouse building loomed up ahead, and a tired employee in jeans and a canvas jacket leaned against its wall puffing on a cigarette.

Rueben's fingers gripped the golf cart's frame. "Marshall. What are you doing?"

Marshall faced Rueben, childlike glee reflected in his old man's eyes. "Taking another shortcut, son. You might want to hold on."

Rueben did, and Marshall guided the golf cart through an open overhead door of the warehouse's façade while the smoking employee stared wide-eyed. The cigarette fell out of his mouth.

The warehouse's interior was dark.

"Oh shit." Rueben recalled his accident with the golf cart in his childhood. Then he felt Aki's warm hand grip his, and he eased up a bit.

"Want to talk about it?"

Rueben gave his head a vigorous shake. "We don't talk about the golf cart incident."

Marshall whooped as he narrowly avoided a forklift transferring pallets of bricks through the warehouse. However, he didn't miss a wooden crate sitting off to the side, and it crunched and grated against the cart's bumper and undercarriage.

Rueben's jaw tightened.

"Hang on, son. We're almost in the clear."

Rueben didn't see how. Through the golf cart's windshield, they were facing a solid wall.

An employee wearing a hard hat was sitting at a desk near the wall. By the look of him, he might've been the foreman.

"Police!" Marshall cupped one hand over his mouth and repeated it. "Police. Now open the goddamned door!"

The foreman leapt up from his seat as if his granny had smacked him. Then, spinning on his feet, his hand latched onto the doorknob of a door hidden along the darkened wall, and he threw it open.

A doorway of light glared back at them, and Marshall floored it through the opening with an excited, "Much obliged!"

Rueben relaxed. Marshall was right. They had made it after all. He glanced at Aki. It seemed she didn't think him a complete wuss for being scared of a golf cart.

Up ahead, they now saw the other agents in pursuit, guns drawn. Pete's shot-up white hoodie was visible far into the distance.

Marshall floored it through the alleyway. "Let's get this bastard."

"Glad for the help, Dad."

"Well, I figured it meant a lot to you, seeing as you were willing to get fake-engaged for it and all."

Aki and Rueben glanced at each other guiltily. "You knew about that?"

"Of course I knew. Who the hell goes cake tasting at eight o'clock at night? And for all the dumbass shit you do, I'd like to think you'd at least know better than to give her what's-her-face's ring."

Marshall scoffed, and Aki laughed and fingered the ring.

Rueben smiled sheepishly. "Why didn't you say anything?"

"I figured you were up to something weird, and whatever it was, you were probably going to need your ass saved. Maybe a phone call to the precinct."

Marshall snorted, but Rueben smiled. It really killed him to say a couple of nice things, didn't it?

A couple of agents on foot on the sidewalk were starting to tire, and the golf cart raced past them. One of them motioned to around the corner of a building. "He's up ahead."

Marshall guided the cart around the corner as Pete's white hoodie disappeared. Pete was in really good shape physically.

Marshall slowly drove past a dumpster in a back alley, and they all scanned behind stairways and buildings. No sign of him.

He asked Aki, "You think he went inside somewhere?"

"No. He's too hot to sit still, and he knows it."

They reached the end of the alley and arrived at a chain-link fence. Reuben spotted Pete about ten yards ahead of them with his fingers poised to climb. There was no time to talk. Rueben jumped out of the moving vehicle and booked it toward Pete.

He reached Pete when he was about halfway up the fence, wishing he had a tranq gun. "Stop it, Pete."

Pete turned, sneered, and abandoned his climb over the fence. He jumped back down to the ground and dusted off his hands. "Ah, you caught up to me. I knew that would happen eventually. There are enough of you, anyway. I'm glad it was you."

Marshall called that he would try to flag down some reinforcements while Aki blocked off the alley in case Pete got past Rueben. Rueben stepped up to his counterpart standing by the fence. "You are not me."

Pete winced. "Yeah, I'm sorry. I really am. You turn into a real asshole later on in life. Or, maybe I turn you into one. Who knows? Chicken or the egg, that eternal question."

"You're not going to do this."

"Do what?"

"Attack the summit."

"Who says I'm doing that?"

"I know you're behind it."

"Why would you think that?"

"Please, don't play dumb with me."

"I'm interested to know what I might have said to give you that impression."

"I saw it on the news footage. When you kidnapped me and took me to your hidden lair in an abandoned skyscraper. You know, the one owned by one of Pout's conglomerates?"

"You know about that place? Shit. That's probably where you found out about Doris. But you know, it's for the best that you know everything now. What I'm doing…it's one of those things that I can do, and you're too worried about doing the right thing."

"Killing half the world's leaders is for the best? What kind of twisted logic is that?"

"It's what you want to do."

"I can assure you that it's not."

"Oh, Reuben. Still so locked up. It'll be a while before you're free. See, you're a nationalist. You believe in a free democracy and get choked up during the *Star Spangled Banner*. That's why you went to work for the CIA—to preserve democracy."

"What's your point?"

"The point is, not even democracy can save the world. Not even a united global government can. It will come and ravage the world no matter what. Like it did…" Pete realized what he was saying and let his words trail off.

Rueben blinked. "What the hell are you talking about? *It* will come? What is *it?*"

Pete cursed. "I've said too much. It doesn't matter. Not really. You'll find out eventually."

"The main thing is, if I don't do what I have to do, you will curse yourself for being in the right place at the right time but not having the balls to do anything about it. So now here I am doing everything that you want to do but can't find the strength to."

Rueben gulped. "I would never try to start a nuclear war. Never."

Pete made a motion with his palm. "Blah, blah, blah."

Rueben shook his counterpart's twisted logic away. "You won't succeed in doing it with me in this timeline."

"How disappointing. I had hoped you'd have found the balls in this reality. I guess I went back too far."

"Reality? Huh? Your bullshit's not going to work on me. I will lock you up in an iron box and kill you if I have to in order to stop you from killing millions of people."

Pete sneered. "What was that?"

"I said, I will kill…you." Rueben realized what he had said.

"Remember what I said about 'never say never?' I'd say you're learning fast the ways of the jumper. You're becoming me much sooner than I would've guessed possible."

Rueben shook his head. "Shut up. That's not what I meant—"

Pete chuckled. "Besides. If you do manage to kill me, I'll come right back and finish the job with or without you, as Bono would say."

"Your pop-culture references are annoying."

"I'm sorry, am I not entertaining enough for you? Should I tap dance? You're still a dancer, right?"

"No. You should die. Die and never come back." Rueben leapt forward in a rage and grabbed Pete's shoulders. Pete laughed as if enjoying it and easily shoved him to the side, where he toppled over two metal trash cans.

Pete stared down at Rueben with disappointment scrawled over his face. "After all that combat training so that you could stop Pout, I would think you'd be a lot better than this."

Rueben picked himself up from a pile of garbage. He shook the remains of a rotten banana peel from his shoulder. "Shut up."

"Oh, and you know what?" Pete crossed his arms. "You eventually start running and working out regularly to try to impress or keep Aki's affection. Spoiler alert, she stops believing you're a mysterious badass. Once she leaves you, you won't set foot in a gym."

"Aki leaves me?"

"Oh, come on. Did you really think you'd hold her attention for that long? She's going through her 'nerd phase' only because you're not Mike, and she's still broken-hearted over him."

The words were everything Rueben feared and didn't want

to hear. With a violent yell, he grabbed Pete by the neck and slammed him against a dumpster.

He grabbed his head and rammed it over and over against the hard metal. He completely zoned out and blinded by rage as if in a dream, he kept repeating the movement. He felt the man's blood run down his fingers and didn't care. He kept ramming Pete's head against the dumpster. Was this what losing it felt like? There was a certain high to it that felt cathartic. Why was Pete letting him do this? It was masochistic. And Rueben was...

He shifted his attention away from Pete and down to the blood on his hands.

That's when Pete finally kicked him hard enough that he fell on the asphalt, scraping over gravel. Sharp, paralyzing pain shot through Rueben's back, and he couldn't move.

Was his back broken? It hurt to move. He grimaced in pain, and Pete drew out a syringe from under his hoodie. He crouched down next to Rueben. "Nighty-night—oomph!"

With a single solid punch, Marshall had sent Pete face-first into the side of the dumpster. Marshall's fist popped like a firecracker, but he didn't even grimace.

Pete rose, and with one finger wiped the blood off his lip. Interestingly enough, there was a piece of thrown-out greasy hash brown smeared onto his pants leg, and he wiped it off. His lips quivered as if he'd sustained a mortal injury, but then he composed himself.

Man, this version of me is weird. Rueben tried to pick himself up, but his back still ached intensely.

Marshall stepped between Rueben and Pete, and Pete froze, his fingers still wrapped around the syringe. Pete's hand began to shake as he spotted someone behind Marshall, standing in the shadows of the alley. His eyes narrowed with confusion or frustration.

At this point, the pain in Real Rueben's back subsided enough that he was able to regain his footing. Marshall took a step toward Pete, but then Pete turned and ran like hell.

It was only then that Reuben noticed the homeless man—the Chicken Man—who'd also been outside the Exit Bar. He caught Reuben's eye. "You're welcome, Rueben."

Then the man walked away.

Reuben's mouth dropped, and he chased after the homeless man. "Wait, wait. Who are you?"

The homeless man cowered as Rueben approached him. "My name's Jim."

"Jim. Okay, so you know me?"

The homeless man didn't answer and instead mumbled and entered a storefront liquor store.

Aki huffed as she arrived on the scene. "What happened?"

"He got away." Then Rueben pointed at the liquor store. "But I know someone who I think has some answers. We're going to talk to him and get them."

CHAPTER TWENTY-FOUR

Sunday, May 21, 9:00 p.m.

Martha and Zach sat in her office in the largely empty precinct.

"So, what have we learned?"

"Other than there's a publishing house in the same tower as One Republic?"

Martha rolled her eyes. "Yes, other than that."

"We've uncovered that One Republic is doing a light show with drones during the One Response pre-show. What does that have to do with anything?"

"How else would you attack the summit?"

"Good point. Do you think Lucas is in on it?"

"I would venture eighty-twenty he is."

"Okay, so we have to find proof."

She paced the room and tapped the dry erase marker against her palm. "Proof. How could we prove that these drones connect to... Where are they now? That's the question."

Zach's face brightened. "Hey, I bet my friend could answer that."

"Your friend isn't going to know about some super-secret bomb plot."

"No, but he might know if there's a storage unit somewhere."

Martha swigged from a bottle of water. "Well, it's worth a try. We've gotten leads on worse ideas."

Zach pulled out his phone and stepped out of the room as he dialed up his buddy.

Martha called Buzz.

He answered with an annoyed, "This had better be good."

"Drones."

"What about them?"

"That's how they're planning to attack the summit."

"We know this. That's what Rueben already said."

"No. One Republic Entertainment is teaming up with GRI to do a light show for the event rally. The light show is going to release two hundred LED drones outfitted with bombs over the summit."

Buzz let the words sink in. "You know this?"

"Pretty sure. We found one of the drones, but it might have been a prototype. We need to find the rest of them."

"You found one of them? Where?"

"The One Republic office. The one we broke into tonight during your jacuzzi soak."

"Oh, right. How'd that go?"

She smirked. "Thanks for your help and all. We couldn't have done it without you."

"Oh, don't be too modest. You underestimate yourself."

"Well. How would you find two hundred drones?"

"It's not that hard. Drones broadcast an IP address, which makes them fairly easy to hack."

Zach came back in, and Martha wrapped up the conversation. "Thanks. I might need you for backup. I'll call you later."

"Ciao, darling."

She ended the call, and Zach sat.

"Who was that?"

"My friend Buzz. He's a scientist, works on contract for the White House."

"Whoa. You know someone like that?"

"Yeah. In fact, I do."

"You think he may be involved with the drone attack?"

It hadn't occurred to Martha until Zach said that. She didn't know Buzz that well, and Buzz was well-connected enough that he could easily orchestrate something like a drone attack. That would explain why, off the cuff, he knew about GRI. As for a motive…God only what went on in that head of his. Plus, he'd been reluctant to help them break into the tower. Still, Rueben trusted Buzz, and Martha trusted Rueben.

She answered Zach the best way she knew. "Buzz is good."

The question hung in the air, though, and Martha tried to squash it. "He knows about drones and how to hack them. What did your friend say?"

Zach drew a deep breath and glanced over his notes. "He said there was a lot of talk about drones, but everyone was really secretive about it."

"Not a good sign."

"Nope. I asked him where he thought they might be stored. He said he didn't know, but the company has a few storage spaces. He gave me a couple of places."

"They wouldn't store bombs in a mini-storage lot."

"No, they wouldn't. So I kept pressing him for more information, and he finally said Lucas and a couple of the other executives like to go with the GRI guys out to someplace in New Jersey."

"New Jersey?"

"Yeah. That was all he said."

"Where? Do you know?"

"Nope. That was all the information he had."

"Okay. Let's try to find places in New Jersey that might be big enough to hold this kind of thing. Also, let's get Buzz…"

She searched her bag and found Lucas's business card, then redialed Buzz and put him on speaker.

"Did you miss me so soon?"

"Yeah. Can you hack into a cell phone?"

"Probably. Why?"

"I have a cell number, and I need to find every address that cell phone has been to recently. Is that possible?"

"Fairly. What's the number?"

She read Lucas's cell number from the card. He repeated it back to her.

Zach jumped in on the call. "Hey, what portal are you using to get in?"

"What?"

Martha chuckled. "That's Zach. He's helping with this."

"You know how to get into secure systems?"

"Eh, I play around."

Buzz laughed. "Well, I do a lot more than play around. It'll take a bit to run this. I'll call you."

"Thanks."

She ended the call, and Zach grinned. "He's a hacker, huh?"

"Oh my God, world-class."

Zach nodded approvingly. "I think I like this guy."

Martha raised her eyebrow. "Let's focus on possible drone locations in New Jersey."

An hour later, both Martha and Zach were drowning in coffee and notes.

Zach rubbed his face. "There is no way to find this out. These drones could be anywhere in that state. It could be in a farmhouse. It could be in a warehouse. It could be...even bad information. All he actually said was that they take business trips to New Jersey a lot. They could be meeting with a client, for all we know."

"Trust me, if they're taking the GRI guys down there, that's where they've probably got the drones. Besides, we're running out of time. It's our best shot to go with it."

"I will admit, GRI creeps me out."

Martha's phone rang, and she wanted to jump up and cheer when she saw it was Buzz. "Buzz, tell me something. Did you get in?"

"I did."

"I'm going to cry right now. Tell me, what did you find?"

"First of all, there are a lot of potentially incriminating emails. No hard evidence, but he's in pretty deep with them."

"Really? How deep?"

"They've kept it all vague for this very reason. But there's enough that Lucas Cameron's in on it."

"I don't know why he'd want to bomb all the world's politicians. I met him, and I got that he was a little bit of a young, rich, hot asshole. If you'd said he was into some shady accounting or something, I'd be quick to believe it. But I didn't get the impression that he's the type to assassinate world leaders."

"Oh, from these emails, he doesn't. It sounds like someone's blackmailing him."

"What do they have on him?"

"It looks like someone has threatened to kill his mother."

Zach chimed in, "Hey Buzz, Zach here."

"Hey, Zach."

"Would you mind forwarding me those emails? I'd like to take a look at them. Also, were you able to search for an IP address on the sender?"

"I did not. Let me run that." Buzz was quiet for a moment, then he chuckled. "Yep. It's bouncing off a tower near Trenton, New Jersey."

Zach did an online search for GRI Trenton and came up with an address. "I just found their offices. It looks like this one is under Marc Woolard." He read off the address to Buzz. "So, you were going to send me those emails, right? I'd like to analyze them."

"Yeah, hold your horses, man. I'm forwarding the relevant ones right now. As far as your other question, I have good news."

"Please tell me you found the address."

"I did. He—and when I say he, I mean his phone—goes to an address outside Trenton pretty frequently. It's about a mile from where Zach found their address. I looked it up, and it belongs to Gerhardt Military Base."

Zach grinned. "A military base? Yeah, that's where you'd hide your bombs."

Zach and Buzz laughed in unison. Martha raised an eyebrow. "So you're sure this is where he goes in New Jersey?"

"Yes. He's been there…let's see…three times in the last week."

"That's where the drones would be. Okay, thanks, Buzz."

"Yeah, thanks, Buzz, and send me those emails."

"Jesus, man. I will."

They ended the call, and Martha grabbed her bag.

Zach looked confused. "Where are you going?"

"New Jersey. You coming?"

Zach glanced around the office. "Right now?"

"No. After the terrorists have a chance to transport the drone bombs to the summit tomorrow. Yes, right now."

Zach jumped up, grabbed his stuff, and sipped one last time from his coffee cup. "Let's go."

They left the office, and the cool evening breeze reminded her that hours earlier, they had narrowly escaped from Lucas's office. Now they were closing in on him. She hoped.

With traffic at this time of night, it was about an hour and a half drive to Trenton, and Zach had his laptop out the entire way. He was reading through the emails from Lucas's phone.

"The light show was supposed to symbolize peace and unity, and the light of a new era."

"A new era, that's for sure."

"The guy from GRI was supposed to be…Marc Woolard and Geoff Van Housen. They've built the drones and have them programmed to dance in the air in formation."

"Formation? What do you mean?"

"It sounds like the drones are programmed kind of like fireworks to make shapes in the air."

"I'd like to see that. Not that they're going to do that."

"No, but they're programmed to make hearts and peace symbols and some flowers... Ooh, and they're going to make all the flags of the countries represented at the summit."

"That's a nice touch."

"Yeah. Then they have a couple of phrases they're going to do in different languages. 'One World. One People. One Planet For All.'"

"Is that the One World campaign slogan?"

"I think. But, I don't see anything that sends up a red flag. I'll have to call Buzz." He pulled out his phone and called Buzz. Within minutes, all talk of drones and bombs was out the window, and Martha was lost listening to them talk about hacking.

Zach launched into a long story that Martha couldn't follow, then ended with the punch line, "Well, you know there are ten types of people in the world—those who understand binary, and those who don't."

Zach dissolved into laughter and heard Buzz laugh through the phone. "That's true, man. All right, call me when you get there."

"Cool." Zach ended the call and turned to Martha. "How did you meet this guy?"

Martha laughed. "Oh, just around. You know there are ten types of people in the world—those who get Buzz and those who don't."

Zach frowned. "That makes no sense. That was only two, and why ten?"

Martha tried to backtrack. "That was what you did with the other joke."

"What joke?"

"You know, ten types of people who understand binary—"

Zach laughed at the joke all over again, and Martha gave up. Some things she would never understand.

———

Gerhardt Military Base was a small compound of concrete buildings. Razor-wire fences surrounded it and guardhouses every dozen yards or so.

Martha parked, and Zach frowned at the buildings. "How do we get in?"

She noticed the uniformed guard staring at their vehicle. "That doesn't look promising."

"Yeah. We can't exactly sneak in like this."

"There has to be a simple way around this, though."

Zach called Buzz and put him on speaker. "Hey, dude. Listen, it's like totally a secure compound. How do we hack in?"

"Gerhardt, right?"

"Yeah."

"Hold on." Buzz typed furiously for a few minutes. "You have access to a website?"

Zach repositioned his open computer on his lap. "Yeah, go ahead."

"Okay, this is what you're going to do. So, Holmes Security guards it, which is bullshit-easy to hack."

"Cool."

"Yeah. I'm going to send you a link. Tell me when you get it."

After a few moments, Zach pulled up a webpage. "Got the link."

"Perfect. Now I've infected their system with a virus that's going to disable all logins. So that means you should have full access to their security system as a guest user. Pretty wicked if I do say so myself. The virus only lasts for up to twenty minutes. It should give you time to override their security long enough to get in."

With a few keystrokes, Zach grinned. "Cool. Okay, I'm in."

"All right. You should be able to do whatever you need to do to get in from here."

"Got it."

Zach was hard at work by the time he ended the call. He grabbed his phone and snapped a selfie. Then he instructed Martha, "Smile."

She smiled, and he snapped a photo.

"Not the best lighting, but it will do. We can't use anything that might be online. Too risky."

"What are you doing?"

He pointed to a menu item on the website. "I'm uploading us as legit guests. That way we don't have to break in. We can walk in."

"Smart thinking."

"Yeah, I met this British lady who did something similar. Her name was Rosie McClintock."

"It didn't work all that well for her."

"Well, I'm adding a few tweaks."

He cropped the two photos on his computer, then uploaded them. "You want to be Rosie again?"

"You know, I've always wanted to have an exotic name…like…"

"No more accents."

"Well, how about Moira? Moira De La Cruz."

She tossed her hair back and laughed.

"You're so goofy. I'm going to be John. John Michaelson."

"All right, here's our coverup. We're federal agents that are working with what's his name? Marc?"

"Woolard."

"Marc Woolard for permitting on the drone show."

She borrowed from Aki's story. "We're working on making sure all the security for the event is top-notch. All the world leaders have requirements, and we need to make sure that the drones used in the show are up to technical requirements and aren't defective."

He looked a little nervous. "That's a lot to remember. You talk."

He uploaded his photo while she touched up her makeup and wrapped a scarf around her hair. The less she could be recognizable as Martha Dragone, the better.

He shut the laptop. "We're good. Let's move."

"Wait. I have an idea." She dug in her purse and pulled out her keys. Then she detached a red toucan figurine from the keychain and tossed it out the window into the grass.

Zach raised his eyes in question, but Martha only winked.

Then John and Moira stepped out of the car and approached the guard tower.

The uniformed guard that had been watching their vehicle was right on top of them. He showed his gun. "Halt. This is a secure area. You're going to need to move on."

"We're on the list. We're federal agents De La Cruz and Michaelson. We're here for a surprise inspection on the drones for tomorrow."

The guard checked the list and pulled out his walkie-talkie. "All right. Jeebs?"

"Yes, sir?"

"Can you show some federal agents the property, please?"

"Copy that, sir."

The guard pressed a button on the fence, and Martha and Zach walked right through. "Jeebs will be with you shortly."

Martha and Zach stood on the sidewalk near the fence and waited for Jeebs. He didn't take long. He was a muscular soldier, early twenties, dressed all in camouflage.

"Hello, welcome to Gerhardt Military Base. I'm Private Jeebs."

Martha effected a cool posture. Too much friendliness could lead people to ask questions. "We're federal agents De La Cruz and Michaelson. We're here to do a surprise inspection on the drones for the summit event tomorrow."

Jeebs looked nervous. "Ummm...okay." He motioned them toward a military jeep, and they all piled in. Jeebs drove them deeper into the base. "We don't get a lot of visitors here at Gerhardt. Usually, the ones we get are the regulars."

Martha appeared nonplussed but surveyed the base with a keen eye. "Lucas Cameron, Marc Woolard."

"Yeah, those guys come a lot."

He drove up to a small concrete building and parked the vehicle. They all stepped out, and Jeebs swiped a security card at the metal door and let them in. Inside was a large lobby with shining linoleum and touch screens on all the walls.

Jeebs walked up to a screen and called up a page. "So, this is where the drones are." He pointed toward a list with numbers on it. "Each of these addresses corresponds with one of the two hundred drones for the light show. We do regular security checks to make sure we can get a signal on each one. And that's it." Jeebs turned to Martha and Zach and shrugged.

Martha glanced around the lobby. "Okay. So where are the actual drones?"

Jeebs looked surprised, then laughed. "Oh no, ma'am. We

can't go in there. That's...that's a secure location. We can just see them on the radar on the screen."

"But I don't want to see the radar. I need to view the actual drones."

Jeebs shifted his weight back and forth. "I'm sorry, ma'am. I can't do that."

"Private Jeebs, do you know what this light show is for?"

"Yes, ma'am. The One World Summit. It's an event."

"Exactly. Do you know who is going to be at the One World Summit?"

"Uh...not exactly. It's a lot of important people, ma'am."

"No. Not a lot of important people. It's all the important people in the world."

"I understand, ma'am. It's just that here on this base we don't—"

"I don't care what you do or don't do. It is my job to protect these important people. I need to visually verify that these aircraft are safe to launch into the airspace around every international dignitary currently in power. I can't certify that on..." She gestured toward the screen in disgust. "Your radar."

"I understand that, ma'am. But I don't have access, even if I wanted to."

"Well, then who does?"

"Mainly Mr. Cameron and Mr. Woolard."

"So you're telling me that there is a locked building on federal property that no one who works on it has access to?"

"Well, I'm sure the captain does, but..."

"But what?" She clapped her hands together. "Get him up. If I can't certify these aircraft tonight, not only will there be no light show, everyone on this base will be subject to legal action."

Jeebs now looked genuinely scared. "Yes, ma'am. I'll find someone."

"I would appreciate that."

Jeebs scurried out of the building. Zach relaxed, but Martha eyed the camera. "Don't drop character."

"You're terrifying. You know that?"

"There's a reason I became a cop."

He chuckled, and another guard came back in with Jeebs. This one was a little older, in his late thirties perhaps. He looked a little more difficult to push around.

"Ma'am, we can't let anyone into the rooms past this lobby. You're lucky that you've even gotten this far. Everything you need to see is on the monitor right here."

She protested with folded arms. "No, it's not—"

He held up his hand and nodded at Jeebs and then the monitor. "I promise you."

With a couple of clicks of the mouse, Jeebs brought up another view. There it was, a still frame of the storage room. It wasn't a live view, but it did clearly lay out its interior. Rows of miniature aircraft devices sat neatly on shelves.

Martha didn't want to see pictures of the drones. She wanted to be in the same room as them so she could inspect them and figure out a way to sabotage them. "That's not what I need to see. I need to—"

The soldier held up his hand and brought up the list view. "See, now if you click on each device number, you can pull up a photo view of the device itself." He demonstrated and treated them to a three-sixty-photo view of a drone identical to the one they had found in Lucas's office. About a foot wide, gray, with four propellered arms.

"That still doesn't show me what I want to see."

Jeebs's superior placed his hand on his hips. "What agency are you with?"

"I'm working with the State Department."

"Huh? What are you really doing? They may have let you onto the base, but I need to see some credentials."

Zach had been quiet so far, and he finally chimed in. He shoved a phone at the man. "We work for the CIA. Here are our IDs."

Martha snuck a peripheral glance at Zach's phone. Buzz had apparently faked them some IDs out of Rueben's and Aki's.

Jeebs's superior raised his arms in surrender. "Fine. Show them to the warehouse and let them in."

She shot the man a withering glance, and he didn't respond. He simply nodded and led the way.

A few minutes later, they came to a door with a keypad. Jeebs entered the code and opened the door. With an arm movement, he ushered them in. Then the metal door clanged shut behind them.

Zach and Martha were now in a huge warehouse room. Just like in the computer photos, metal shelves held the devices as well as several tables with aluminum foldout chairs around them.

Martha gingerly picked one up. "Does this feel a little heavier than the one in Lucas's office?"

Zach picked one up. "Yeah, it does."

She inspected it carefully. It had the standard blue LED light. Then she looked a little closer. "Oh my God."

"Yeah," Zach said. "It has a digitally controlled bomb on it."

She started checking them all. They were all the same. "These can't go out." Martha pulled out her phone to send photos. As soon as she pulled up her message thread for Rueben, she had no reception. She looked at the thick metal construction all around. "There's no reception in here. How about you?"

Zach pulled out his phone and found the same. "We can take photos and send them later."

"That's what we're going to have to do."

As soon as she said that, there was a gruff, knowing chuckle, and a man wearing a white hoodie and shades stepped out from the shadows behind a shelf of drones. The hoodie was torn and scuffed up as if the man had recently been in a fight. "You couldn't stay away, could you? I guess I'm not surprised."

Zach turned to her, and Martha shook her head. "Pete."

Pete laughed snidely. "You don't know what you're dealing with, honey."

She delivered a swift kick to Pete's chest, and he laughed, grabbed her leg, and shoved her to the ground. "That move doesn't work for you, does it?"

She crawled away from Pete and Zach grabbed an aluminum chair and smashed it over his head. Pete whipped around, and Zach's eyes widened.

Martha knew the guy was more trouble than Zach had bargained for. "Leave him out of this."

"You should have thought of that before you brought him here. He's part of it now." Pete lifted the chair with one hand and bent off one aluminum leg. He raised it like a stake and lunged at Zach. Zach ran, and Pete chased him, laughing all the way. "Run, Forrest, run. I think you need to go back to Alabama where you belong."

Zach grabbed a metal pipe off a counter and lunged at Pete with it.

"Very good." Pete deflected some of the blows with the

chair leg, his metal body armor absorbing the rest of them. "You have some instincts. Officer Dragone might make a cop out of you yet."

Zach's eyes narrowed, and he got in a few good licks with the metal pipe before Pete doubled him over with a knee to the gut.

Martha grabbed another lead pipe from the counter and smashed it over Pete's head. He cursed, and it distracted him long enough for Zach to kick Pete in the shin.

"Enough of this," Pete growled and stepped toward them like a bully, reaching toward each of them. His calloused palms enclosed around each of their throats, and he lifted them off their feet, shoving their backs against a shelf full of drones.

Martha flailed about to try to find another weapon, but her vision was already starting to blur. Her last thought before she blacked out was whether he would simply tie them up...or had they angered him enough that he was about to kill them.

CHAPTER TWENTY-FIVE

Sunday, May 21, 11:35 p.m.

Rueben and Aki sat in a dive bar booth across from the homeless man, Jim. The bar was dimly lit, with mahogany booths and art deco-style lamps hanging over each table. It reminded Rueben of a speakeasy, and he wondered if this had been the case at one time. It was New York, after all.

Jim appeared more than uncomfortable in the civilized environment, and Rueben wondered if inviting him out for a drink was the best way to get information from him.

Maybe Jim would have been more comfortable sitting on the street with a bucket of Hurley's fried chicken. Every noise startled him—the door opening, dropped change, the *clank* of glasses... After any sudden sound, he would stop and crane his neck as if alerted to some hidden danger.

Once, when the cash register slammed, jangling coins on its way shut, Jim almost jumped up from the noise.

Rueben calmed him down. "It's all right, man. It's only a cash register. Nothing to be afraid of." Reuben tried to make light of it. "Well, I take that back. We should all be scared of the cash register. It's a giant silver monster that eats your money."

He wiggled his fingers in a creepy alien motion, and Aki smirked, but Rueben had made it worse for Jim. He started to bolt for the door.

"Hey, hey, hey. I was joking, man. Sorry, bad joke. Bad joke. There's no monster."

Jim marginally calmed, but at least he sat.

Drinkers sat more or less quietly over glasses, and a pool game elicited the occasional laugh.

The waitress came by to take their orders, and Jim ordered, "Four orange juices only in a paper cup. Must be in a paper cup."

The waitress seemed a little confused, but Rueben nodded at her. "I'm picking up the bill. Whatever he wants."

She wrote it down. "Okey-dokey."

After she left, Jim squirmed in the booth, his wild red hair sticking out from every angle. Rueben finally got a good look at him and noticed he wasn't a whole lot older than the guy.

He figured Jim was maybe mid-twenties or so, with scraggly facial hair and large wire-rimmed glasses. He wore an open blue-and-red plaid shirt with a black t-shirt underneath.

Rueben turned to Jim. "So Jim, what we invited you—"

Jim grabbed all the sugar packets out of the condiment rack and began to arrange them in rows. "The rule of balance, everything in balance, and balance it will be. Sugar comes from sugar cane and salt from the mines or the sea. Never mix them up, or you will see just how much is not the sea."

Rueben and Aki glanced at each other. Maybe this was a bad idea after all.

Aki smiled gently at him and tried to enter his world. "You like sugar, Jim?"

"Sugar rots your teeth. Bad, like fried chicken. But tastes like ice cream."

"Mhhmm…ice cream. What's your favorite flavor?

He still sorted the packets, but his answer was sure and quick. "Ugh. I hate ice cream."

"You don't like ice cream?"

"Food must satisfy the stomach, not the soul."

"I think they can do both."

Jim didn't answer and continued with the sugar packets. They had to be arranged out on the table, then gathered, and arranged again. Rueben tried to follow a pattern, but there was none.

Aki continued trying to soften Jim. "Hey Jim, can I ask you a question?"

"Question request accepted."

"Thank you for that. What do you know about Rueben?"

Jim continued to sort the packets on the table, over and over, with no discernible pattern. "He's a Repeater."

"A Repeater? What does that mean?"

"It means he repeats. He has had many, many lives, and he repeats in a loop and a loop-the-loop."

Rueben's stomach froze. This guy knew? He was certainly no schizophrenic with déjà vu experiences as he and Buzz had guessed. The man remembered more than bits and pieces. Rueben stammered, "You're right. How do you know that?"

"He lives in many, many worlds. Sometimes he's good, and sometimes he's bad."

Reuben leaned forward. This guy might've been straight-up nuts, but so was his life. If Jim knew something about how this thing worked, he didn't care how crazy he was. "Many worlds? Like multiple universes?"

The waitress came at that moment to deliver the drinks. "Here you go, four orange juices in paper cups."

Jim grinned and inserted all the straws and meticulously arranged the cups on the table, appearing to check for symmetry.

The waitress frowned. "Is he...okay?"

Reuben answered quickly, "Sorry, you'll have to forgive my brother. He's on leave from county for his birthday. We'll have him back in an hour."

"Ahh..."

Jim answered, not looking up from his drink, "Not his brother."

The waitress leaned in over him and yelled slowly, "Can. I. Get. You. Anything. Else?"

Jim clasped his hands over his ears, and Rueben waved dismissively at the waitress, and she nodded at him knowingly before leaving.

Rueben sipped his beer and picked up the conversation from before the waitress had appeared. "Do you mean multiple universes?"

Jim leaned over the orange juice cups and took a sip from each, one by one, then went back to organizing the sugar packets. "Not your brother. Carolyn is your mother."

Rueben nearly choked on his beer. "How do you know my mother?"

"I talk to her often. She smells like cookies."

Rueben stiffened. "You don't know my mother. She's been gone for fifteen years."

With big flamboyant movements, Jim raised his palms

high in the air in a gesture of confusion. "So...where oh where did she go?"

Rueben didn't want to talk about his mother.

He was about to tell him as much, but then Jim continued, "That is the question you must answer. The quest on which you must embark."

"I'm not on a quest for my—"

The phrase "my mother" got stuck in his throat. "I'm not looking for Carolyn Peet. What I want to know is, are you stalking me?"

"Sometimes he's good, sometimes he's bad. But he must quest to find the dream where the time loops end."

Aki chimed in, softer than Rueben. "Hey, Jim. Rueben wants to know how you know so much about him. Can you tell us about that?"

"Request granted. He jumps."

Aki frowned at the answer. "Jumps?"

"Jumps. Like a frog. To universes." He arranged the packets on the table in a circle and jumped his finger over them. "Bad Rueben, that is. It's a time loop. He jumps. Like a frog. In a loop. Loop-the-loop goes the frog."

Rueben tried to wrap his brain around whatever Jim was attempting to say. "Bad Me travels between universes and is somehow stuck in a time loop?"

"Universes. Like TV."

"TV?"

"TV isn't real. It's in the air. Universes are in the air. Nothing is real. It's in the air. And bad you...is the stuck frog. Stuck frog. Stuck frog."

He jumped his fingers across the packets, and oddly, Reuben was starting to figure it out. He was saying that all

these realities weren't a time warp, that they were simultaneous universes.

"How many universes are there?"

He answered quickly, "A lot. A lot, a lot, a lot. I'd say seven
thousand. Yeah, seven thousand sounds right."

"There are seven thousand universes in the air like TV
signals?"

"You live in seven thousand universes. Some we are
friends. Some we are not. And some…" He encircled his eyes
with his fists and peered through them like binoculars. "Some
Jim is invisible man that Rueben can't see."

"You mean I ignore you."

Jim finished arranging the packets and now piled them
into a tall stack toward the back of the table. "And some…
Jim's brain not scrambled like eggs."

Reuben's heart went out to the guy. There was a universe
out there where he was normal? How difficult it must be to
know that your brain was scrambled.

"This is my favorite one."

"Your favorite what?"

"Universe with Rueben. He is kind on this one. Tries to
help, but eggs don't unscramble." Jim wrinkled his nose.
"Rueben that ran away…he's a bad man. I don't like him. Bad
froggy. Bad froggy. Stuck bad froggy, go away."

No matter how much some of this stuff lined up with
Buzz's reasonings, Rueben wasn't sure if anything this guy
said was true. There simply wasn't a way to prove it. "So I
travel to a different universe when I die?"

Jim's head shook erratically. "No. Good Rueben travels
back in time. Bad Rueben can too, but he can also travel
between universes. No universe is safe from him. Good
Rueben's universe is not safe from him."

Hm. That kinda made sense. It also sounded like nonsense. Aki frowned at him, but Rueben turned back to Jim. "Say I… believe you. How do I get Bad Rueben out of my universe?"

"That…is the quest you must take. Like a hobbit to find a nest."

CHAPTER TWENTY-SIX

Monday, May 22, 8:32 a.m.

Rosa brought out a tray and served morning coffee and Twinkies to Rueben and Aki. The pair had rounded out an hour waiting in Buzz's living room.

"Mr. Buzz will be down shortly. Just give him a few minutes."

She left, and Rueben smirked at Aki. "That's what she said verbatim when we got here. How much would you bet he's not even up yet?"

Aki sipped her drink. "No bet."

They both laughed.

Earlier, Aki had called Sven and gotten relieved of her duties at the summit today. She'd explained that she and Rueben were chasing down a lead that might be related to the summit's security, which wasn't a lie. If they didn't find a way to stop Pete, they'd probably end up at the summit anyway.

Now Aki sank into the cream leather couch and shut her eyes. "It's like falling into a cloud and getting a massage."

Rueben cleared his throat and prepared to imitate his

buddy Buzz's voice. "I've never understood that expression." When Aki giggled, Rueben continued in Buzz's voice. "Clouds are composed predominantly of empty air amid tiny particles of ice. Why would someone think they can float on them? They'd plummet to their death."

Aki opened her eyes to make sure it really was Rueben talking. "Thank you, Buzz."

Rueben winked and switched back to his voice. "Everyone seems to have some kind of religious experience on that couch. I don't get it. It's a good couch and all…"

She shut her eyes, sipped her drink, and leaned deeper into the leather. "Shut it, Peet. That's an order from a superior officer."

Rueben smirked. "Superior officer, huh? Well, if you're looking for a religious experience, I could set you up with one that is quite a deal more…enjoyable." As soon as the words were out of his mouth, he realized how stupid they must have sounded. What was he thinking? They weren't play-acting at being engaged anymore. He was going to push Aki away like Pete had said would happen. Should he try to warp back and say something different?

Luckily, Aki chuckled. "Is that right?'

Rueben sighed. "Oh, that is so right. If you come over here, I'll show you exactly what I mean."

She laughed harder, but then Buzz walked in with tousled hair, a bathrobe, slippers, and an irritated expression. "Do you have any idea what time it is?"

Rueben glanced at his watch. "8:42 a.m."

"This hour is not for human beings. This is the hour of poultry mating calls and Catholic schoolgirls in pigtails. Why are you banging on my door so damn early? Rosa! Rosa!"

"Yes, Mr. Buzz?"

Buzz whined as he sank into his chair. "Get me some-thing...something to numb this dreadful headache of mine."

"I'll bring you your usual: one aspirin and one beer."

She left, and Buzz leaned back into his chair. "So, what is this meeting about?"

Rueben started. "Well, we do have less than twelve hours before Pete bombs the U.N. building."

"Crikey. You're right. Damn hangover. Rosa!"

Rosa came dashing in with a beer and aspirin on a silver tray. Buzz took them both, and she left.

Aki studied him. "Are you sure you should be drinking now of all times?"

Buzz exchanged a look with Rueben and Rueben said, "He performs better with alcohol. Usually. It calms him. Works differently for non-geniuses like you and me." *I hope,* Rueben thought. It did seem that Buzz was drinking more and more frequently and in greater quantities lately.

Buzz washed down the aspirin with the beer. "I'm listen-ing. Go ahead."

Rueben and Aki looked at each other, then back at Buzz. Finally, Rueben dove in. "Okay, so the whole time warp thing?"

"Uh-huh."

"We've semi-confirmed the thing about Evil Rueben being me from another universe."

Buzz scoffed and took another sip of beer. "Evil is relative."

"Oh?" Aki shook her head. "Are you arguing that Pete is perhaps Good Rueben?"

"Well, no, not necessarily. I just don't think we should judge the guy's motives until we fully understand them."

Rueben nearly exploded. "His motives? I think he made his

motives clear. He intends to bomb the U.N. and start a global nuclear war. How much more understanding do we need?"

Buzz irritably tapped the arm of his chair. "Although I may lack emotional IQ, there could be a good reason for him to want to achieve this. In his mind, Pete is probably the good guy of his story."

Rueben didn't say anything.

Buzz finished his beer, belched, and set the bottle on a coffee table. "Can we please get to the point? Now that I'm up, I have projects to work on."

Rueben swore. "Buzz. Sometimes…"

Buzz cleared his throat. "Guys, guys. This is not how you cure a hangover."

Rueben was exasperated. "If we don't stop Pete, he's going to start a nuclear war. We're talking about billions of lives hanging in the balance. Global instability and chaos. This is really important, and we need to bring our A-game to the table.

"Yes, yes." Buzz stood and paced the room as he did when he thought deeply. "May I ask how you confirmed this about Pete?"

Rueben didn't want to tell him it came from the crazy homeless guy. Eh, what the hell. It wasn't like this whole time-warp thing could get any weirder to Buzz. "You remember the homeless guy we keep running into?"

Buzz tapped his fingertips together. "Oh, yes."

"His name is Jim. He's a veritable nutcase. Can't keep one thought together."

"Yes, the homeless man you keep running into. Not a warper, but he's involved in this. I've been watching him."

Rueben sat up. "You've been watching him?"

"Yes, I've been watching him for over a year."

"What?"

"Organic Jim? A homeless man who eats organic?"

"Maybe we're talking about the wrong guy. I've only seen this guy eat fried chicken."

Buzz raised a finger in a scholarly way. "Jim is a complex man. The fried chicken he eats counteracts the organic greens he eats. Think yin and yang."

Rueben looked puzzled. "Why Hurley's Chicken? I've had it before, and it's not out of this galaxy or whatever their slogan is."

Buzz chuckled. "Well actually...See, there's a reason Jim only eats Hurley's."

Aki made a "go on" gesture with her hand.

"Hurley's," Buzz said, "is one of Jim's time portals."

"What?"

"Why, yes. He wasn't always how he is."

"Crazy?"

"Exactly. He used to own a chain of Hurley's Chicken restaurants. Then he somehow—I'm not sure how—became active in the time world. Now, the only way he comes in or out of universes is through Hurley's locations or places where a Hurley's used to be."

Rueben's eyes widened. "That's why he's always sitting outside eating the chicken."

"Right. In another universe, he was sitting at Hurley's eating the chicken, and he arrived in ours, still eating his chicken in the same spot."

Rueben nodded. "I had no idea. How did you know? This is critical information—why didn't you tell us?" Rueben eyed the beer bottle sitting beside Buzz.

Buzz recoiled a bit. "Because until you came along, he was one of the only people I knew of that had these sorts of powers. I've researched his files and have even talked to him a little. You can't talk to him much."

"No, you can't." Rueben overlooked the fact that Buzz had been hiding information from him. Sometimes Buzz put the mad in mad scientist. "But you believe it's legit?"

"I didn't fully until you came along. Now he's starting to make more sense. His powers are different than yours. He can't go back in time. Only through universes. Of course, it might not be a power at all but some kind of advanced technology."

"Jim says Pete can jump back and forth between universes. Something about being in a loop, like a frog. Pete is stuck here and brings ruin to our world or something. That only me accomplishing some sort of quest would get him out of our universe."

"Did he tell you what kind of quest it might be?"

"Something about my mother? I don't know."

Aki paced the room in thought. "Rueben, when I said I knew you had secrets. I could never have imagined all this—" She paused. "Wait. So your mom is also Evil Rueben's—"

Rueben held up a palm. "Can we still call him Pete? Come on, help me out here."

Buzz sipped his drink. "Again, 'evil' isn't technically correct—"

Aki held up her hand. "Guys, there is a national terrorist attack occurring in less than twelve hours. Can we please save the ethics debate for another time?"

Buzz looked disappointed, and Rueben was relieved. He never did do well at challenging Buzz to debates. He used to get creamed in their dorm room discussions. Yeah, that entailed what they did in their dorm room.

Buzz acquiesced. "Fine, fine."

Aki continued, "Why would Pete want to do this?"

Rueben thought about this for a minute. "I don't know. Why would Alternate Universe Me do such a thing?"

Buzz's eyes twinkled. "Maybe you're a conspiracy theorist."

"But I'm not a conspiracy theorist."

Buzz sipped his drink and cocked his mouth into a dubious smile. "Really? And where is it you work again?"

"What does that have to with anything? Pete is not me."

Buzz shook his head. "Touché. I wish Dr. Eduardo Nunez was here. He might know how to stop Pete."

Rueben wanted to pull his hair out. "Let's try to focus on what we can control."

Buzz picked up a laptop, toyed with it before tossing it back onto a couch, and sat up. "You're right. The time for academics is past. We have to come up with a plan."

Aki paced the room again. "Killing him is out. He'll come back."

Rueben found a stress ball under the couch. He laid back and tossed it up and down as he thought. "He kicks our asses every time we even get close."

Aki agreed.

Rueben sighed. "You don't even know how many times I've been up against him. He wins every time."

She frowned. "You said he's already killed me twice?"

Rueben nodded and tossed her the stress ball.

Her eyes flashed, and she smacked the ball away in midair. "This bastard's going down."

Buzz rubbed his hands together. "But the question remains...how? We can't kill him. We can't beat him with brute force."

Rueben remembered Buzz's homemade taser that had

twice shocked the piss out of him—figuratively speaking. "We can't beat him with technology, either. His is better." Rueben's eyes shot to Buzz. "Wait, what about that shiny cube device you found at the barn? You said it might be able to help stop Pete. Cap his powers like he capped mine or something."

Buzz hung his head. "I've been poring over it all night. It's so advanced. Either it's not fully finished, or it's broken, and I don't fully understand the technology to complete it."

"An alternate Buzz built it, right? Why can't you figure it out?"

"Because you can't fix a circuit board from an internal combustion engine manual. I don't know how. Given time, I'd be able to figure it out, sure. But... we're dealing with technology that integrates with the time warping gene."

"But," Rueben said, "you have expertise in nanobots. You put one in me to track my warping."

"True, true. I'll run some more simulations." He glanced down at his watch. "Maybe I can still figure it out in time."

They were quiet for several moments.

Aki finally said, "Has anyone heard from Martha?"

Buzz raised a hand. "She was investigating a lead last night. Probably sleeping now."

Rueben studied Buzz's face. His friend's brain was obviously in overdrive now. He wasn't focused on Martha but on trying to figure out how to crack the shiny cube conundrum.

Aki pulled out her phone and put a call to Martha on speaker. It went straight to voicemail. "That's weird. Even if she was sleeping, why would she turn off her phone? She knows we're all working on this and today is Monday."

Rueben had a bad feeling about Martha's silence.

Next to him, Buzz cradled his iPad on his lap and doodled complex math equations while studying what his computers had been able to tell him about the shiny cube. Rueben remembered Buzz covering their dorm room walls with what he called his "thinking scribbles." They were black ink only, usually cubes and arrows, and this weird little gnome man with a wizard hat who periodically changed jackets and shoes.

Buzz had conveniently been out of town when the RA came calling about those. Rueben had ended up painting the room in the middle of the night to avoid having to explain to Marshall why a five-hundred-dollar "damage fee" had shown up on his tuition bill.

Damn Tim Cook. Apple came up with a way that Buzz didn't have to pay the price for his "thinking scribbles."

Aki broke into his trip down memory lane. "Rueben, why does your alternate universe self have to be such a straight-up psychopath?"

Buzz's eyes twinkled, and he tossed the iPad on the couch. "That's it. We're dealing with a psychopath."

Aki snorted. "Gee, you're quick."

He ignored her. "There's only one way to win with a psychopath."

Rueben picked up the stress ball Aki had swatted away and glanced up at Buzz. "How is that?"

"He's not playing by any rules but his, and he doesn't give a shit. So, we do the same. Boys and girls, the only way to fight a psychopath, is with psychopathy. With rage. With…"

Aki turned to Buzz, a light bulb going off in her head. "I know just who to call to give us a unique perspective."

Rueben held his index finger up. "Don't. No. Don't even say his name."

She ran her tongue over her teeth. "Mike Fury."

CHAPTER TWENTY-SEVEN

<u>Monday, May 22, 11:03 a.m.</u>

Rueben donned his hearing and eye protection as he stood waiting for the robot to set up the targets. After his extensive combat training for the Pout mission as well as his CIA field agent training, he'd come to find the shooting range a good place to relieve some stress. Also, the fresh air felt good.

He stood in an outdoor pavilion on a wooden platform Buzz had fully stocked with guns and ammo. The man could have gone with typical human form cutouts for target practice, but Buzz being Buzz, said that if he was going to have a shooting range, he was doing it his way.

That is, with robots and booze.

Sometime after the Pout debacle, Buzz had devised an apparatus to create a shooting range with beer bottles and cans. Rosa emptied all of Buzz's discarded libations into a separate trash can inside the house. Then, an underground pneumatic tube sucked the empties to a receptacle in the shooting range. Once someone switched on the shooting range, a robotic hand reached into the receptacle and set up all the targets. It reset them once they were all shot down.

Rueben was alone now, and he tightened his lips and pulled the trigger. He hit an empty beer bottle dead-on from thirty yards. Then he turned his aim upon the rest of the empty bottles sitting in a neat row beside the glass shards. The robot set up the next batch of bottles, and Rueben shot faster than the robot could reload. He ran out of ammunition, and instead of reloading, tossed the weapon on the ground, grabbed another, and shot faster.

Aki edged up into the pavilion from behind, her footsteps vibrating the wooden platform. He didn't turn. He fired at the next batch of bottles, blasting them cleanly apart with a single shot each. A red light flashed for a break, and the robot began to sweep all the glass shards into a recycling bin. There was a surprising amount of glass to clean up.

Aki was a few feet behind him now. "Hey."

Rueben turned to Aki. "Hey. Sorry for walking out on you guys. I needed to clear my head."

"Mike?"

Rueben nodded. "Yeah, I don't like the guy."

Aki considered Rueben's words and sighed. "You must think I'm an awful person then. Suggesting he come...but I thought he could help."

Rueben understood. He wasn't normally like this, jealous or whatever, but Mike got under his skin. He reached out and touched Aki's arm. "It's all good. You're probably right. Mike might be able to contribute some good information about Pete and how he thinks and acts."

Aki smiled. "So, we good?"

Hm. Were they? Maybe he should ask. "Aki, can I ask you something?"

"Sure."

"Do you think we might have something? You and me?"

She grabbed his hand in hers and met his eyes. "I think we do."

"But what you said about dating other agents…"

Aki winked. "A girl can make exceptions, right?"

"Yeah, but…"

"I get the feeling this conversation might be about something else." Aki settled her hands on her hips.

He had to hand it to her. She did know him pretty well. "I know this isn't the case, but I feel like Pete is my responsibility. Even though he's not me from the future or whatever, he's still a version of me."

"Rueben, you are nothing like that nutjob. I'm sure there's a reason why he is as he is, and that's not on you. Don't let him or his actions get under your skin. It's probably part of his plan to get you off-center."

She had a way of making things seem so easy, but were they really? Rueben opened his mouth to counter, but she pressed a finger to his lips. Her finger was warm and soothing, and it tingled his lips. "Rueben Peet, I know we haven't known each other for long, but I know what kind of person you are. You help people. You take care of your dad every day. You watch out for your friends. You even care about strangers: you listened to Jim when most people might think he's crazy, and you stayed behind at the cake shop to console Laura after Pete destroyed it."

She placed a warm palm against his cheek. "You're nothing like Pete. Maybe he used to be like you at one time in his universe, but he's not you and never will be."

Rueben gazed into Aki's eyes, a smile forming on his face. Then they kissed, quick and hard and he gripped her tight.

"Thanks. I needed that," he said into her hair before pulling away from her.

"Don't mention it." She raised her eyebrows. "We have enough to worry about trying to keep straight Buzz's 'Rules for Repeaters.' I mean, seriously, how many more rules do you think are out there?"

Rueben laughed. "I don't know, but we should probably head back to our friends."

Glad that he knew where the two of them stood now, he took Aki's hand in his, and she walked with him back toward the mansion.

Buzz's garden was in full May bloom, with carnations and lilies dotting the bushes and birds flitting overhead. They walked in silence. They reached the Japanese section of the garden, a half-finished area that started and ended with Buzz's ninja phase. There was an imported Japanese cherry blossom tree that shaded a koi pond with a fountain.

Underneath the cherry blossom tree, he stopped. She turned to face him, and a pink petal fell from the tree, floated down past her dark hair, and stopped at her black boots. He held her chocolate eyes in his, then smiled ruefully and rubbed her hand in his.

Soft and feminine, with pink-tipped acrylic nails and a charm bracelet that jangled with each movement.

He whispered, "You're perfect. You know that, right?" He cupped her face with one hand and leaned in to kiss her, slowly this time. Her lips seemed meant for his, and they stayed locked together for some time as his hands found her lower back and hers searched up his shoulders. Eh, their friends could wait a little longer, couldn't they? Then her phone rang.

"Shit." Aki pulled back and dug her phone from her pocket.

The conversation lasted only a few seconds, then Aki turned to Rueben. "It's Mike. They need us in there."

CHAPTER TWENTY-EIGHT

Monday, May 22, 11:54 a.m.

When they got back to the mansion, the scene was completely different. There were three people gathered in the living room, laughing and talking.

Three people, as in Buzz, Mike Fury, and…

He did a double-take. "Dad?"

Marshall sat on Buzz's couch wearing a plaid button-down tucked into a pair of jeans. Unsurprisingly, he was holding a beer. Mike sat beside him with a matching bottle, grinning with delight at whatever Marshall had said. Marshall looked relaxed and chilled there with his friends, and Buzz stood awkwardly in the entryway.

"Hey, son. Glad you could join us."

Rueben stared at him in confusion. The cumulative total of two minutes Marshall had spent making small talk with Buzz at the Exit Bar on Friday night was the most he had talked to him since Rueben had met Buzz. Now he was invited to Buzz's mansion?

Marshall attempted to explain. "It looks like you guys got yourself in a pickle here."

Rueben sighed. Of course, Marshall would take the opportunity to throw their debacle at him. They hadn't gotten a chance to discuss what had happened. Of course, that was assuming any of them really knew what had happened. That was why he and Aki had come to Buzz's in the first place, to figure it out.

Rueben smiled sheepishly and rubbed the back of his head. "Yeah, I'm sorry about how the scene at the cake shop went. Then the guy got away."

"Crazy, that's an understatement. A shit-show is more like it."

Everyone laughed, and Rueben affected a thin-lipped smile. No one else knew that the comment was Marshall's biting sarcasm. Rueben kept relatively quiet, though. He wasn't about to lay into his dad right in the middle of the investigation. "You're joining our little band of justice warriors?"

They all laughed at the name, and it got repeated a couple of times.

Marshall shrugged. "Well, you kids already dragged me into this kicking and screaming. So, I'm involved. I might as well throw in my lot."

Aki apologetically grimaced as she searched Rueben's face. "Yeah, Buzz called him. We think he might be able to add something."

Add something? Sarcasm, bigoted political rants, and insults?

Marshall frowned and started to stand from the couch. "Look, if you don't want me intruding on your space and your friends, I get it. I can take a hint."

Shit.

"No, no, Dad. We can use your expertise. You know more about criminals and psychopaths than any of us do."

He sat back down. "You're damn right I do. You kids got yourself into an awful mess. You're going to need all the help you can get."

Mike Fury, still sitting next to Marshall, reached upward to offer Rueben a "bro handshake" that stretched across the better part of the couch area.

In his late twenties, Mike was tall and well-built, and right now, his biceps practically popped out of his tight black t-shirt. He had spiky dark hair and wore wraparound shades backward on top of his head. "'Sup, Robert."

God, Rueben hated this guy.

He shook Mike's hand and corrected him. "Rueben."

"Yeah, that's what I said, Robert." Mike sat back down and grabbed his beer off the end table. Then he flashed a dazzling smile at Marshall. "So, Marshall man, finish that story you were telling with those Canadian milk bastards. Did you bust them?"

Rueben considered grabbing one of Buzz's statues and bashing it against Mike's skull. Isaac Newton stared at him in bronze, and he thought about it. What goes up must come down, after all. But instead, he grabbed the last beer off the abandoned silver tray and popped it. The Canadian milk bust story was Marshall's *Moby Dick*, and he'd heard it over and over again all his life.

It was an unsolved case from his days on the police force involving raw milk smugglers across the border and some farmers' co-ops that got cozy with a bunch of local small-town grocers. Long story short, many people died from milk poisoning, and when the cops came to investigate, nobody knew anything. Eventually, the feds outranked the local police, and not even they could find anything. As it turned out, it wasn't the milk that had poisoned the people, but a case of SARS, and the agency was involved in it. Talk about messy.

"One of the deaths was this little girl, and the mother begged me to bring her justice. That's my greatest regret on the force. That I couldn't find out who was responsible and couldn't get 'em prosecuted anyway. Once the case was closed, I told her I would find out who was responsible if it was the last thing I did on this Earth."

Mike appeared to wipe a tear. "Dude, you're a white whale, man. I'm telling you. Good people are hard to find these days. People that care about their fellow man."

Marshall nodded ruefully. Mike rambled on, "I've seen things, and let me tell you, this world is a fucked-up place. No one gives a shit about anyone but themselves. You can't count on anyone."

Marshall shook his head vigorously. "Don't I know it. Government bureaucrat bastards. Not a damn one of them cares about the American people. They only care about lining their pockets at the expense of the hard-working taxpayer."

Marshall sat up straighter and turned to Mike fully. "You know, I remember a time when people respected the government and the president. There was a time in this country when the government commanded respect."

Mike grinned and listened to the tale of an era he'd never inhabited. "Man, I can't imagine that."

Marshall shook his head vehemently. "Yeah, I know you can't. It was before you, you know. You're about Rueben's age. It was long before any of you were born."

Marshall leaned even closer and wagged his finger at Buzz and Mike, a captive audience. "But it was a different time in

America, let me tell you. When the president, he would get on television...." Marshall banged the side of the couch for emphasis. "You listened. Let me tell you, let me tell you... people would stop in the street to watch the storefront televisions to see what the president of the United States of America might have to say. That was the way it was. It was a time when the American flag meant freedom and hope and prosperity to everyone worldwide. It was a time when people would see that flag, and regardless of creed or nationality, they would know it meant freedom. Freedom, and Michael Jackson."

Everyone laughed, and Marshall smiled. It was such a rare sight for Rueben that he almost felt like he was watching a stranger.

Marshall leaned back into the couch. "Now they poisoned Michael Jackson, and if the president has something to say, well, it's just another day in the news, and half the Internet has something to say right back."

Everyone laughed in agreement except Rueben. Marshall's political rants were legendary, and Rueben had heard them all —about five hundred times more than he ever wanted to. "Um, are we going to save the world or relive the good ol' days?"

Marshall narrowed his eyes at Rueben. "Please excuse my cynic of a son. His liberal education and a government job have indoctrinated him."

Rueben could have taken the bait, but Aki's words had straightened him out. It was time to get things rolling. He glanced out at his friends. "Has anyone heard from Martha yet?"

They all looked at each other. Aki frowned. "I still haven't been able to get hold of her."

Buzz straightened his shirt collar. "I tried to ping her cell phone, but it's not showing up anywhere. It's going to take me time to track her recent GPS. Maybe she's got it turned off?"

Marshall appeared concerned. "I hope she's all right. Let me call her."

He pulled out his phone, and Buzz stood and motioned for everyone to gather in the foyer. It was a massive room, all in pristine white marble with a winding double staircase.

"Everyone has been briefed on the situation, right?" Buzz said. It was his mansion, and he was taking the lead on this operation.

Mike cleared his throat and adjusted the waist of his pants. "Yeah. We've got an underground lead on a possible terrorist attack at the summit. We believe it's an unidentified white male who goes by the name of 'Pete.' You folks foiled his attempted kidnapping of my man Marshall, and now he's at large."

Rueben, Aki, and Buzz all looked at each other. Marshall was still on the phone leaving Martha a voicemail. Buzz nodded. "Bare bones, yes, you're up to speed. I have surveillance footage of the attack at the bakery. We're going up to the theater for a viewing."

Mike grinned. "A theater? This guy should be on like, Science Channel Cribs."

Buzz's face lit up, and he must have stared at Mike for a good thirty seconds just smiling. Rueben groaned. It was everything Buzz didn't need to hear.

Marshall finished on the phone. "I can't get her. It's going straight to voicemail. That's unusual for her. I left her a voicemail, sent her a text. Son, did you say something to piss her off, maybe?"

Rueben bit his tongue and stepped out of the foyer to take

some deep breaths. Between Mike and Marshall, this was becoming a nightmare. He spotted a gilded bust of Isaac Newton on the console table. How many of these did Buzz have in here? He picked it up; it must have weighed ten pounds. It was perfect. He tossed it across the room, and it hit a window.

"Shit."

Rueben rushed toward the window and crouched to check the damage. Good, he hadn't broken it. But, the commotion echoed in a side room, and out came the most beautiful woman Rueben had ever seen. Well, he'd seen her before.

"Hello, Binnie."

Binnie was a tall, leggy brunette, and her voluminous dark hair fell in soft waves against a perfectly fit and curvaceous body. Today she was dressed in a tight red dress that accentuated every curve. His pulse raced, and he gulped back his attraction. Her black heels had to have been about four inches, and she moved effortlessly across the marble floor.

Her red lips curved into a blissfully seductive smile. "Hello."

She leaned against the windowpane in front of him and drummed her red fingernails against the sill. She flexed her toned and silky legs as she crossed them. "Looking for something?"

"Not you."

She pouted, and her brown eyes registered hurt. "Have I done something to offend you?"

He scoffed. "Other than the day you killed me, no."

She pursed her lips. "I don't remember that."

"Of course you don't. Because I warped back in time and also because you're a—"

Her voice dropped to a low whisper. "Are you angry with

me, Rueben? Have I been a bad, bad girl? Would you like to…punish me?"

"Look, Binnie, I appreciate what you're doing here. Really. I get it. But that's not my thing."

She held his eyes, and he rose from the floor. She fingered his shirt, and he started to wonder if everything he knew about her was wrong. It would sure be nice to believe. After all, this was clearly the most beautiful woman he'd ever seen in real life.

And she wanted to have sex with him? Aside from the fact that Rueben would never betray Aki like that, there was also the problem with Binnie.

He pushed her away. "Binnie, you're a robot."

"What?"

"You're not real. I know that—"

She slapped him hard across the left cheek. Rueben had never had a woman slap him before, and it hurt.

Rueben rubbed his cheek. Binnie flipped her hair, and her silver earrings jingled. "How dare you talk to me like that!"

"Sorry, I don't mean to offend, but it's true."

Her eyes widened, and she shook her head. "Oh my God. Talk about toxic masculinity and the objectification of women. I can't even right now. I just…I can't even with you."

Her reaction and the way she moved were so human that he had an inkling of doubt. She was a robot, right? She had electrocuted him to death once in the middle of a lap dance. Buzz had said she was a robot right before he died, right?

She got up from the windowsill and sashayed out of the room, her heels echoing through the house. He felt bad for being rude to her, and he didn't mean to. But it wasn't like she had feelings or anything. Right? He replaced Isaac Newton on his pedestal and looked the physicist in his blank gold eyes. "He didn't create an emotive robot, did he?"

Newton had no response, and Rueben patted him on the head before turning back toward the foyer where the others had long since gone into the theater.

Rueben found the theater room upstairs; he had been there a few times before to watch movies with Buzz. Although, movie night with Buzz typically consisted of Buzz salivating over some kind of mind-bending science lecture or AI documentary. Both lost Rueben before Rosa even arrived with the popcorn. He was usually asleep after the first twenty minutes. The fully reclining chairs were great for that.

The room was done in gold and red, consistent with the taste of the person who'd designed the place. Two rows of plush red velvet chairs, four each, stood in the center of the room in front of a screen that Buzz had once bragged was a hundred inches high and a hundred eighty inches wide. No one should ever have to watch stem cells magnified to a hundred inches tall. There was just something fundamentally wrong with that. Now, Jessica Alba, that was another story.

Red velvet curtains with gold fringe flanked the screen, and it had a tiny wooden platform in front. Rueben wondered if Buzz ever gave lectures from this room. He started to wonder if Buzz ever did any work. As much money as he had, he mainly saw Buzz wander around in his pajamas and get drunk. Then again, Rueben's boss at the CIA only had the vaguest idea where he was at the moment, so it was all about the same.

Along the walls were three faux archways in gold, with

bas-relief carvings of African wildlife and cherubs. The ceiling was framed with a circular gold rim, with dome bulbs about every foot, giving it a more modern feel. A projector hung in the middle of the circle, pointed at the screen.

Everyone was already seated when Rueben arrived, and Rosa was passing out popcorn. Buzz wasn't there, but the screen flickered on and off, and Rueben assumed he must be in some control room.

Rosa smiled and handed him a bowl and a beer. "Mr. Rueben, it's always good to see you."

He took them and smiled. After what he had just been through with Binnie, Marshall, and Mike, he needed some alcohol. Besides, he'd heard Buzz mention earlier to Aki that they had plenty of time to sober up before the U.N. bombing went down this evening.

Rosa peered at Rueben's cheek. "What happened to your face?"

He frowned, and she scurried away.

Buzz came back in the room holding a remote control. "Okay, people. What we have here is the security footage from the bakery. We're going to go over it and see if we can come up with some clues for how to capture him."

He shook the remote to underscore his point. "And remember, I said 'capture.' We are not on a mission to kill. None of us want to go to prison, me least of all."

They all laughed, and Buzz kept going. "So, our plan is to capture him and hold him off until the end of tonight so he can't execute whatever scheme he has for the keynote address that's in...yikes...about eight hours."

They all whistled and checked their watches.

"That's right. So the purpose of today's viewing is to study how our assailant moves and to see if we can discern any other details on how we can beat this guy. We're all a bunch of experts here in our respective fields—"

Buzz stopped and smiled at the back of the room. "Hello, Binnie."

Rueben turned to look at her. She gave him the worst look and smiled at Buzz. "Hey, Buzz." She sat on the edge of a chair and flexed her legs. "Don't let me be in the way."

All the men in the room sat captivated, and Aki groaned.

Marshall finally found his tongue. "Buzz, who the hell is this?"

Buzz waved. "This is Binnie. Don't worry. She's totally cool. She's also totally—as they say—DTF."

That met with whistles and laughs. Mike was the first to try. "Why don't you come over here, Binnie? Let's get to know each other."

"Ohh...you're hot. I'd love to get to know you."

Rueben wanted to throw up. "Are we going to watch the footage or have an orgy?"

Mike laughed. "Who says we have to choose?"

Buzz and Mike laughed, and Binnie sat on Mike's lap. They whispered sweet nothings, and Buzz turned on the footage.

The surveillance film was silent and jumpy, and Rueben worried that Mike would see the end where it revealed the two Ruebens. This would be too difficult to explain, and given that he trusted Mike Fury about as far as he could throw him, the last thing he wanted was to explain his quirky little secret. He hoped Buzz wouldn't be that careless. He cleared his throat toward Buzz and gave him a questioning glance.

Buzz winked and shook his head. "Don't worry. It's all taken care of."

The footage started with Marshall sitting at the table alone and bored, surrounded by empty cake samples. Marshall took a bite of something, made a face, and pushed it away. He checked his phone.

Aki showed up, disheveled, and Marshall gave her an odd look.

Rueben didn't see it the first time, but now he recognized that look. That was his *I don't buy your lie* face that Rueben remembered from growing up. Man, he didn't get away with anything when he was a kid.

What was he thinking? He didn't get away with anything now. If Rueben had been the one out there, Marshall would have launched into a sarcastic, insult-laden interrogation until he forced Rueben to tell the truth. As it was, he didn't say anything to Aki.

Now in the theater, Marshall scoffed. "That is the worst imitation of sex hair I've ever seen."

Aki turned toward him. "What do you know? I could look like that."

"Nobody looks like that. Especially not after bathroom sex."

Rueben buried his head in his palm. "Dad, really."

"Nah, that's not the way a woman looks after she's been freshly schnogged over a bathroom sink. That's what a woman thinks she looks like, but it's not what she really looks like."

Aki's eyes got big. "And you would know this, how?"

Marshall winked. "I was in the Navy as a young man. "

Mike whistled and clapped. "Marshall's got the con."

Buzz cheered and high-fived Marshall, and he continued, "But I'm a gentleman. I don't share those stories in mixed company."

Aki raised an eyebrow. "You will find I can hold my own out there with the boys."

Marshall nodded at her. "I'm sure you can. But it's how my parents raised me. And how I raised Rueben, too. Not that he remembers."

"Dad, really. Would you shut down the sarcasm machine for one night?"

Aki laughed and ruffled her hair to make the guys laugh. Fortunately enough, Pete entered the bakery on the screen, with his hood up and sunglasses on. Everyone got quiet.

Buzz pointed him out to Mike. "That's our man."

Mike's expression turned serious, and he watched the frame intently with Binnie still on his lap. Rueben was interested to know what Binnie might have to say about the footage. Since she was, in essence, a computer, her analysis might be worth listening to.

Pete alternated fighting with everyone in the bakery. Ernie, Gus, Aki, Rueben, Marshall. It was embarrassing how badly he kicked everyone's asses. But, Rueben mused, since Pete was really himself, *he'd* actually whooped all of them, right? He sat back and watched his moves. He could learn a lot from himself.

Mike was the first one to comment. "He's not consistent."

Buzz stared into the screen. "How do you mean?"

"Look at the way he kicks there. It's like, he's great with the reflex and the release, but on the follow-through, he just bumbles it. Replay it."

Buzz backtracked a few seconds and slowed the speed down. Indeed, Pete lifted his leg to kick Ernie and sent great force into Ernie's stomach. Ernie's facial expressions contorted, and then he recoiled before hitting the ground. But a second before Ernie hit the ground, it was almost like Pete lost his balance a little.

Mike peered closer. "Replay it again." Buzz replayed the clip, and Mike leaned forward. "Yeah, it's like he's…dragging his left leg. But only slightly."

Aki set her popcorn down. "Oh my gosh, he's right. See if he does it the whole time."

Buzz forwarded to the next clip of Pete kicking. This time it was at Rueben. Rueben grimaced at the idea of kicking his ass. But once he got over that, he noticed they were right. "It's like it's injured or something."

Marshall pulled out his glasses and edged forward on the seat. "Play another one. I think I notice a pattern."

Buzz forwarded to another kick. This time Pete kicked Aki.

She shook her head. "Same thing. There's something there with that left leg."

Marshall pointed at the screen. "No, see how that recoil looks so jerky?"

Everyone in the room agreed in unison. *Jerky* was the word they were all searching for.

Marshall wagged his finger. "That's something seniors would recognize. That's a hip problem. He's had some kind of hip injury or replacement. That's the only way someone ends up moving like that. But he's so young. It would surprise me if he's had something like that."

Buzz tapped the remote against his finger and peered at Binnie. "Hm. A metal hip replacement…"

They all watched the footage for a few minutes. Ernie wrestled Pete to the ground, and the tape ended.

Mike groaned. "Where's the rest of it?"

Buzz winked at Rueben. "That was all I was able to get from the shop owner. She's pissed that he tore up the shop."

Marshall scratched his forehead. "You know, I think I might have an idea to catch him."

Everyone looked at him, and he removed his glasses and hung them off his shirt. "I know the metal pin in his hip wouldn't be magnetic, but I glimpsed that fancy hi-tech body armor beneath his hoodie. Now that's definitely magnetic."

Aki, Buzz, and Rueben agreed, but they were confused.

Marshall paused. "So, we could use a magnet. One of those giant magnets that they attach to the cranes to move stuff around in junkyards."

Rueben leaned back in his seat. That was a good idea. Marshall continued, "We lure him into a fight, then the magnet will stop him as long as none of us are carrying any metal."

Buzz nodded slowly. "I can't think of a single reason that wouldn't work. Unless it's some non-magnetic alloy...probably not, though."

Aki smiled. "You've still got it, old man."

Marshall narrowed his eyes at her. "I guess I deserve it after the bad sex hair comment."

She laughed, and Mike high-fived Marshall and mimed a worshipping gesture. "I just got to say, dude, you are badass. Seriously, I wish my dad was that badass."

Rueben had to admit that Mike was good with people. In less than an hour, he'd made closer friends with Marshall than Rueben had in twenty-five years.

Suddenly, Buzz clapped for attention. "Okay, so we have to come up with a concrete plan. Marshall, do you know where to get one of those magnets?"

Marshall shrugged. "Sure, there's a scrapyard in Brooklyn.

The guy that owns it, well, let's just say he owes me some favors. I'll call over there and arrange to get one."

"Perfect."

Marshall pulled out an old-school flip phone from its hip holster, and Buzz turned to the remaining three.

Rueben stood and leaned against the chairs, clenching the chair back.

Buzz kept going. "I'm not sure why Pete hasn't tried to come after us again. He must be busy making preparations for his attack on the U.N. building. So, we need to figure out how to lure this guy into a trap—and without the CIA's 'help.' How do we do that?"

Rueben spoke up. "Well, it would depend on where he is right now."

Aki nodded. "Too bad we don't have a cell or anything for him."

"Yeah, all we have is that footage from last night. If we can tell where he was going after that…"

Buzz snapped his fingers. "I'll get back into the city CCTV cams and try to follow him all night and all day until we can get a current location. Although I doubt I'll be able to find much on him… Remember how good he was at evading security cameras back when we were tracking Pout the same way? Back when he was just a guy in a white hoodie with stripes on his shoulders?" He paused. "But you know, I could try to triangulate the signal he was using to track Marshall's cell phone."

Rueben scoffed. "You may be a genius, but I don't think that's possible. There's no way that Pete is still using that signal. He would know that we could trace it."

"Ah, young grasshopper, my AI's experimental predictive algorithm says it can."

Aki and Rueben nodded at each other, and Mike whistled. "Nice, bro. What do you need me to do? I'm ready for duty, boss."

Rueben rolled his eyes and had an idea. "Why don't you stay here and keep watch on Buzz in case Pete shows up?"

"Right on! If he does, I'll show ol' Metal Hip how to fight like a real man. Good idea, Robert."

Buzz nodded in approval and turned to Aki. "Why don't you guys come up with a location to lure him to once we find him? We can set it up with that magnet. Then we've got him."

Aki nodded. Marshall got off his phone. "We'll meet up with my buddy in an hour. He's got a big one we can use."

This set off a round of applause, and Aki and Mike went into high gear. Rueben was about to join their planning party when Marshall came up to him. He had an odd look on his face and dropped his palm on Rueben's shoulder. "Have a beer with me."

Rueben cleared his throat in surprise. "Um, sure." Was he about to share a true father-son moment with Marshall?

Marshall cocked his head toward the door. "I'm sure Buzz has some kind of mini-bar in here somewhere."

"I think he has one in every room."

Marshall and Rueben both laughed, and Rueben scratched his head in confusion. He couldn't even remember the last time he'd shared an actual laugh with his dad.

"I think the main house bar is in the game room."

They headed down the long, carpeted hallway toward the game room. Rueben shoved his hands in his pockets. Now with his temporary moratorium on sarcasm and insults, he didn't know what to say to his dad. "Good idea about the magnet."

Marshall's eyes glazed over. "Well, it'll get the job done."

That was all there was to say about that. They arrived at the game room, and Rueben opened the door.

Marshall scoffed. "When you said game room, I thought you meant pool tables."

Rueben laughed. "No, I meant video games."

Lit up by a sleek blue light, the game room had a row of eight screens, each about fifty-five inches, mounted into the wall. It was two rows of four, all of which had the same login screen for Call of Duty. Sitting before the screens were two rows of black leather chairs, each with a small tabletop hosting a video game controller.

Marshall rolled his eyes. "I thought it was too good to be true that he was a grown-up."

There was the old Marshall. Now the world was normal.

Rueben pointed toward the counter, a long, sleek black marble fixture. "Bar's over here. You can quit whining and get back to your regular, drunk-ass self."

Behind the counter was fully stocked, and Rueben reached underneath and opened a cooler. He slid a beer across to Marshall, who scowled as he twisted off the top. "You know, if you'd seen what I'd seen on the force, you'd be in therapy like the rest of your pussy ass generation."

Rueben grabbed a beer for himself and held it to his forehead to calm his rising blood pressure. "Maybe I need therapy. That's my problem."

Marshall scoffed and nearly choked on the drink. "You've got just one?"

Rueben sighed long and hard. "You know, you sit and talk about your glory days on the force, but you know, you're not dead yet."

Marshall's eyes flashed at him. "What is that supposed to mean?"

"It means you're not dead. You can't keep living in the past, on some washed-up stories about...Canadian milk smugglers."

Marshall slammed his drink on the counter and stared at him. "You got a lot nerve, kid. You don't have a damn clue about what it was like out on the force, day in and day out—"

Rueben sighed again. "I'm sure I don't. But you know, we're doing something pretty great here. *I'm* doing something pretty great here, and you don't even notice it. You're still so wrapped up in the past with the police force."

Marshall gestured helplessly around the room. "I'm here, aren't I? And I came up with the winning idea that none of you kids had a clue how to execute."

Rueben shifted in his seat. Marshall was right—he was investing in this new adventure. That's not exactly what he was trying to say. The words danced around in his head, and he couldn't spit them out. The beer probably didn't help.

Just say it, Rueben. Just say what you want to say. Tell him, "Why can't you ever be proud of me?"

He looked over at Marshall slumped over on the barstool, wild gray hair sticking out in all directions with a brown bottle in front of him. His dad toyed with a stray paperclip on the counter, and Rueben couldn't say it.

He wished he could be one of those people that, fuck it, didn't care what their parents thought of them if they thought of them at all. He wished he could be completely free from his childhood and family life. But the truth was, Marshall needed him, and without Rueben, Marshall had no one. But he still couldn't say what he wanted to say.

Marshall looked up at him and caught him staring. "What?"

Rueben shook his head and rose. "Forget it. Thanks for the beer."

Marshall sighed and rubbed his temple. "Rueben."

Rueben turned to face him but didn't answer.

"That's not what I wanted to tell you."

"Then what did you want?"

He played with the paperclip, then flicked it across the room. "I saw your mom."

Rueben's eyes widened. "What?"

"At the Exit Bar."

CHAPTER TWENTY-NINE

Monday, May 22, 1:05 p.m.

"What do you mean you saw her?"

Guilt dripped from Marshall's face. "She was there, at the bar."

"Did you...talk to her at all?"

"I tried to. I rushed off after her when I saw her, but then everything went down with that hoodied psychopath, and she disappeared again."

"She ran away again? She just..." Rueben choked back the hurt. He never could talk about Carolyn.

Marshall sighed. "I have to tell you the truth about something."

"Okay."

"The day she left...it wasn't exactly like I told you."

"You didn't tell me anything. She was there in the morning when I left for school and gone when I got home. I never saw her again. Except...maybe after the gunman took off."

"Yeah. That's the thing...there's more to it. A lot more."

"I'm sure there was. I always hoped one day I'd figure it

out. I mean, did you come home to find her in bed with another man or something?"

Marshall recoiled. "God, no. I need you to know that. Your mother was never unfaithful to me." Marshall sipped his drink and stared into the distance. "There's just so much...so much you don't know. And I should have told you the whole story. Maybe then you wouldn't be so fucked about women."

"I'm not fucked about women."

Marshal raised his eyebrows. "When was the last time you got laid?"

"I am not having this conversation with you."

"Fine, fair enough. But I don't think things are as peachy between you and Aki as you'd like to think. But I digress. A talk for another time, maybe. Let me explain what happened that day." His voice dropped to a low tone, and he twirled the beer cap on the counter as he spoke.

"The day on the bus?"

"Yeah."

That was a defining moment in Rueben's life, and he had so many questions about that day and no one to answer them. Certainly not Marshall, anyway.

"She showed up at the police station that day, before the incident."

"I didn't know that."

Marshall nodded. "Yeah, she was frazzled and completely freaked out. She'd kept calling my cell babbling about some kind of uh, premonition."

Rueben's ears perked up. "Premonition?"

"Yeah, I, uh, didn't know what the hell she was going on about. She said she had a feeling something bad was going to happen, and I needed to get to a certain street, and she knew where the guy was going to get on the bus. I had no idea what she was talking about. She was babbling on like a crazy person. So, I told her I was busy. So she shows up at the station and almost gets herself arrested trying to get to me in the station. I finally found her, and she keeps telling me the same stuff, only it makes a little more sense this time. She starts talking about your bus and that I had to save you."

Marshall sipped his drink and frowned, and fiddled with the beer cap some more. Rueben listened intently now. She had a "premonition?" She knew where the attacker was? He knew exactly what that sounded like.

Did she have the power?

"So, you know, my mind immediately goes to that movie *Speed*, and so I rush out to the bus. She rode with me in the car, and the whole time she was telling me what to do, and where to turn, and even what he was going to say."

"How would she possibly know this stuff?"

"I'm telling you a goddamned story. Just shut up and listen for once."

Rueben leaned on the counter and sipped his beer, and he suddenly had this recollection of the attacker's words. He had asked for them to bring a girl to him. "Hopper."

Marshall scoffed. "Yeah. I don't know who the hell Hopper was or why this guy was so obsessed with him or her."

Rueben whispered to himself, "Just like Jim said. Frog. Hopper."

Marshall narrowed his eyes. "What are you mumbling about?"

Rueben shook his head. "Never mind."

"Don't 'never mind' me. I'm trying to tell you a story, and you can't even sit for two minutes and respectfully listen. See, this is why we can't ever have a civilized conversation. You can't listen to a damn thing. You just have to blah, blah, blah, put in your two cents without ever thinking that someone else might have something useful to offer."

Rueben scowled and didn't take any of Marshall's accusations to heart. It was just his usual babbling. Marshall set the beer down. "I should have known I couldn't talk to you about this stuff. I've got to go. I've got to get to Brooklyn."

Marshall rose from the barstool and stormed out of the room.

Rueben held the bottle to his forehead. Why did things always end like this with him? And right when Marshall was about to give him information on his mom that he had been waiting on for over ten years.

Ugh. Maybe he shouldn't have said all that stuff about his dad's past being irrelevant. That was harsh. But Marshall pushed buttons, and he said things and didn't say things that he wouldn't say or do to anyone else. Why couldn't he get along with this man? Buzz, Aki, and even Mike Fury got along great with him. Why couldn't he?

For a moment, he considered killing himself with a corkscrew behind the bar to warp back and avoid the fight with his dad. But that was something Pete had predicted he would do. Dying to fix tiny mistakes. He wouldn't do that. As Aki had said, he was nothing like Pete. He'd man up and accept the consequences of his actions.

He at least owed Marshall an apology for how he'd talked to him. He sighed and got up to find him. Then Aki burst into the room. "We've been looking for you everywhere. Why haven't you been answering your phone?"

Rueben stammered and searched his pockets for his phone. Sure enough, four missed calls from Aki in the last twenty minutes. Damn, he'd switched his phone to silent when he'd gone into the theater. "What's going on?"

"Buzz found him."

"Pete?"

"Yep. He's in some shithole motel almost to New Jersey."

"Great. Let's get a plan together."

"Right. Marshall is going to meet his guy. The one hooking us up with the industrial magnet. Now we have to scope out a good area and keep sights out for Pete. You up for it?"

"Yeah. Let's move."

CHAPTER THIRTY

It was early afternoon now, and Rueben and Aki sat in the Porsche outside the MidCity Inn in New York just across the bay from New Jersey. This was where their intel, namely Buzz's cyberstalking, had it that Pete was staying. They needed to keep an eye on him. The others were creating a trap while Rueben and Aki were supposed to secure the target.

Now here they were, alone, the two-story building forlornly rising to their left. It was an eyesore of a structure—sagging bricks, grimy four-pane windows, and overgrown sidewalks. A couple of ne'er-do-wells in hoodies hung around on the sidewalk, smoking and casting paranoid glances down the block.

Rueben smirked. "Yeah, the Porsche was a good idea. We fit right in here. No one could possibly notice us now."

She laughed. "You're right—we should have taken your Mazda. No one would think a thing in this neighborhood."

"Okay, lay off on the Mazda. I'm just saying that we could've chosen a better cover."

They were partially shrouded by trees now, and so far that had kept them out of view. But the longer the stakeout went on, the more Rueben was sure someone would blow their cover. They waited, and Rueben pulled up the hotel's Wikipedia page on his phone.

"Did you know there was a movie set here once?"

She tapped her fingernails against the steering wheel and watched out the window. "Oh yeah? *Saw*?"

He laughed. "No, it featured some rock star, Hugo Hill. Have you heard of him?"

"No."

He skimmed the webpage. "Apparently, he was quite the thing at one point, and he was, I quote, 'moved by the cultural significance of the building.'"

"Oh, God. I don't like him already."

Rueben scanned the rest of the page. "God, the reviews are terrible. 'Not even Hugo's star power could save this contrived effort, based around a sophomoric script and actors that appeared freshly plucked out of a groundlings class.'"

They both laughed, and Aki shook her head.

Rueben set his phone on his lap and watched the building. Beside him, Aki raised her eyes as if lost in a memory. "Did I tell you I wanted to be an actress when I was a kid?"

He searched his memory. "I don't know if that was before I warped back in time or not, but you did at one point."

She laughed. "I'm going to have to get used to that."

They were quiet for a few minutes as Rueben considered Aki's words. Did she mean she'd have to get used to that because she wanted to continue working with him after they somehow found a way to stop Pete? Or because she wanted to be in a romantic relationship with him?

"You may not believe it, but I was good at acting," she said.

Rueben cleared away the thoughts in his head as he sat up straighter. "I'd watch you act, Lady Macbeth." He put a slight Victorian English accent on the last two words.

She leaned against the car window and laughed. "Okay, tell me something about you I don't know."

He smiled ruefully. "I'm…I'm pretty boring. Just an average, middle-class vanilla white guy."

"You are miles from average."

He ran his tongue over his teeth and studied her for a moment. "Okay, I'm going to show you something. I haven't shown anyone this in like…years."

She raised an eyebrow, and he picked up his phone. She watched the building while he pulled up a video file. "Okay, so one time a few years ago, I did a movie with some old friends."

"You were in a movie?"

"Well, it was an old friend of mine. He did an indie film cause he's like that. And he needed a bunch of actors, so he recruited me to play a mad scientist."

She laughed hard. "It's not like you didn't have any inspiration."

"Buzz and I hadn't talked in a while, so I didn't draw that much from him. But yeah, it was this really awful movie. So bad, and it was so much fun. The director had full-on artistic meltdowns, and the whole thing was just so funny…later."

Her eyes widened, and a grin lit up her face. "Oh my God, I have got to see this, like…now."

He pulled up the file and held his phone out in front of them so that they had to scrunch up shoulder to shoulder to both see the screen. Beyond the phone, they could both still see if Pete came out. He pushed play. "So this is my scene."

In it, Rueben was in a lab coat, plastic goggles, and a bad

wig. "I alone have created a device that will catapult humanity into its next evolutionary leap...hahaha!"

Film Rueben threw up his arms and laughed maniacally, and Aki chuckled. "Yeah, I... It's a lot different having met Buzz."

"Yeah, but this is the best. I get a song. "

Aki dissolved into laughter and touched Rueben's wrist. "A song?"

"Yeah, I don't sing, but I spent a week learning *The Eureka Dance*."

"*The Eureka Dance*? Oh, I have got to see this."

He laughed hard. "Oh, it's bad. It's so, so bad."

Film Rueben busted out moves that looked like a lone imitation of a Backstreet Boys routine. There were spins, kicks, and a double-footed jump. "That was seriously the most difficult part of the whole movie. We had to do that like ten times."

"Oh my gosh. This is *epic*. You're a really good dancer."

The song was a dubbed-over rap song that bragged, "I found a solution, the only solution, to rectify the human condition..." and so it went. Aki laughed harder, and the song continued with Rueben now prancing around with a beaker full of purple liquid. "I'm not Dr. Who. I'm not Dr. House. I'm not Dr. What-Ails-You, I'm the one, the one, the one that you want... I'm Dr. Von Ziegelman."

With that, Film Rueben crossed his arms and stared into the camera like a badass while his character name reverberated.

"Dr. Von Ziegelman?"

"Yeah. I think he played Mad Libs with German last names."

"Uh-huh. Whatever happened to this friend?"

"Uh, last I heard, he delivered pizza."

"Maybe a more suitable occupation for him."

"Yeah, I think so."

They both laughed and watched the hotel for a few minutes. The sidewalk hoodlums had gone now, and the outside of the hotel was empty. Aki replayed *The Eureka Dance* one more time while Rueben kept an eye on the hotel.

From the corner of his eyes, Rueben watched Aki's long fingernails tapping against the phone screen. She was so much different than he had ever thought she was when he had met her at work. He always knew she was strong and confident, but she was also down to earth and kind, and around Mike, maybe a little insecure.

Her dark eyes caught his. His heart hammered against his ribs, and he couldn't miss the sweet scent of her perfume filling the car. An undeniable magnetism had built between them, and he wanted nothing more than to reach over and touch her. Without taking his eyes off her, he twisted in his seat and leaned forward, her breath warm and moist against his face. His lips found hers.

The mere touch of his skin against hers sent a warming shiver through him, and he was acutely conscious of everywhere that his body met hers. His tongue traced the soft fullness of her lips and explored the recesses of her mouth, sending the pit of his stomach into a wild swirl.

He leaned back and searched her face, and she drew him back to her and hungrily devoured him. His lips seared a path down her neck, her shoulders, and she emitted the softest moan that sent shivers of delight coursing through him. He knew where this was going, and he savored the moment, delighting her, planting kisses over her neck, and slowly working his way down.

Suddenly she pushed him off. "Shit."

He sat up, alarmed. "What? What?"

She started the engine and pointed toward the sidewalk. "Pete."

He looked out the window, and sure enough, Pete sauntered along the hotel's sidewalk toward a green Ford Escape parked on the curb. He wasn't hard to spot—he was still wearing his trademark white hoodie and shades.

"Shit. He's on the move." Rueben lifted his phone and called Buzz. "We're a go. Let's get this party started."

Pete got into the green car and pulled away from the curb.

Aki calmly pulled out onto the road and followed him a few cars back as Rueben fixed his hair and clothes. Man, his alternate universe future self was such a buzzkill.

CHAPTER THIRTY-ONE

Aki and Rueben followed Pete's green Ford Escape, hurtling down the highway and careening through traffic. Pete was a borderline reckless driver, and following his quick turns and fast speed nearly resulted in multiple wrecks. Aki deftly maneuvered the little Porsche in and out of traffic, avoiding detection.

A split-second left turn with no signal left them without a line of sight on him, and now they were six cars behind him. Aki banged the steering wheel. "Shit. He suspects someone's following him."

"How do you know that?"

"Mike gets paranoid as hell, and when he thinks there might be some possibility of being followed, he drives like an asshole just in case."

Rueben groaned at the mention of Mike. "And here I thought we were supposed to get Pete to chase us—not the other way around."

Aki veered onto the shoulder and sped around the corner,

causing drivers and pedestrians to yell and curse at her. "Shit, he's going to get away."

Rueben scanned the traffic on this street. "I know this area. The next street over runs parallel. Let's take that one and catch up with him at the cross street."

She turned off and took the next street over, leaving Pete to think he was home free. They maneuvered through a busy city block with pedestrians and shops every which way. She tapped her fingernails against the steering wheel impatiently. "We're going to lose him this way."

"Let's track him, then." He hit the walkie-talkie button on the console. "Okay, Buzz, you're tracking us, right?"

"Roger that. What the hell are you doing? You deliberately turned away from the suspect."

"Yeah, we're trying to make him think we've lost him. You've got him on satellite, right?"

"Yep. He's heading west—it looks like he's making for the Garden State Parkway."

"Jersey? He's going to New Jersey?"

"I don't know. It looks like it."

"What would he have to do in New Jersey?"

Suddenly, Buzz remembered. "Gerhardt Military base outside Trenton."

"What?"

"Yeah, that's where he's headed. That's the lead Martha was pursuing. Martha called me last night. She was trying to break in."

"That would have been useful information." Rueben tried to hide his irritation, but he couldn't get the image of Buzz sitting and drinking beer this morning at his mansion out of his mind. There was no way around it—his friend had a drinking problem.

Couldn't dwell on that now though. "Martha is still missing. Maybe something happened to her, and she's still there."

"It seemed like a simple recon mission for her—she's a very capable lady."

"What was the mission?" Rueben asked.

"We tracked some drones out there."

Rueben's eyes widened. "Drones?"

"Yeah."

"For crying out loud, man. Where's your head at? We all need to know this stuff."

"I know. I know. I'm really sorry. But with the confirmation that the multiverse is real...I mean, can you imagine the possibilities? My brain is literally exploding with ideas for the future—"

"There won't be a future if we don't stop Pete."

Buzz was quiet for a bit. "I messed up. I really did. But I've also been tinkering with that silver cube. I've been routing most of my brainpower and computer resources into cracking it. I'm almost there. I know it."

"Good. That's good." Rueben sighed. "Back to Martha. Where is that military base at?"

"I'll send you the address."

"Great."

"I've pulled up a satellite visual on the Escape. He's getting on the Garden State Parkway. It's highly probable that he's going to that military base."

Aki swerved onto a side street that would lead her straight to the Garden State Parkway. They could barely see Pete in the distance.

Aki cursed. "Too bad Martha wasn't here. She could call for a police barricade. Buzz, in case she's not at the base and since you can't ping her phone, can you have someone go by her house? And then see if there's any Jane Does in the hospitals or…morgues, that could be Martha?"

"Yes. Got it."

"Where are we on the magnet?"

Buzz was quiet for a second, then responded, "Marshall has acquired it. He and his buddy are transporting it now. It's in a semi, I think."

"Damn. Yeah, a magnet that big should work."

"That's what we're thinking. But it's a pain in the ass to transport and move."

Rueben laughed. "That would be a problem."

"Yeah. Maybe the magnet plan wasn't such a good idea after all. We're still trying to figure out a place to trap him. We'll give you more details. Just don't lose the suspect."

They were on the highway now, crossing over the bay, and could see the Ford Escape a few vehicles ahead.

"Roger that. We've got him in our sights, headed south on Garden State Parkway. Thanks, Buzz."

Rueben ended the call and settled in for a long drive. He did a search on his phone for Gerhardt Military Base. "It looks pretty secure. We're going to have to figure out how to get in, and I'm not sure Buzz can help us right now with his plate as full as it is."

As they neared the base, Pete stopped for gas at a gas station rest stop, and Aki parked way in the back to avoid him seeing them. Suddenly, she grabbed her phone and scrolled through the contacts until she found the one she was looking for. After dialing the number, she turned to Rueben. "I know someone who can help us."

A voice answered on the other line.

"Hey, Captain Dave, it's Aki from the New York office.

Yeah, yeah… You're welcome. I was happy to help. Hey, can you do me a favor really quick?"

Rueben sighed. Aki had old contacts and closed cases all over the world. What did she see in him?

"Yeah, I need an ID badge to get into a base. Can you get me a general contractor code? Thanks. And, tell your wife I said hi. Oh, you're so sweet. Well, I can't tonight, but I love her cooking, and we'll have to set up a night soon. Thank you, Dave."

She ended the call and rolled her eyes.

Pete was still in the gas station, and Rueben took the cue. "Who's that?"

"A military captain I worked with on another case. He keeps wanting to set me up with his son."

"Oh, yeah? What's the deal with the son?"

"He's gay, for one thing."

"Ah."

"He doesn't want to tell his parents yet, so he asked me out as a one-time cover-up date."

Her phone *beeped* with a text, and she smiled. "This is it." She tossed the phone to him; the screen displayed a QR code.

"This should get us in?"

"According to Captain Dave, it should."

Rueben checked his phone's GPS map. "About another half an hour at this point. I sure hope the drones are at the base. That way, we can end this once and for all."

Aki nodded. "I can't believe he didn't tell us about Martha and the drones this morning. The U.N. bombing is only a few hours away."

"I don't know. I guess he didn't know how it went or if it was relevant at all with Martha not there."

Aki scoffed. "That's a flimsy reason. I blame the man's excessive reliance on chemical brain alteration."

"You don't know him as well as I do, but he has been drinking more than usual of late. When this is all over, I'm going to have to talk with him."

Up ahead of them, Pete turned down a long, empty side road. Without any traffic between them, there was no way to hide from Pete now.

Rueben chided her, "Bad choice for a follow car."

"I know, I know. I didn't hear you complaining when we were chasing him through the city streets, though."

He smiled ruefully and scratched the back of his head. "Yeah, that was pretty hot."

She laughed, and the GPS announced their imminent arrival at the base. Sure enough, Pete slowed. He arrived at Gerhardt Military Base, a secure complex with high, razor-wire fences and armed security guards.

Aki peered through the gates as she tried to pull in inconspicuously. They hid behind a grove of trees and watched Pete park and get out.

He flashed an ID at a security guard, who opened the door and let him in. They waited to see if he would talk to anyone, but he kept walking until they couldn't see him anymore. It seemed odd they would let Pete in with his hood up and his sunglasses over his eyes.

She unbuckled her seat belt and switched off the engine. "Let's go in."

Rueben followed her out of the car. The silence of the military complex was an odd change of pace from the busy city traffic they had been navigating.

They stealthily approached the entrance, and Aki whispered to him, "If we don't have to use that code, the better. We want to stay off the radar."

"Right. Off the radar."

They reached the same door that Pete had gone through. An armed security guard with a rifle across his chest addressed them.

"Secure area. Military personnel only."

Aki smiled at the guard and started to say something, but then she noticed a tiny red object in the grass off to the side. Watching her closely, the guard allowed Aki to bend over and pick it up. It was a red toucan with the name Petunia inscribed on it. Rueben's eyes widened. "Martha's keychain."

Aki turned to him. "What?"

Rueben held up the red bird. "This keychain is Martha's. It's a joke. Petunia's her little keychain friend that goes on ride-alongs with her. It's a whole thing. Only I know about it."

Aki stared at the keychain. "You're sure it's hers?"

He looked around for her car but didn't see it anywhere. "I'm positive. That confirms that she was here. She may have dropped it for me to see in case they got in trouble."

He pocketed Martha's keychain and flashed his CIA badge to the guard. He didn't let him see the name to stay somewhat off the radar. But knowing Martha was missing and likely still on this base, he didn't care much about his cover.

"We're federal agents. Do you know where this lady is?" Rueben showed him a picture of Martha on his phone.

The guard shuffled his feet. "Um. I don't know. I haven't seen her since last night. She uh, came here asking about the drones. That's all I know."

Rueben and Aki looked at each other, and Rueben demanded, "We need to see the drones."

"It's a secure area. If you're a federal agent, then come back with credentials."

Aki flashed her QR code. "Let us in."

The guard gulped. "Look, there's something seriously screwy going on. I don't know what it is. I just don't want to go to jail. Promise me you won't screw me over."

"Promise."

He opened the door, and Aki and Rueben stepped onto the base. The guard stood at his post again, and Rueben knew better than to milk him for more information. He would likely alert his superiors that they were on the base. Then there would be real trouble.

He called Buzz. "We have a confirmation on the drones. They're here on this base. The security guard has confirmed them."

"Um, okay." It sounded like Buzz was distracted, probably working in his lab.

"Buzz, what's going on? Are you focusing?"

"I am, in fact. You might think I'm not pulling my weight, but I have a contingency plan in case you and Aki can't stop the drones from being released from the base to attack the summit. I'm getting into position as we speak."

"Contingency plan?"

"It's not important right now. Oh, and that shiny cube...I think I know what the problem is now. Turns out it was damaged. I think I can fix it and use it against Pete. If it works, it will land me on the cover of *CR* for sure."

Rueben rolled his eyes. Buzz had wanted to get on the cover of *Contemporary Research* for years. "Buzz, if we fail, there will be no *CR* at all."

"There will. The world will just be short some world leaders, prompting global anarchy and...um. Never mind."

Rueben cut in, "Buzz, have you located Martha yet?"

"I had Rosa call her landlord to check her place, and I've electronically scoured the records of all the hospitals and morgues within a hundred miles. Nothing."

"That might be a good thing." Rueben patted the keychain in his pocket. "She's probably still here on the base."

"If you find her, I need her intern."

"Intern?"

"Yeah. Last night she had an intern with her. An affable and rather energetic fellow named Zach. Look, Mike and I are getting into position to counter the drone attack if it comes to that. When you find Zach, connect me to him."

"Gotcha."

Rueben got off the phone, and so did Aki. "That was the office. We're getting backup. We're in over our heads."

Rueben nodded. "Probably a good idea. We've got to rescue these guys."

"These guys? Just Martha."

"No, she has an intern with her. Some guy named Zach."

"Never heard of him."

"Hmmm… All right, let's come up with a plan."

CHAPTER THIRTY-TWO

<u>**Monday, May 22, 3:34 p.m.**</u>

When Martha came to, her head throbbed, and her throat felt parched. She swallowed to move the fluids in her mouth, but it didn't do much good.

Where was she?

It took a few seconds for her to place the warehouse and the shelving. It looked bigger in person than it did on the computer monitor. This was the drone room on the military base.

Every muscle in her body cried out in pain, and her wrists felt weighed down. That was when she noticed the ropes. Thick, coarse ropes in layers around her chest and arms.

Someone had tied her to a chair.

A vague headache formed from the back of her neck and radiated up. Had she been drugged? Bright sunlight streamed down from a skylight above her. Her stomach rumbled with hunger.

What time is it? What day? Then she thought about Zach

and twisted her head around, but she didn't see him anywhere. Where was he? Was he okay?

The events of the night before came back to her slowly. The drive to New Jersey with Zach. Zach. Poor Zach. She'd gotten him into all of this.

While she was somewhat used to the real danger that often accompanied Rueben's quests, Zach wasn't. He was only an intern. She tried to look around to see if she could find him, but she couldn't move. The ropes were too tight.

She wiggled around and only managed to scoot the chair a little, then she stopped. The aluminum chair was a bit flimsy, and if she tipped it over onto the floor, she might be able to break free from the chair. She recalled how easy it had seemed for Pete to bend off the chair leg when he was lunging for Zach earlier.

She shifted as much as she could to relieve some of the pressure on her joints. Her back popped a little, and she was able to coax some feeling back into her rear. She licked her lips for moisture and tried to take note of everything around her. That's when she saw the telltale white hoodie.

Pete.

Presently, he was crouched in front of a shelf, his back to her. It looked like he was typing a code or message on a touchscreen on one of the drones. Upon closer look, all of the drones seemed to have touchscreens on them.

She cleared her throat. Her voice was hoarse. "What day is it?"

"Monday," Pete replied flatly, resuming his work.

Monday? Well, that was good, wasn't it? The sun was still up so that meant they could still stop the attack before it happened. She needed to put on a brave face and stay calm until a moment of escape presented itself. Maybe she could get some information from her captor.

"Whatcha got over there, Pete?" Her voice sounded hollow in the silent room, but she had to force it. Once in Afghanistan, she'd taken a course on what to do if anyone ever kidnapped her. One of the guidelines was to play nice with your captors.

Pete didn't turn around. "I'm playing with my new toys."

"Oh yeah? A little old for toys, aren't you?"

He laughed and launched one of the drones into the air. He let it buzz around the ceiling. Then it came to rest in its previous place on its shelf. "Not these kinds of toys."

"What are you going to do with them?"

"I'm going to blow them up."

"That's very *Toy Story* of you." The course prohibited sarcasm, but she was rusty. Rusty, pissed, and hungry.

"This is hardly a child's game. I play on a much more sophisticated level."

"Yeah, I can see that."

He tapped on the touchscreen of another drone. This time there was a *beep*, and Pete recorded a short, threatening message in a language she couldn't understand. Russian, maybe?

Pete pressed the screen, and his words played back to him. He was recording messages on some of the drones? But why? Hadn't Rueben said these drones were supposed to drop bombs?

"What are you trying to accomplish?"

"What do you mean?"

"Obviously, you want to attack the World Summit."

He laughed hard and long. It had a manic quality that sent shivers down her spine. "I don't want to attack it."

"You don't?"

"No. I want entire nations destroying nations. In the nuclear war that results."

She glanced at the shelves upon shelves of drones. She didn't count them, but there appeared to be about two hundred of them. How exactly was he going to start a nuclear war with them?

The drones had small compartments for bombs, but they weren't big enough to carry enough explosives to level the U.N. building. "Don't you care about any of the people that are going to get killed when these drones...do what you want them to do?"

"It wasn't an easy decision. But I have to do it."

"Why? Why do you have to do it?"

"You wouldn't understand." He finished working on his current drone, and with a few taps on its touch screen, he released it to go back onto its shelf. Then he got up and retrieved a black backpack from the back of the room.

He pulled out a small decal of a flag belonging to a country Martha couldn't place and adhered it to the side of the next drone. After tapping something on its touchscreen, he glanced up at Martha. "I know you think I'm a terrorist."

"Aren't you, though?"

He didn't answer.

"Who the hell are you? And what do you want with me? I'm one little street cop. How much can I possibly get in the way of your little plan of global anarchy?"

"You know the answer to that as well as I do."

"What do you plan to do with me here?"

"I want you to wait. Once the plan is past the point of no return, then I'll release you. But not until then."

"Why keep me alive? And when is the point of no return?"

"All in time, dear Martha. All in time."

"Quit saying my name that way. You don't know me. And your plan will never work."

"Oh yes, it will."

"There are too many people who know what you're doing. You've left too many footprints."

He didn't say anything, just started working on the next drone.

When she started to open her mouth again, he got up and walked over to her. Then he leaned down next to her and threw back his hood and took off his sunglasses.

Martha gasped. It was the first time she'd seen Pete's face up close.

And even though she knew he wasn't actually Future Rueben, it was most definitely Rueben's face aged by about twenty years.

Aki and Rueben stood with Jeebs in the lobby of the building with the drone monitors. He showed them the various images of the drones on the monitors. "If you want to see the drones, this is how you do it. Period. No exceptions. Captain's orders."

Rueben raised an eyebrow at the preemptive refusal. "Captain's orders, huh?"

Jeeb's blue eyes flashed coldly. "That's what I said. Now, here are the drones, and that's what they look like, and here are the specs on each one, like I showed the other agents. Anything else you need to see?"

Aki perked up. "How long ago did the other agents leave?"

"I can't tell you that, ma'am. Now, if you've finished here, it's almost chow time, if I may."

Aki smiled. "Oh yes, of course. Unfortunately, we need to make quite a few notations before we can be on our way. Please, don't let us keep you."

Jeebs turned on his heel and left the building without another word. They waited until they heard a vehicle pull away.

Finally, Aki spoke. "We need to find where these are. That's probably where Martha and the intern are at."

"They have to be on this base somewhere."

They ventured down a hallway and found a coded door. They couldn't get in.

Rueben pointed at a scanner above the keypad. "Try your code."

She pulled her phone out and scanned the code, but it didn't open the door. "Damn."

Aki examined the door to see if there was any way to break in. "This thing is completely electronic. There is no way to open this door other than with a code."

Then Rueben had an idea. "I saw a metal door on the ride over here that looked like it was cracked open. It's outside."

Her face brightened. "Let's go."

They ran out of the building, but as soon as they got outside, a tight group of soldiers burst around the corner in their afternoon jog. They were all in camo and chanting, "Left, right, left."

Rueben and Aki scrambled back inside and hid out of view from the windows. They could still hear the soldiers chanting.

She whispered, "I thought it was chow time."

"He said it was almost chow time. Maybe he was worried he would miss dinner."

The noise calmed, and Rueben peered out the window. One more straggler jogged past, and Rueben ducked out of sight again. He ventured back up and saw no one. He looked in both directions and still didn't see anyone. "Looks like the coast is clear. Let's go."

Rueben and Aki stepped out of the building, warily scanning for anyone else. The base seemed empty again. He motioned to her and took off in the direction of the open door on the backside of the building.

As soon as they got there, they saw it. It was a metal door with fading red paint, and it looked like it was cracked open about half an inch.

Aki commented, "I'm surprised you noticed that from the Porsche."

"It was open more when I saw it. I guess the wind blew it shut some."

"That means we'd better hurry."

Shrubs protected the door, and they had to pick their way through the branches. A Jeep whizzed past, and they ducked behind the bushes. The vehicle stopped about thirty feet away, and two soldiers got out and casually chatted.

"I'm just saying, like if you had to choose."

"Between Kim K. and J. Lo?"

"Yeah."

The two soldiers got closer, and Rueben crouched as low as he could. Aki scrunched down beside him.

The conversation continued. "I don't know, man. That's a hard choice. They both got that booty, but they're both a little high maintenance, you know what I'm saying?"

"I know what you're saying."

They were inches away from Rueben now. If they looked over the top of the bushes, they'd see them.

"I mean, you know, a man's gotta get paid to get with that."

"I hear you, man. I hear you."

The two soldiers swung the metal door wide open and entered as they talked. "Plus, like I said, they're old as fuck. I'd go with the younger ones, like that Kylie…"

They disappeared into the building, and the door floated shut behind them. Rueben's heart raced, and he scrambled to catch it without being detected. He wasn't going to make it, though.

Rueben reached into his pocket and fished out Martha's red toucan keychain as he dove toward the closing door. Falling on his chest, he extended his hand and barely managed to wedge the keychain into the doorway as the door closed on it. He looked up from the ground and found that Petunia had caught in the crack and successfully prevented it from closing.

The soldiers' conversation was distant, but he could still hear it.

"Yeah, now Kylie…she's hot. I wouldn't mind, you know… with her."

The other soldier laughed. Then Rueben couldn't hear them anymore as he lay on his chest. Aki was still hiding in the bush behind him, and she shot him a questioning look. He winked in response, and she visibly relaxed.

Still prostrate in the dirt, he held up a finger. He waited for a few more minutes for the soldiers to get far enough away, then he glanced around outside the bushes. He couldn't see anyone.

He rose and dusted off his clothes, and Aki did the same. He opened the door and pocketed Petunia the plastic toucan. They both entered the building.

The back of the building had a short hallway with offices on either side. Clearly, the two soldiers worked back here, so they were somewhere. Rueben and Aki leaned against the wall and crept slowly along the hallway. They didn't see anyone. Where had the two guys gone?

They crept deeper inside. One of the two guys suddenly stepped out of an office. Luckily he turned back to address his buddy and didn't see Reuben and Aki out in the open. "But Khloe, she looks too fake."

Rueben held his breath, and every muscle in his body tensed. They had credentials to be on the base but not breaking in back here. If anyone caught them, they would likely go to jail. Well, Sven could get them out of it, but it would be an ugly process. That was if the guards didn't shoot them on sight.

Rueben carefully felt his way back along the wall. He saw a door nearby. He felt around until he found a doorknob and eased it open.

The conversation between the two guys continued. "They all look fake, though."

"That's true. That's the point of that whole family. Especially that dad."

They doubled over in laughter, and Rueben darted behind the door and grabbed Aki with him. They shut the door behind them, and in the darkness, it appeared they were in a closet of some kind.

Rueben smelled cleaners, and it was small enough that Aki pressed against the same wall he was, and he was stepping on her foot. There wasn't room for the both of them in here, and there sure wasn't time right now for them to adjust.

From outside the door, one of the soldiers commented, "Did that closet door just open?"

Rueben froze. He still had his hand on the inside doorknob, and he felt a lock against his palm.

"I definitely heard something. Is someone back here?"

With a subtle palm movement, Rueben twisted the lock and felt it click.

"I didn't see anyone come in."

Rueben squeezed his eyes shut, held his breath, and lifted his hand off the doorknob.

The soldier tried the door. "It's locked."

Only a door separated them from the soldiers.

"Whatever. Let's go. It's chow time now."

"If there's someone in here and we don't check it out, it's our asses. Go get the keys."

Rueben's stomach froze. *Busted.* They would have to fight these guys who were clearly in much better shape than he was. Then they'd radio for backup, and the whole horde of United States troops guarding this base would be on their asses like white on rice.

"Dude, I don't even know where the keys are. We'll have to call someone, and it will take forever."

"We have to do it right and file a report of suspicion."

"A report of suspicion? Come on, really? You think some crazy homeless dude is hiding in the cleaning closet? How would a homeless guy even get in here? There are, like, twenty armed guards outside and a security fence. I can barely get in here half the time."

"You said you saw it open too."

"I don't know what I saw. I *heard* something. It could have been a mouse. Come on, dude. I'm hungry. Let's go."

"Fine. Let's go."

The metal door slammed shut, and Rueben counted to ten before he exhaled. Then he felt along the wall and found a light switch. He flipped it on. They were in a janitorial closet no bigger than a bathroom stall.

He repositioned himself to get off Aki's foot. "That was close."

"Yeah. We don't have much time. The one guy's onto us. All he has to do is compare notes with Jeebs, and they'll figure it out. We have to find Martha and Zach and those drones fast."

"Yeah."

Rueben opened the door, and they all but fell out of the closet and into the hall. Rueben made sure to lock the closet in case the soldiers came back later to check. They hurried down the short hall, up a flight of steps, and found another door with a keypad at the end of the hall. They tried it. It was locked.

Aki motioned to him. "Do you have your wallet on you by chance?"

"Yeah."

She peered at the door locking mechanism. "This one will work. Give me a plastic card."

He pulled out his wallet and handed her the first rewards card he could find.

She smirked when she saw it. "You shop at IKEA?"

He shrugged. "I like the style, okay?"

She raised an eyebrow.

"Okay, and they have good lamps."

"Lamps? You buy lamps?"

"Yes, I buy lamps. Mainly because Buzz said... Never mind. Are we going to break into this room or not?"

She grabbed the card and shoved it between the door and the frame. "I can't see anything."

"Maybe you need one of my lamps."

She silently chuckled. After a bit of finagling, the door popped open. She held her finger over her mouth, and they crept in. It was a tiny office with a concrete floor, and they had to be careful with even their footsteps.

The office reminded him of going into the office area of a mechanic's shop. There was a messy wooden desk and a computer whose manufacture date looked like it was before Rueben was born. A couple of crinkled papers lay on the desk, and some tools and screws.

Rueben took out his phone and snapped photos of everything. Then they noticed the office had a door on the far wall next to a window overlooking a large warehouse area.

That was when they saw Martha.

"Oh, thank God. She's still alive." Rueben wiped a hand across his forehead. That was the only relief they got. Martha was in the middle of the room, tied to a folding metal chair. She appeared to be talking to someone, although they couldn't see who. He was standing between rows of shelves containing drones.

Aki ducked beneath the view of the window, and Reuben did the same. They needed weapons. Suddenly, his eyes lit up, and he felt in his pocket. He triumphantly retrieved Buzz's spinning top, careful not to activate the blades. He turned to Aki. "Hey, do you have any weapons on you?"

Aki looked at him. "No. Why would I? We wouldn't have been able to get past the checkpoint."

"Yeah," Rueben said. "But women have places to hide things." He flinched when Aki crooked an eyebrow at him.

"What exactly are you saying?"

"Um, it's just that on TV, whenever a woman is undercover in, like, a tight dress or something, she always has a weapon and her badge concealed somewhere…um, uh never mind."

Aki smirked and then said, "Who do you think Martha's talking to?"

Rueben stared through the window down at the shelf of drones concealing Martha's kidnapper. Suddenly a swatch of white hoodie came into view. "It's Pete."

Martha wiggled against the restraints around her wrists, and she thought she noticed a shadow of guilt pass over Pete's face. "You think you could let me go, here, Pete? I mean... Rueben. This hurts like hell."

"You don't know true pain."

"Just let me go."

"I can't."

"Yes, you can."

"No. I don't trust you in this world."

Fair enough. If he let her go, she'd probably kick his ass. Or at least try to, anyway. She didn't know if she could with his metal body armor or whatever he had on under his hoodie.

Pete continued with his drones. He looked so alone.

"Why are you doing this, Rueben? Why are you really doing this? I don't buy your fake Guy Fawkes historical bullshit for one minute. It was a smokescreen for something else. Tell me why you're doing this."

"You wouldn't understand."

"Try me."

He raised an eyebrow and continued to load the bombs inside the drones. "This world is the hardest."

"Why?"

"Everyone dies."

"Isn't that what you're trying to do?"

"That's not what I mean. I mean...everyone I care about

347

dies over and over again. There's no way out. No matter how many times I try to save them, they keep dying. Believe me, I've tried everything. In over seven thousand tries, I still can't save them."

"Seven thousand?"

"Yeah. I just want to be free from all of this."

"Look, there has to be some other way. You don't want to do this."

"But I do."

"Reuben, this isn't you."

"This isn't me when I was in my twenties, no. That's the Rueben you know."

"No, I know the real Rueben. We grew up together."

"Oh, hell. Like I remember any of that."

She wondered if Pete, being from another universe, had an alternate version of herself as his childhood friend. If so, had things happened as they had in this universe?

Evil Rueben continued to inspect each drone, sometimes placing a decal of a country's flag onto the side, and sometimes he'd record a voice message in a foreign message. But why? Martha watched him closely. "It reminds me of that time you built a rocket."

"What?"

"In seventh grade, you wanted to build a rocket that went into space. You spent all summer working on it and mowed lawns for the parts. You'd read all these books and convinced yourself that you could get it to launch. All you needed was this one little part, and it would be complete. You saved up all your money, and…this kid, you remember Perla Jaxson?"

He didn't say anything. He just kept working.

"She was this girl down the street, and someone stole her bike. She was devastated, and her mom said it would be a while before she could get her a new one. They didn't have much money. So, you started a crowdsourced campaign for her bike. Do you remember that?"

A slight smile played about his lips, but he didn't say anything. That was good. It meant his universe was like her universe.

"Only no one donated, so you put in all your rocket money and gave it to her. She never knew it was you."

He raised an eyebrow. "She never bought a bike. She took the money and bought a curling iron and new makeup. Incidentally, she suddenly became hot and popular and completely uninterested in me."

"That's how that ended up?"

"As I recall. But you were there considerably more recently than I was. So I trust your memory over mine on that."

Martha suddenly did seem to remember Perla turning into something of a snot after the bike incident. Had that had to do with buying beauty products with Rueben's bike money?

"That's not the point. The point is, you're a nice guy. You're not like this. Killing a bunch of human beings, regardless of your reasons, is wrong."

"Wrong? There is no right and wrong, Martha. There are only rules and rule-followers."

There was a clear difference between Rueben and Pete. For a moment, she'd been talking to Rueben, and now he was switching back to Pete.

"Think about what the fallout is going to be in this timeline after you do this. Is that what you want for all of us? For the people you care about?"

He slammed the screwdriver down. "That's just it. You're all going to die. Especially you. You're going to die soon, and it will be a horrible death."

Martha's stomach froze, and she felt the color drain from her face. "How?"

"Never mind. Just leave me in peace."

He worked on his drones for a few more moments. She tried to get to his soft side again. "Remember when we were kids, and we built that bike ramp? God, that thing had to have been at least six feet high. How did we not die?"

He didn't respond, but she could tell he was holding back a chuckle. "Remember that one time a bunch of us went to that party at Bret Williams's house? It was great until the cops busted it up. Everyone got arrested but you.

"We were all running like hell, and you grabbed a throw blanket and hid under the couch. I don't know how you fit under there. We all went to jail, and our parents had to bail us out. You were sound asleep in your bed at Marshall's curfew. We all got grounded, and you didn't have anyone to hang out with, so you kind of grounded yourself."

He raised an eyebrow as his lips rose in slight amusement, but he still didn't say anything. He grabbed a screwdriver from his backpack and started to loosen a screw on one of the drones.

"Damn. How you put up with Marshall all those years, I will never know. He was all right before the whole...thing. Once Carolyn left, he flipped a switch."

Pete's movements were tense now, but she kept going.

"The thing I most remember about Carolyn was that she always had cookie dough in her freezer. She would bring it out sometimes, and we'd all have cookies and milk."

He turned to face her, his eyes wild. "Don't. You. Dare."

"I'm sorry, I'm sorry."

"If you don't shut that hole in your face, I will shove this screwdriver down your throat until you do."

For the first time, she was really scared. This alternate universe Rueben was not the Rueben she had grown up with. This was someone else. And she feared he was capable of anything.

Rueben and Aki crouched down low under the window in the office and watched the exchange between Martha and Pete.

They watched the exchange until Pete stepped out from between the shelves and gestured at Martha with what appeared to be a weapon.

Rueben's eyes widened, and he turned to face the door leading down into the warehouse. "We have to rescue her."

"Wait. Wait. I've called for backup."

"But it may be too late. We've got to go in."

"We don't have any weapons, and this guy's a psychopathic killer."

"What do you suggest, that we sit here and watch her get killed?"

"No. I think we need to come up with a better plan than an ambush. It hasn't worked for us in the past, has it?"

Rueben had to admit she was right. "What if we alert the base staff?"

"Right. The first thing they'll want to know is why we're sneaking around, and by the time we get around to explaining ourselves, it will be too late. Besides, they have Pete in there in the first place. For some reason, they trust him."

"Well, I'd feel a lot better with more than this razor blade top." Rueben rifled through the desk drawer and found a sharp metal letter opener. Man, he didn't want to have to use it, but if Pete threatened Martha, he'd have no choice. "I'm going in with this."

Aki winced. "That might do." She snooped through the office for another makeshift weapon and found only a heavy paperweight in the shape of a small sea bass. She shrugged. "Better than nothing, I guess."

Rueben and Aki slowly opened the door next to the window and descended sturdy metal stairs, sneaking silently against the wall. The shadows helped conceal them. They heard muffled voices but couldn't make out what Martha and Pete said. Slowly, keeping a watch out for any extra guards, they snuck up to the middle of the room.

Pete was speaking. "It's a useless existence. I keep living, and everyone around me dies. So this time, everyone will die with me."

Martha's eyes widened as she spotted them behind Pete. She kept going, maintaining eye contact with Pete, keeping him distracted. "What if you stayed in one timeline, and you were like the rest of us, trying like hell not to die?"

"Don't try to tell me how to live my life."

"Why not? You want to tell the rest of us how to end ours."

Pete smirked, and Rueben and Aki snuck up behind him.

Martha fidgeted her knees together awkwardly. "I have to use the bathroom."

Pete sighed and set the screwdriver on a shelf. "You're not going to try anything funny, are you?"

"No. I really need to pee. Can you please untie me?"

He rolled his eyes and approached her.

As soon as his attention focused on the ropes, Pete's eyes narrowed on Martha, and he drew his silenced pistol and leveled it at her head. "I see what you're trying to do. So you thought you could escape when I untied you? I'll show you—"

Rueben snuck forward, closing in on Pete from behind, the razor blade top in one hand, the metal letter opener clutched in the other like a knife. No, like a shiv. He suddenly felt unclean, like a criminal. Like Pete...but Rueben heard the click of Pete's gun cocking and he let fly the top, twisting it in a vicious corkscrew manner.

The top went flying across the room, landing upon the floor with a click. Pete's gun was swinging around as the razor blades sprang out. He fired at it, missing on his first two shots and hitting it on his third.

It was the perfect distraction and bought Rueben the time he needed to close in the rest of the distance to Pete. Realizing too late that this was some trick, Pete was in the motion of turning the gun back on Martha when Rueben thrust the letter opener hard into Pete's back.

Pete stumbled, then whipped around, the blade still lodged in the back of his body armor. "Ow." He felt at the wound in his back irritably with one hand and sucked in a sharp breath. "Who stabs with a letter opener? Hah. I knew it wouldn't be long before you two showed up."

He scrunched his face with pain, then reached back and ripped the letter opener from his back. He held the bloody knife, and it dripped on the floor. "Good. You're getting better at this. I can see you've been practicing."

Rueben scoffed. "Stop playing the timeline card. It's not as predictable as you make it seem."

"Yes, it is. I knew you were coming. I prepared for your arrival."

"How so?"

Pete fingered his gun and waved it in front of him. "Silencer. And I have at least two bullets with each of your names on them."

He gestured toward Rueben. "Of course, then you'd warp back in time and try to stop me a different way. No matter. You can't go back farther than the Exit Bar, and if you like, we can keep going around and around until the end of time."

His gaze sharpened on Rueben. "I'll never stop. I will eventually complete my mission."

Aki snuck around Pete and worked on trying to free Martha.

Rueben knew his best bet was to keep Pete talking. "Your little suicide mission?"

Pete scoffed. "Oh, my mission isn't to die. No, no. You catch on slow. Not that I should fault you for that. You haven't evolved yet into the strongest version of yourself that you can be." He pointed to his chest. "Me. However, you're making quite the accelerated progress...I mean, stabbing me with a letter opener? That's cold."

"I am not you."

"Not yet." Pete sneered. "Welcome to the dark side."

Suddenly, Aki did a spin kick and staggered Pete a bit. "Shit. I always miss that one."

Martha shrugged off her bindings as Pete's gun slid across the floor. Throwing the heaping coils aside, she lunged out of the chair to grab it. But Pete was faster, and he hip-checked her, sending her sprawling to the floor. Aki picked up the silenced pistol and fired at Pete's chest. The bullet ricocheted off.

Pete stripped the gun from her hand in a swift backhanded sweep as he spun on one heel while simultaneously lifting one boot and planting it against Aki's midriff. He kicked out, sending her sliding along the floor.

"I still got some of your dance moves, kid." Pete grinned as he watched Aki collide with one of the tables in the room.

Rueben clenched his teeth as he stepped toward Pete. "Then why don't you try to use them on me?"

He swung his fist at the older version of himself, but Pete sidestepped. Then Pete punched, and Rueben barely danced out of the way. With Pete caught mid-swing, Rueben brought his shoe up, kicking Pete broadside just below the ribs.

Grunting, Pete clutched his side as he repositioned himself across from Rueben like a matador might a bull.

Rueben couldn't help but smile at his training and dance footwork paying off. "You've lost a step or two, senior."

Pete made an exasperated face and punched forward. Rueben sidestepped again, realizing too late that it was a feint, and Pete clobbered him where his neck met his shoulder with a solid fist.

Rueben collapsed to his knees, seeing spots, as Pete walked around to face him.

"Stay. The. Hell. Away." With that, Pete slugged Rueben across the cheek and Rueben slumped onto his chest.

Pete took off down an aisle of shelves at a brisk jog.

Rueben meanwhile moaned and turned his head to check on his friends. Martha was also lying on her chest. Blood matted her hair to her forehead where she must have struck a table when Pete had hip-checked her. She was still breathing, though. A few yards away from Martha, Aki groaned and rubbed her head.

"You've failed." Rueben turned his head again to face the far wall of the warehouse as Pete smiled and pushed a button on the wall. With a series of *clicks* and some hydraulic *whirs*, the entire warehouse wall parted down the middle, and both sides slid back like the opening of a hangar.

Outside was a private parking area they hadn't yet seen, with the green Ford Escape. Pete tapped on a tablet, and all two hundred drones in the room came to life as one, lifting from their shelves and hovering in midair.

Martha and Aki were still on the floor, but Rueben managed to stagger to his feet as drones swarmed him and buzzed past him like bees. With a satisfied laugh, Pete stood with his arms akimbo as the drones darted out the now-open side of the warehouse. They ascended into the sky, and like a flock of birds, disappeared from view.

Rueben raised a hand uselessly. "No..." His throat felt parched, and he knew that Pete had beat him. One of the drones lingered behind and jabbed Rueben with a cattle prod. With a zap of electricity, Rueben fell to his knees. The drone buzzed off into the sky to join the rest of the flock.

Pete pulled a tiny key from his pocket. He tossed it into the air and caught it with flair. Then he flicked it onto the floor. "That's the key to closet 1A. You can free Zach if you'd like. I told you, I don't want to kill you. But I will if I have to. As Marshall might say, 'It's all over but the crying.' There's nothing anyone can do to stop things now."

Pete pulled his car keys out of his pocket and climbed into the stolen Escape.

That's when soldiers rushed around both sides of the open warehouse. They poured in with rifles raised, surly expressions on their faces.

"Shouldn't have interrupted chow time," Jeebs said, and his fellow soldiers nodded in grim agreement.

"This is all a big misunderstanding—"

Jeebs cut Rueben off. "Shut it. Not another word or we'll shoot."

Rueben glanced up into the sky and watched hopelessly as the straggler drone became a dot up in the sky and disappeared.

CHAPTER THIRTY-THREE

Monday, May 22, 5:40 p.m.

Buzz stood on the rooftop of the Mount Olympus Grand Hotel, ten blocks from the U.N. building. Sixty stories below him, the streets were empty, blocked off by police before the day had begun. Peering over the edge of the roofline, Buzz let the music from the concerts outside the summit reach his ears.

"Dude, man, is that Springsteen? Wish I was at that concert." The voice came from Mike Fury, standing a few yards behind Buzz in jeans and a leather jacket.

Zach cleared his voice from beside Mike as he raised his eyes from the tablet in his hands. "I had two tickets to it, you know."

Mike turned to Zach and slapped a strong hand on Zach's shoulder. He smirked and cocked his head over his shoulder toward the center of the hotel's rooftop. "I say screw it. The real party is right here. Glad you were resourceful enough to join us." He winked exaggeratedly, but it came off as cool and confident instead of awkward. "Amiright?"

Zach turned and gulped. Standing in three rows of ten, like Rockettes lined up for a show, were thirty leggy Binnies, dressed in tight-fitting gray silk blouses complete with sparkly silver miniskirts and black fishnet stockings beneath plunging to silver laced up boots. They stood at attention, the world's sexiest robot army. Except, of course, they looked perfectly human.

The thirty Binnies wore fantastical silver flight goggles over their eyes and a compact futuristic device on their wrists that looked like some kind of hand cannon straight from a sci-fi flick.

"Y-yeah," Zach agreed. "Party's here all right."

All this Buzz watched from his peripheral vision as he scanned the sky above the cityscape beyond. After checking the laptop resting in front of him on the raised lip of the roofline, he spun on his two assistants.

"Let's get our heads in the game. The drones will be here at any moment."

"Yes, sir, Boss Man!" Mike saluted while Zach cleared his throat.

"Are they on the radar yet?"

Buzz shook his head and lowered his fingers back to his laptop's keyboard. He tried to hack back into the central "brain center" that controlled the drones' collective movements while in swarm formation but found that he was still locked out.

From the time Pete had released the drones from the military base, Buzz had been successfully hacking into their preprogrammed flight pattern and altering it at intervals. Inevitably, the drones' program would kick Buzz out, and they'd begin rerouting back to their destination. Then Buzz would run a hacking application in the background until the digital backdoor was open again—then he'd add a lengthy detour to the drones' route.

He'd found that he couldn't alter their destination—the U.N. building—but he could slow them down. Maybe they'd even run out of battery before they even reached their target, but he wasn't counting on it.

He recalled listening to Rueben's, Aki's, and Martha's interaction with Pete via a microphone patch-in on Rueben's smartwatch. He'd had to divert his resources to his contingency plans after that. Aside from Zach, who had escaped the base on his own, Buzz hadn't heard from any of his friends since.

Buzz's White House connections had allowed him to rent out the hotel's rooftop even though it was in a controlled zone and had gained assurances that no government rooftop snipers would harm them.

With a chuckle, Buzz recalled walking down the streets of New York, him and Zach and Mike, surrounded by thirty Binnies while sewer smoke drifted up from all around them in an alley. It was like a wall poster of some badass action film, the gang fully assembled and ready to kick some ass.

Himself, his laptop tucked under his arm. Zach, readjusting his novelist's pencil behind his ear. Mike, toting dual machine guns. The Binnies blowing kisses to heart-struck men and women with their faces pressed up against the windows of their homes as they observed the procession.

Luckily Buzz had enough Binnies on standby in his mansion's subbasement—never know when you're going to need thirty sexbots, er, robots—and Mike had been able to commandeer and drive a school bus from his mansion out to the blockade around the summit.

Zach had met them at the roadblock, where they'd walked

the rest of the way. It was fortunate Zach had been able to escape the closet on the military base as well as steal a Jeep with skills he'd picked up from "book research."

Zach had escaped before Rueben and Aki had found Martha and confronted Pete. After finding his cell phone outside the closet and calling Buzz, Buzz had directed him straight to the blockade for their last stand in case Pete released the drones. Zach had been concerned about Martha. Buzz had assured him that Rueben and Aki had it covered, that Pete outmatched Zach.

Wiping off a bead of sweat forming on his forehead, Buzz hoped that his decision had been the right call. What if Pete had incapacitated Rueben and killed Aki and Martha?

Buzz's laptop *beeped*, signaling it was time to do his hacking. He input a few route changeups, and the drones' guidance system ejected him again.

He wiped his forehead again with his sleeve. With his slowing down the drones, if Rueben, Aki, and Martha had managed to escape the military base—they had to have, right? —they might still be able to reach the summit before the drones finally struck. But it would be awfully close. Hopefully, it didn't come to that.

Buzz had been working on this plan ever since Rueben and Aki had left, and if the drones didn't run out of battery, he'd hard-coded their flight path to fly a mere seven feet over this hotel rooftop on their way to their final target.

Yes, the world's final defense against global nuclear war stopped and ended with a rooftop containing a super-genius, a muscle man, a competent hacker and novelist-wannabe, and thirty smoking-hot robochicks.

Buzz didn't discount their chances. He'd thought of everything, but he knew how actual outcomes could differ from hypotheses.

He checked his laptop one more time, his fingers poised over the keyboard to reroute the drone swarm yet again as soon as his hacking program let him back into their system.

From behind him, Mike Fury uncapped a flask, took a swig, and tried to hand it to Zach.

"No way."

"Aw, come on, be a man."

Zach waved his hands emphatically, and Mike shrugged. He turned to Buzz. "You want some, Boss Man?"

Buzz turned and held out his hand. Mike nodded and tossed the flask to him. Buzz, not being an athlete, completely missed the flask. He picked it up. *Damn. With my brain calculating its velocity and the best angle for which to catch it, I shouldn't have dropped it.*

Picking up the flask, Buzz uncapped it and prepared to throw back a gulp.

"Wait," Zach called. "You're our leader. You can't get drunk right before we go to war."

Mike nudged him. "We're drinking *because* we're going to war."

Zach shook his head. "Well, I'd rather be a sober liability than a drunk asset."

Mike thought about that. "Hey. That's pretty good. You ever think about being a writer?"

Buzz was about to toss the flask back to Mike when his laptop beeped. Then again. Then again.

"Let the war games begin."

Buzz tossed Mike the flask and turned to his laptop. Catching the flask, Mike slid it inside his leather jacket and shouldered his machine guns. Zach readied his tablet in both hands.

"Men, to your positions," Buzz ordered.

He ran and ducked behind an AC unit with a section jutting out that was perfect to place his laptop on. Meanwhile, Zach and Mike took cover behind opposite corner walls of a rooftop outbuilding where they'd both be able to peek around the corner to attack.

"What about us, Master Buzz?" the Binnies called in a unified sexy swoon.

"Ladies, battle formation."

"Yes, sir, Master Buzz." The Binnies moved as one well-oiled machine, spreading out their three lines to cover more space as well as to provide adequate social distancing in case one of them took fire and exploded.

Peering out over his cover, Buzz saw a black cloud approaching. A cloud of drones.

"Ready, people?"

"Yeah," the Binnies cried.

"Yep," Zach said.

"Bring it!" Mike roared, and Buzz turned to see the man with a lit cigar balanced between his teeth. A chill gust of wind chose that moment to flip the flaps of his leather jacket open to reveal the crisscrossing ammo belts wrapped around his chest.

Buzz turned back to the front. As the black cloud grew bigger, a seed of doubt niggled in his mind, and he recalled dropping the flask. He was good, right? He was in control?

If he had to be honest with himself, he'd been resorting to drink to calm his nerves more and more here lately. Ever since their last mission. The Pout mission. Where he'd been held at gunpoint in a van by a crazed trucker.

Could he redeem himself now? Or would he break under pressure again, right when the world needed him most?

Now, directly ahead of him, the illusion of the black cloud started to dissolve into individual drones.

"Steady, people. Steady. Don't fire till you can see the blacks of their touchscreens."

Nerves started to worry at Buzz like a dog chewing on a piece of meat. What if he failed? He needed a drink.

He reached down toward his chest and remembered he'd tossed the flask back to Mike.

Now he could hear the collective buzzing of the drones. Heh. Buzzing. Like his name...

Focus. Focus!

His troops were counting on him to get the job done. The whole world was depending on him. Him?

Directly ahead, the drone swarm narrowed into two single-file lines and began their descent toward the rooftop, as Buzz had programmed them to do.

Any moment now. Any moment now...

Moonlight reflected off the touchscreens of the two lead drones.

"Fire!"

CHAPTER THIRTY-FOUR

Buzz's laptop screen showed a zoomed-in satellite image of the rooftop so clear that Buzz could read the serial numbers off the drones if he were so inclined to snap a screenshot of them. He wasn't inclined to snap a screenshot of them though—he wanted to disable and kill every last drone that got past the Binnies and Mike Fury.

While the drones had been out of range, Buzz had only been able to redirect their flight route. Now that the drones were in such proximity to them, Buzz's laptop and Zach's tablet could do some real damage to them.

The first of the Binnies fired their wrist-mounted microwave hand cannons—patent pending—at the lead drones. The concentrated bursts of microwaves were completely invisible, but the weapons made a soft *pew! pew!* sound for the benefit of human ears.

The first two drones dipped in the air before plummeting to the rooftop, their internal circuitry fried. The two nearest Binnies, anticipating the drop, stepped out of the way with precise aplomb. Identically, the Binnies took down the next pairing of drones and then the next. The drones crash-landed on the roof, exploding in magnificent bursts of red and yellow and orange and black smoke.

"All right!" Zach whooped from across the roof.

Then the program running the drones wised up, and the drones separated from their dual lines. They were still seven feet over the hotel's expansive rooftop, but they had spread out, making them much more of a challenge for the Binnies to hit.

Now it was Buzz's and Zach's turn.

Tracking the oncoming flow of the drones on their screens, Buzz and Zach began frantically tapping on targets and queueing up strings of attacks upon the drones' internal components. Propellers froze up. Internal gyroscopes signaled that down was up and up was down. Essentially, the drones that got past the Binnies braked and tilted and hovered in place.

A war cry erupted from Mike Fury's chest. "My turn!"

Semi-automatic gunfire erupted from Mike's weapons as he lined up his targets and fired. All his shots connected. Even if they hadn't, he was firing specialized rounds Buzz had designed for the government—patent pending—that would disintegrate into a harmless cloud of dust particles when they connected with the target or if they missed and traveled farther than a hundred feet. Mike's shooting today wouldn't harm any civilians.

Buzz relished the sounds of propellers locking up and bullets pinging into the drones' plastic bodies. Explosions soon rocked the sky.

Buzz did a mental fist pump. *All right!*

Thirty seconds into the attack, Buzz checked the progress

bar at the bottom of his laptop screen. They'd destroyed nearly thirty-one percent of the drones, and so far, none had made it past them.

This was going even better than Buzz's best predictions.

They say the tide of battle can shift like the current of the wind, and it wasn't long before the black clouds of the exploding drones began to obscure the battlefield.

"Ah shit, I can't see nothin'." Mike's words came like a bad tiding to Buzz's ears.

Zach's words, at least, gave him a heads up. "The drones are forming up again or something. I think...I think they're about to—"

The first bomb dropped onto the rooftop.

"...go on the offensive."

That's when the first Binnie went up in flames. They'd suffered their first casualty.

Nor would it be the last. Some of the drones started to vary their height against Buzz's hard-coded flight pattern. Some of the drones had forward-mounted machine guns, and Buzz watched as a stream of bullets rock-shocked a Binnie to her back, and she lay there, unmoving, her gaze fixed upon her master's face.

You're slipping. You can't handle the pressure after all

Buzz smacked himself to clear the words from his mind. The constant machine-gun fire of the drones sounded like an angry mechanic mosquito in his ears.

"Everybody! Take cover!"

He grabbed his laptop and collapsed to the rooftop with his hands over his neck. He hoped Zach and Mike were doing the same. They couldn't warp back in time like Rueben if they died, and if Rueben had been kidnapped by Pete again, he might never warp back. Might never undo his failure.

Buzz suddenly thrust his hand into his pocket and rubbed his thumb over the flat shiny surface of the cubed device he'd liberated from the barn. He'd finished it right before they'd left for the hotel, but he didn't want to use it. It was a last resort, and the results were, well, final.

He wiped more sweat from his head and checked his laptop screen. The Binnies were still *pew! pewing!* away at their targets but drones were now getting through.

Buzz felt sick to his stomach.

The rooftop rumbled and shook as another Binnie blew up. Then another. Drones continued to buzz past.

He noticed that not all the drones seemed to have guns or bombs. Some of them had stickers of flags on their sides. Others emitted a short prerecorded message in a foreign language as they whizzed by. Was this part of Pete's plan?

Even worse, had Pete already planned for this "last stand" atop the hotel? Had this scenario already played out and he didn't remember because Pete had warped back? Was this all some game played by immortal time-warping gods that mere mortals couldn't hope to win?

Suddenly Buzz was jarred back to reality by the ripping blasts of Mike's twin machine guns. The man now had them on full auto, and he wasn't conserving his ammo. "Yeah. Take that! Haha. How you like that? Want some more?"

Mike drew a breath as he reloaded. "Come on, men! We got this! Back to it! Yo, Boss Man. You got this. Back to—"

A drone's bullet struck Mike in the side of the leg, and he staggered to one knee. He kept firing. "Haha! You think you can kill me? I'm Mike Fuckin' Fury! Take that, you ugly—"

Another bullet winged him in the arm, and one of his machine guns clattered to the rooftop.

Then, from out of the chaos of battle, Zach's voice shouted, "For Fury!"

Buzz watched as the drone targeting Mike suddenly jerked and swiveled and aimed its gun at a fellow drone. Then the drone began rapid-firing upon its fellows. Explosions once again lit up the night sky.

Nice thinking, Zach. Real nice thinking.

With renewed hope, Buzz turned back to his laptop, his fingers ready to spam out some damage to these drones. Would it be enough? He didn't know. An awful lot of drones had already gotten through their line, and more continued to do so.

He and Zach and Mike would continue the attack until the last of the drones passed overhead. And then…

Well, then they'd take the fight down to the streets if they had to. They'd fight, and they'd fight some more. They'd fight until global nuclear war began if they had to. They would fight.

CHAPTER THIRTY-FIVE

Monday, May 22, 6:56 p.m.

Rueben and Aki struggled to hold on to something—anything—in the back of the military Jeep. They screamed as Martha took a sharp turn and they fell into each other. Gripping the wheel, Martha began to weave her way through NYC traffic, a borrowed police strobe light stuck to the vehicle's bumper.

Aki sat up and straightened her hair, only to get tossed sideways again. "Martha, can you please manage to stay on the road?"

The last hour had been a bumpy ride. Back at the military base, edgy soldiers had surrounded them. As they were about to escort Rueben, Martha, and Aki to the brig—Zach had already escaped the base—Aki's CIA reinforcements showed up and straightened everything out.

The military base had even loaned them this Jeep and some guns, and some off-duty soldiers had been able to slow Pete down as he fled in his green Ford Escape. The soldiers had reported Pete's position over the Jeep's radio as he neared the city, and Martha had eventually caught up to him.

It was hard to imagine that Pete had been able to elude capture in a Ford Escape—a rather ordinary SUV that could easily flip if taking a turn too sharply—which only proved Pete's driving prowess. Of course, maybe he'd died and warped back a few times in the process to make it so far. Regardless, Pete left a trail of disgruntled drivers and the occasional fender bender in his wake.

Martha found an opening in traffic and gunned it, while up ahead, Pete ramped up onto the sidewalk, sending pedestrians screaming and running for cover.

"Jesus. He's getting off on this, isn't he?" Aki fell into Rueben, then sat up. "Tell us what your evil twin is thinking."

Rueben thought for a second and tried to get into Pete's mind. The worst part was that it wasn't so hard. "He doesn't give a shit. He has nothing to lose, nothing to gain, and the whole world is one giant video game. He can reset whenever he feels like it, and nothing matters."

Aki held on to the seatback as Martha agreed, "I've seen that. How do we stop him?"

Aki replied quickly. "By ourselves, I'm not sure we can."

Martha pulled out her phone and put it on speaker while she took another sharp turn to pursue Pete. "I'm calling in help." She completed the turn, narrowly avoiding a bus. The bus horn blared at them, and the passengers gestured at the Jeep.

Pete was straight-out playing with them. What was his game?

Martha conversed with some fellow cops on the force for a few moments, and a few minutes later, she'd arranged for cop car barricades a couple of blocks ahead in all directions.

Suddenly Aki cried out, "Fly! Windshield!"

Rueben focused on the black speck on the other side of the windshield. Aki was right. "I bet that's Pete's mini-drone." Probably the same one that had implanted the nanobot "capper" in him at the Exit Bar.

The fly flew off. Then it was inside the vehicle. It landed on the dashboard and emitted a tiny electric spark.

The Jeep died.

Its mission complete, the fly took flight again and buzzed toward the back seat as if to gloat in Rueben's face. Rueben eyed it closely, raising his palms to strike.

"Can't beat meee," a tinny speaker warbled from the mini-drone.

Rueben brought his palms together in a mighty clap. "Oh yeah?"

Aki took Rueben's hand. "Rueben, that was very—"

"We've got to get out and go!" Martha yelled, opening her door. "We can't let him get away."

Traffic was hanging back from the Jeep, and they were all able to climb out. They sprinted after the green SUV, following it on the sidewalk as it took a turn. Up ahead was the police barricade.

Martha drew her gun, and the three of them hustled down the street.

Ahead of them, the Escape barreled up to the barricade and showed no sign of slowing down. Rueben's heart quickened. Was Pete going for a suicide mission?

Then, right before he reached the barricade, Pete opened the driver's door and rolled out into the street, a black backpack strapped to his back. His vehicle continued, hitting the police barricade at full force.

In a massive orange blast, the vehicle exploded. Pete must have rigged it with one of his bombs.

People screamed and ran for cover, and glass from the windshield and nearby storefronts rained down onto the street. In the commotion, Rueben spotted Pete making a break for it down an alley.

He motioned to Aki and Martha. "Go, go, run, run."

The three ran after Pete, and Martha grabbed a police radio from the officers gathered there and radioed in that the suspect was on foot. "We have reason to believe he's headed to the U.N. building."

The barricade scene was still in chaos, and Rueben overheard someone on Martha's radio talk about injuries. With all that glass and fire, of course, someone had gotten hurt.

He saw Pete about a quarter-mile ahead in his signature white hoodie, running with the precision of a track and field athlete. Rueben was keeping up now, but he knew that his endurance was fading. He didn't appreciate his future self showing him up like this, especially not in front of Aki. He'd have to take up running after this.

Rueben summoned every ounce of energy in his reserve to keep up with Pete. *Do it for Aki. Do it for Aki,* he repeated in his mind like a mantra as he closed in on Pete.

Then Pete slipped down another side alley, and they pursued him down a narrow, brick-walled space. There was nothing here but a dumpster and some undergrowth in between two tenement buildings. Then, much to Rueben's astonishment, Pete started Spider-Manning up the wall.

"What the fuck?"

Then Rueben realized Pete was climbing up a series of small metal pipes. Once he got to the second story, he smashed in a window and crawled inside.

After glancing at the vertical and probably difficult-to-climb pipes, Martha and Aki looked at Rueben questioningly.

The trio instead scrambled toward the front entrances of the building, but they were all locked.

With one swift kick, Martha broke down a door. The threesome entered a dark and dank apartment hallway. One of the hallway lights buzzed and flickered with the commotion, and residents peeked out through doors, only to scurry back inside. A woman in a dirty housedress stood with a crying baby on her hip, and the whole place smelled like cigarettes and urine.

The three of them raced down the hall toward a chipped and broken wooden staircase and up to the second floor. That level was a maze of green painted doors and ratty carpet, with occasional graffiti on the wall.

Aki leaned against the wall, brandishing her gun around the corner. "Where would he have gone?"

Rueben didn't have an answer to that. He figured they would find him dashing through the hall and catch him. Now that it was empty and silent, he didn't know where Pete would be.

Rueben remembered one time watching a show about some bounty hunter and remembered how he had handled a situation like this. He nodded at Aki and Martha. "Let's make some noise. Let's piss everyone off until someone tells us something."

Martha, Aki, and Rueben smiled at each other and went down the hall yelling, "Pete, come out, you bastard. We've got you surrounded." They kept yelling at the top of their lungs and started kicking doors.

Residents screamed inside their homes, and children wailed. Rueben kicked in a door and caught two burnouts sitting on a couch. They nodded when they saw Rueben. "You see an older version of me in a white hoodie come through here?"

"Dude, oh my gosh. Yeah. You look like him. But younger."

"So you know where he went?"

"Nah, man. He says he don't smoke no more. Hey, look, man, I'm up in the clouds." The stoner gestured at the ceiling with one lazy hand, his face illuminated by a TV playing Bevis and Butt-Head.

Rueben shut the door, but at least he knew that Pete frequented the place.

The noise plan worked because Pete came out with a wide grin. He tugged on the straps of his black backpack on his back to make sure they were snug. "You've got me surrounded, huh?"

The three of them turned toward him, and Aki pointed her gun. "Freeze."

"No, I don't think so. I'm not going to let you take me alive. And if you kill me, well, we'll just do this dance again."

Rueben sauntered up to him. "You're not going to get away with this."

Pete shrugged. His hands were bare, weaponless. "Yes, I will. If not this time, next time. Instead of fighting me all the time, you should thank me. I'm doing you a favor, you know."

Pete set his arm on Rueben's shoulder, and Rueben pushed it off. The next thing he knew, they were wrestling on the floor, with Martha and Aki jumping in to wrangle with Pete.

A couple of the residents came into the hall. One was a giant hulk of a man with tattoos and a toothy grin, wearing nothing but a pair of tighty-whiteys. "Hey, we don't need no cop shit up in here, Jared. Don't be bringing that shit up in my house."

"Jared?"

Pete smiled at Rueben. "We have many names and many lives."

The distraction was enough that Pete got a solid punch into Rueben's gut and sent him flying backward in pain. Then police car sirens sounded outside, and Pete took off on foot down the stairs.

Tighty-Whitey Man cursed up a blue streak and lumbered back into his apartment, searching for a gun. "I'm going to kill you, bringing that shit up in here." He reappeared in the hallway, chasing Rueben down the stairs and firing shots the whole way down.

Rueben shook his head at Martha and Aki midway down. "There has to be another way."

Rueben pursued Pete outside, glad when Tighty-Whitey ran out of bullets and luckily hadn't hit him or Aki or Martha. Once outside, they saw Pete in the distance, about twenty yards down the block, getting farther and farther from the scene.

Aki panted and checked her phone. "That's the direction of the U.N. building. He's headed there. This was a decoy to lose us."

Martha scoffed. "Or to lure some of the cops away from the summit. Now they're tied up for the next half hour investigating the scene. Too bad this isn't my jurisdiction."

A sudden buzzing sound brought their attention up to the sky. Bright colorful lights droned past them. Martha pointed up. "The drones for the light show. They're here."

Rueben watched them with dread. These weren't light-show drones. They were killing machines.

Aki cursed. "What do we do?"

Rueben rubbed his forehead. Then he had an idea. He

pulled out his cell phone and dialed Buzz. He'd tried to call him earlier, but Buzz hadn't answered. Surely Buzz wasn't drunk again. Not when they needed him most.

CHAPTER THIRTY-SIX

<u>**Monday, May 22, 6:42 p.m.**</u>

Buzz beelined through the empty city streets, his gaze so focused on the drone that he nearly ran right into a parking meter. Behind him, he heard Zach ask if he was okay. And behind Zach, Mike Fury limped along, his wounded leg and arm tied off with strips of his t-shirt so he wouldn't bleed out.

When he was a kid, Buzz's mom used to call it "Buzz-Zone," by which she meant he had an abnormal capacity to zone in on something and completely lose sight of anything else. That's what he was in right now as he ran through the streets, following the path of the drones.

He'd done all he could to slow down the drones with his computer hacking. The drones had almost reached the U.N. building, but Buzz had managed to program a couple more detours into their flight pattern. He, Zach, and Mike clutched microwave hand cannons taken from some of the fallen Binnies atop the rooftop.

Now Buzz raised his microwave hand cannon and lined up his shot on the drone. He stopped, held his breath, and pulled the trigger. *Pew.* The drone's propellors stopped mid-hover, its forward momentum carrying it into the path of a street lamp where it exploded into tiny bits.

Mike cheered from behind him. "Hell ya, bro."

Buzz's eyes tracked another drone. He kept his neck craned so high it hurt, and he wondered if he would get it stuck in the pose as people did in yoga.

Zach sprinted up behind him, completely out of breath. "Man, you almost lost Mike and me back there."

Buzz kept his hand cannon raised to the sky and gestured for Zach to do the same with his. "You have to aim carefully."

Buzz pointed at the drone he was currently watching. "See that one? The way it's traveling, if I stand here and aim at a forty-two-point-five-degree angle, I can get it." Buzz lifted his hand cannon, positioned it, and waited for the drone to pass at the perfect angle.

Zach raised his hand cannon. *Pew, pew, pew, pew, pew. Pew.* He struck the drone before Buzz even had a chance. "Or you could do it that way."

Buzz narrowed his eyes at Zach. "Science is based on precision and respect for the process. If it's all a big joke to you—"

Zach sighed. "I'm not disrespecting science. I just want to shoot a cool gun, okay?"

Buzz eyed Zach warily.

"Oh, come on, this whole thing is because you wanted to play Ghostbusters."

Buzz laughed. "That I did. That I did."

A drone flew overhead, and they both whistled the *Ghostbusters* theme song and aimed wildly at the sky. Invisible bursts of microwaves shot into the air, and some of the drones exploded into fireballs when they struck the walls of buildings or the pavement. With the streets cleared of bystanders, the debris didn't harm anyone.

Zach laughed. "Dude, this is better than virtual reality."

Buzz laughed, and they followed the drones down through the city, shooting at the sky. As they neared the U.N. building, Buzz checked the progress bar on his laptop. There were still eighty-odd drones aloft. Not even the Ghostbusters could save this neighborhood.

CHAPTER THIRTY-SEVEN

<u>**Monday, May 22, 7:13 p.m.**</u>

Rueben figured Pete had to be going to the U.N. building. He hadn't when he'd kidnapped Rueben and held him in that basement for three days, but in that version of the timeline, Pete hadn't had to worry about Rueben and company getting in the way.

So, after Martha had commandeered a police car, Martha, Aki, and Rueben now waited for Pete at the U.N. building. At least, they hoped they had beaten him there. There was no sign of chaos and carnage yet, so Buzz must have figured out how to either slow down the drones or reroute them to buy them some time.

The concerts had already wrapped up in anticipation of the world leaders taking the stage at 7:30 p.m. Rueben surveyed the area surrounding it, as he had seen Aki and Mike doing when he'd watched this scene play out in that basement. He spotted the blond reporter and her cameraman, filming the stage and waiting for the keynote speech. It was funny what the news team had selectively chosen not to display.

On one side of the building, protesters against the One campaign waved signs, citing communism and incorporating the One logo into the communist hammer and sickle flag. They chanted communist slogans along with the One propaganda.

Next to the anti-communist chanters were the conspiracy theorists who protested against the global elite and one world government.

"We are not your slaves."

"1984 ends with 1776."

On the other side of the building, kept separate by a line of security guards in riot gear, the One supporters sang Bob Marley songs and waved One posters.

As tense as the situation was with those two groups, nearest to Rueben's position were the Cavemen, a group of anti-establishment, chaos-driven protestors hell-bent on returning to pre-government eras.

For full-on anarchists, they sure knew how to coordinate their outfits. Fred Flintstone had nothing on them.

It was also the perfect environment for Pete to infiltrate— tense, crowded, and full of chaos.

Aki had alerted building security, and they were all on the lookout for "the bomber in the white hoodie." No one in command seemed to put much stock in that though, even after the incident at the police barricade. Rueben and Martha had tried their best to persuade those at the top that something big would go down soon, but it seemed it was up to them to save the day.

The three of them stood in the shadows near the protestors, watching the street.

One of the Cavemen in the loincloths pulled out a slingshot and killed a pigeon pecking at some garbage. Everyone gasped.

The Caveman grabbed the dead bird off the ground, much to everyone's disgust. He crouched on the sidewalk, and Rueben was glad he wasn't directly in front of him because the loincloth didn't appear to have much "crouching coverage." He rubbed two stones together, and in less than a minute, had built a fire and began to roast the bird.

The protesters all gasped and screamed, and some threw things at the man. A couple of the protestors even threw up.

Security was right on top of him. "Sir, sir, you can't do that here."

The Caveman with the ZZ Top beard responded, "It's my right to live how I want."

The protestors all exploded with applause and cheering. The man in the loincloth had adequately made his point, and suddenly he was on their side.

The police officer wasn't amused. He grabbed the man up by his forearm. "Yeah, now you're going to jail."

"That's against the culture of global unity."

The protesters screamed in agreement, and the line of security guards all turned to them militantly. "All of you, we're shutting this down. It's now a security risk. Let's go. All of you."

Cops in riot gear arrested Loincloth Man and started ushering the protesters away. They reluctantly cooperated, and two officers saw the trio standing waiting for the Hoodie Bomber. "Let's go, people. We're shutting it down."

Good, Rueben thought. With fewer people here, there would be less cover for Pete. And, if Pete's drones did succeed and start attacking, there'd be fewer people to get hurt.

Aki pulled out her phone. "It's too hot out here. We have to get to another entrance." She tried to make a call, but they kept getting jostled around by the masses, and Rueben was even smacked in the head by a protest sign.

"We have to get away from here."

Aki and Martha said in unison, "Agreed."

They managed to push their way out of the crowd and toward another entrance. Aki dialed and redialed numbers on her phone. "I can't get through to anyone."

A group of chanters nearly knocked Martha over. "What?"

Aki yelled, "We have to get to the east entrance. That's where security is, and if we can get there, we can get backup."

Rueben only figured out what she said after thinking about it. He couldn't make it out in the crowd.

They snaked their way through the people and found the east entrance. Security was less swamped there, and when the trio all flashed badges, they were instantly let through.

They stood on the other side of security and tried to formulate a plan.

Rueben and Martha looked at Aki. "It's almost 7:30. Your call here. Where to?"

"This way."

They were almost to the door of the east entrance when a line of drones buzzed toward the building, lit up like bright flashing Christmas tree lights.

Rueben's stomach tensed. "Oh no. It's about to start." He turned to the nearest police officers and summit guards. "We have to get these people out of here now!"

Out in front of the building, people began to applaud. World dignitaries started to step up to the main stage. The news teams alternated their focus between the drone light show and the world leaders.

Up in the sky, the drones formed a giant pink peace sign.

Then they morphed into a smiley face. Then they started dropping bombs in front of the building.

Fire and chaos began to sprout up everywhere.

"Shit." Rueben turned and collided with an obstacle. He whipped around to find none other than…his alternate future self in his scuffed and torn white hoodie, dark shades, and black backpack.

Pete flashed a wide, toothy smile. "And so it begins."

Aki reached for her gun. "Not so fast."

Pete shook his head. "This again? Don't you people ever learn? Doris, pulse."

His metallic glove sent Rueben, Aki, and Martha sprawling, along with the security stationed around them at the entrance. Pete easily sprinted past them into the building while outside bombs rained down and drones shot out the windows of the U.N. building with mounted machine guns.

Rueben, Aki, and Martha chased after Pete into the foyer. Pete turned to face them, and Rueben yelled, "Doris, disable."

Pete's glove powered down, but the man still smiled. Aki lined up a shot on Pete, intending to disable him with a shot to the leg, but suddenly several drones buzzed into the room and swarmed in front of Pete like bees. Aki fired several shots, but every time, one of the drones intercepted the bullet and fell to the ground.

Martha held fire from her gun. "How do we defeat him?"

Rueben gritted his teeth. "I don't know. Maybe Buzz can help." Rueben speed-dialed his friend. Buzz's phone rang and rang as Pete made it inside.

Now drones circled Martha, Aki, and Rueben, blocking them from venturing farther into the building. Martha and Aki picked them off one by one, but by that time Pete was already gone.

Aki got on her phone. "The bomber is in the building. I repeat, the bomber is in the building."

Buzz wasn't answering so Rueben tried to think what Buzz would say. *Buddy, you got to think like Pete. What would you do?*

Rueben didn't know Pete's full plan, but it involved setting off a global nuclear war. To do that, he probably needed some world leaders for leverage.

Turning around, Rueben spotted some bodyguards ushering world dignitaries into a stairwell contained behind a hidden panel in the wall.

That's it. Pete would be going upstairs too. He'd probably done his homework. He probably knew the location of the safe room where security would whisk the leaders away. Too bad Rueben didn't.

"Rueben, get down!"

Aki threw herself at Rueben as a particularly large drone buzzed toward a nearby window from the outside. The two landed beside a lavish-looking lobby couch as part of the wall exploded inward.

When the dust started to settle, Rueben noticed he and Aki held onto each other in a tight embrace.

He blinked at her. "Umm. Thanks." They helped each other up.

She nodded. "Don't mention it. Partner."

Rueben turned, beaming. Then he spotted several people wounded from the blast. Some were guards and officers. Others were news reporters and onlookers who had come inside during the bedlam. Martha was stooped over a portly man in a gray suit, making sure he was okay.

Rueben tried to locate the hidden stairwell through the smoke and found it again. Security teams gathered around their heads of state still ushered them up the steps. Radios and phones chattered and *beeped*. Building alarms sounded, and every screen in the building simply broadcasted, "Lockdown."

On the opposite side of the foyer, Rueben spotted a flash of white hoodie and a door closing on another stairwell. Pete was heading up. Meanwhile, the drones gathered outside the building were still dropping bombs and firing guns at the law enforcement and security agents on site. They were the perfect distraction.

Pete had thought this through, down to the contingency plan of if he had to come down here to the U.N. building himself to get the job done.

Rueben was about to take off toward the stairwell Pete had entered when he heard Aki mutter, "Oh shit."

He turned, and time seemed to slow as he watched in helpless terror as a drone buzzed through an open window, pivoted in mid-air, and sighted in on Aki with its machine gun.

"No..."

Rueben reached out, but it was too late. There was nothing he could do to stop the drone from killing Aki. Pete was going to kill Aki a third time.

The drone's machine gun made a snicking sound as it prepared to fire.

Aki tensed her legs to throw herself to the side, even though she wouldn't be fast enough.

Pew. Pew. Pew, pew, pew.

The drone's machine gun tilted downward, and one of its

propellors stopped. Then it did a three-sixty and rammed straight into the wall, exploding in a blast of light and debris.

Rueben whipped around to see none other than Buzz and Zach with what looked like some kind of sci-fi wrist blasters in their hands. Buzz wore a satisfied smile. "I do what I can."

Rueben laughed and high-fived Buzz. "Inspector Gadget strikes again. What kind of weapons are those?"

"Microwave hand cannons," Zach said proudly.

Buzz added, "Patent pending."

"Nice." Rueben smacked Buzz on the shoulder. "Way to utilize microtechnology for the good of humanity."

"I thought so."

Mike Fury limped inside the foyer then, his machine gun gripped in one hand, his leg and arm tourniquets stained with blood. "You guys go on without me. Me and the Binnies will stay out here and save who we can."

"Thanks," Rueben said sincerely, setting aside his petty annoyance with the guy. Maybe he'd been too hard on Mike. Also, the dude looked like the friggin' Terminator.

After Mike stepped back out, Rueben and his friends briefly surveyed the damage. The world leaders had all gone up the stairwell. The hidden panel once again displayed an ordinary-looking wall.

"Follow me." Rueben led his friends to the wall. He got the panel open and saw a wounded security guard sitting against the wall at the base of the stairwell.

Rueben bent to check on the man. He was in pretty bad shape, but he'd live. He was a bit woozy, though.

Rueben had an idea. "We're here to stop the bomber. Do you know which floor the safe room is on?"

"Twenty-first floor. Room uh...2109."

Rueben gave him his thanks. He'd leave the hidden panel

open so that the medics could find him when they entered the building. Then Rueben started up the stairs. His friends followed.

As they ascended the stairwell, explosions and gunfire continued to pierce the night outside. Rueben shook his head. "This is a disaster."

Buzz shook his head and sucked in a breath. "You're telling me. I'm missing my bubble bath and cocktail and evening massage." It was supposed to be a joke, but no one laughed.

Martha shook her head. The climb up the stairwell hadn't seemed to affect her much yet. "Buzz, the last thing you need is more cocktails. Great job, Zach. Just be careful with how much you let this guy influence you."

Zach shook his head. "You're all a bad influence."

They all bobbed their heads in agreement.

Martha added, "Probably. Just stop before homemade guillotines get involved."

Zach made a face. "Homemade guillotines? You guys are funny. I think."

Martha, Buzz, and Rueben glanced at each other and cleared their throats. While Martha and Buzz didn't remember killing Rueben that way when training for the Pout mission, they'd seen the nanobot watch footage of it in Buzz's secret computer room.

Zach's eyes widened. "Wait, guillotines? You guys are joking, right?"

Buzz wrapped his arm around Zach's shoulder as they continued to climb the steps. "You have so much to learn, young grasshopper."

"Clearly. 'Let them eat cake,' I guess."

Another explosion sounded from outside. Rueben heard someone cry out in pain and he winced. Finally, he stopped on the step he was on and faced his friends. He met Aki's eyes. "Guys. If we keep going, we might still stop Pete's full plan from happening. But...the cost has been too high. We weren't as prepared as we were for the Pout mission."

He angled his head toward the sound of the bomb blasts and gunfire. "Too many people have been injured and killed, and with my powers, I can't let that happen. I'm going to have to die to warp back and reset all this." He tried not to let Zach's dropped mouth distract him. "We'll do it right this time. We know what we're doing. We know what we're dealing with. We can fix it."

That's when Buzz shook his head. His lips were taut, and Rueben didn't think he'd ever seen his friend's face so serious. "No. Actually, I don't think you should do it." They all looked at him, confused.

"What are you saying?" Rueben said.

Buzz reached into his pocket and retrieved the small shiny cube. Everyone's eyes focused on the tiny needle projecting from one of its surfaces. "It's ready."

"That's great..." Rueben let his words trail off. "We can use it against Pete now. Right?"

"Yep. According to my super computer's computations, once you stick Pete with this needle, the nanobot you'll inject into him will bond to him at the genetic level. It will immediately and indefinitely disable his ability to warp if he dies."

Rueben stared at him. Buzz had done it. Found a way to defeat Pete. "How'd you figure it all out? You said it was, like, twenty years advanced."

Buzz gave a sly grin. "I studied the nanobot capper that

Pete implanted in you via data collected through the original nanobot that I use to monitor your warps. The nanobot in the shiny cube is way more advanced.

"My supercomputer helped me understand how I could incorporate the framework of your Exit Bar cap into a permanent warping cap in the shiny cube's nanobot. It's very complex stuff, and I wouldn't have been able to do it without my computer."

Rueben thought it over. "You're saying that if I inject Pete, it'll severely hobble him. Without his warping power, if we stop him, he can't go back and try it again."

He paused as another explosion sounded from outside. "I can't let all those people die out there. Not when I can warp back and stop it. Why don't you want me to warp back? Then you can give me the shiny cube—"

Buzz looked exasperated. "Do you realize how lucky we've been to get to this point? People have died, but if you warp back to try to save them, Pete might surprise you or knock you out again.

"Who knows if Pete is watching us right now with another one of his little fly surveillance drones. If he finds out about this device, he'll warp back and kill me at the Exit Bar over and over again so I can't make it. This is our last hope, and if we don't use it now, the world as we know it could be reduced to ashes once Pete accomplishes his plan."

"I don't know—" Rueben started.

"This is more serious than Pout's plan," Buzz said. He turned to Martha and Aki and Zach. "We're not just trying to save NYC. We're trying to save the entire world."

Zach fidgeted and smiled weakly for support while Martha looked almost sick. "Rueben, that's a tough call to make. I'm…glad it's not up to me."

Aki stepped up beside Rueben and brushed her hand against his. She swallowed. "I support whatever decision you choose."

Rueben weighed both options. If he made the wrong choice, he might not be able to fix this situation.

Buzz looked at him beseechingly, the shiny cube resting on his palm.

Rueben took it and slid it into his pocket. "I'll do it. I'll go and try to stop Pete. I'll make sure he doesn't see the cube coming until I have a good opening so that he doesn't warp back. But I'm going to need you guys' help."

They all nodded tensely.

Pete was a formidable foe. A few months ago, Rueben might have had some trepidation. But now... He gazed around at all his friends. There was a time when every hero had to stand up and be brave. This was his time.

Rueben cleared his throat. "As Marshall would probably say if he were here, 'It's time to take off the training wheels.'"

His friends chuckled softly, looking at him for leadership.

"I say, let's go be heroes."

He waited, and his motley crew applauded and echoed, "Let's go be heroes."

CHAPTER THIRTY-EIGHT

Room 2109 lay just up ahead.

Rueben and company hung back a few rooms from it, leaning against the wall as they recovered from the stair climb.

When Rueben stood to move, Buzz stopped him. "I think it's best if Zach and I hang back. To provide tech support, and stuff."

Rueben nodded, and Buzz held out his hand. Thinking he meant to shake, Rueben extended his hand, and Buzz pressed a razor blade top into his palm.

"Uh, heh. Also whipped up one of these before we left the mansion. Prototype was easy to reconstruct. Those blades are sharp. Give Pete hell, all right? Then, you know, inject him."

"I plan to," Rueben said.

"Be safe, buddy."

Rueben exchanged glances with Aki and Martha. They were ready. As they crept the short distance to Room 2109, they noticed that all the wall paintings were crooked.

What was that about?

Rueben slid up to the door and placed a hand on the golden knob....

The door burst open then, and a security guard in a black suit angled his gun out at Rueben.

"Don't shoot!" Aki said.

Too late. The gun had already gone off in Rueben's face.

Monday, May 22, 8:42 p.m.

This time around, Rueben called, "Friendly," as he slid up to the door and knocked.

The security guard carefully cracked open the door and lowered his gun.

Rueben glanced past the man in the doorway. He could see several other bodyguard-type men standing in front of a wall of foreign dignitaries.

"Who the hell are you?" the man in the doorway said.

Rueben turned to him. "CIA." Aki nodded, and Martha said she was with the police. "We're looking for a man. Forties. Last seen in a white hoodie—"

"Ze ghost man!" one of the dignitaries cried out from behind the bodyguards.

Rueben, Martha, and Aki's eyes perked wide. The man in the black suit nodded briskly. "Yeah. Creep already came through. Before we were fully situated. Blasted us with some sort of air burst or something." He angled his head at the crooked pictures on the wall. "Never seen anything like it before. Took a few of the world leaders."

Martha stepped forward. "Who'd he take with him?"

"Don't know, ma'am. This isn't the only safe room in this building. The leaders were split up and distributed to different wings of the building. But the man...he went that way."

Aki groaned. "So he could be anywhere now."

Rueben thanked the man and the door shut in their faces. Calling Buzz and Zach over to them, Rueben said, "Can you two patch into the building's security feed? We have to locate and stop Pete."

"Already on it, buddy. That's what we were doing."

Zach started, clutching his tablet. "Got something. Twentieth floor. Right below us. White hoodie—aw crap." The intern met all their glances. "Feed just went dead. He must've known we were in the system."

Rueben gritted his teeth with resolve. They had to move before Pete figured out their plan. "Let's go."

They rushed to the nearest stairwell and Rueben threw open the door to the twentieth floor. Immediately, a metallic gauntlet flew right at his face. Rueben ducked the fist and shouted, "Doris, disable," right as Pete was saying, "Doris, pulse." The gauntlet shut down, and Pete threw another fist.

Rueben leaned back and managed to block it, allowing his combat training to take over. "We don't have to do this. We don't have to fight."

"Oh? You suggest we all sit around the campfire and sing—"

They exchanged a few punches, neither getting in a solid hit.

"—kumbaya?"

Rueben grunted as he knocked Pete's kick wide. "It would be a start."

Pete scoffed. As he danced and bobbed, his torn and bullet hole-ridden white hoodie certainly did resemble a ghost. The drawn-up hood concealing his face was the finishing touch, except ghosts didn't typically wear black backpacks. "You know, you're different. This whole universe, it's different."

Pete and Rueben circled each other out into the hallway with their dukes up. Martha and Aki stepped through the stairwell doorway with guns raised, but they didn't have a clear line of sight for a disabling shot.

Rueben huffed in a breath, fatigue starting to set in. So far he hadn't had an opening to stick Pete with the cube. "How about we make a deal?"

"Deal? Are you nuts? Why would I make you a deal?"

"Look, how about we both give each other what we want?"

Pete grinned. "Oh. And what do you know of what I want?"

"I know you don't want to do this. Not really. You said I wouldn't understand..." Rueben blocked a punch then knocked aside Pete's kick. "I've been trying to figure out a reason why you would want to start a global war. There's only one reason I can think of."

Pete didn't look convinced. "Go on."

Rueben met his gaze. "You're doing this because you feel like it's the only way to achieve your goal. I think...this must be the least bad option of a bunch of bad options you face."

Pete spat. "You. You know nothing."

"I disagree. You're not technically me. I'm not technically you. But we understand how the other thinks. Your mission clearly pains you. The measures you took not to kill my friends—shadows of your friends from your universe. I think you're lonely. You have to be. This isn't your home."

Rueben dropped his fighting stance and took a few steps

backward in the hallway toward Martha and Aki. He was about ten feet away from Pete now. "I don't think your actions are out of spite. I think...I think they might even be out of love."

Martha and Aki exchanged confused glances, their guns still raised over Rueben's shoulders but they didn't fire. Buzz and Zach hung back in the stairwell.

Pete's coal-like eyes bored into Rueben. Pete raised a hand threateningly, then dropped it. Suddenly, he clutched his hands to the sides of his face, his fingers digging into his cheeks. He screamed.

Then he flew toward Rueben in a rage.

Rueben slid his hand into his pocket and gripped the cube. This was it.

He let Pete come to him. He let Pete slug him across the jaw. Then he jabbed the cube upward, the needle poking into the side of Pete's neck as Rueben collapsed backward.

Pete stepped back, clutching a hand to his neck. "What did you do? What did you do?"

Suddenly, the futuristic body armor beneath Pete's torn hoodie began to *beep*. A robotic voice said, "Repeating ability. Negated."

"What? No!" Pete's eyes became animalistic as they fell on Rueben.

"It's not too late to stop," Rueben said calmly, but it was like talking to an ambushed wild tiger. Pete prepared to leap at him.

Rueben already had Buzz's top in his hand. Now he let it rip, the blades extending along its curved sides as it spun in mid-air toward Pete.

"Agh!"

The top's blades sliced through the sleeves of Pete's hoodie as he raised his hands in defense. Turning on a dime, Pete flew down the hallway like a wraith. "This changes nothing! You can't stop me!"

Aki made to rush past Rueben, but he caught her arm.

"Wait, he could have another trick up his sleeve."

Pete disappeared around a corner in the hallway, and a door opened and closed.

Buzz stepped forward from the stairwell, holding his laptop. He positioned the screen toward Rueben.

"Got the cameras back online. If Pete's got a trick, I don't see it."

Rueben observed the laptop screen. Pete stood in a hotel room with five world leaders bound and gagged and kneeling on the floor by him. The room was a mess. It had a wide window on one side, and it was open, allowing wind into the room that rippled Pete's torn hoodie. Pete unshouldered his backpack and set it on a fancy, heavy-looking coffee table beside him.

Aki shook her head. "He's about to do something."

Martha nodded.

"On me," Rueben said.

They stopped to the side of a door, the carpet in front of it marked by blood drops. Rueben nodded to Martha and Aki, and they kicked open the door in unison. Rueben stepped inside.

The room was just as on Buzz's screen.

A dignitary cried, "Don't kill me."

Pete turned toward Rueben with the backpack already cinched over his shoulders. A silenced pistol in his hand aimed at the dignitaries along the wall. "Ready for the grand finale?"

On the coffee table beside him sat a block of plastic explosives stuck to the table's surface. Wires protruded from the bomb, connected to a ticking timer device.

"Don't let him do it," a female world leader said, and a big man beside her whimpered.

Rueben said, "If that bomb goes off, you die for real."

Pete cocked an eyebrow at him. Blood dripped down his sleeve from where the razor top had nicked him. "Sorry, but this bomb has to go off." While keeping his gun trained on the world leaders with one hand, Pete lifted the front of his hoodie and tapped some buttons on his metallic body armor. Five drones buzzed through the open window into the room.

These drones looked different from the other drones; they were heavily armored, with front-facing camera lenses and claws dangling beneath their bodies. Each one hovered in front of the coffee table for a close-up shot of the bomb before buzzing over to face the dignitaries.

Each drone had a flag decal that corresponded to the world leader it was in front of.

"You're probably wondering what my plan is. Maybe you've already figured it out." Behind him, the bomb's clock timer ticked. "You can't stop it now. This is only one room of dignitaries out of several throughout this hotel."

He motioned at the drones with his free hand. "I positioned my most specialized drones at the back of the swarm. So they wouldn't get destroyed.

"As we speak, they are now blocking off all ingoing and outgoing transmissions except for theirs. See, they're wirelessly transmitting video feeds as well as ransom messages or threats to either their own country or their rival's country, framing them. Starting wars, if you will, between nations with already tense relations. Russia and Ukraine. Pakistan and India..."

"Then you're going to kill all the world leaders?" Rueben asked, his throat tight and dry. The bomb continued to tick.

Pete shook his head. "Only in this room. I mean, look who I've got rounded up." With the pistol, he indicated two proud men kneeling next to each other. "The president of the People's Republic of China and the supreme leader of North Korea. Don't say I never did anything good for this world."

"I have a clear shot," Aki said from beside Rueben.

Martha stood on Rueben's other side. "Me too."

Rueben shook his head for them to wait. "You can't do this. You can't execute whoever you think deserves it—"

"That's rich." Pete chuckled. "Coming from a CIA spook."

The bomb's timer continued to tick, and Rueben felt time running out.

"I must admit," Pete wiped the perspiration from his forehead. "I didn't see things happening like this. I mean, capping me? I should have killed Buzz right from the start. He's too smart for his own good."

Aki edged up against Rueben's shoulder. "He's stalling."

"Hah. Stalling?" Pete sneered. "Now, how would that benefit me? I can't warp. You have all the leverage. I'm a dead man."

Rueben stared into Pete's eyes. "I don't think you really want to die."

Pete started to back toward the wide-open window.

"Don't move!" Rueben said.

Pete smirked as he backed another step toward the window. "Just a friendly word of caution. If you try to cut a wire or remove the bomb from the table's surface, it'll blow.

And that's a heavy table. Mike Fury might be able to lift it. But you...by all means though, try to prove your manhood for Aki. She'll leave you in the end anyway."

Suddenly, Pete spun toward the window, and both Aki and Martha started firing, their pistol shots clanging off the back of Pete's body armor as he dove out the window.

Rueben rushed to the window to watch him fall. It made no sense—then some sort of specialized parachute burst from Pete's back, thrusting him upward. A few moments later, Pete swooped gracefully through the air with his middle finger raised, disappearing around the corner of a skyscraper.

"Rueben!" It was Aki, standing at the coffee table, studying the bomb. "Fifteen seconds."

Rueben wondered if he should try to lift the table and throw it out the window, but he wasn't as strong as Mike Fury. He had to be himself to fix this. He had to solve this his way.

He turned to the doorway where Buzz and Zach stood with their electronics held before them. "Guys, can you hack these drones?"

"Yeah—"

"Do it and have them carry the coffee table outside the window."

Without a word, Buzz and Zach tapped rapidly at their devices.

"Nine seconds..."

Rueben stood his ground, watching as the five drones buzzed away from the world leaders and turned haphazardly to face the coffee table. Then with jerky motions, they hovered over the table. Their claws clamped onto its edges.

"Six seconds..."

Propellers stopped and restarted, motors burned under the table's weight. Smoke issued from some of the drones.

Martha gasped.

Rueben stared resolutely at the bomb.

The drones lifted the table and buzzed out through the wide window.

"Take them up!" Rueben said.

Motors whined. Fire engulfed one of the drones. Then the table disappeared upward into the sky.

A moment later, an explosion rocked the building. Miniscule splinters of debris rained down outside the window. Rueben and Aki exchanged nervous, happy glances, and everyone in the room let out a collective sigh.

CHAPTER THIRTY-NINE

Sometime later, Rueben and his friends finally had clearance to leave the twentieth floor. There had been questions and questions and more questions, and they did their best to offer general answers that didn't involve time warps or Pete or multiple universes.

For a time, Rueben and his friends still held their breath. They'd saved them, but had they *saved* them? Would what happened with the drone attack still prompt global war?

They'd tensely watched from the hallway as security teams escorted the world leaders back to the ground floor. Surprisingly, most of them were smiling and patting each other on the backs.

The president of the United States was there too but didn't approach or say anything to Rueben or his friends. Rueben sighed as the president stepped onto an elevator with six bodyguards.

Aki punched him lightly on the arm. "Cheer up. It's usual for us agents not to get any of the praise. It's part of the job.

I'm sure Sven will gobble up the accolades on behalf of the CIA. Unless he's fired for not foreseeing this whole mess in the first place."

When they were finally able to leave, Rueben said, "Well, will it be the stairs?"

Buzz shook his head. "Fuck no. We're taking the elevator."

Rueben smirked. While they waited for an elevator car, he yawned, noticing how scuffed up and dirty his clothes were. He also had plenty of cuts and scrapes that would need tending to. Nothing like the scar across Pete's face, but...

For a few moments, he wondered how Pete had gotten that scar and also the metal hip. Pete was a Repeater, and yet he'd allowed these things to happen to him. Why? And where was he now?

He turned to Buzz, who was poring over his laptop. "Has global war broken out yet?"

"Nah. The media is saying, and I quote, 'Ironically, the peace summit couldn't have gone better...' Hah. If the schmucks only knew what we had to go through."

"I'd say," Zach agreed coolly.

Martha smiled. "With Pete unable to warp anymore, he's pretty much out of the picture in regard to being a serious threat to anyone."

Rueben rubbed the back of his head. "Hopefully."

Aki winked at him. "Mortality bites, amiright? Besides, if Pete does show his face, he's toast. You're a Repeater. If he steps out of line, we'll track him down and deal with him. We did good today. We won, and the entire world gets to keep on spinning."

Buzz high-fived her while juggling his laptop. "Not bad, not bad, people. I think this deserves a bubble bath and champagne."

The elevator doors slid open, and they stepped in. When they were almost to the first floor, Buzz's mouth dropped open. "Oh shit. Rueben. You might want to take a deep breath and compose yourself before we step outside."

Rueben stared at him. "What do you mean?"

Buzz closed his laptop. "Umm...you need to see."

The elevator slid open, and as soon as they stepped off into the debris-strewn main lobby, crowds packed in, applauding. They were everywhere. Camera bulbs flashed, and people shoved microphones in their faces.

"Tell me, did you know of the drone attack before the summit?"

"Who was the suspect and what do you believe his motive was?"

"What's your take on the One campaign?"

"Are you familiar with One Republic Entertainment?"

"Did the bomber have any connection to Alister Pout?"

"Is Mike Fury single?"

The questions came faster than Rueben could process, let alone answer. He threw out a couple of vague answers. These reporters didn't even know who he was. He'd just happened to step out of the elevator after the president.

"Could we get an exclusive?"

Somewhere in the crowd, he caught sight of his and Aki's boss Sven Larson weeding his way through the throng.

"Is the suspect still at large?"

"What do you believe was his plan?"

Sven reached the front of the crowd and stood before the reporters. "I'm Sven Larson, State Department. We're proud of our heroes today, but in the interest of national security, we'd like to debrief them before they take any further questions. Thank you."

Sven winked at them and frowned at Zach and Martha. Then he patted Buzz on the shoulder. "Buzz, good to see you again."

"Hey, Sven. Always a pleasure."

Yolanda Martinez arrived downstairs, and the reporters zoned in on her like flies on hot shit, and Sven was able to corner Rueben and Aki. "I want to take you two out to dinner sometime soon."

Rueben stared at Aki. He didn't know about Aki, but Sven had never invited him to anything. Not lunch or drinks or even coffee. Now he wanted to take them to dinner?

Aki answered for both of them. "We'd love that."

Their boss scrutinized them. "You're a 'we,' huh?"

Aki blushed, and Rueben looked like he didn't know— which he didn't. Then Aki's smile melted his heart as she said, "Yeah. We're a 'we.'"

Sven nodded and stroked his chin. "Well, after what you guys did...I'm sure we can allow it. Try to keep it on the down-low at the office, will ya?" Then he winked and left the building. Rueben made a fist-pumping gesture and Aki laughed.

Yolanda Martinez was now shouting at the reporters closing in on her and probably asking her stupid questions.

Rueben turned to Aki. "We have to get out of here."

"Agreed."

"Let's go find the others."

They looked around for Martha, Buzz, and Zach, but now a new batch of reporters was closing in on them. One was particularly aggressive, a blond woman that Rueben recalled seeing on the news footage from when Pete had kidnapped him. "I need to talk to him," she called.

Rueben grabbed Aki. "It's not safe here. You've heard of people getting mobbed by paparazzi, right?"

It wasn't exactly paparazzi, but it sure felt like it. Cameras and live video feeds were everywhere. It bothered him more than a bit considering they were both CIA agents. They needed their anonymity.

"Rueben, Rueben Peet."

Damn, who had leaked his name to them? Rueben held up his palm. "No comment."

"Please, I need just a minute."

He ignored the blond reporter and kept walking. Then he heard it. "Please, Mr. Hash Brown…I need to talk to you."

Rueben stopped dead in his tracks. His blood ran cold, and his stomach froze. He whipped his head around. "What did you call me?"

He saw her face then, and his whole world stopped. The blond hair had thrown him off. "Mom? Is that you?"

AUTHOR NOTES RAMY VANCE
JUNE 15, 2021

I may write about super heroes and people with special abilities – but a hero, I am not.

As for special abilities? I so wished I had Rueben Peet's ability to 'repeat' after my less than graceful attempt to save my son...

My kid, John, had decided to climb up one of those tube slides common in playparks. This is one of the more noble pursuits of children his age and something I would have taken no issue with had he not chosen to climb the *outside* of the slide.

I should note that the slide is high enough to serve as a perch for any peeping tom seeking to spy into a second-floor window.

Upon reaching the top, he got stuck, a situation only exasperated by how windy the day was and that my 1-year old daughter, Orla, was climbing an equally challenging, albeit much closer to the ground, pursuit of her own.

The priority was obvious. If John were to fall from such a

height, he'd break a bone if he was lucky (I shudder to think of what would have happened if he was unlucky).

I grabbed Orla and placed her in the hands of a stranger – social distancing be damned. And then, in a manner uncharacteristic to my natural athletic abilities, I climbed up the structure and ran across the obstacle course created by sadistic city-planners to challenge children at play.

I achieved my goal and got across... albeit with all the grace of flummoxed pug.

Upon reaching to the other side, my heart sunk when I realized the wooden wall that stood between us was six feet high.

It is amazing how panic, accompanied by a complete disregard of self, offers clarity. Things actually did slow down as I assessed my best course of action. There were two bolts used to attach different sections of the wall. Placing a foot on each, I used my momentum to *half* hoist myself over the edge.

I can only imagine the amusement of onlookers seeing an overweight, middle-aged man teetering over a jungle-gym wall (this is the moment I wish I could 'repeat').

With my shorter-than-average arms, my son's rescue was in doubt.

Yelling for him to reach up, I realized that I didn't have the strength or agility to stay lodged on the wall *and* lift him over.

With my options limited, I did the only thing I could think of and hoisted him straight up as I allowed myself to fall backwards.

We landed with an audible thud that left a very visible bruise.

His response to his father's Herculean efforts? "I'm OK, Daddy. I fell on you and you're soft."

Soft, indeed.

I have since enrolled in a Parkour course to prepare for the next, inevitable rescue.

Joking aside, John has expressed interest in the sport and we have found a course for beginners (6 and up). After the slide incident, I think it a good idea to enrol him.

His mother, not so much.

And herein lies my greatest challenge as a parent. My role is constantly moving away from protector and toward encourager: Test your limits, my wee ones. Climb the outside of slides. Try not to hurt yourself. And should you get stuck, I will endeavour to save you despite my short arms and even shorter comings.

And if you do fall, know I will be there to help you stand again. Forgive my tears when I do, for even though you don't understand this now, one day you will learn that the expression, 'this hurts me more than it does you', is painfully accurate.

--

I really hope you liked *Die Again to Save the World* and will continue to enjoy the series. It was a gamble to write it the way we did. After all, heroes are meant to know what they're doing.

But real people aren't and we don't get 'do-overs'. Rueben does. As bumbling as he is, at least his heart is in the right place. Just maybe that, couple with his 'warping' abilities, will be enough to save the day.

If only barely.

Thank you for not only reading this story but these author notes as well!

As I type this, one part of the United States was slammed with a Tropical Storm a couple of days ago that flooded areas and caused massive destruction in the southern states.

Fifteen hundred miles to the west, there is a multi-year-long drought in many states that might get to a point where perhaps millions are affected because there will not be enough water.

So yesterday, I went searching for the latest technology related to desalinization.

Total freshwater on this planet is 2.5 – 2.75% of total water, so oceans and seas are the rest at about 97%.

The amount of water used (here in the USA) is by farming and ranching. Something like 70% of freshwater.

So, the amount we need for drinking is a rather small percent considering most freshwater is in ice sheets at the moment.

Essentially, we have the water; it just isn't in locations where we need it.

I found some technology which (in a nutshell) is a permeable sheet with *really* small holes. The H2O molecules will pass through, the salt (NaCl) won't. To accomplish this separation doesn't require much energy, and we are left with the salt and other microscopic molecules.

Yes, I know. I'm majorly oversimplifying.

Because my brain creates stories, answers if you will, I quickly thought about using large magnifying glasses to heat up the oceans to cause evaporation. Well, space-based magnifying glasses because I think large and don't ever have to worry about budget.

Then the whole "zapping oceans from space" issue where you accidentally burn up a ship comes into play. Or accidentally fry a few thousand fish by accident. Maybe we cause a flash algal bloom or some other massive ecological oops.

There is *always* a downside, it seems.

Regardless of my sci-fi-based shenanigans, I would like to understand how we could use natural solutions to fix the problem. For example, what would happen if we piped water to a naturally hot area that could evaporate the water more effectively?

Well, then we have concerns about how did we get the water into the pipe in the first place? Using any sort of suction is going to cause problems with plant and ocean life getting sucked into the intake pipes.

Another idea, another problem to solve.

Further, the ionic bonds of NaCl are very strong (and we would have a LOT left over after the water evaporated), plus it's a pain to break them apart. It takes thousands and tens of thousands of pounds of pressure to move them to Na_3Cl and

$NaCl_3$, something postulated by lead researcher Artem Oganov at the State University of New York in Stony Brook and confirmed by an experiment.

Not that we have any use for the substance that we know of at the moment.

So, we are stuck with a LOT of Salt. Not sure what to do about it unless we can use it for table salt. Should be easier to acquire than digging deep underground in salt mines, one would think.

Or, you know, we could create another dead sea on this side of the world and charge people to float in it for their health.

Ok, I've rambled long enough on this thought, and I appreciate you coming along for my inadequate mental effort to stave off the world's water problems.

I am no closer to answering any questions about what is going to happen in the future, but I am thankful that people who are way more intelligent than I am are working on the problem(s).

I hope you have a fantastic week or weekend, whichever is appropriate, and thank you for reading our stories!

Ad Aeternitatem,

Michael Anderle

OTHER BOOKS BY RAMY VANCE

Other Middang3ard Books

Never Split The Party (01)
Late To the Party (02)
It's My Party (03)
Blue Hell And Alien Fire (04)

Death Of An Author: A Middang3ard Novella

Dark Gate Angels
Dark Gate Angels (01)
Shades of Death (02)
The Allies of Death (03)
The Deadliness of Light (04)

Dragon Approved
The First Human Rider (01)
Ascent to the Nest (02)
Defense of the Nest (03)

Nest Under Siege (04)
First Mission (05)
The Descent (06)
Sacrifices (07)
Love and Aliens (08)
An Alien Affair (09)
Dragons in Space (10)
The Beginning of the End (11)
Death of the Mind (12)
Boundless (13)

Other Books by Ramy Vance

Mortality Bites Series
Keep Evolving Series
Fatebound Series
Welcome to the Dragon Show Series

BOOKS BY MICHAEL ANDERLE

Sign up for the LMBPN email list to be notified of new releases and special deals!

https://lmbpn.com/email/

For a complete list of books by Michael Anderle, please visit:

www.lmbpn.com/ma-books/

CONNECT WITH THE AUTHORS

Connect with Ramy

Join Ramy's Newsletter

Join Ramy's FB Group: House of the GoneGod Damned!

Michael Anderle Social

Website: http://lmbpn.com

Email List: http://lmbpn.com/email/

Social Media:

https://www.facebook.com/LMBPNPublishing

https://twitter.com/MichaelAnderle

https://www.instagram.com/lmbpn_publishing/

https://www.bookbub.com/authors/michael-anderle